STEVE ORLANDO

WRITER, CREATOR

GARRY BROWN

ARTIST, CREATOR

LEE LOUGHRIDGE

COLORIST

THOMAS MAUER

LETTERER

ARIELLE BASICH

ASSOCIATE EDITOR

JON MOISAN

EDITOR

COVER BY GARRY BROWN
& LEE LOUGHRIDGE
LOGO DESIGN BY ANDRES JUAREZ
COLLECTION DESIGN BY CARINA TAYLOR

MY PAST LIFE
RETURNED FROM
THE DEAD
TO CLAIM YOU

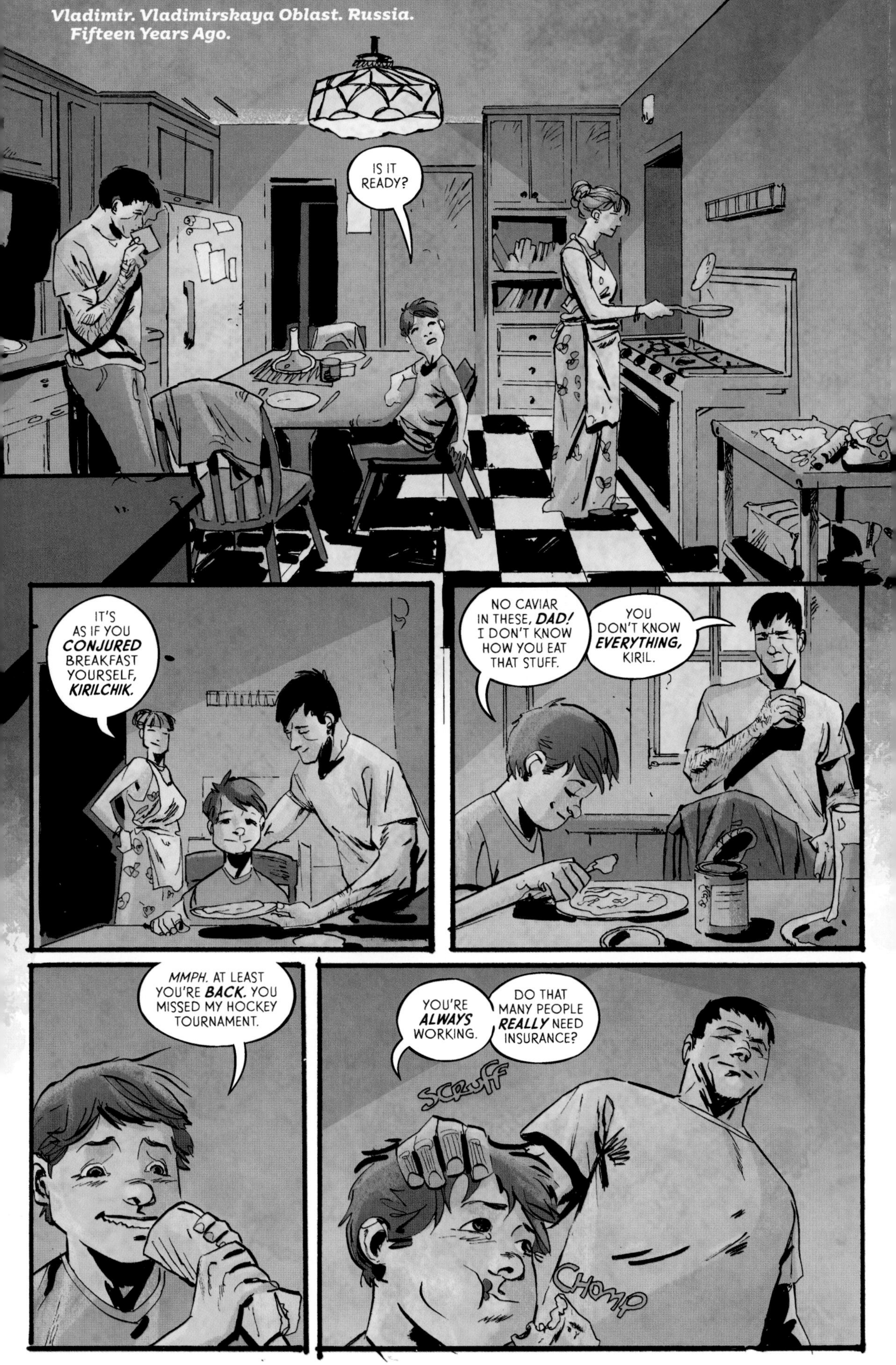
Vladimir. Vladimirskaya Oblast. Russia. Fifteen Years Ago.
IS IT READY?
IT'S AS IF YOU CONJURED BREAKFAST YOURSELF, KIRILCHIK.
NO CAVIAR IN THESE, DAD! I DON'T KNOW HOW YOU EAT THAT STUFF.
YOU DON'T KNOW EVERYTHING, KIRIL.
MMPH. AT LEAST YOU'RE BACK. YOU MISSED MY HOCKEY TOURNAMENT.
YOU'RE ALWAYS WORKING.
DO THAT MANY PEOPLE REALLY NEED INSURANCE?
SCRUFF
CHOMP

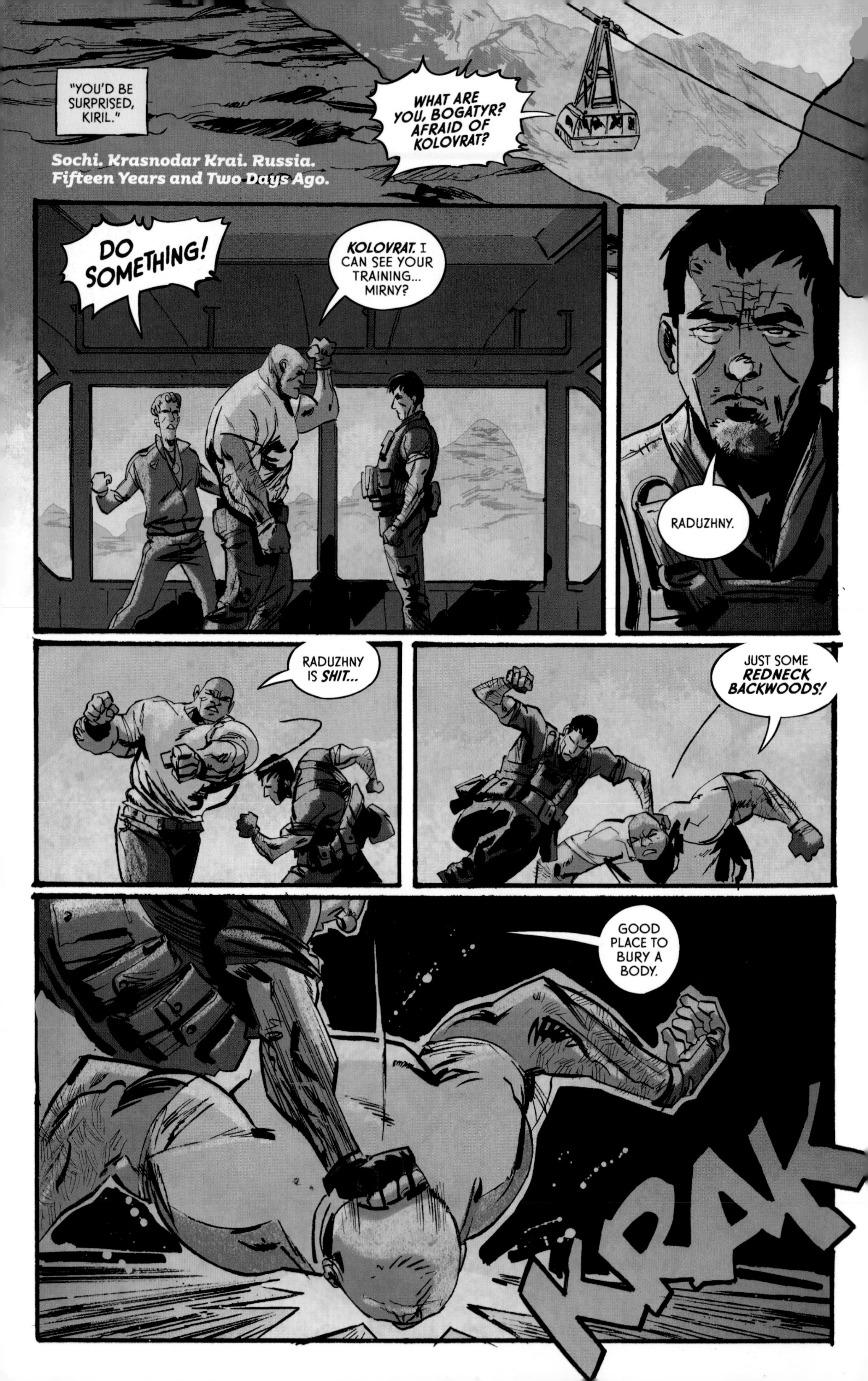
"YOU'D BE SURPRISED, KIRIL."
WHAT ARE YOU, BOGATYR? AFRAID OF KOLOVRAT?
Sochi. Krasnodar Krai. Russia.
Fifteen Years and Two Days Ago.
DO SOMETHING!
KOLOVRAT. I CAN SEE YOUR TRAINING... MIRNY?
RADUZHNY.
RADUZHNY IS SHIT...
JUST SOME REDNECK BACKWOODS!
GOOD PLACE TO BURY A BODY.
KRAK

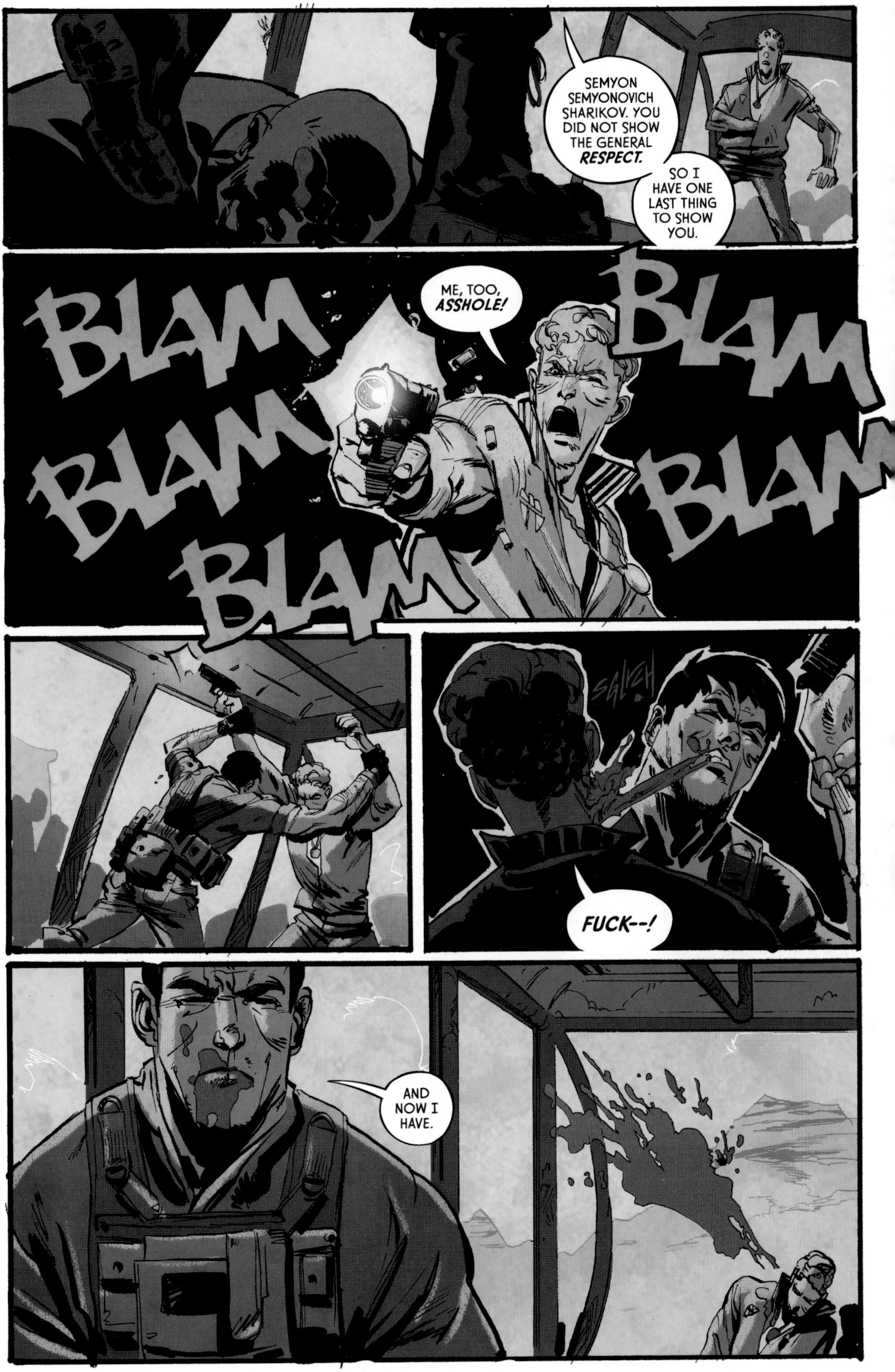
SEMYON SEMYONOVICH SHARIKOV. YOU DID NOT SHOW THE GENERAL RESPECT.
SO I HAVE ONE LAST THING TO SHOW YOU.
BLAM BLAM BLAM
ME, TOO, ASSHOLE!
BLAM BLAM
SGLCH
FUCK--!
AND NOW I HAVE.

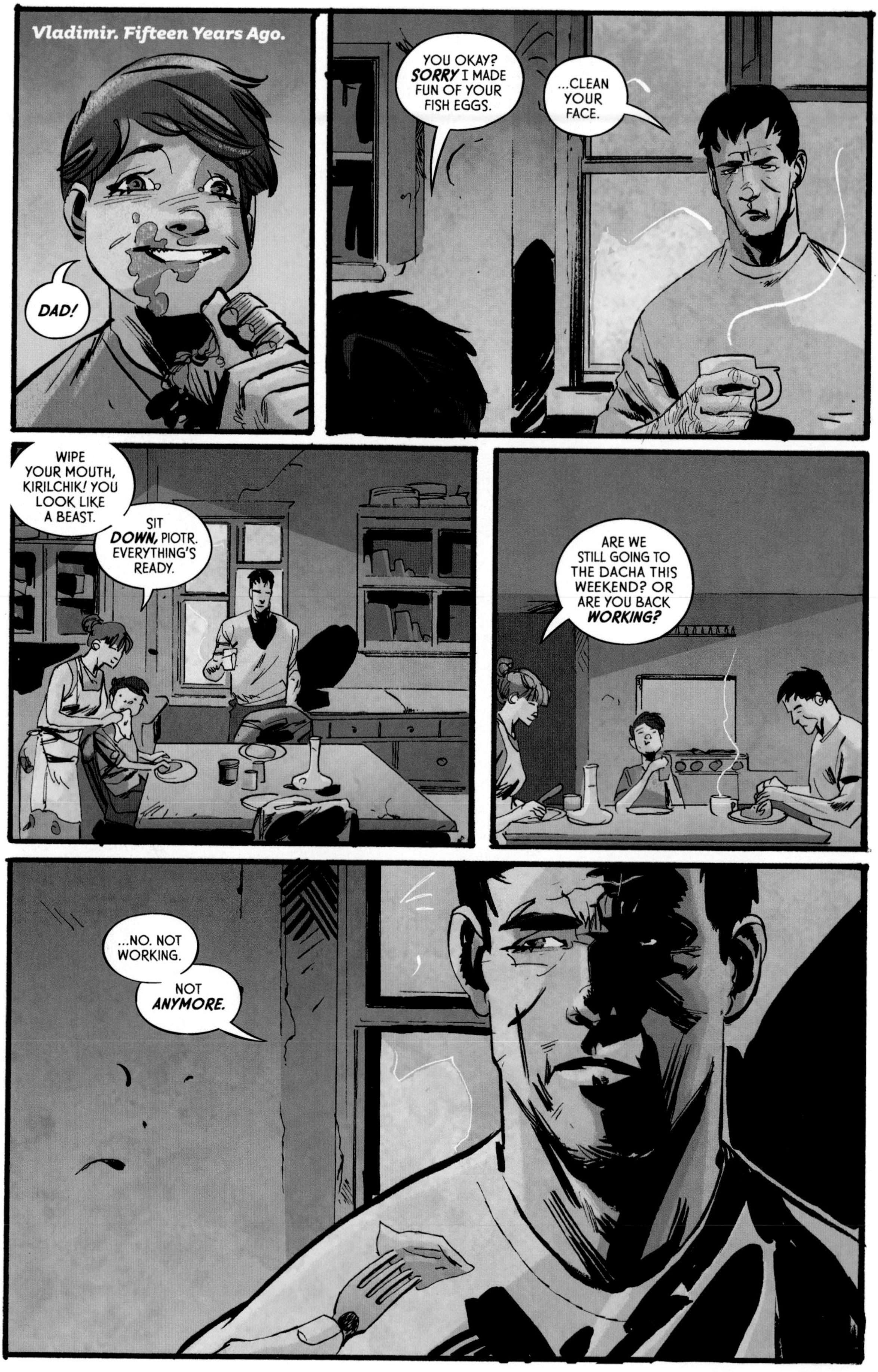
Vladimir. Fifteen Years Ago.
DAD!
YOU OKAY? SORRY I MADE FUN OF YOUR FISH EGGS.
...CLEAN YOUR FACE.
WIPE YOUR MOUTH, KIRILCHIK! YOU LOOK LIKE A BEAST.
SIT DOWN, PIOTR. EVERYTHING'S READY.
ARE WE STILL GOING TO THE DACHA THIS WEEKEND? OR ARE YOU BACK WORKING?
...NO. NOT WORKING.
NOT ANYMORE.

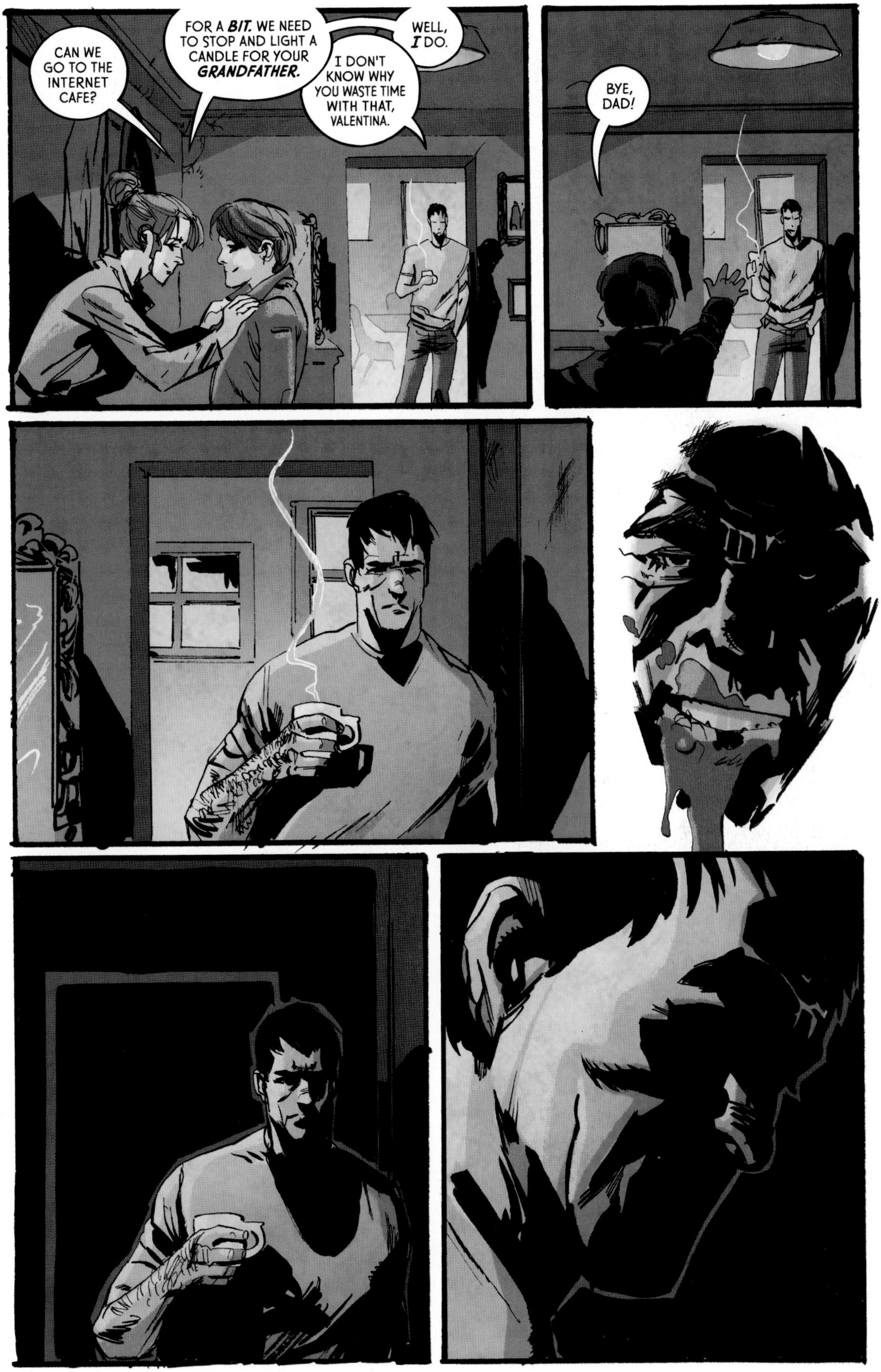
CAN WE GO TO THE INTERNET CAFE?
FOR A BIT. WE NEED TO STOP AND LIGHT A CANDLE FOR YOUR GRANDFATHER.
I DON'T KNOW WHY YOU WASTE TIME WITH THAT, VALENTINA.
WELL, I DO.
BYE, DAD!

Vladimir. One Year Ago.

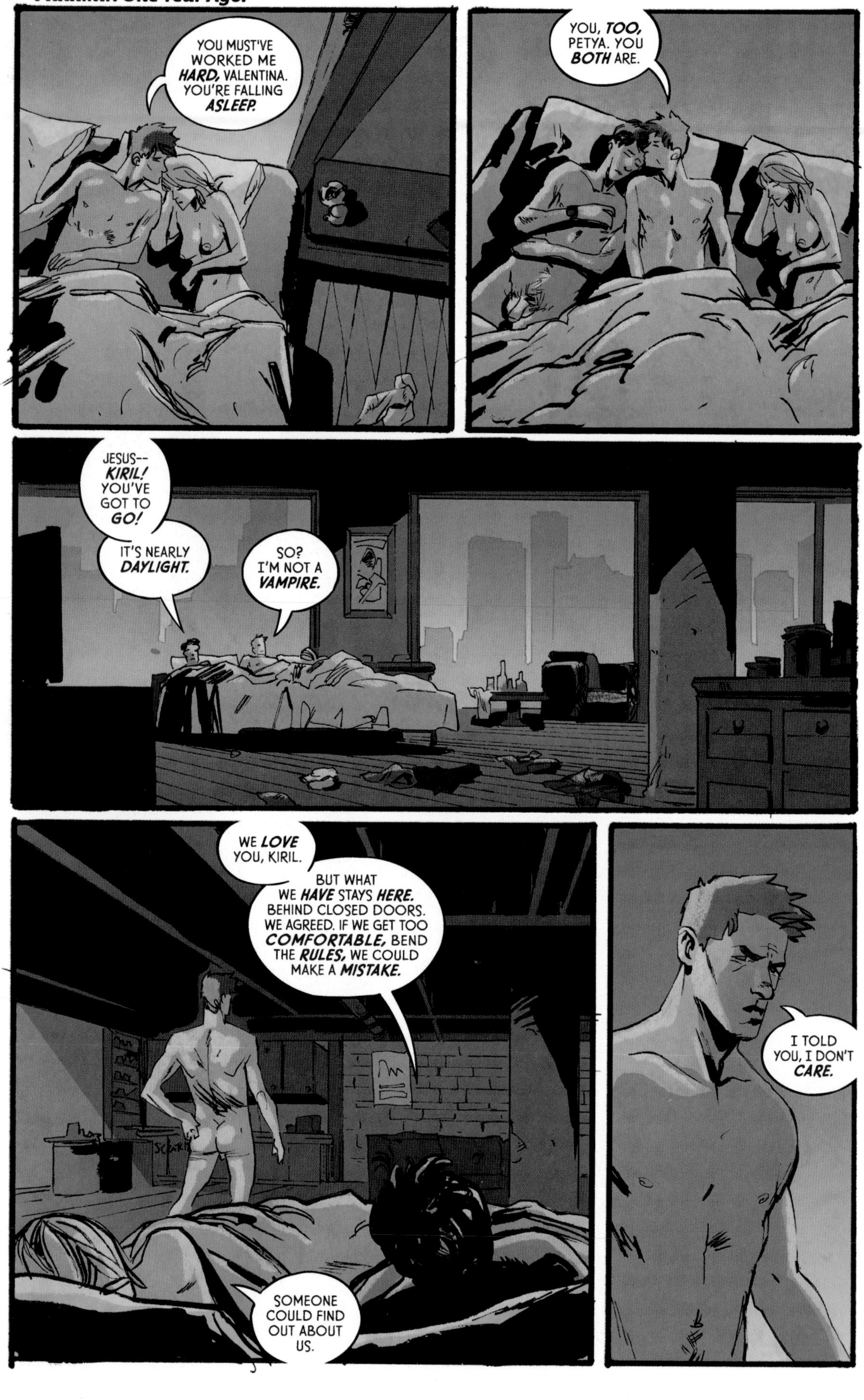
YOU MUST'VE WORKED ME HARD, VALENTINA. YOU'RE FALLING ASLEEP.
YOU, TOO, PETYA. YOU BOTH ARE.
JESUS-- KIRIL! YOU'VE GOT TO GO!
IT'S NEARLY DAYLIGHT.
SO? I'M NOT A VAMPIRE.
WE LOVE YOU, KIRIL.
BUT WHAT WE HAVE STAYS HERE. BEHIND CLOSED DOORS. WE AGREED. IF WE GET TOO COMFORTABLE, BEND THE RULES, WE COULD MAKE A MISTAKE.
SOMEONE COULD FIND OUT ABOUT US.
I TOLD YOU, I DON'T CARE.

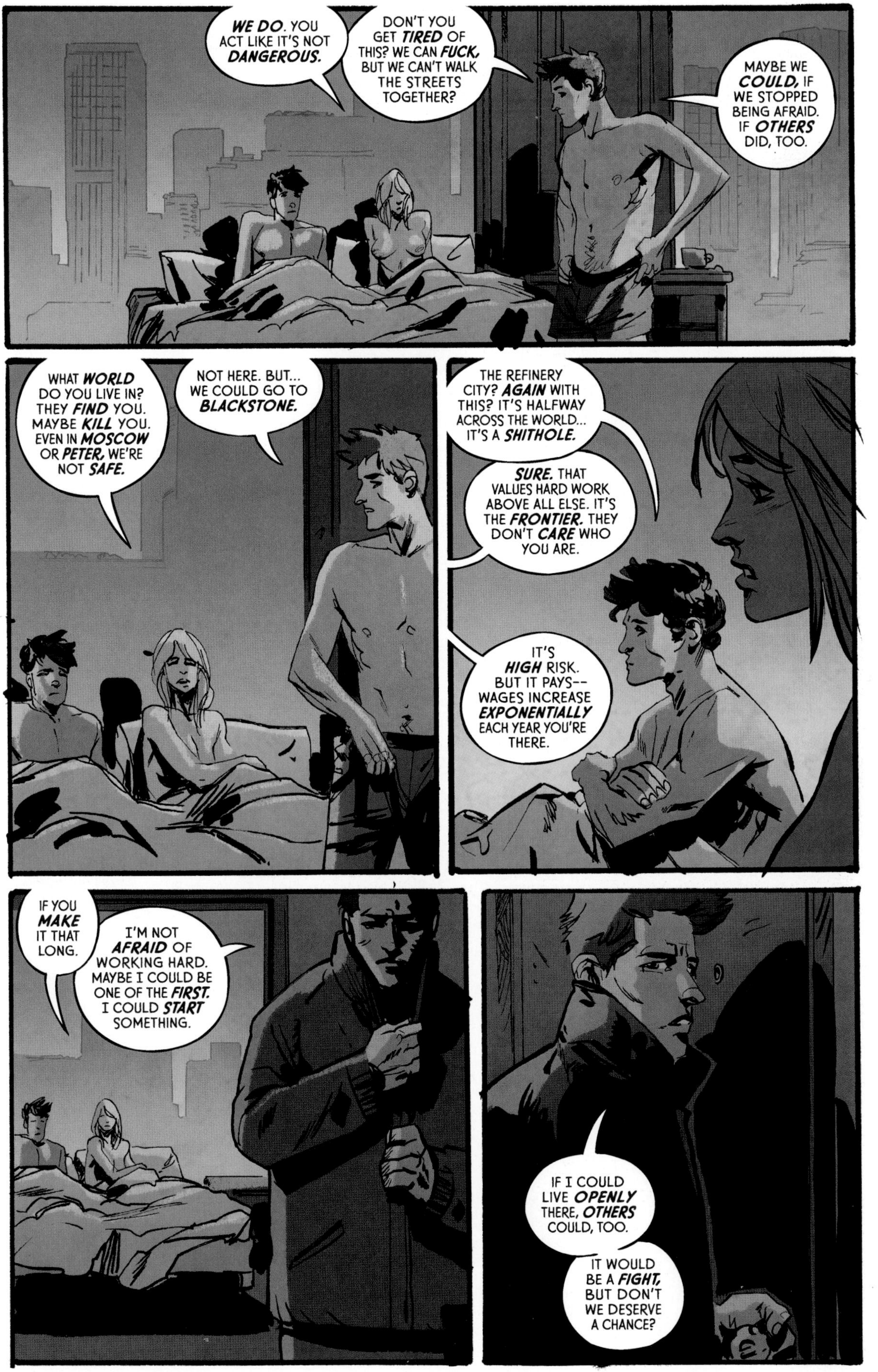
WE DO. YOU ACT LIKE IT'S NOT DANGEROUS.
DON'T YOU GET TIRED OF THIS? WE CAN FUCK, BUT WE CAN'T WALK THE STREETS TOGETHER?
MAYBE WE COULD, IF WE STOPPED BEING AFRAID. IF OTHERS DID, TOO.
WHAT WORLD DO YOU LIVE IN? THEY FIND YOU. MAYBE KILL YOU. EVEN IN MOSCOW OR PETER, WE'RE NOT SAFE.
NOT HERE. BUT... WE COULD GO TO BLACKSTONE.
THE REFINERY CITY? AGAIN WITH THIS? IT'S HALFWAY ACROSS THE WORLD... IT'S A SHITHOLE.
SURE. THAT VALUES HARD WORK ABOVE ALL ELSE. IT'S THE FRONTIER. THEY DON'T CARE WHO YOU ARE.
IT'S HIGH RISK. BUT IT PAYS-- WAGES INCREASE EXPONENTIALLY EACH YEAR YOU'RE THERE.
IF YOU MAKE IT THAT LONG.
I'M NOT AFRAID OF WORKING HARD. MAYBE I COULD BE ONE OF THE FIRST. I COULD START SOMETHING.
IF I COULD LIVE OPENLY THERE, OTHERS COULD, TOO.
IT WOULD BE A FIGHT, BUT DON'T WE DESERVE A CHANCE?

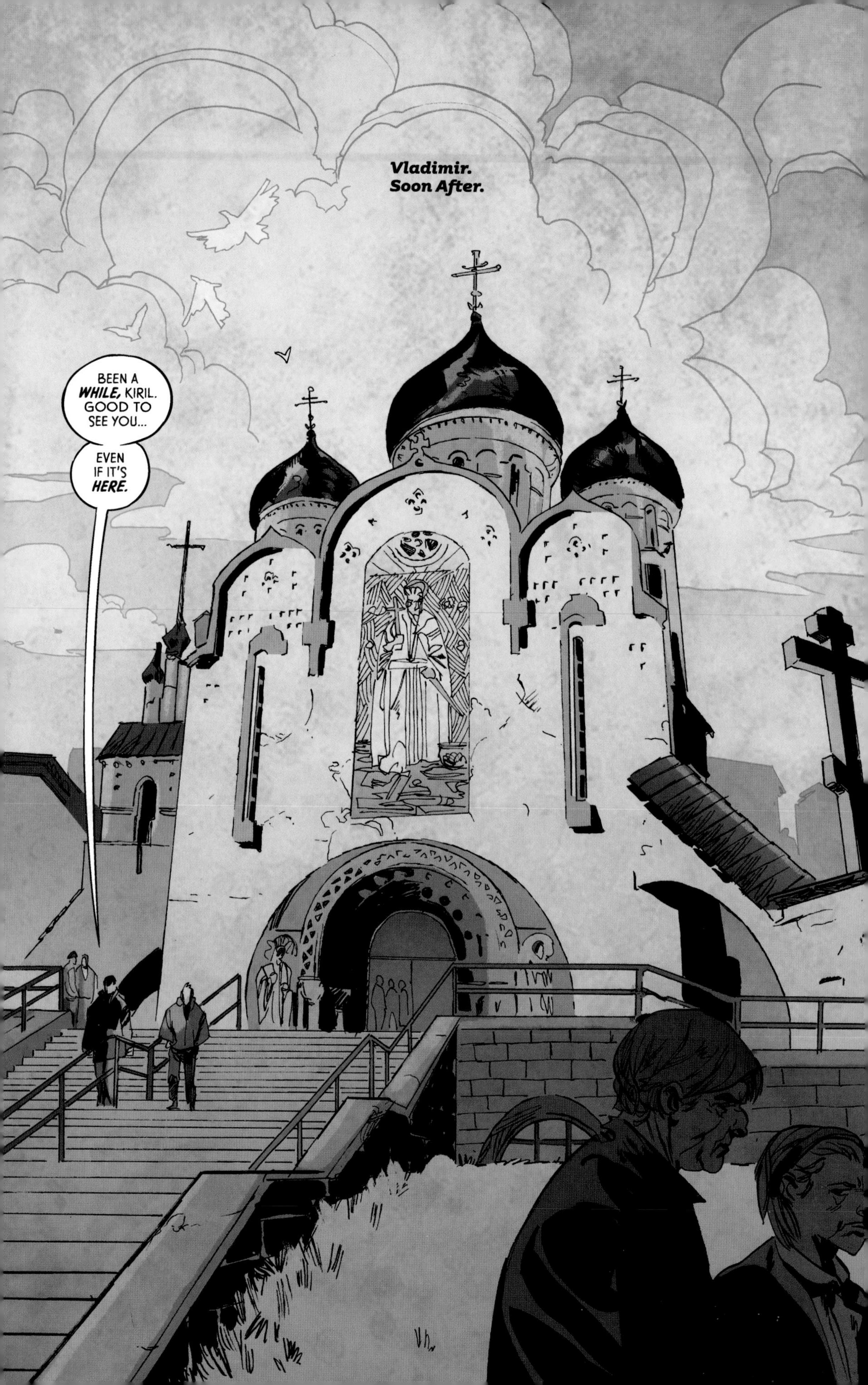
Vladimir.
Soon After.
BEEN A WHILE, KIRIL. GOOD TO SEE YOU...
EVEN IF IT'S HERE.

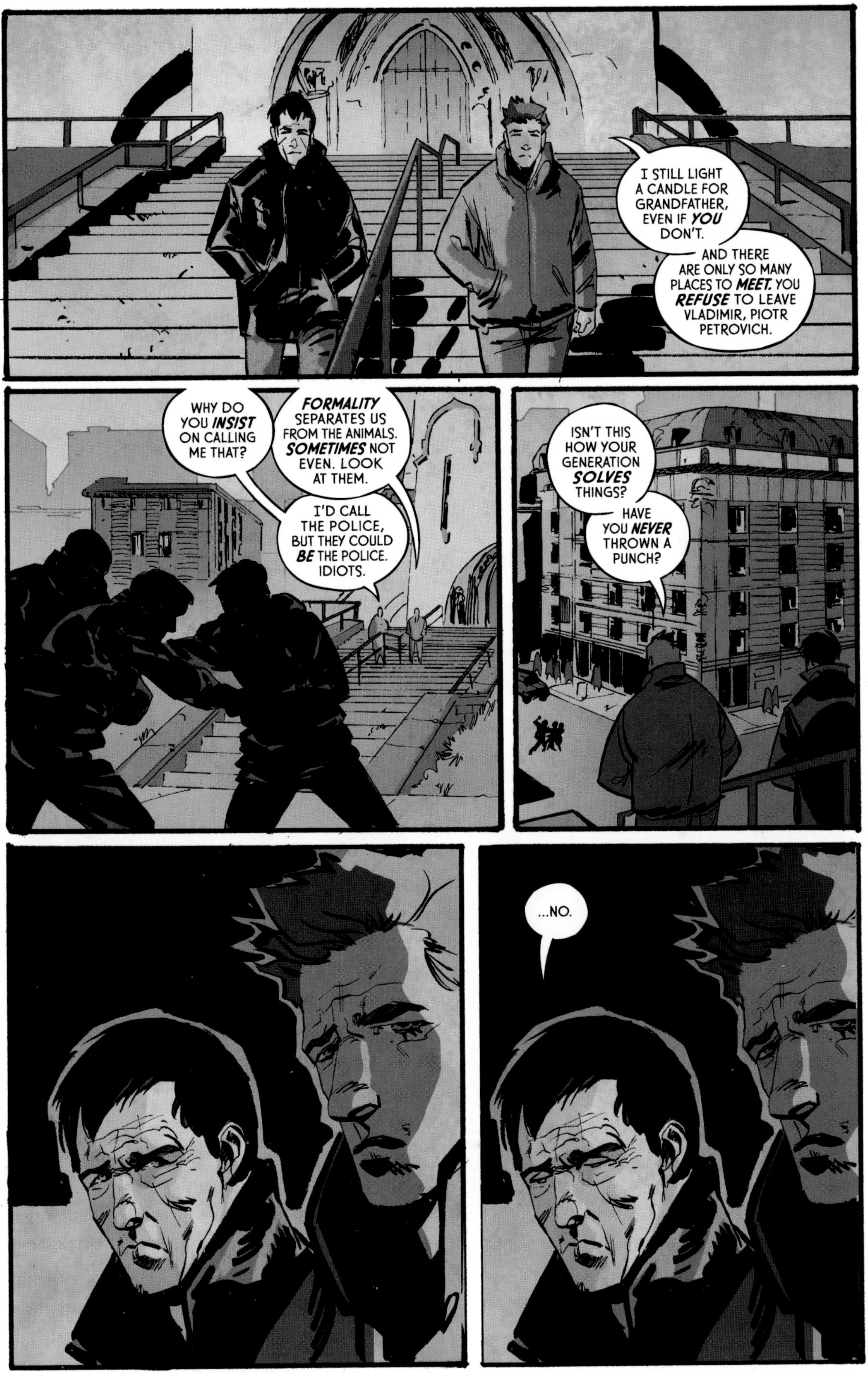
I STILL LIGHT A CANDLE FOR GRANDFATHER, EVEN IF YOU DON'T.
AND THERE ARE ONLY SO MANY PLACES TO MEET. YOU REFUSE TO LEAVE VLADIMIR, PIOTR PETROVICH.
WHY DO YOU INSIST ON CALLING ME THAT?
FORMALITY SEPARATES US FROM THE ANIMALS. SOMETIMES NOT EVEN. LOOK AT THEM.
I'D CALL THE POLICE, BUT THEY COULD BE THE POLICE. IDIOTS.
ISN'T THIS HOW YOUR GENERATION SOLVES THINGS?
HAVE YOU NEVER THROWN A PUNCH?
...NO.

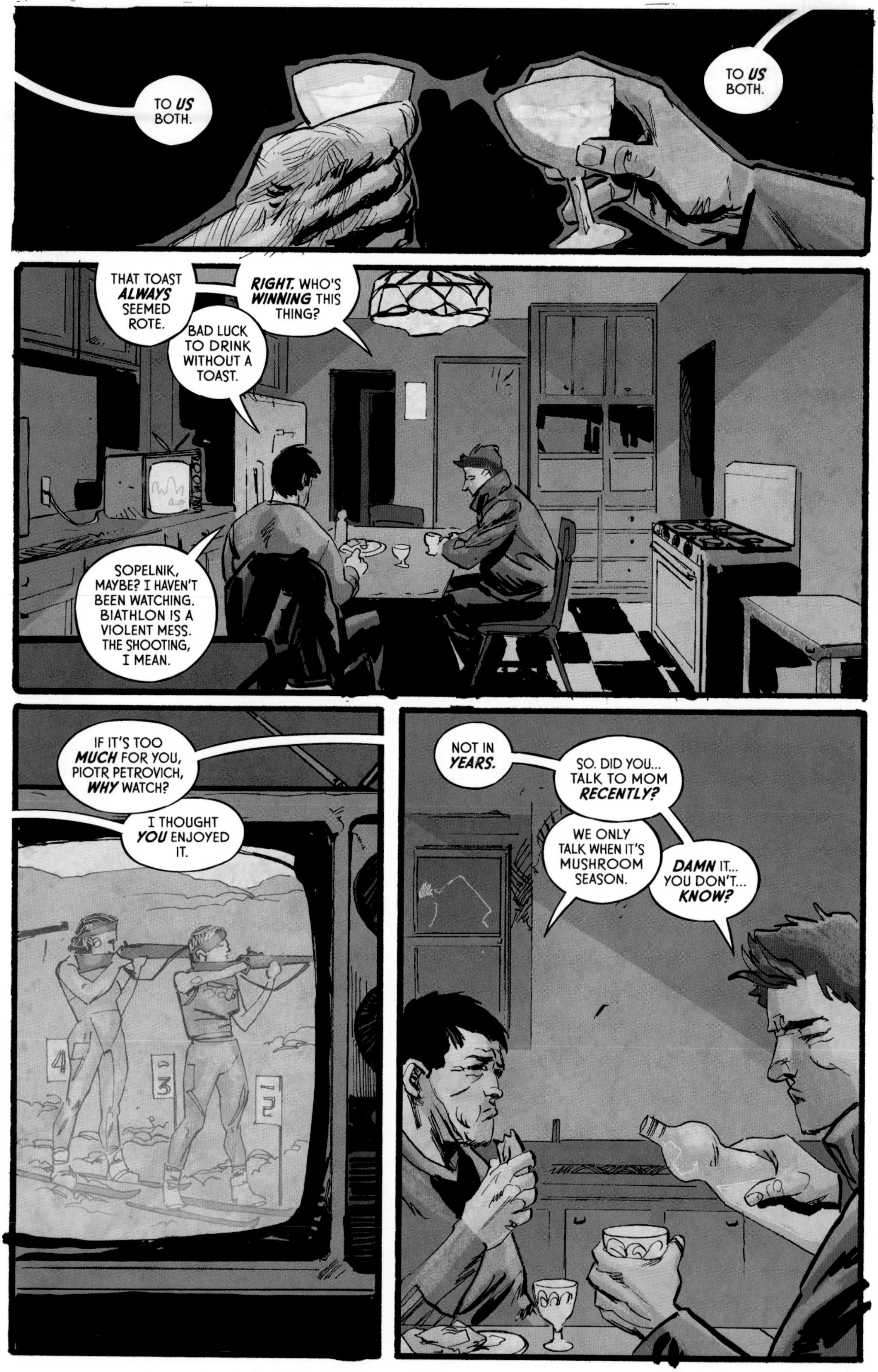
TO US BOTH.
TO US BOTH.
THAT TOAST ALWAYS SEEMED ROTE.
BAD LUCK TO DRINK WITHOUT A TOAST.
RIGHT. WHO'S WINNING THIS THING?
SOPELNIK, MAYBE? I HAVEN'T BEEN WATCHING. BIATHLON IS A VIOLENT MESS. THE SHOOTING, I MEAN.
IF IT'S TOO MUCH FOR YOU, PIOTR PETROVICH, WHY WATCH?
I THOUGHT YOU ENJOYED IT.
NOT IN YEARS.
SO. DID YOU... TALK TO MOM RECENTLY?
WE ONLY TALK WHEN IT'S MUSHROOM SEASON.
DAMN IT... YOU DON'T... KNOW?

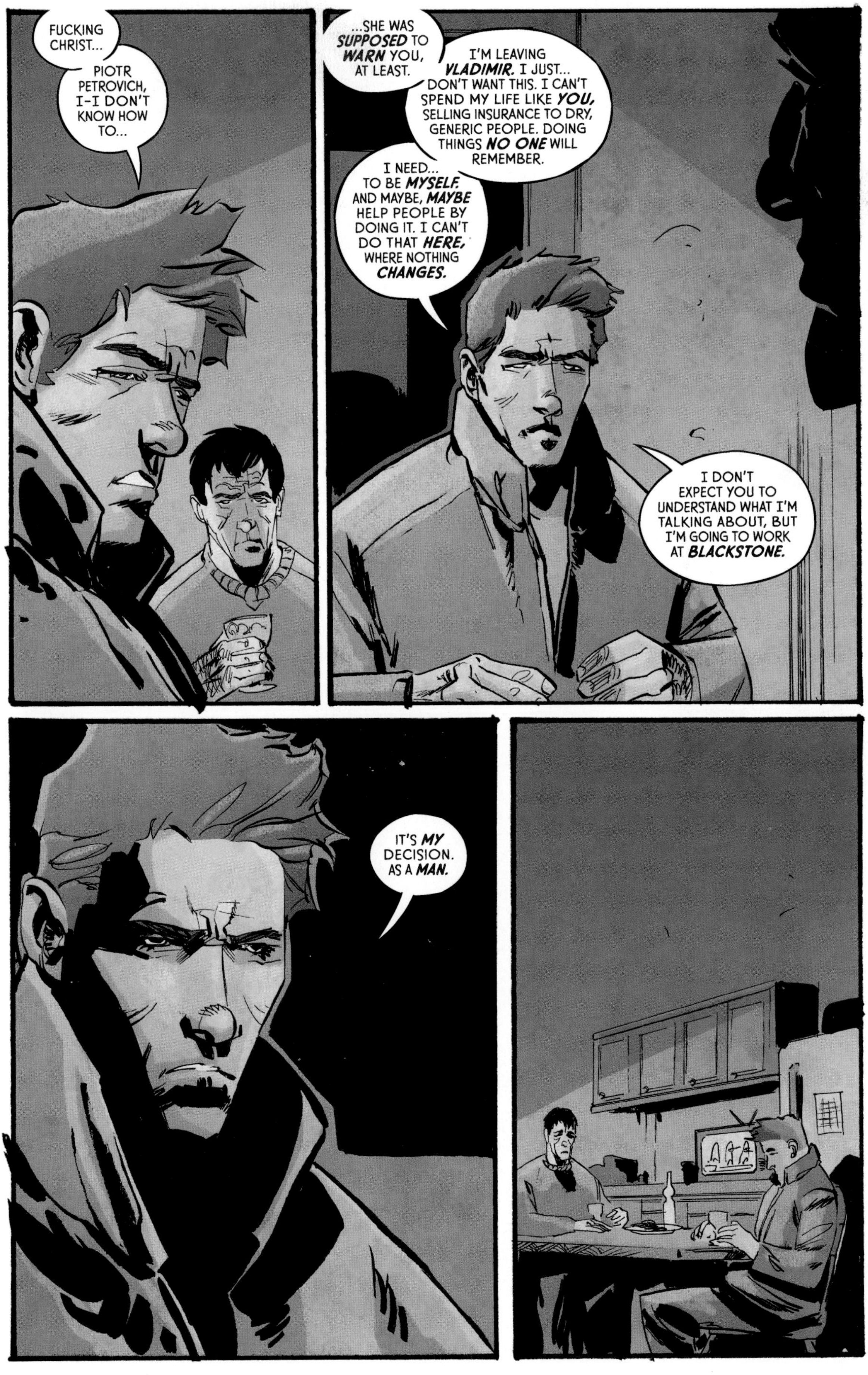
FUCKING CHRIST...
PIOTR PETROVICH, I-I DON'T KNOW HOW TO...
...SHE WAS SUPPOSED TO WARN YOU, AT LEAST.
I'M LEAVING VLADIMIR. I JUST... DON'T WANT THIS. I CAN'T SPEND MY LIFE LIKE YOU, SELLING INSURANCE TO DRY, GENERIC PEOPLE. DOING THINGS NO ONE WILL REMEMBER.
I NEED... TO BE MYSELF. AND MAYBE, MAYBE HELP PEOPLE BY DOING IT. I CAN'T DO THAT HERE, WHERE NOTHING CHANGES.
I DON'T EXPECT YOU TO UNDERSTAND WHAT I'M TALKING ABOUT, BUT I'M GOING TO WORK AT BLACKSTONE.
IT'S MY DECISION. AS A MAN.

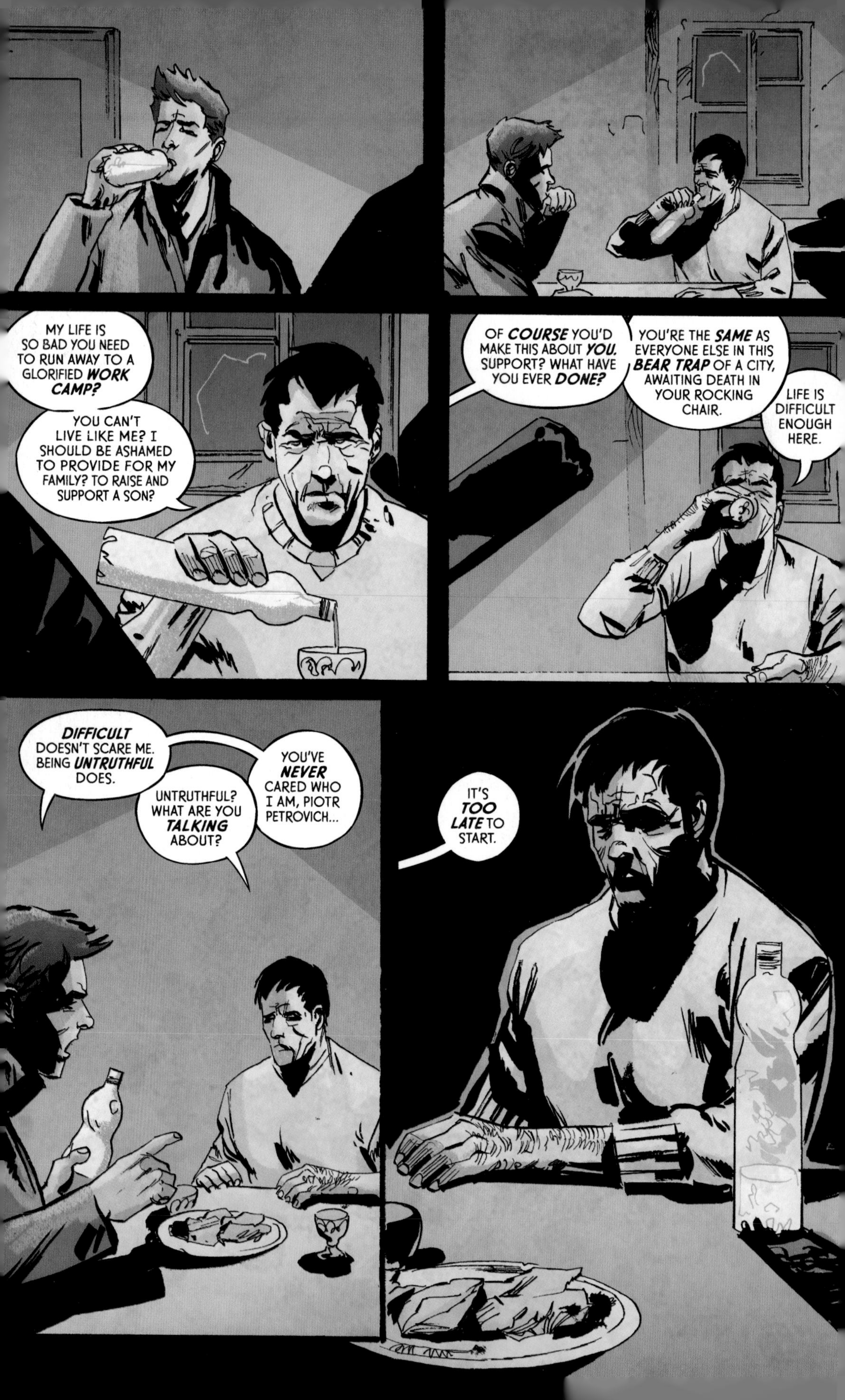

MY LIFE IS SO BAD YOU NEED TO RUN AWAY TO A GLORIFIED WORK CAMP?
YOU CAN'T LIVE LIKE ME? I SHOULD BE ASHAMED TO PROVIDE FOR MY FAMILY? TO RAISE AND SUPPORT A SON?
OF COURSE YOU'D MAKE THIS ABOUT YOU. SUPPORT? WHAT HAVE YOU EVER DONE?
YOU'RE THE SAME AS EVERYONE ELSE IN THIS BEAR TRAP OF A CITY, AWAITING DEATH IN YOUR ROCKING CHAIR.
LIFE IS DIFFICULT ENOUGH HERE.
DIFFICULT DOESN'T SCARE ME. BEING UNTRUTHFUL DOES.
UNTRUTHFUL? WHAT ARE YOU TALKING ABOUT?
YOU'VE NEVER CARED WHO I AM, PIOTR PETROVICH...
IT'S TOO LATE TO START.

One Year Later. Now.

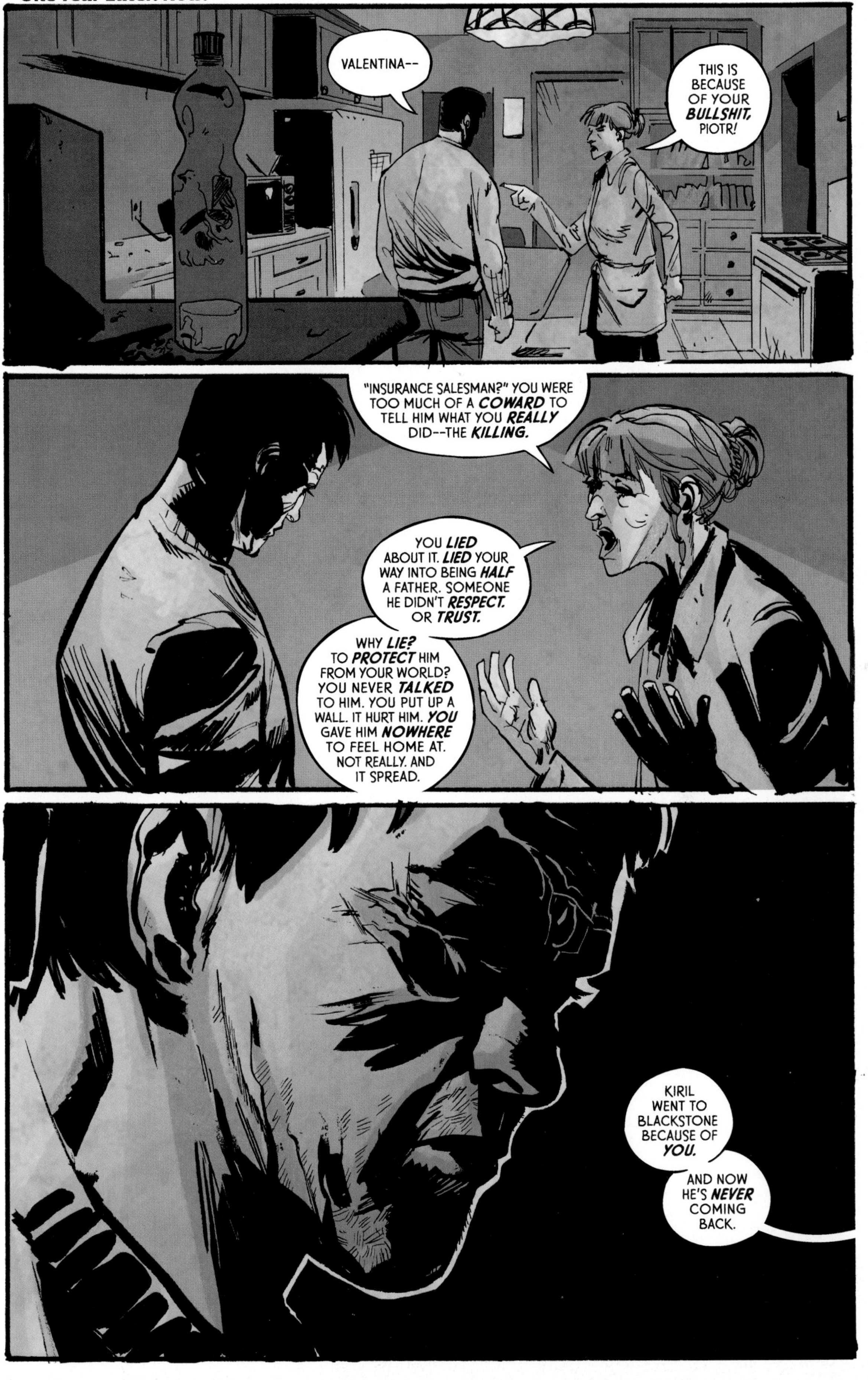

VALENTINA--
THIS IS BECAUSE OF YOUR BULLSHIT, PIOTR!
"INSURANCE SALESMAN?" YOU WERE TOO MUCH OF A COWARD TO TELL HIM WHAT YOU REALLY DID--THE KILLING.
YOU LIED ABOUT IT. LIED YOUR WAY INTO BEING HALF A FATHER. SOMEONE HE DIDN'T RESPECT. OR TRUST.
WHY LIE? TO PROTECT HIM FROM YOUR WORLD? YOU NEVER TALKED TO HIM. YOU PUT UP A WALL. IT HURT HIM. YOU GAVE HIM NOWHERE TO FEEL HOME AT. NOT REALLY. AND IT SPREAD.
KIRIL WENT TO BLACKSTONE BECAUSE OF YOU.
AND NOW HE'S NEVER COMING BACK.

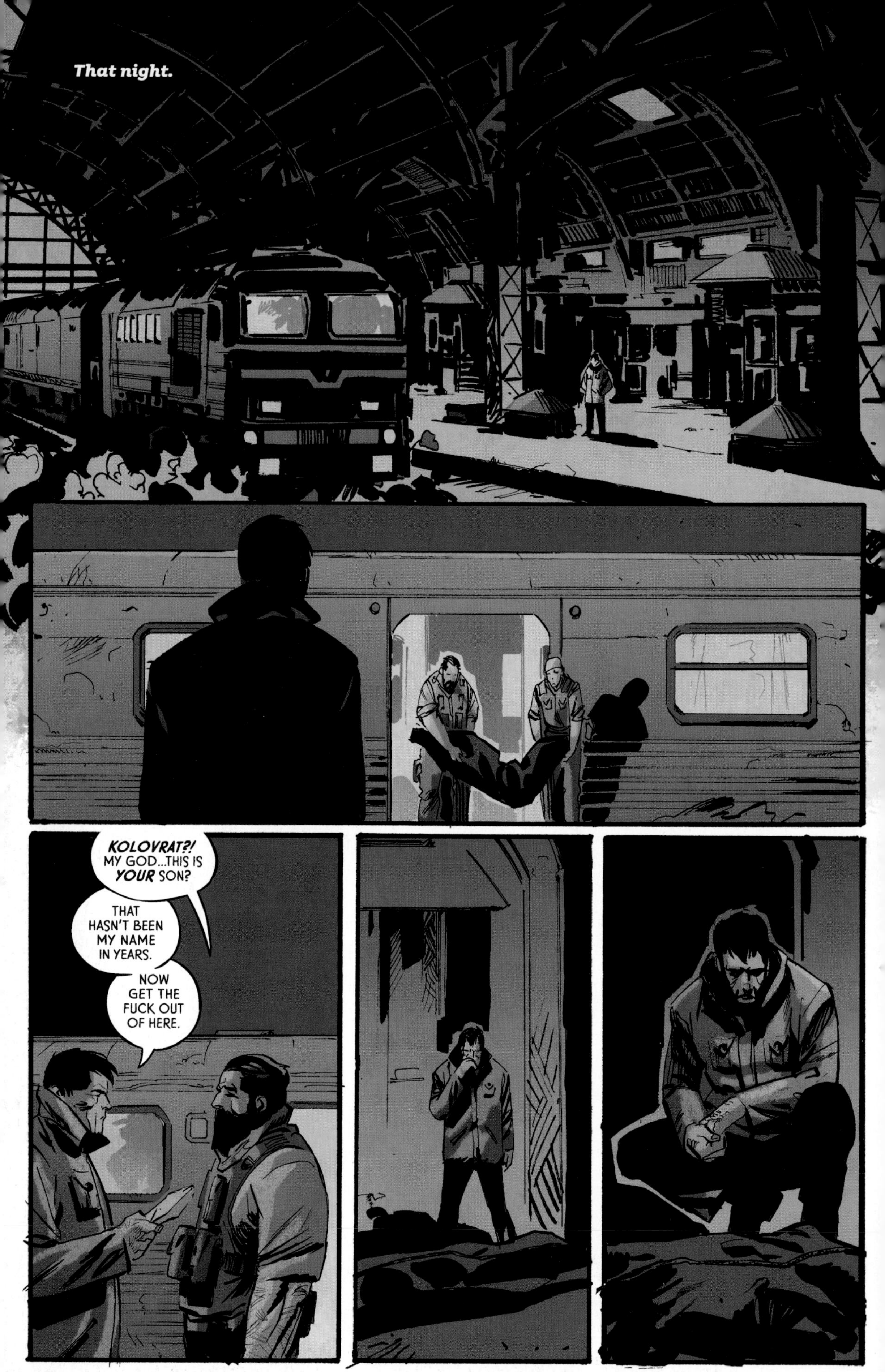
That night.
KOLOVRAT?! MY GOD...THIS IS YOUR SON?
THAT HASN'T BEEN MY NAME IN YEARS.
NOW GET THE FUCK OUT OF HERE.

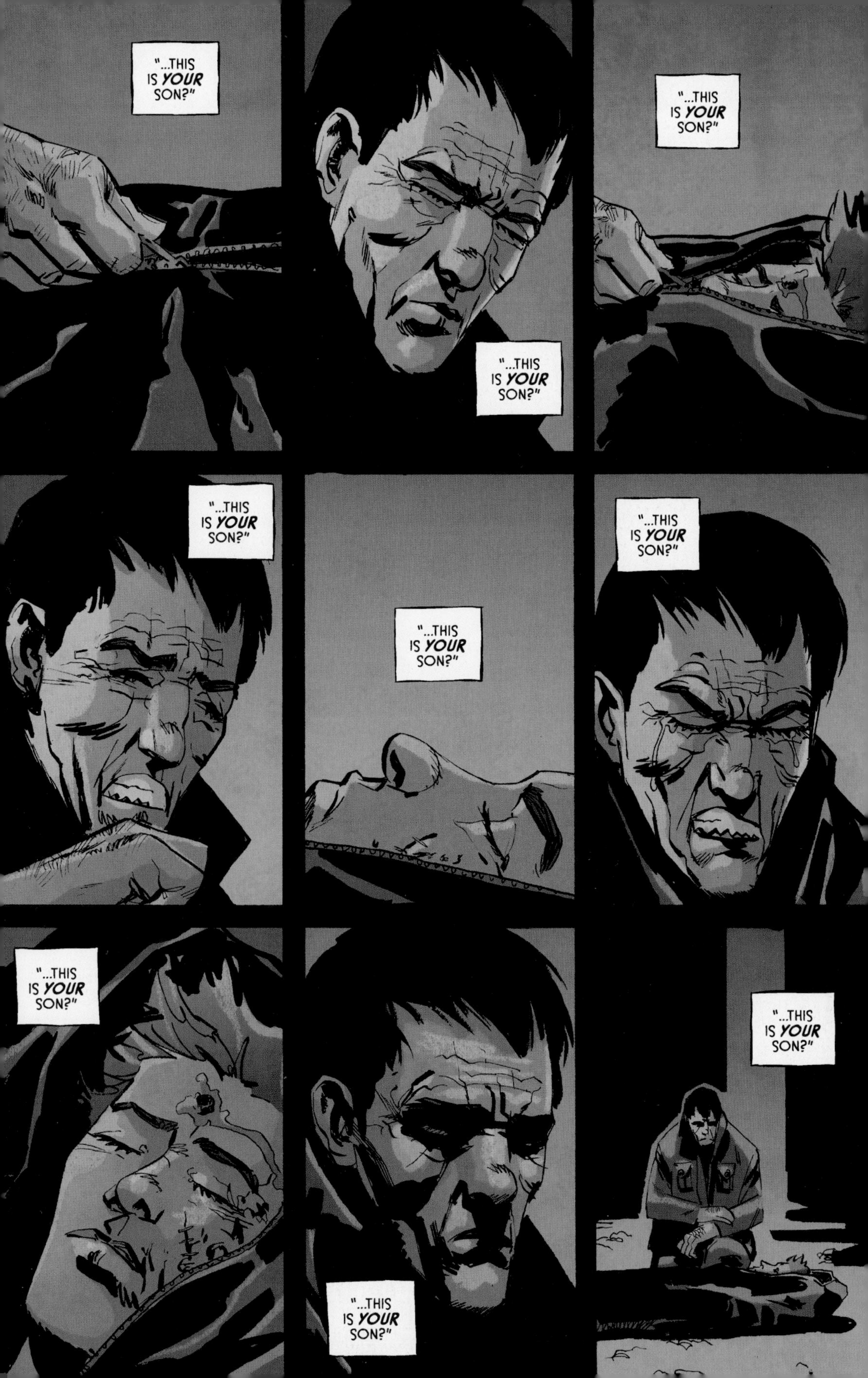
"...THIS IS *YOUR* SON?"
"...THIS IS *YOUR* SON?"
"...THIS IS *YOUR* SON?"
"...THIS IS *YOUR* SON?"
"...THIS IS *YOUR* SON?"
"...THIS IS *YOUR* SON?"
"...THIS IS *YOUR* SON?"
"...THIS IS *YOUR* SON?"
"...THIS IS *YOUR* SON?"

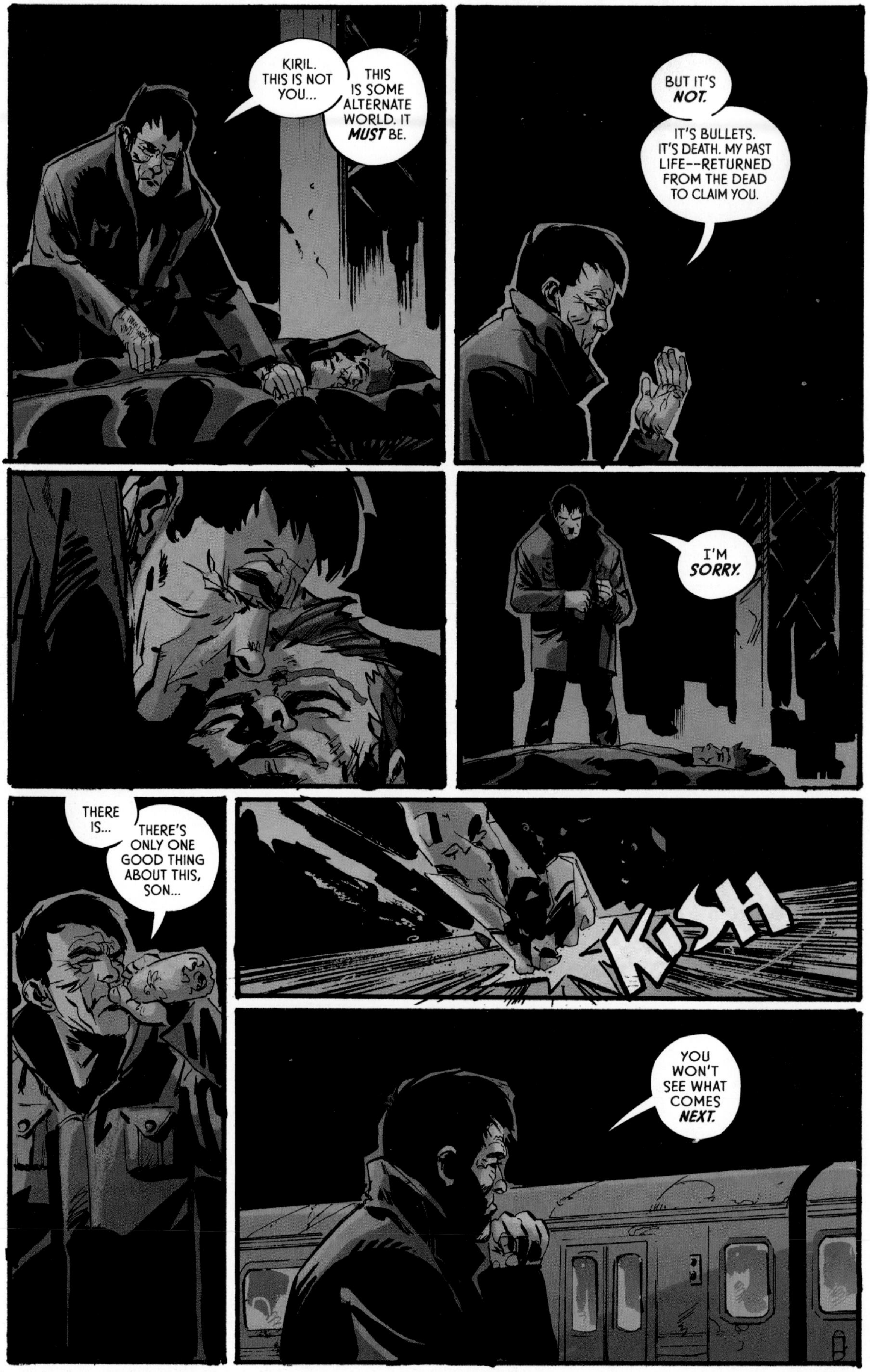
KIRIL. THIS IS NOT YOU...
THIS IS SOME ALTERNATE WORLD. IT *MUST* BE.
BUT IT'S *NOT.*
IT'S BULLETS. IT'S DEATH. MY PAST LIFE--RETURNED FROM THE DEAD TO CLAIM YOU.
I'M *SORRY.*
THERE IS...
THERE'S ONLY ONE GOOD THING ABOUT THIS, SON...
KOSH
YOU WON'T SEE WHAT COMES *NEXT.*

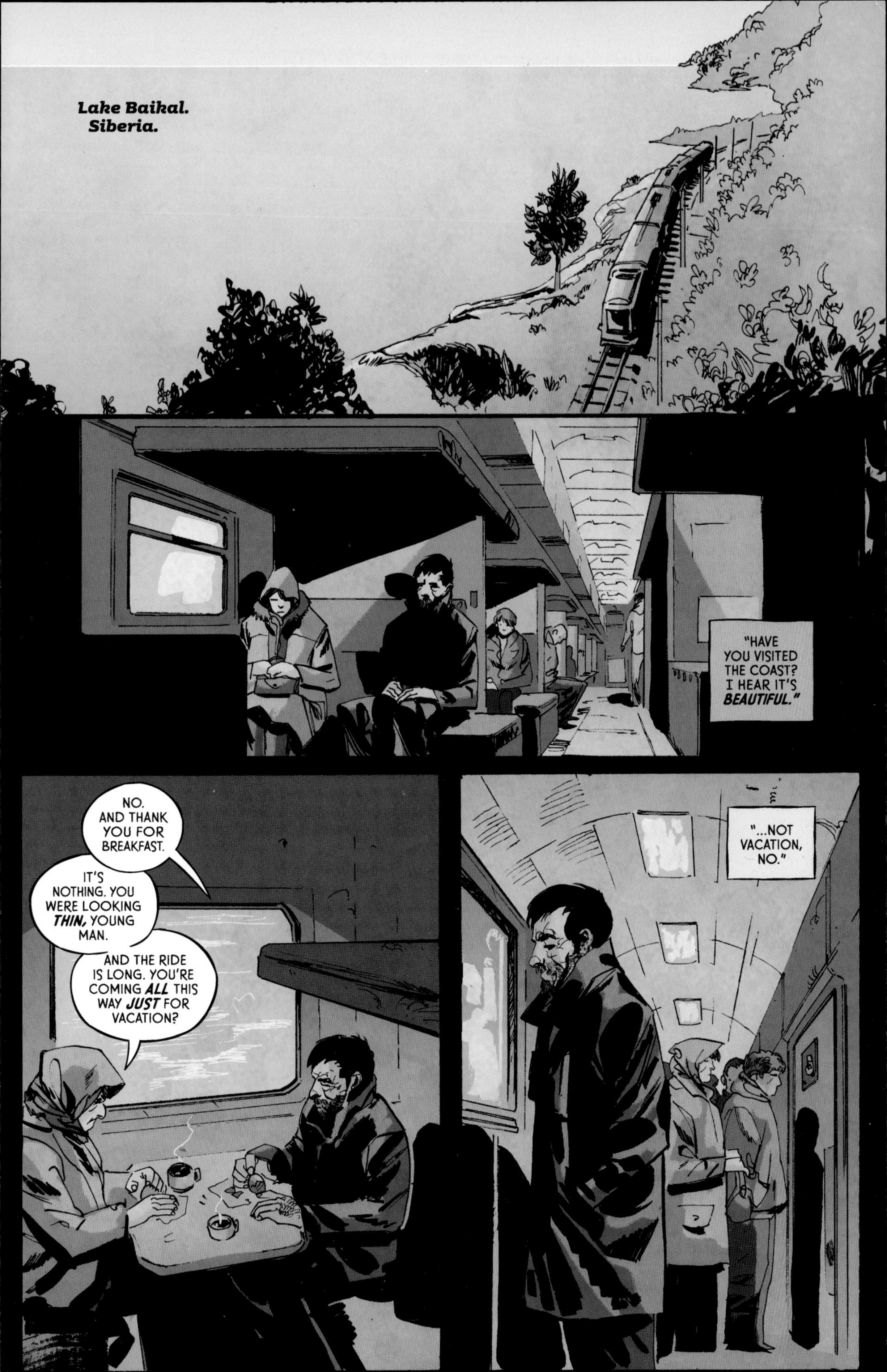
Lake Baikal.
Siberia.
"HAVE YOU VISITED THE COAST? I HEAR IT'S BEAUTIFUL."
NO. AND THANK YOU FOR BREAKFAST.
IT'S NOTHING. YOU WERE LOOKING THIN, YOUNG MAN.
AND THE RIDE IS LONG. YOU'RE COMING ALL THIS WAY JUST FOR VACATION?
"...NOT VACATION, NO."

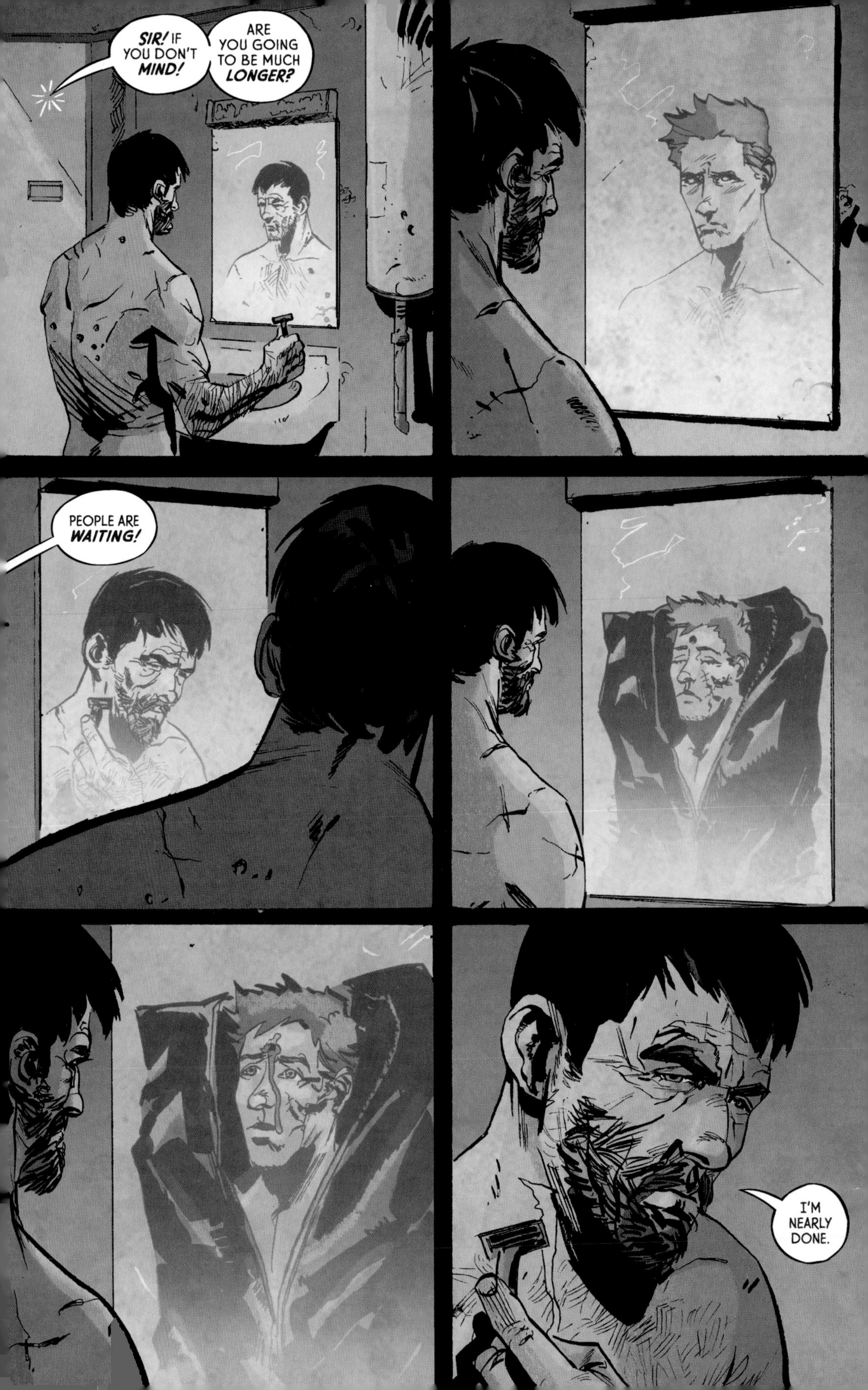
SIR! IF YOU DON'T MIND!
ARE YOU GOING TO BE MUCH LONGER?
PEOPLE ARE WAITING!
I'M NEARLY DONE.

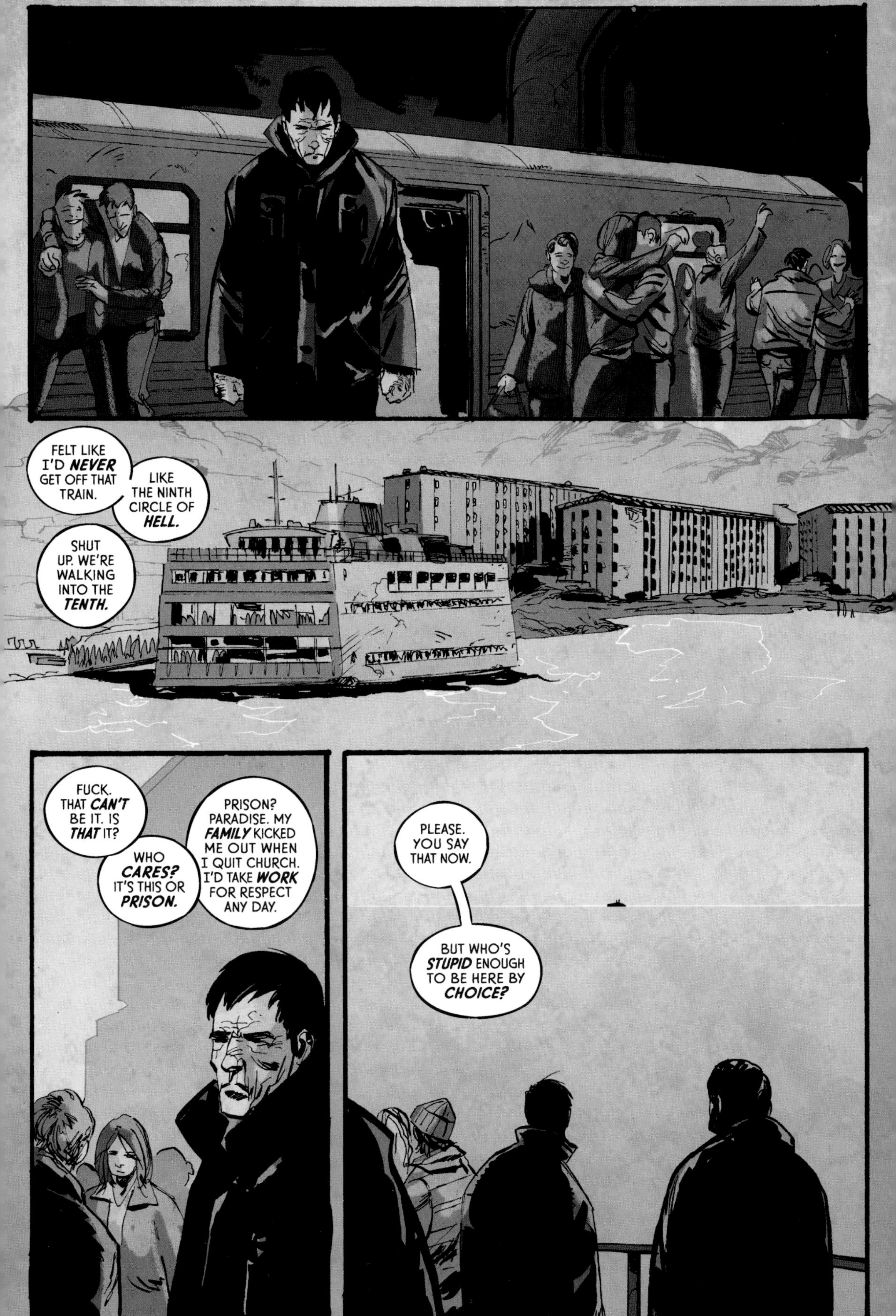

FELT LIKE I'D NEVER GET OFF THAT TRAIN.
LIKE THE NINTH CIRCLE OF HELL.
SHUT UP. WE'RE WALKING INTO THE TENTH.
FUCK. THAT CAN'T BE IT. IS THAT IT?
WHO CARES? IT'S THIS OR PRISON.
PRISON? PARADISE. MY FAMILY KICKED ME OUT WHEN I QUIT CHURCH. I'D TAKE WORK FOR RESPECT ANY DAY.
PLEASE. YOU SAY THAT NOW.
BUT WHO'S STUPID ENOUGH TO BE HERE BY CHOICE?

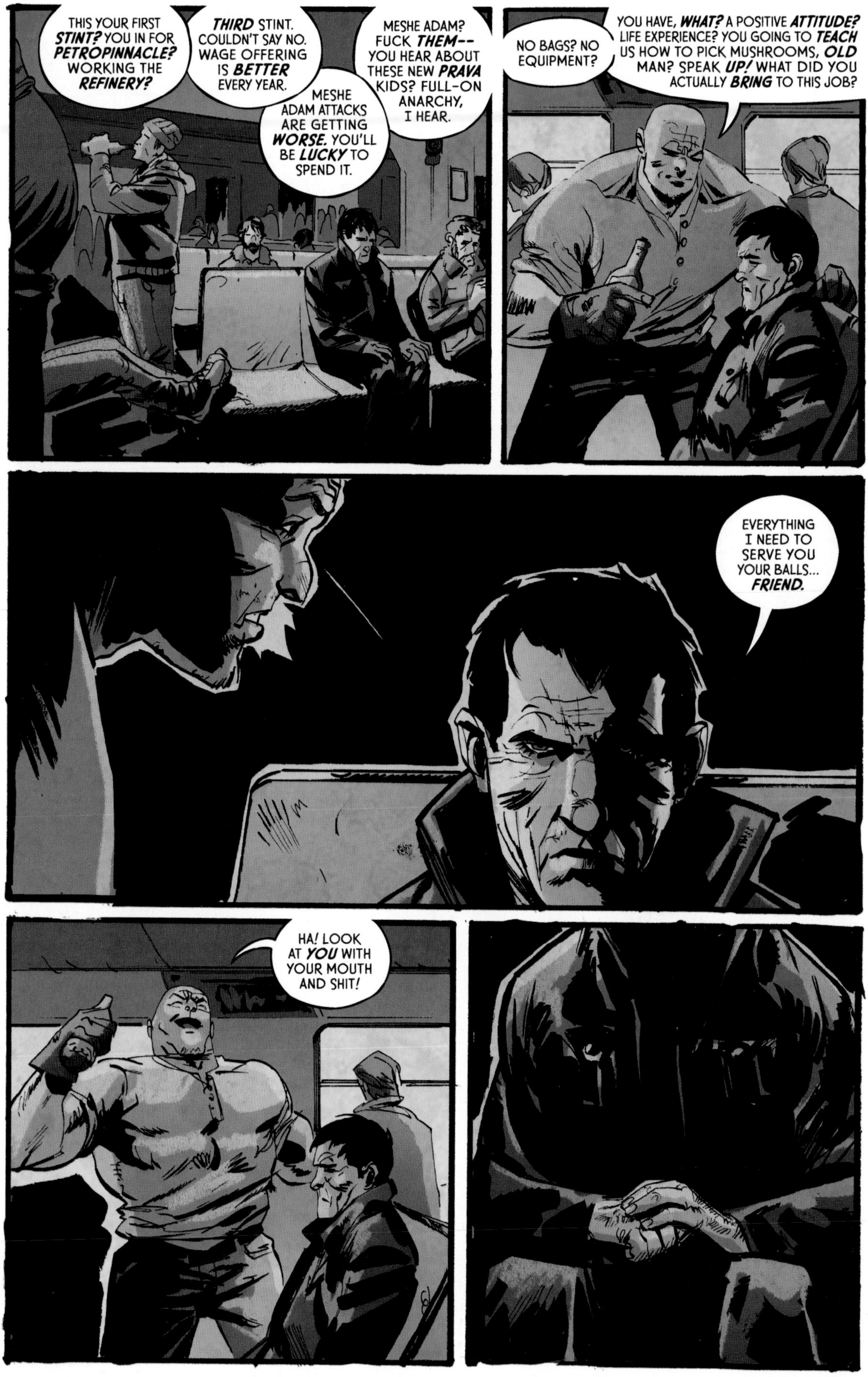
THIS YOUR FIRST STINT? YOU IN FOR PETROPINNACLE? WORKING THE REFINERY?
THIRD STINT. COULDN'T SAY NO. WAGE OFFERING IS BETTER EVERY YEAR.
MESHE ADAM ATTACKS ARE GETTING WORSE. YOU'LL BE LUCKY TO SPEND IT.
MESHE ADAM? FUCK THEM-- YOU HEAR ABOUT THESE NEW PRAVA KIDS? FULL-ON ANARCHY, I HEAR.
NO BAGS? NO EQUIPMENT?
YOU HAVE, WHAT? A POSITIVE ATTITUDE? LIFE EXPERIENCE? YOU GOING TO TEACH US HOW TO PICK MUSHROOMS, OLD MAN? SPEAK UP! WHAT DID YOU ACTUALLY BRING TO THIS JOB?
EVERYTHING I NEED TO SERVE YOU YOUR BALLS... FRIEND.
HA! LOOK AT YOU WITH YOUR MOUTH AND SHIT!

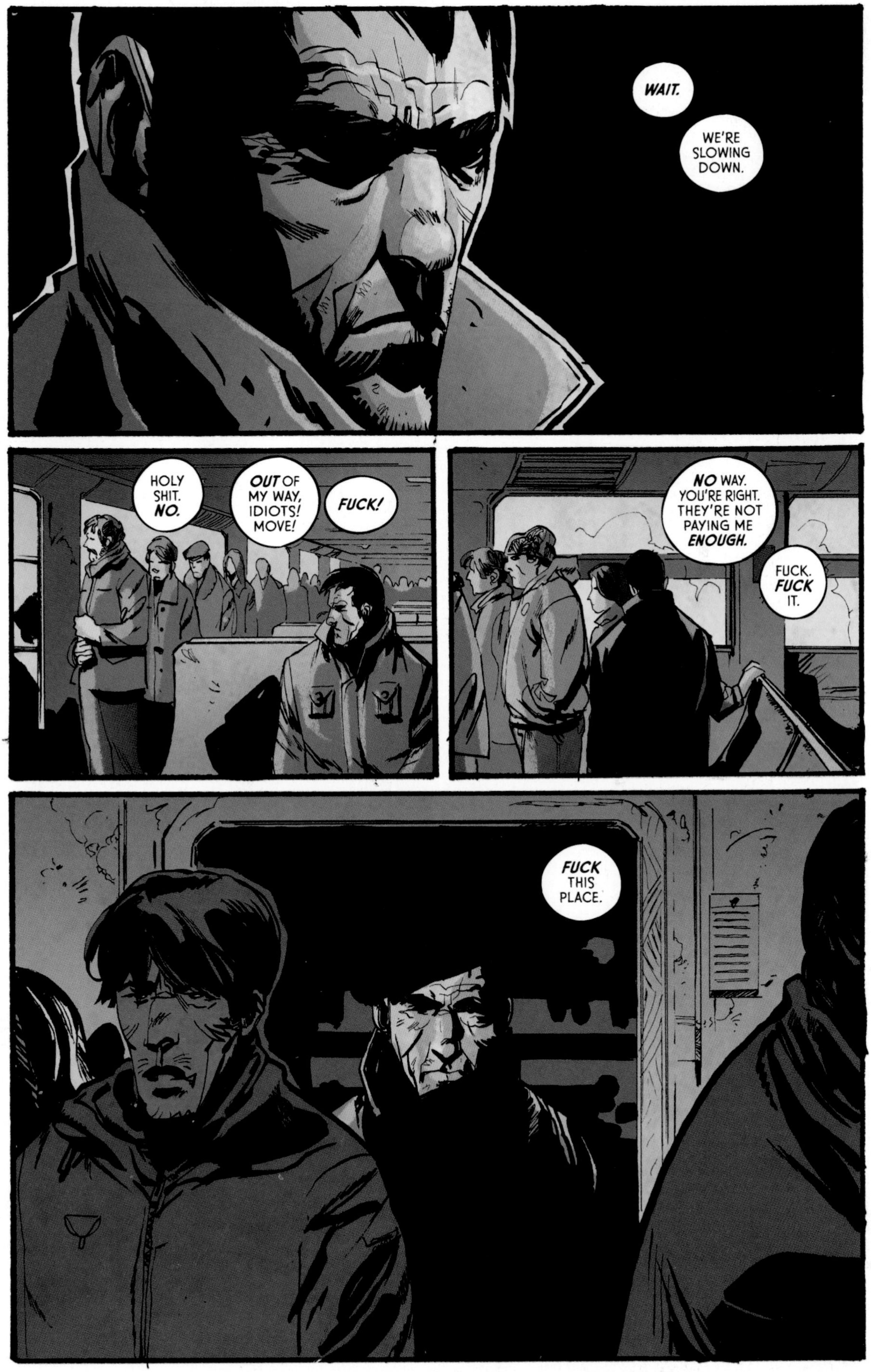
WAIT.
WE'RE SLOWING DOWN.
HOLY SHIT. NO.
OUT OF MY WAY, IDIOTS! MOVE!
FUCK!
NO WAY. YOU'RE RIGHT. THEY'RE NOT PAYING ME ENOUGH.
FUCK. FUCK IT.
FUCK THIS PLACE.

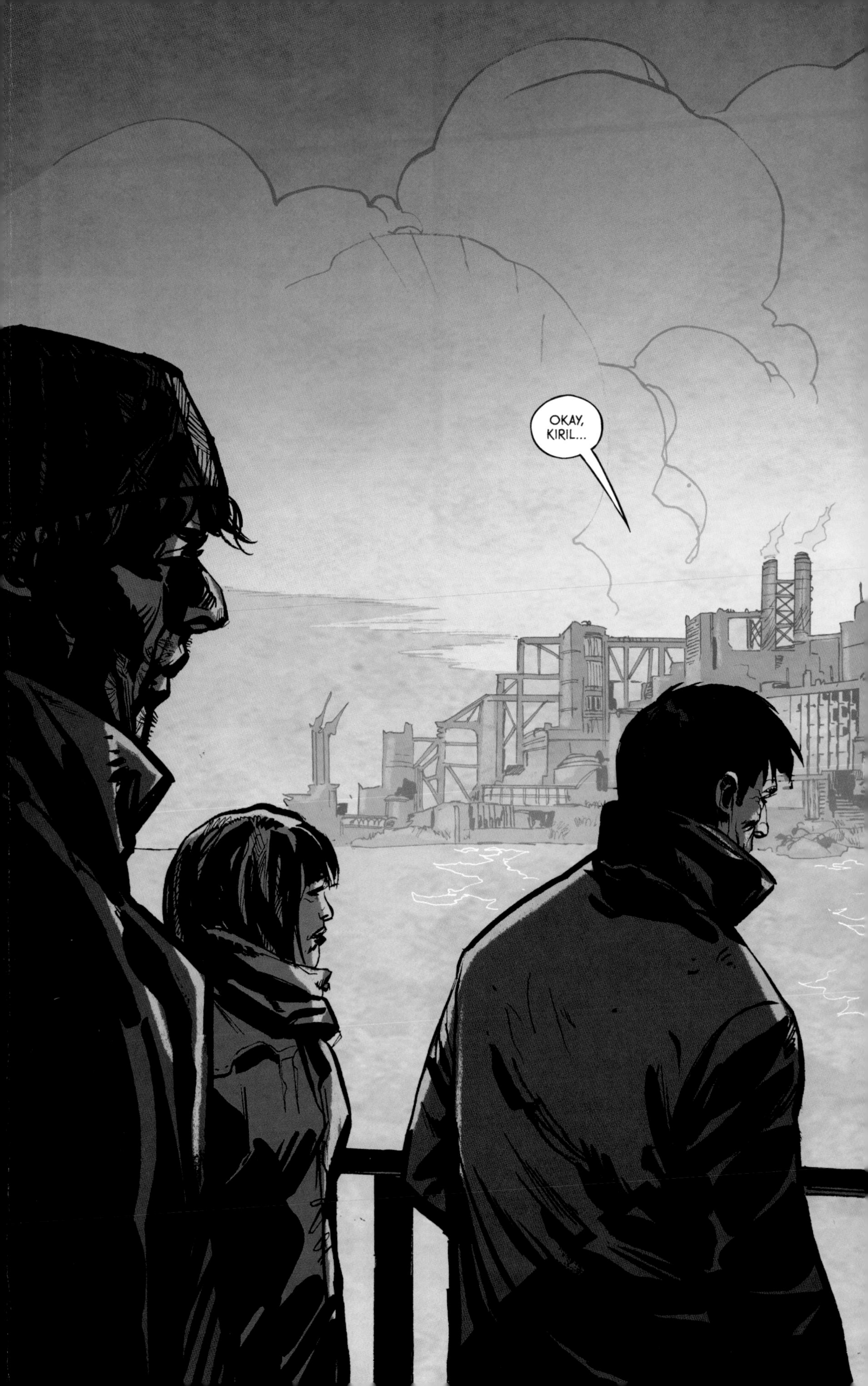
OKAY, KIRIL...

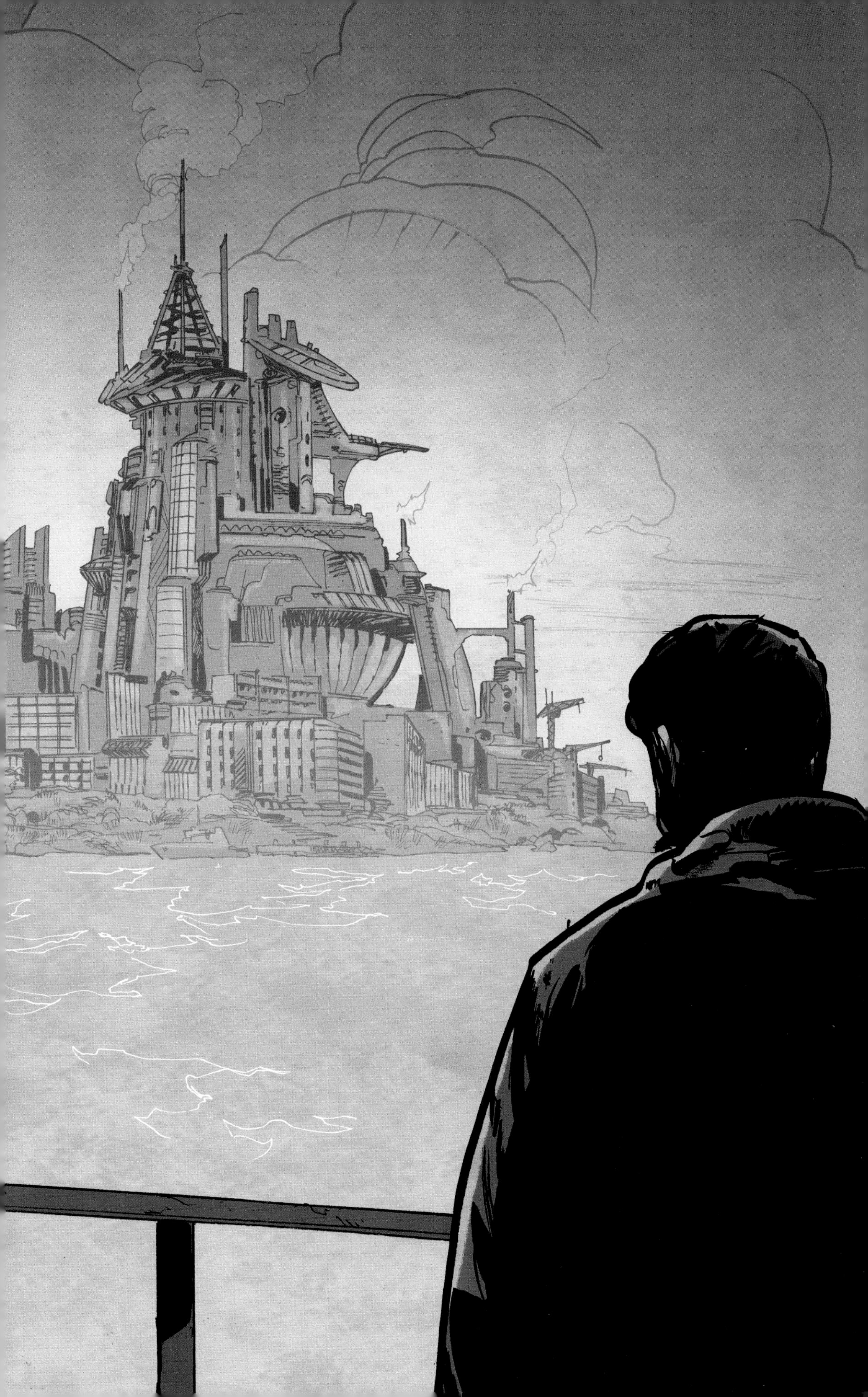

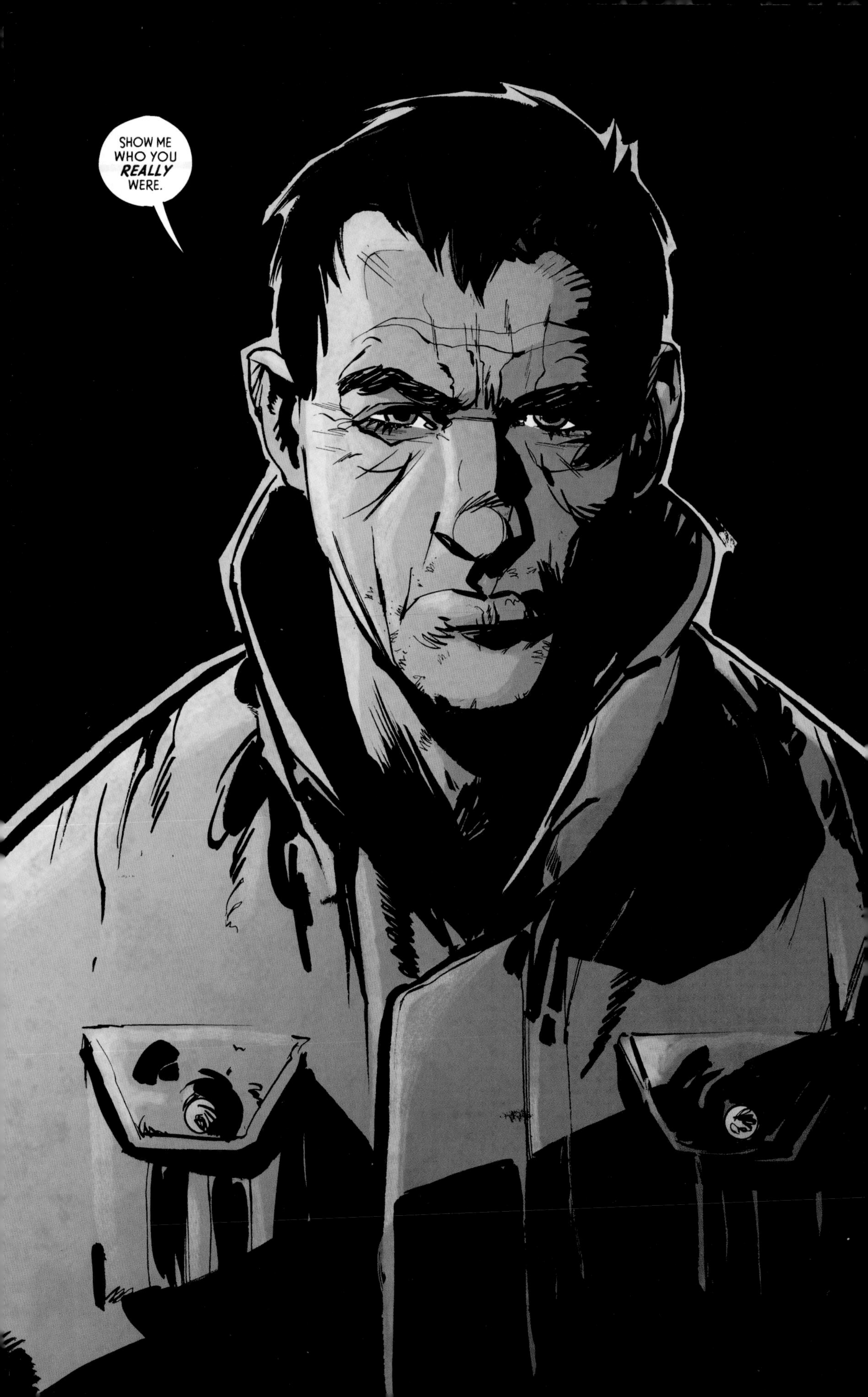
SHOW ME WHO YOU **REALLY** WERE.

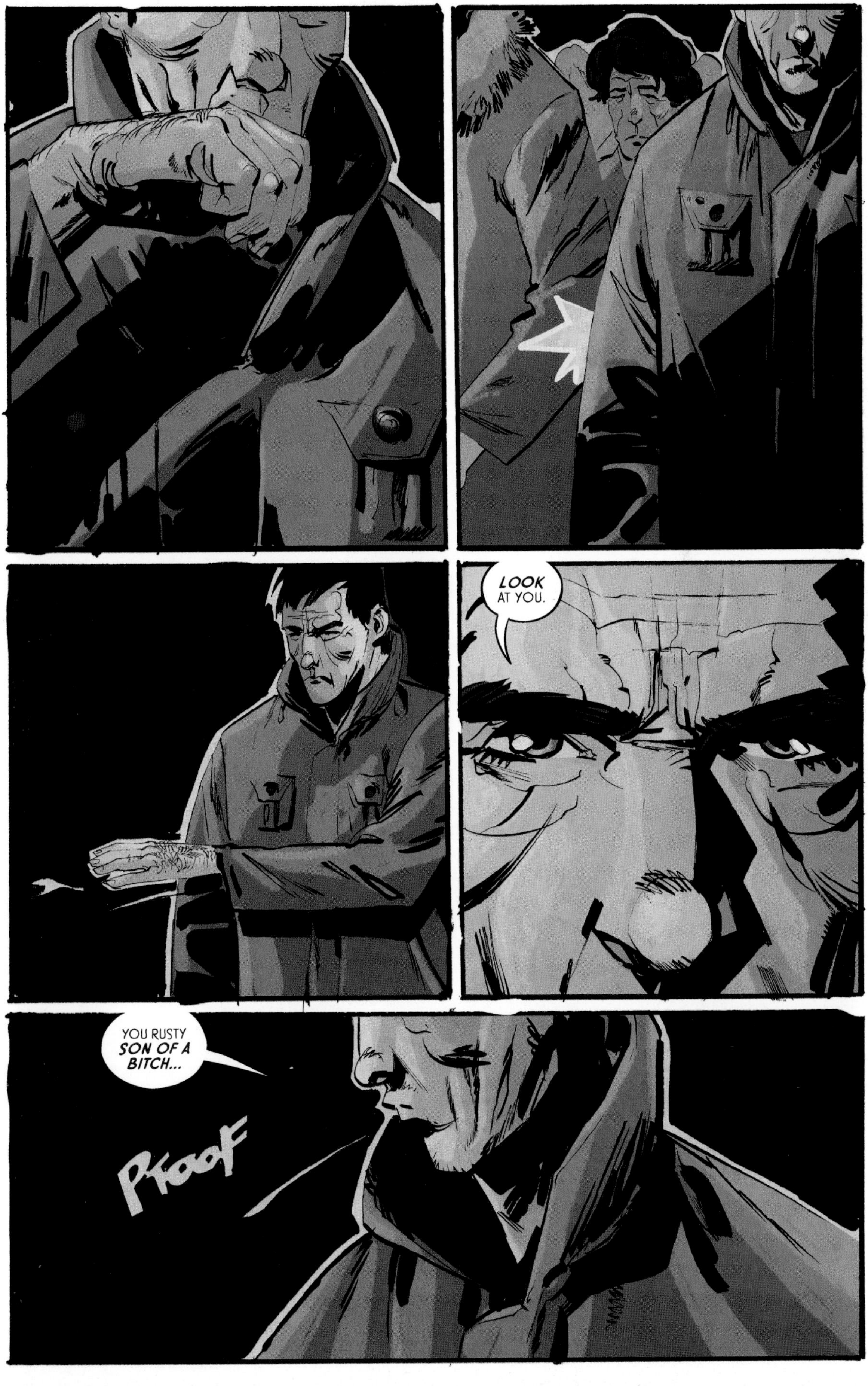
LOOK AT YOU.
YOU RUSTY SON OF A BITCH...
PFOOF

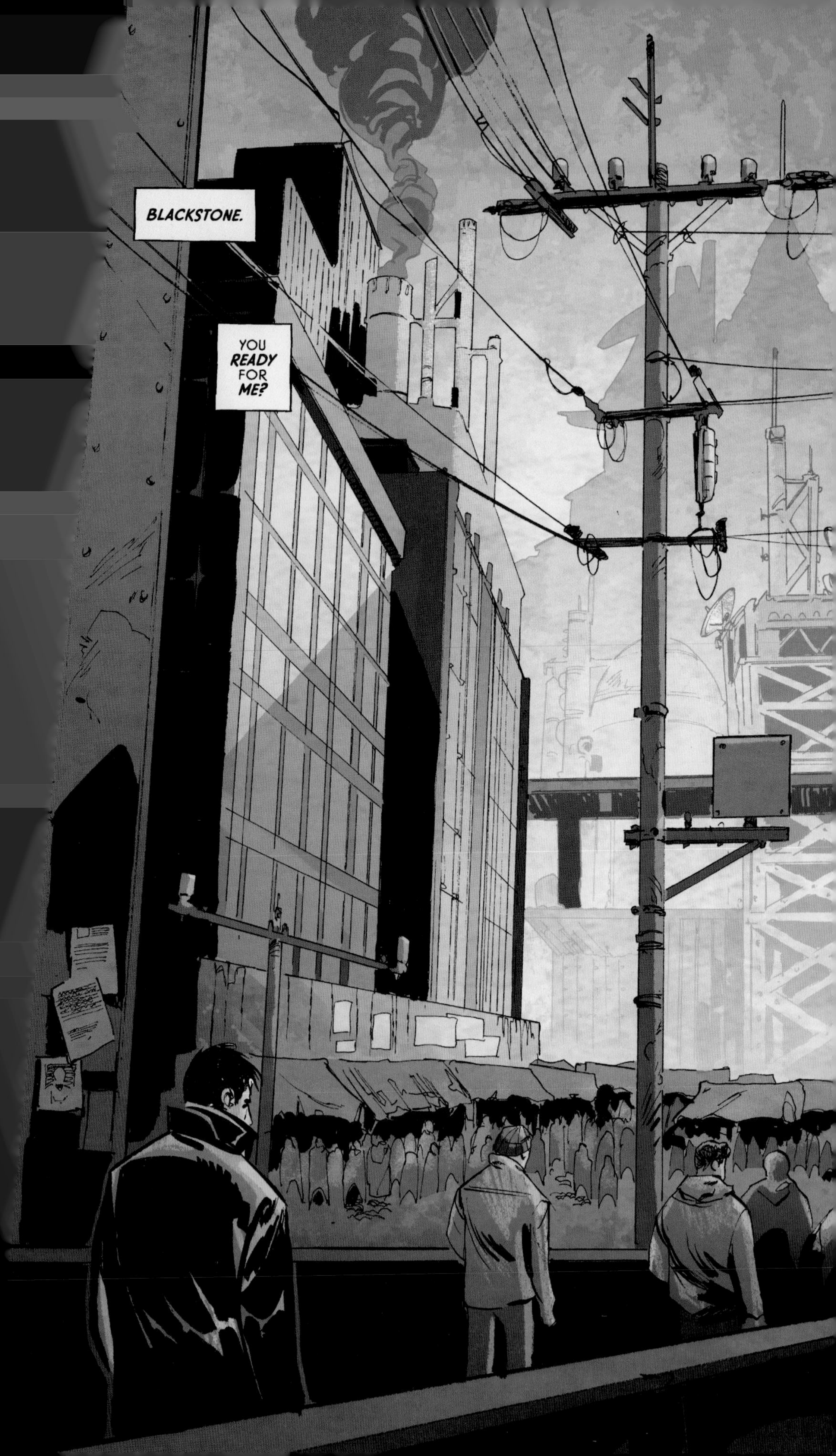
BLACKSTONE.
YOU READY FOR ME?

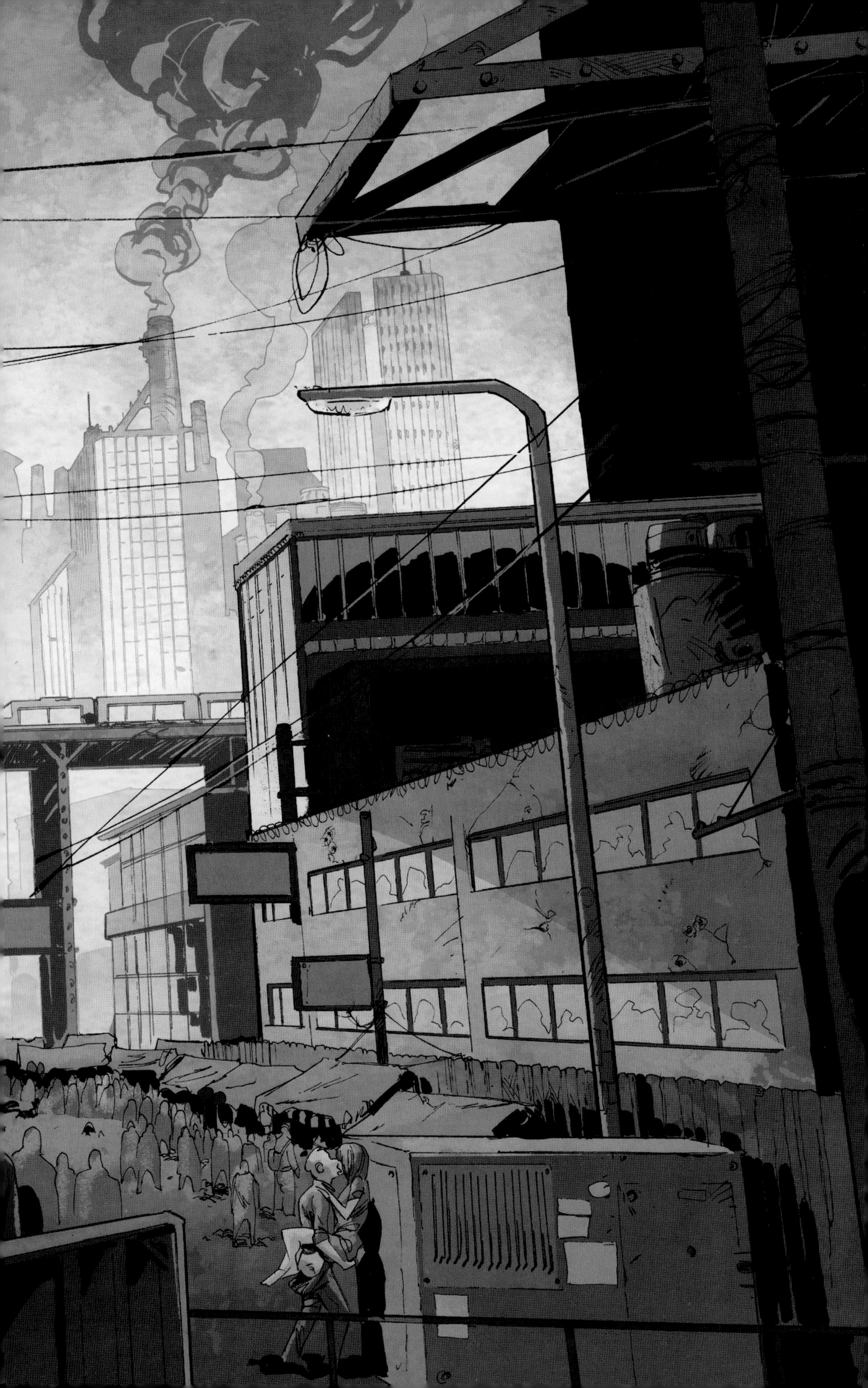

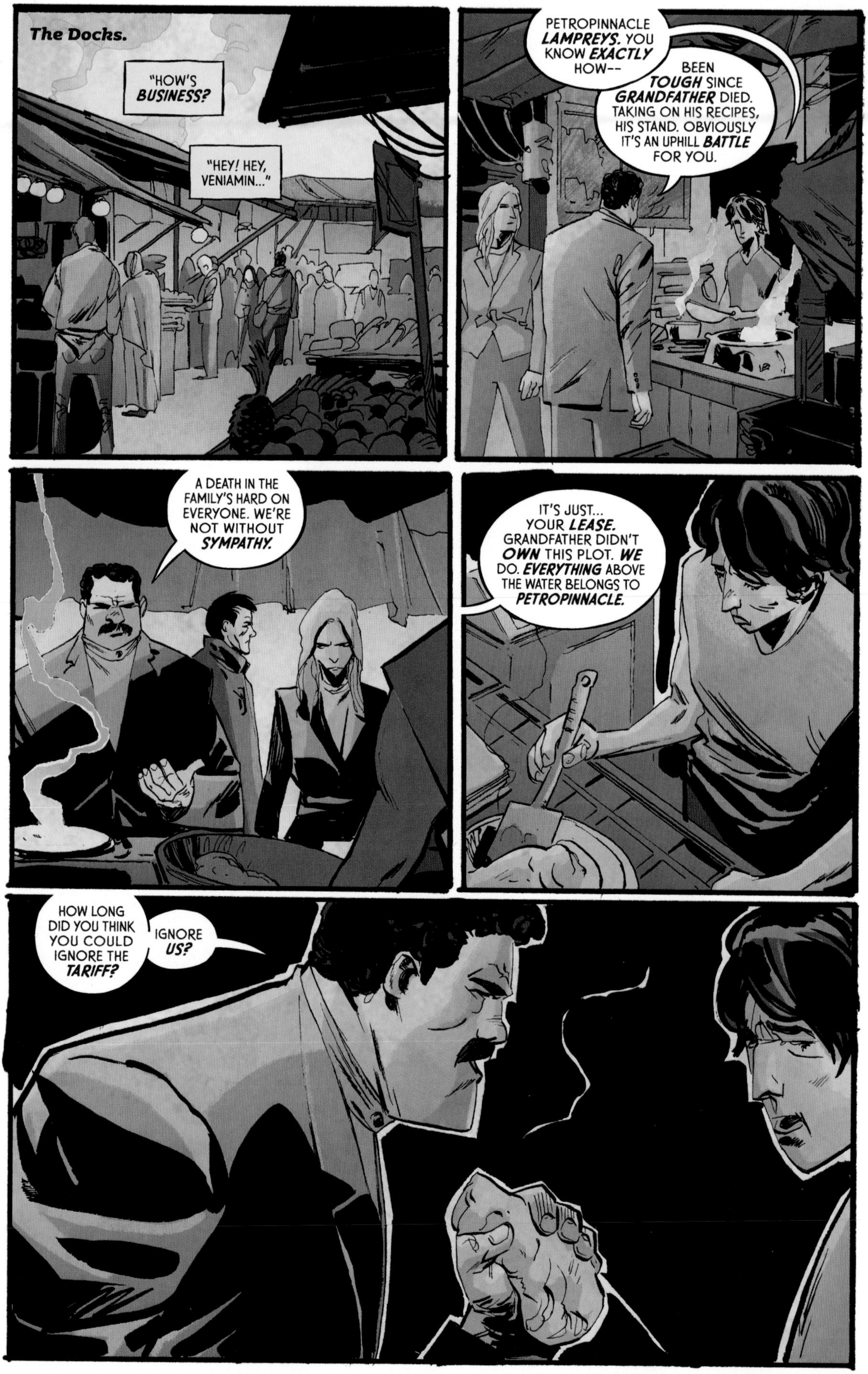
The Docks.
"HOW'S BUSINESS?
"HEY! HEY, VENIAMIN..."
PETROPINNACLE LAMPREYS. YOU KNOW EXACTLY HOW--
BEEN TOUGH SINCE GRANDFATHER DIED. TAKING ON HIS RECIPES, HIS STAND. OBVIOUSLY IT'S AN UPHILL BATTLE FOR YOU.
A DEATH IN THE FAMILY'S HARD ON EVERYONE. WE'RE NOT WITHOUT SYMPATHY.
IT'S JUST... YOUR LEASE. GRANDFATHER DIDN'T OWN THIS PLOT. WE DO. EVERYTHING ABOVE THE WATER BELONGS TO PETROPINNACLE.
HOW LONG DID YOU THINK YOU COULD IGNORE THE TARIFF?
IGNORE US?

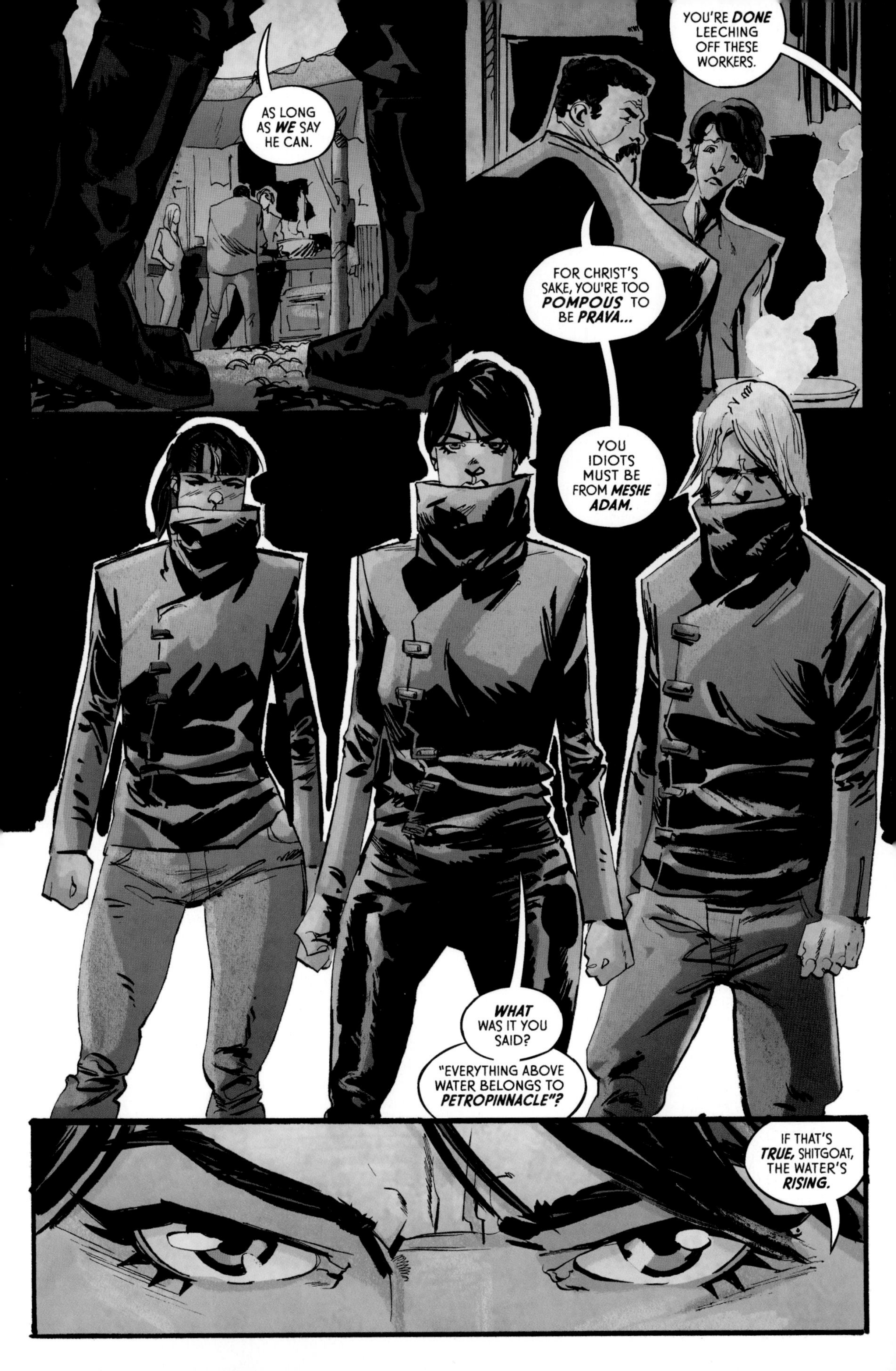
AS LONG AS WE SAY HE CAN.
YOU'RE DONE LEECHING OFF THESE WORKERS.
FOR CHRIST'S SAKE, YOU'RE TOO POMPOUS TO BE PRAVA...
YOU IDIOTS MUST BE FROM MESHE ADAM.
WHAT WAS IT YOU SAID?
"EVERYTHING ABOVE WATER BELONGS TO PETROPINNACLE"?
IF THAT'S TRUE, SHITGOAT, THE WATER'S RISING.

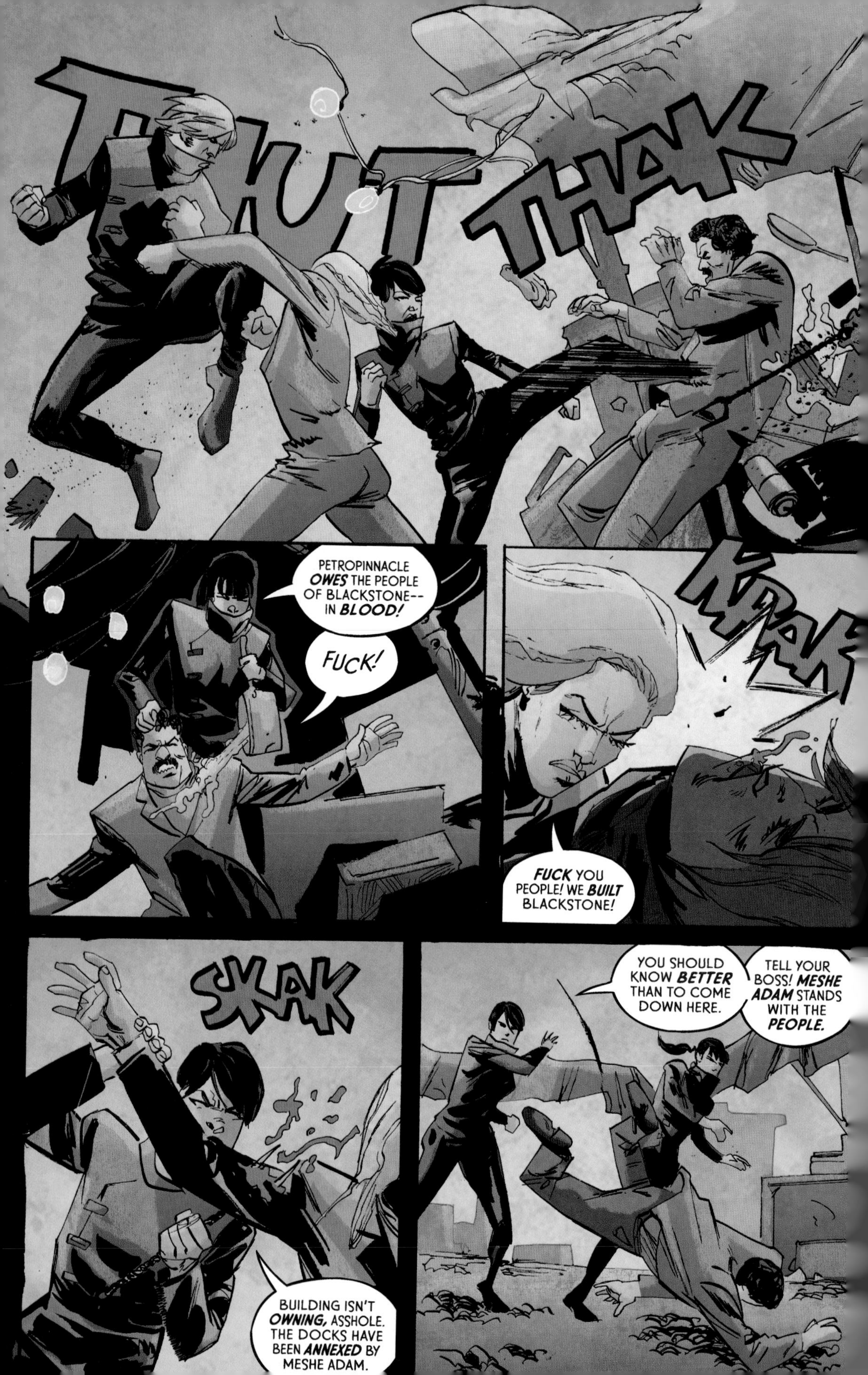
THUT
THAK
PETROPINNACLE OWES THE PEOPLE OF BLACKSTONE-- IN BLOOD!
FUCK!
KRAK
FUCK YOU PEOPLE! WE BUILT BLACKSTONE!
SKLAK
BUILDING ISN'T OWNING, ASSHOLE. THE DOCKS HAVE BEEN ANNEXED BY MESHE ADAM.
YOU SHOULD KNOW BETTER THAN TO COME DOWN HERE.
TELL YOUR BOSS! MESHE ADAM STANDS WITH THE PEOPLE.

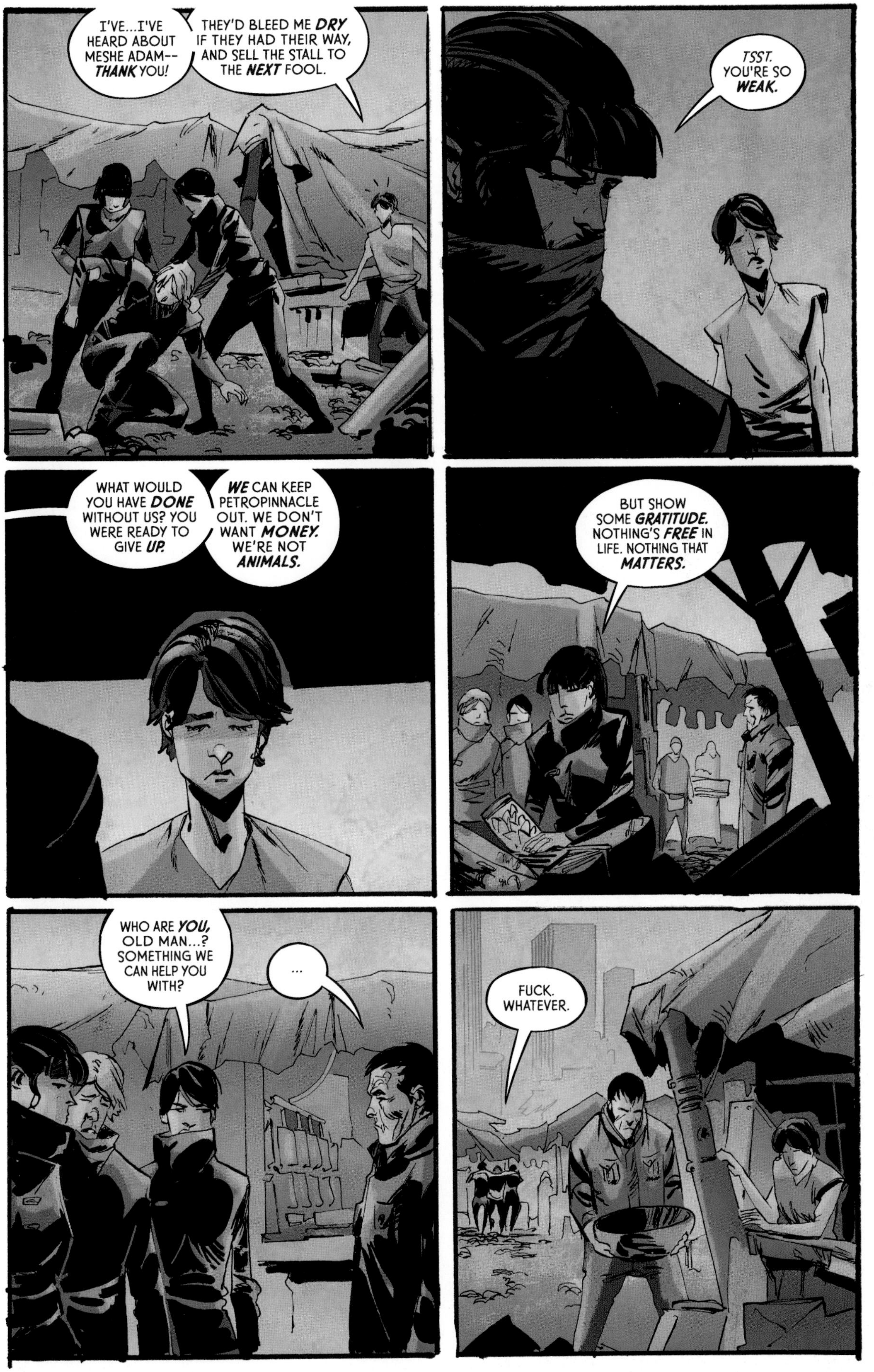
I'VE...I'VE HEARD ABOUT MESHE ADAM--THANK YOU!
THEY'D BLEED ME DRY IF THEY HAD THEIR WAY, AND SELL THE STALL TO THE NEXT FOOL.
TSST. YOU'RE SO WEAK.
WHAT WOULD YOU HAVE DONE WITHOUT US? YOU WERE READY TO GIVE UP.
WE CAN KEEP PETROPINNACLE OUT. WE DON'T WANT MONEY. WE'RE NOT ANIMALS.
BUT SHOW SOME GRATITUDE. NOTHING'S FREE IN LIFE. NOTHING THAT MATTERS.
WHO ARE YOU, OLD MAN...? SOMETHING WE CAN HELP YOU WITH?
...
FUCK. WHATEVER.

In minutes.

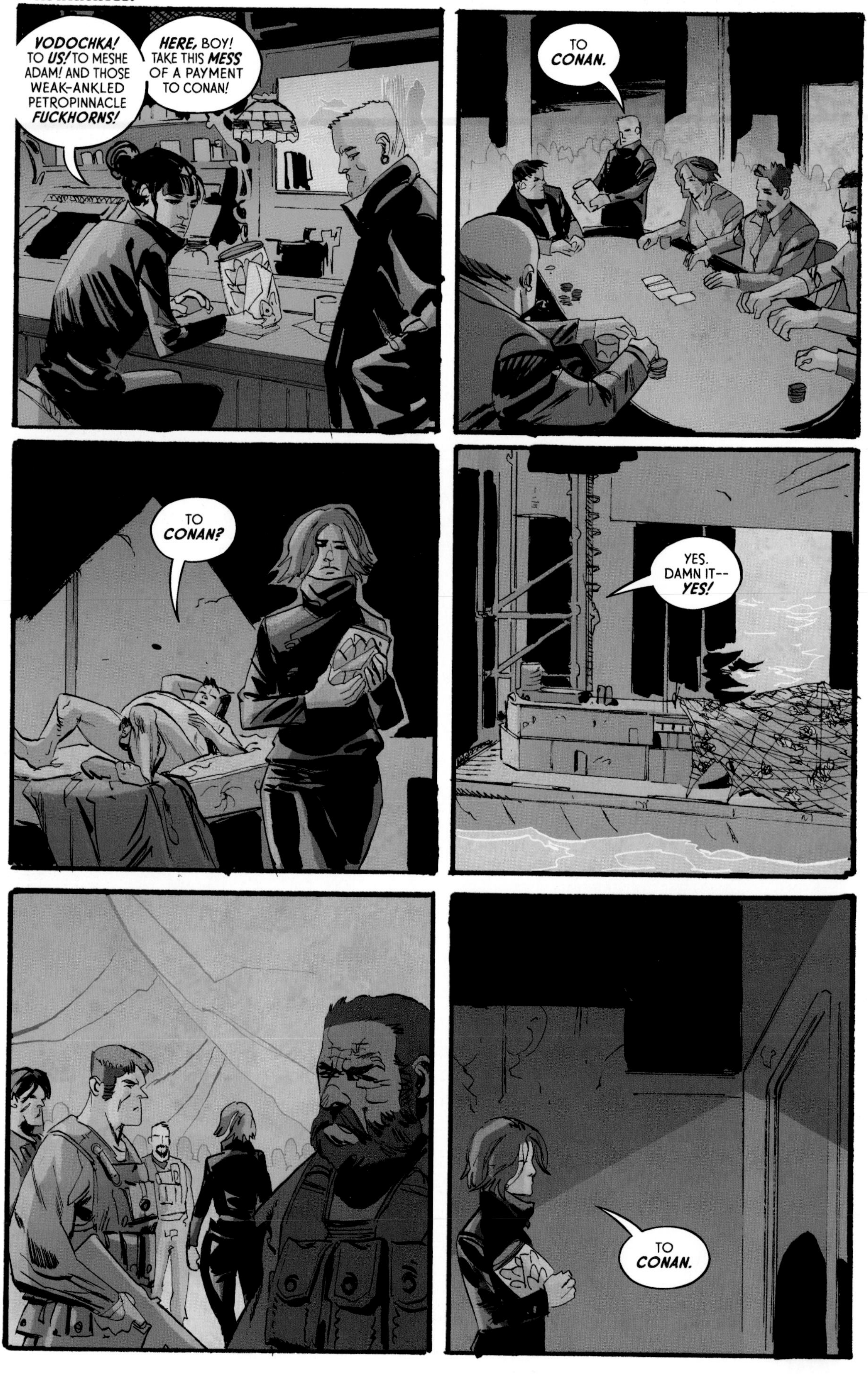
VODOCHKA! TO US! TO MESHE ADAM! AND THOSE WEAK-ANKLED PETROPINNACLE FUCKHORNS!
HERE, BOY! TAKE THIS MESS OF A PAYMENT TO CONAN!
TO CONAN.
TO CONAN?
YES. DAMN IT-- YES!
TO CONAN.

Meshe Adam Keep. Floating beneath Blackstone.

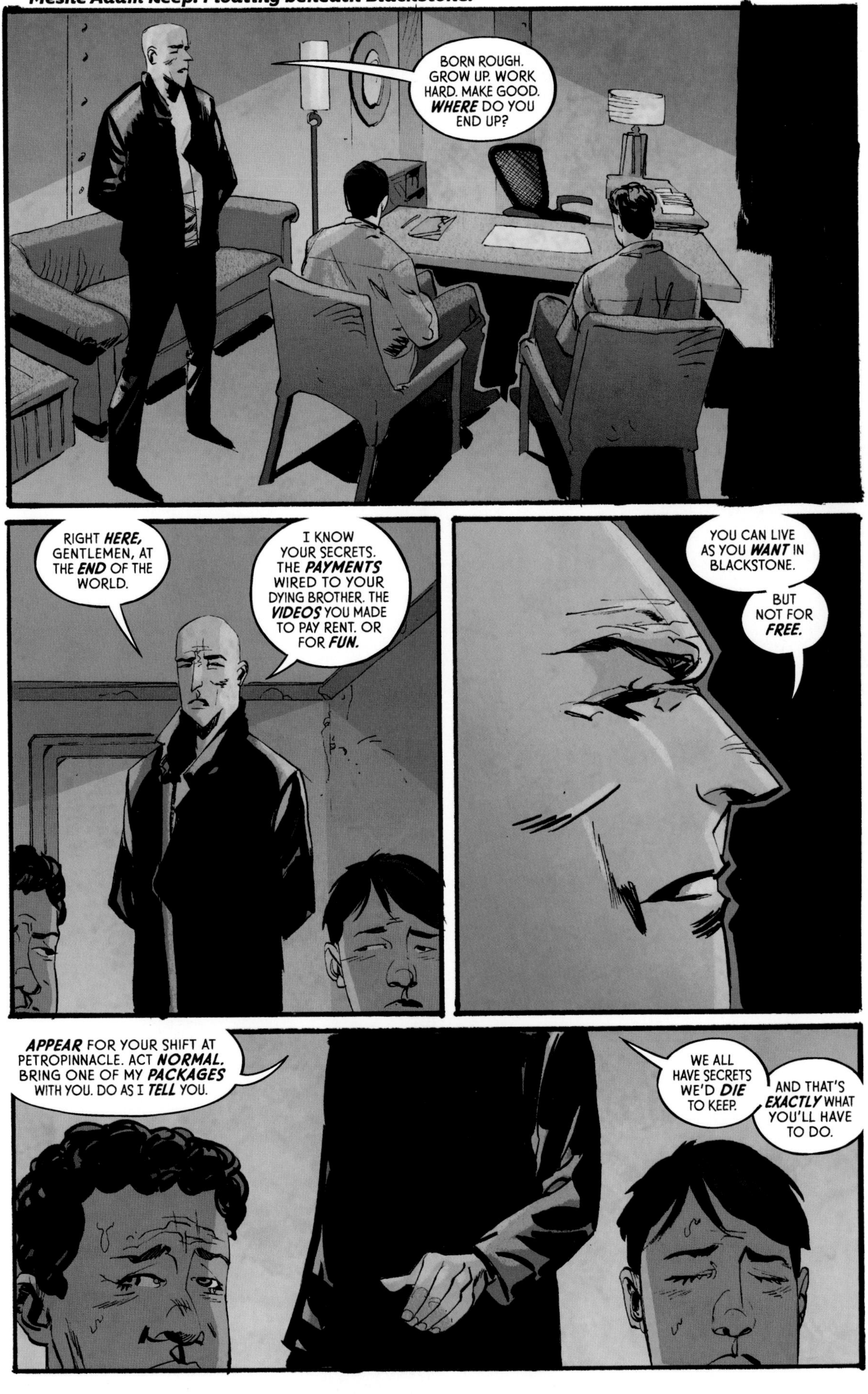
BORN ROUGH. GROW UP. WORK HARD. MAKE GOOD. *WHERE* DO YOU END UP?
RIGHT *HERE,* GENTLEMEN, AT THE *END* OF THE WORLD.
I KNOW YOUR SECRETS. THE *PAYMENTS* WIRED TO YOUR DYING BROTHER. THE *VIDEOS* YOU MADE TO PAY RENT. OR FOR *FUN.*
YOU CAN LIVE AS YOU *WANT* IN BLACKSTONE.
BUT NOT FOR *FREE.*
APPEAR FOR YOUR SHIFT AT PETROPINNACLE. ACT *NORMAL.* BRING ONE OF MY *PACKAGES* WITH YOU. DO AS I *TELL* YOU.
WE ALL HAVE SECRETS WE'D *DIE* TO KEEP.
AND THAT'S *EXACTLY* WHAT YOU'LL HAVE TO DO.

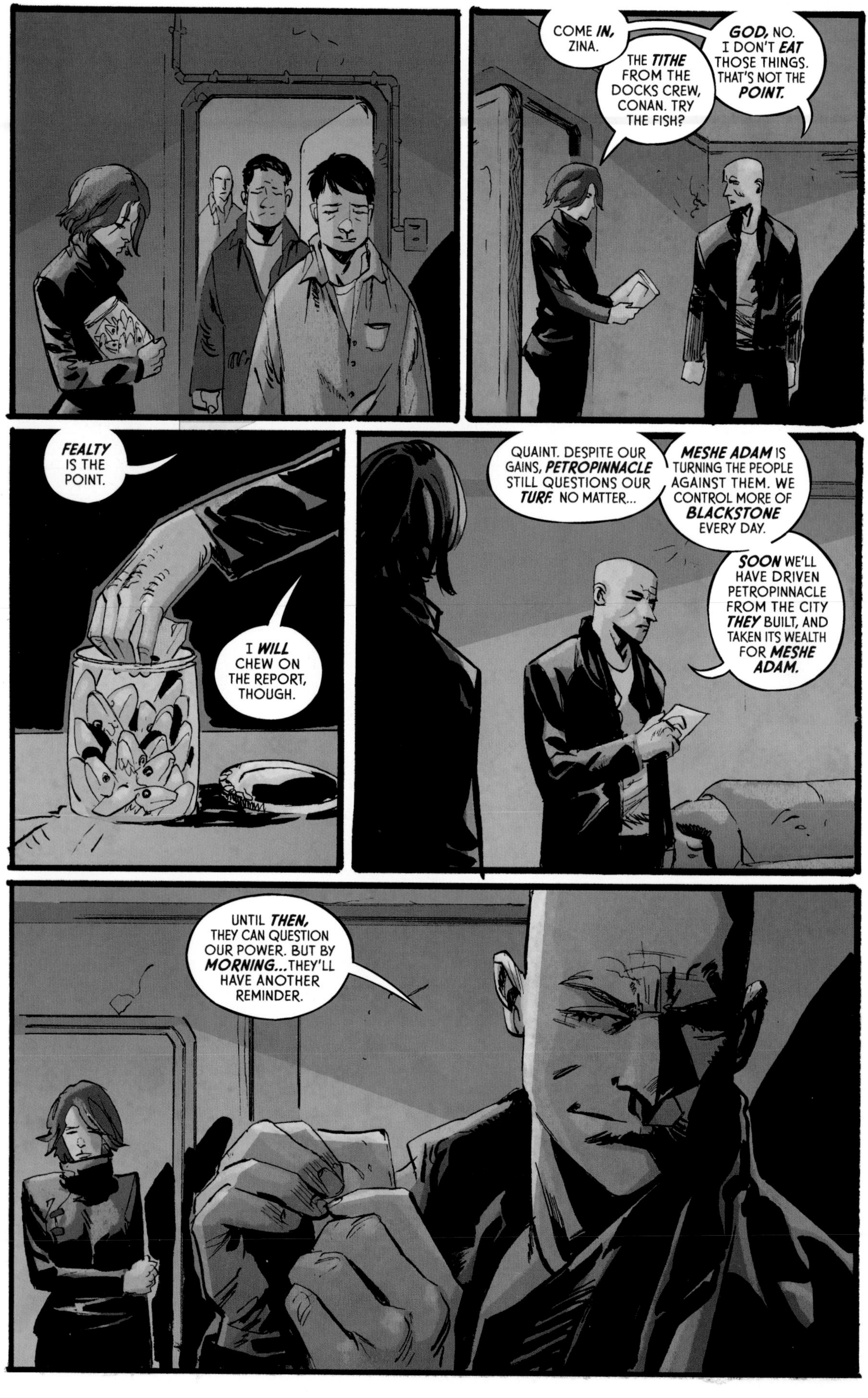
COME IN, ZINA.
THE TITHE FROM THE DOCKS CREW, CONAN. TRY THE FISH?
GOD, NO. I DON'T EAT THOSE THINGS. THAT'S NOT THE POINT.
FEALTY IS THE POINT.
I WILL CHEW ON THE REPORT, THOUGH.
QUAINT. DESPITE OUR GAINS, PETROPINNACLE STILL QUESTIONS OUR TURF. NO MATTER...
MESHE ADAM IS TURNING THE PEOPLE AGAINST THEM. WE CONTROL MORE OF BLACKSTONE EVERY DAY.
SOON WE'LL HAVE DRIVEN PETROPINNACLE FROM THE CITY THEY BUILT, AND TAKEN ITS WEALTH FOR MESHE ADAM.
UNTIL THEN, THEY CAN QUESTION OUR POWER. BUT BY MORNING...THEY'LL HAVE ANOTHER REMINDER.

The Docks.

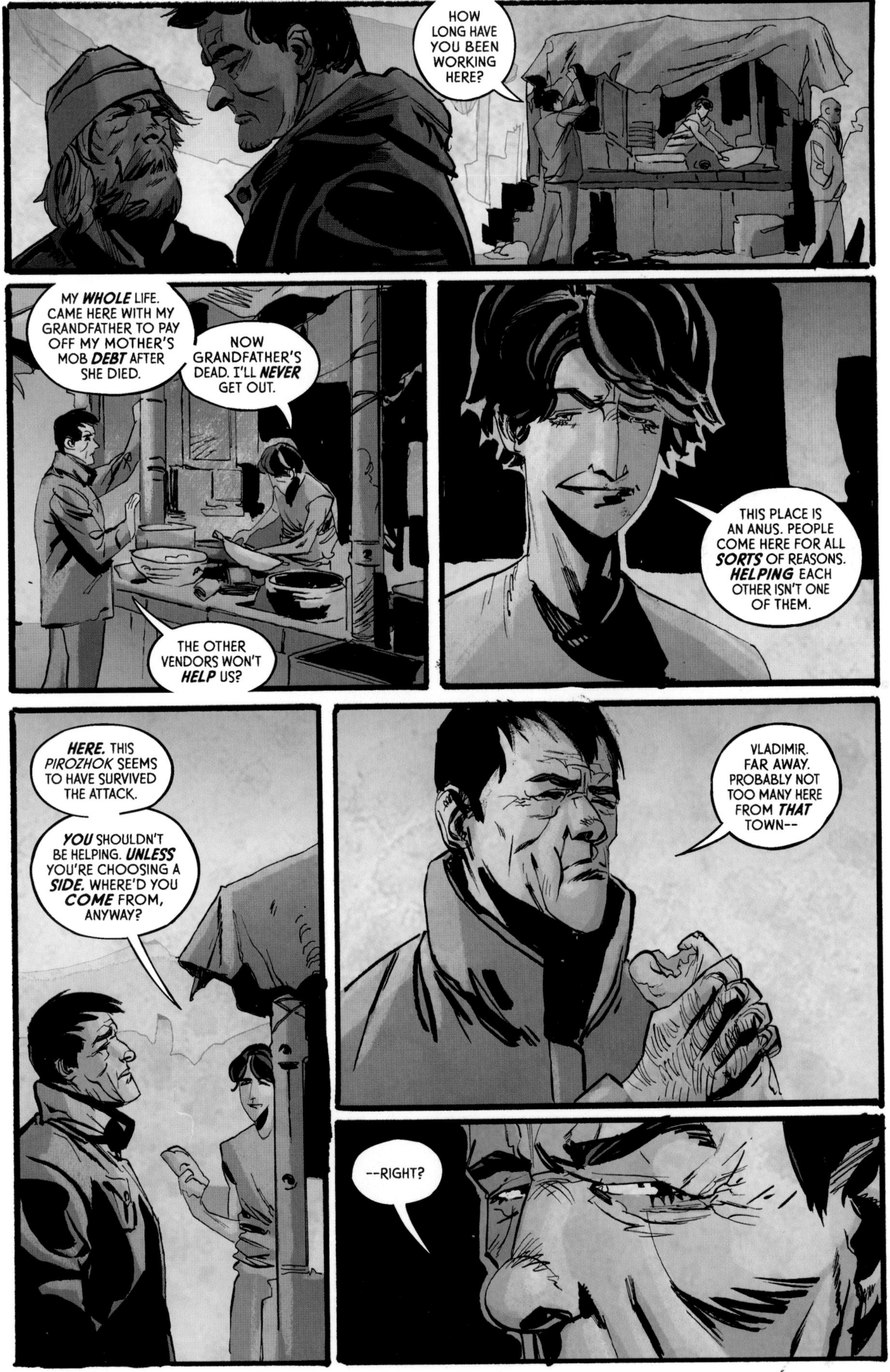
HOW LONG HAVE YOU BEEN WORKING HERE?
MY WHOLE LIFE. CAME HERE WITH MY GRANDFATHER TO PAY OFF MY MOTHER'S MOB DEBT AFTER SHE DIED.
NOW GRANDFATHER'S DEAD. I'LL NEVER GET OUT.
THE OTHER VENDORS WON'T HELP US?
THIS PLACE IS AN ANUS. PEOPLE COME HERE FOR ALL SORTS OF REASONS. HELPING EACH OTHER ISN'T ONE OF THEM.
HERE. THIS PIROZHOK SEEMS TO HAVE SURVIVED THE ATTACK.
YOU SHOULDN'T BE HELPING. UNLESS YOU'RE CHOOSING A SIDE. WHERE'D YOU COME FROM, ANYWAY?
VLADIMIR. FAR AWAY. PROBABLY NOT TOO MANY HERE FROM THAT TOWN--
--RIGHT?

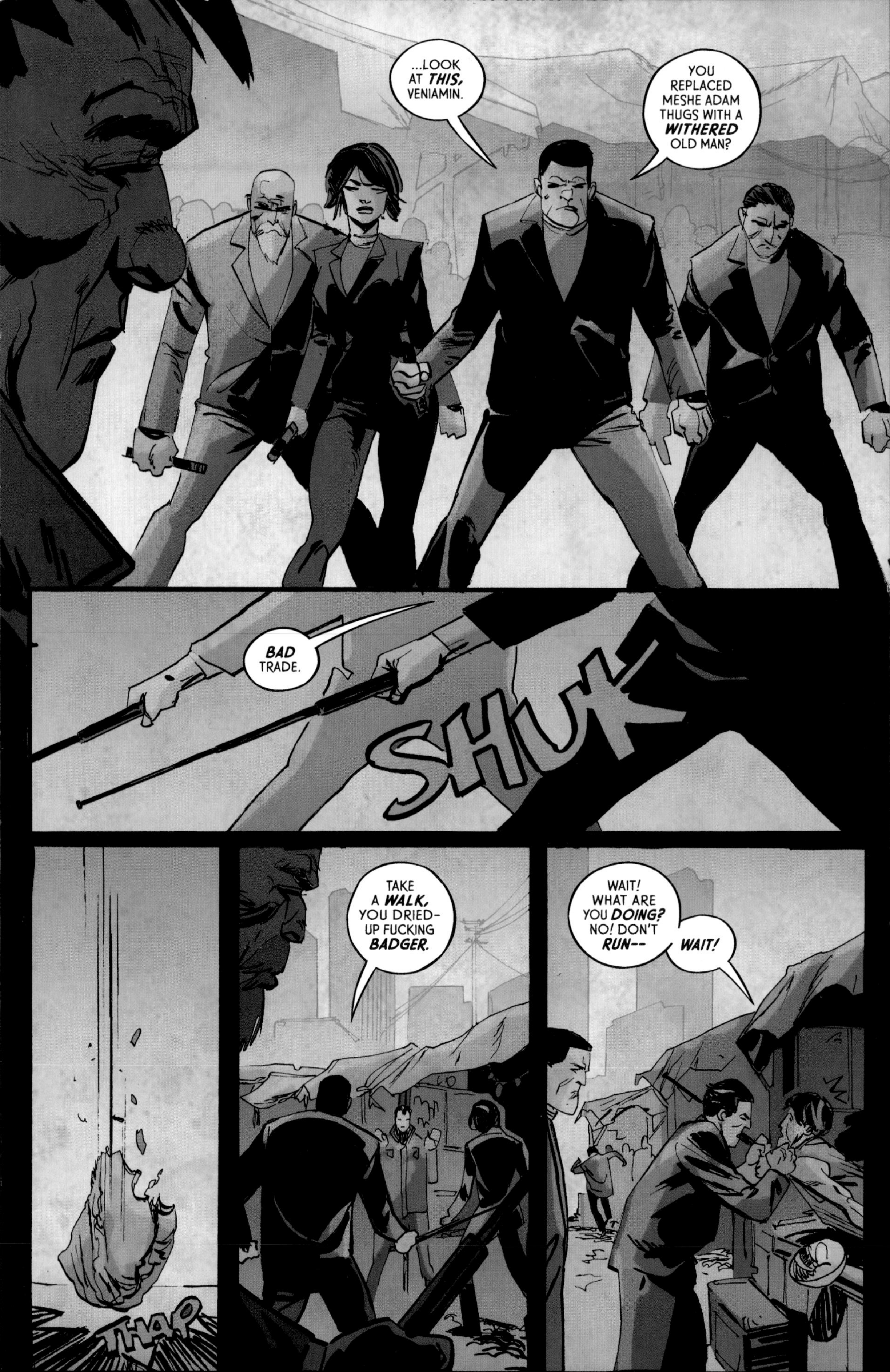
...LOOK AT THIS, VENIAMIN.
YOU REPLACED MESHE ADAM THUGS WITH A WITHERED OLD MAN?
BAD TRADE.
SHUK
THAP
TAKE A WALK, YOU DRIED-UP FUCKING BADGER.
WAIT! WHAT ARE YOU DOING? NO! DON'T RUN--
WAIT!

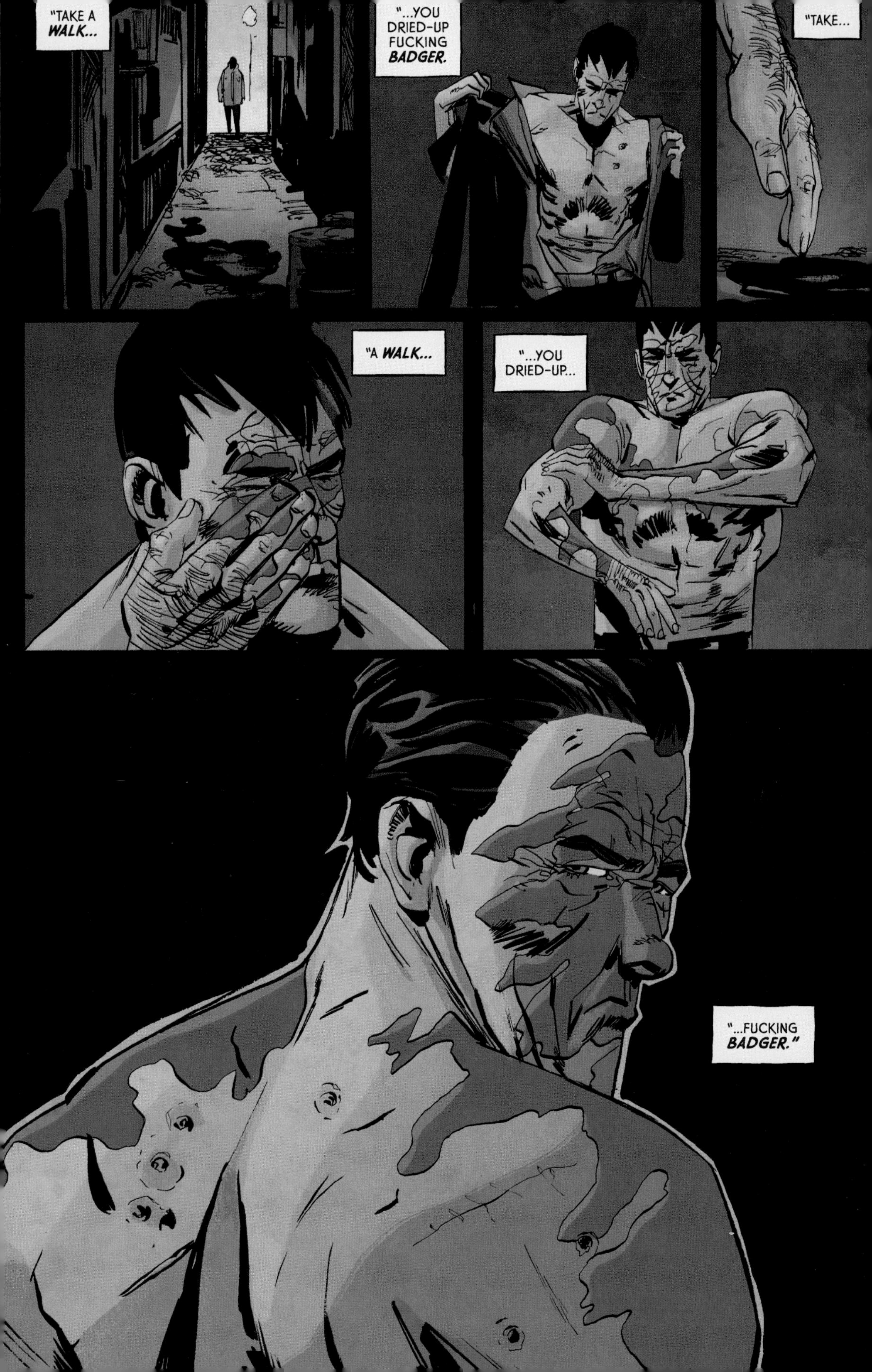
"TAKE A WALK...
"...YOU DRIED-UP FUCKING BADGER.
"TAKE...
"A WALK...
"...YOU DRIED-UP...
"...FUCKING BADGER."

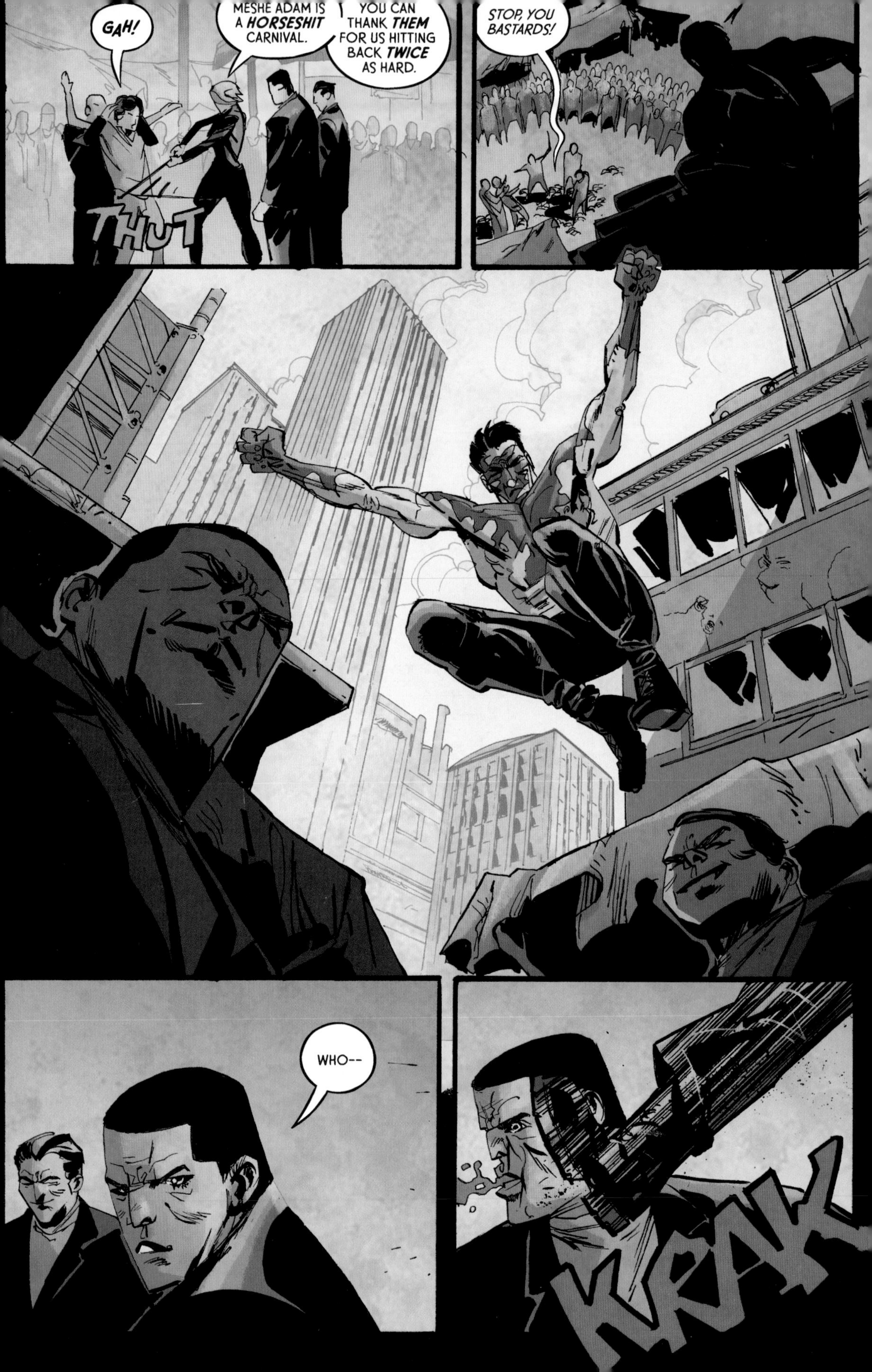
GAH!
MESHE ADAM IS A HORSESHIT CARNIVAL.
YOU CAN THANK THEM FOR US HITTING BACK TWICE AS HARD.
THUT
STOP, YOU BASTARDS!
WHO--
KRAK

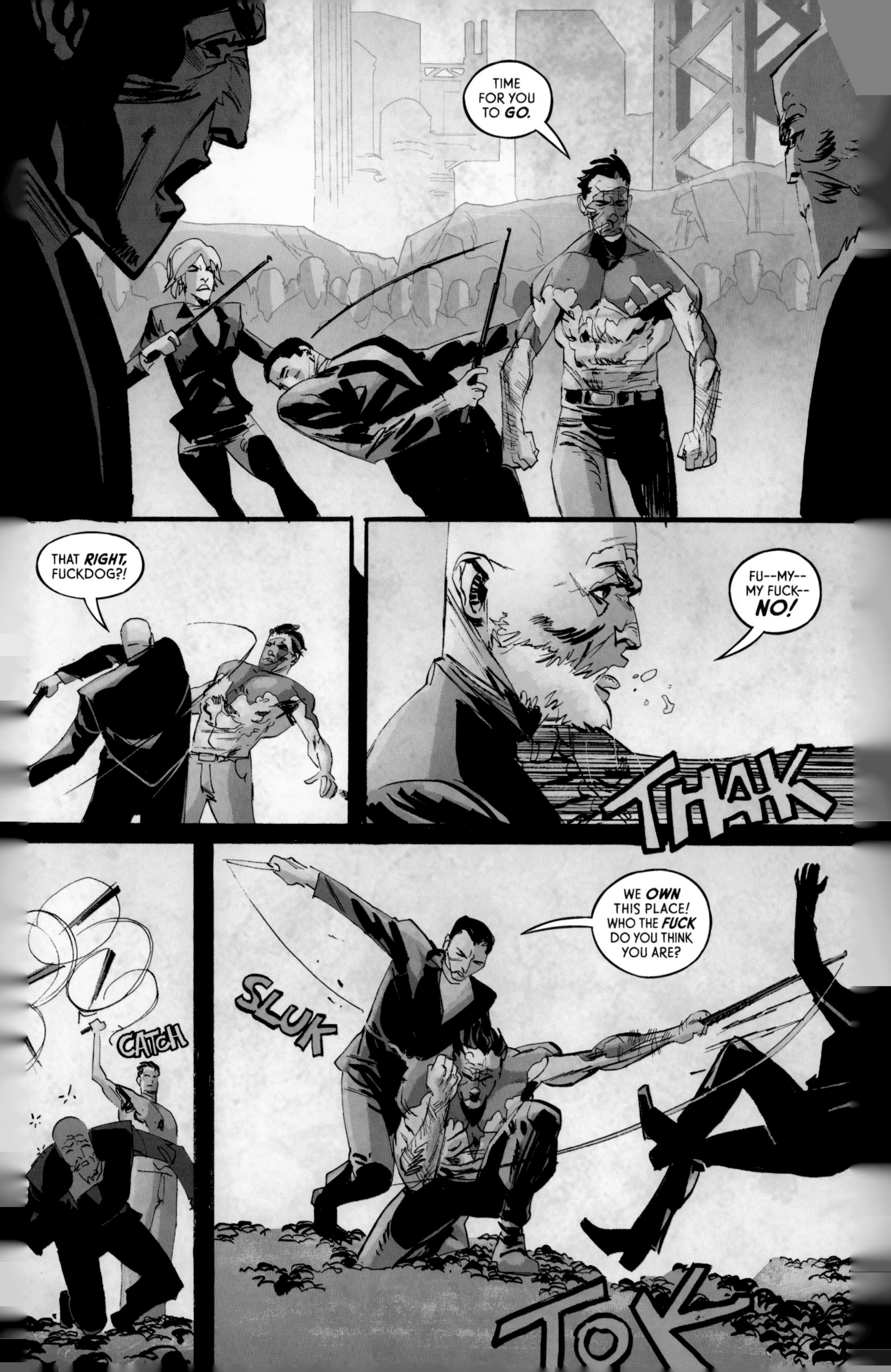
TIME FOR YOU TO GO.
THAT RIGHT, FUCKDOG?!
FU--MY-- MY FUCK-- NO!
THAK
CATCH
SLUK
WE OWN THIS PLACE! WHO THE FUCK DO YOU THINK YOU ARE?
TOK

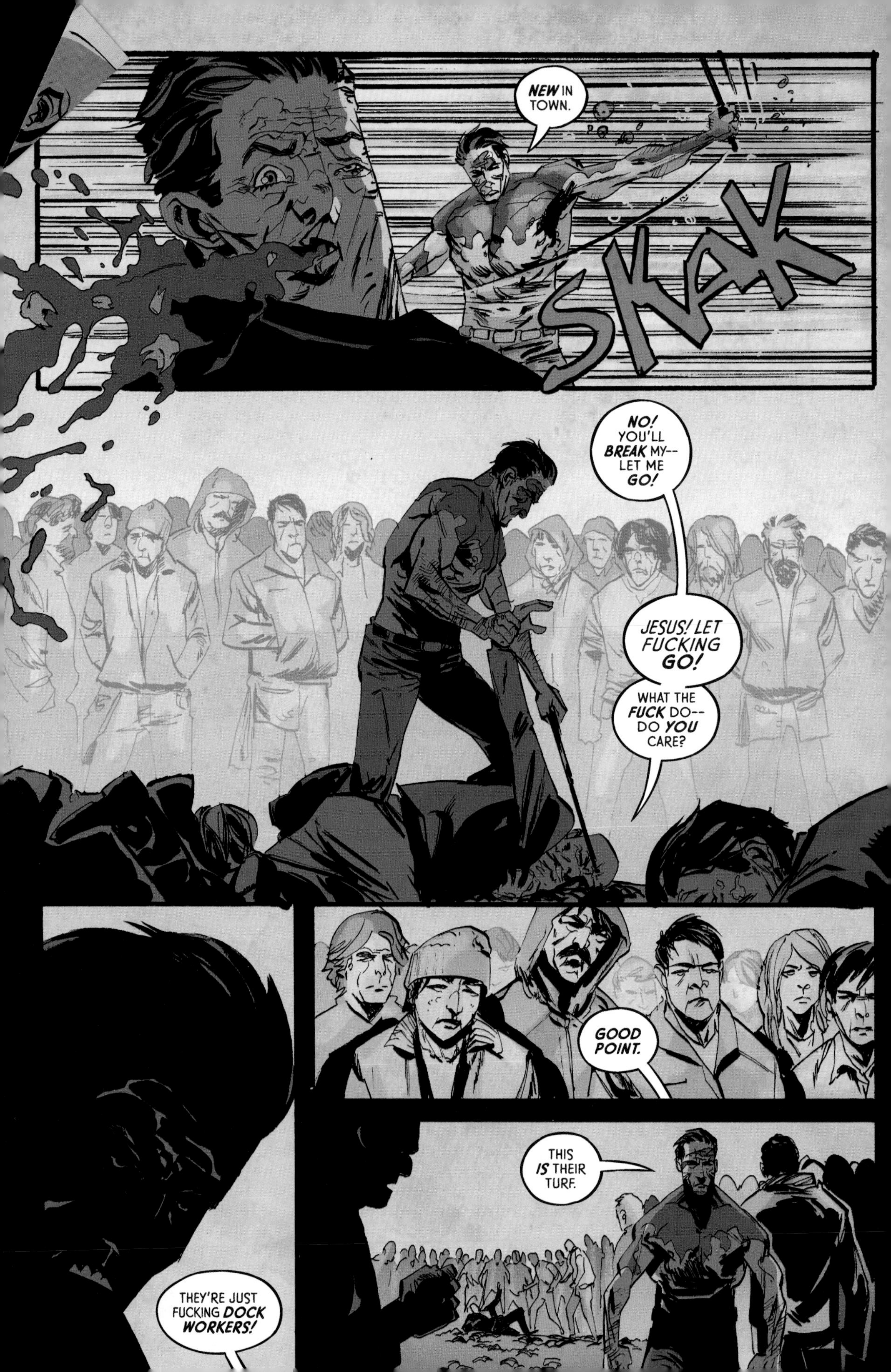
NEW IN TOWN.
SKAK
NO! YOU'LL BREAK MY-- LET ME GO!
JESUS! LET FUCKING GO!
WHAT THE FUCK DO-- DO YOU CARE?
GOOD POINT.
THIS IS THEIR TURF.
THEY'RE JUST FUCKING DOCK WORKERS!

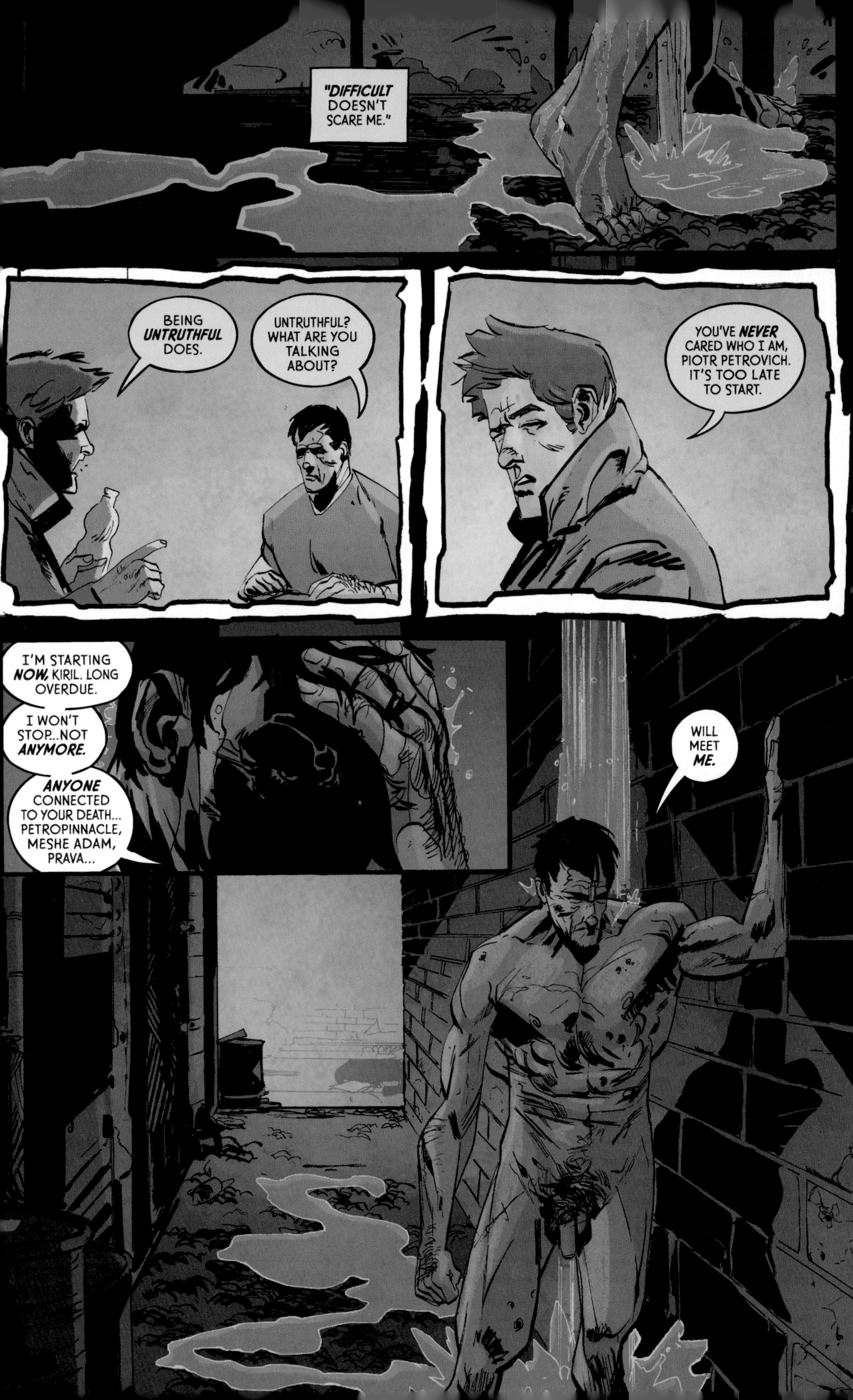
"DIFFICULT DOESN'T SCARE ME."
BEING UNTRUTHFUL DOES.
UNTRUTHFUL? WHAT ARE YOU TALKING ABOUT?
YOU'VE NEVER CARED WHO I AM, PIOTR PETROVICH. IT'S TOO LATE TO START.
I'M STARTING NOW, KIRIL. LONG OVERDUE.
I WON'T STOP...NOT ANYMORE.
ANYONE CONNECTED TO YOUR DEATH... PETROPINNACLE, MESHE ADAM, PRAVA...
WILL MEET ME.

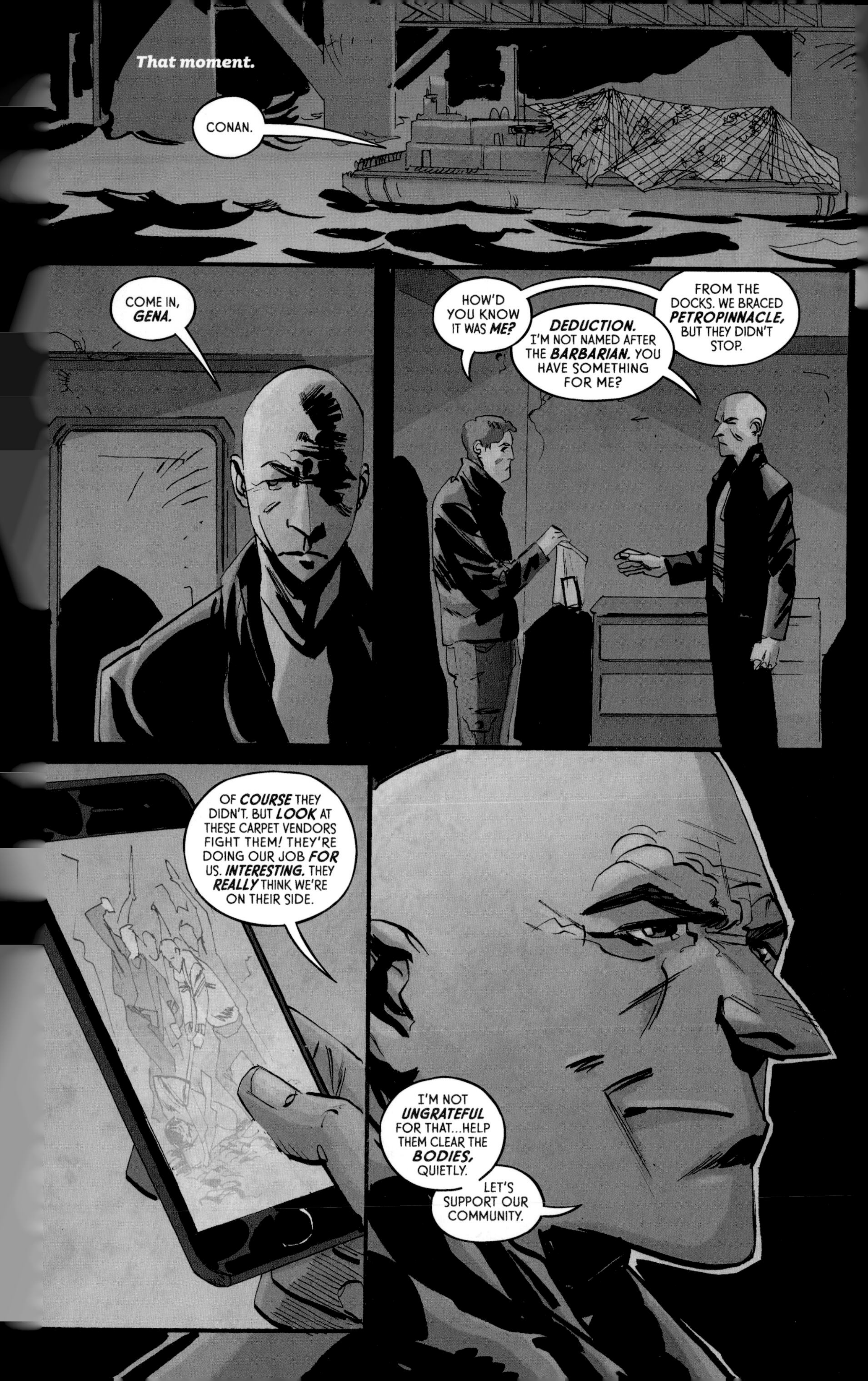
That moment.
CONAN.
COME IN, GENA.
HOW'D YOU KNOW IT WAS ME?
DEDUCTION. I'M NOT NAMED AFTER THE BARBARIAN. YOU HAVE SOMETHING FOR ME?
FROM THE DOCKS. WE BRACED PETROPINNACLE, BUT THEY DIDN'T STOP.
OF COURSE THEY DIDN'T. BUT LOOK AT THESE CARPET VENDORS FIGHT THEM! THEY'RE DOING OUR JOB FOR US. INTERESTING. THEY REALLY THINK WE'RE ON THEIR SIDE.
I'M NOT UNGRATEFUL FOR THAT...HELP THEM CLEAR THE BODIES, QUIETLY.
LET'S SUPPORT OUR COMMUNITY.

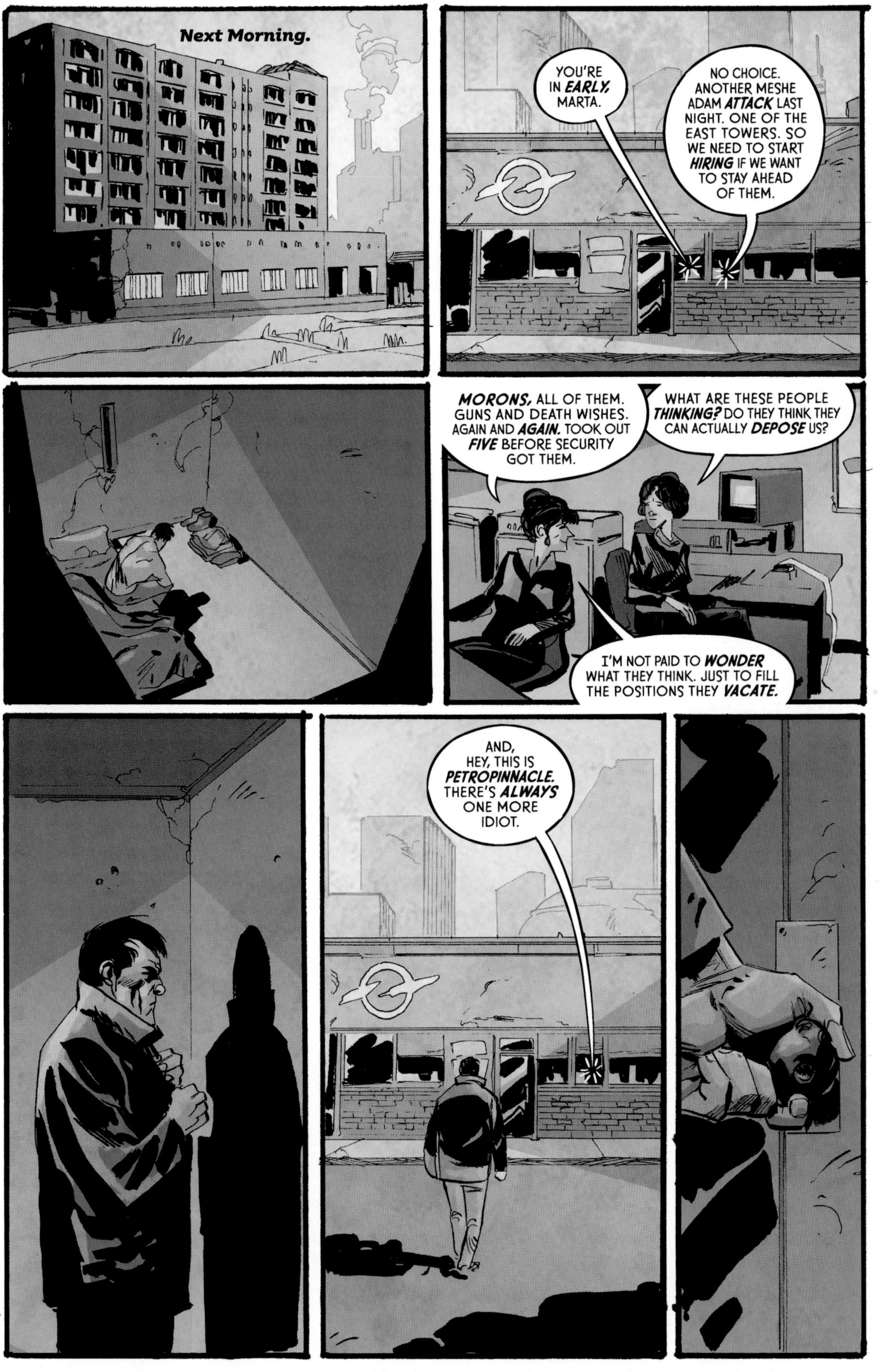
Next Morning.
YOU'RE IN EARLY, MARTA.
NO CHOICE. ANOTHER MESHE ADAM ATTACK LAST NIGHT. ONE OF THE EAST TOWERS. SO WE NEED TO START HIRING IF WE WANT TO STAY AHEAD OF THEM.
MORONS, ALL OF THEM. GUNS AND DEATH WISHES. AGAIN AND AGAIN. TOOK OUT FIVE BEFORE SECURITY GOT THEM.
WHAT ARE THESE PEOPLE THINKING? DO THEY THINK THEY CAN ACTUALLY DEPOSE US?
I'M NOT PAID TO WONDER WHAT THEY THINK. JUST TO FILL THE POSITIONS THEY VACATE.
AND, HEY, THIS IS PETROPINNACLE. THERE'S ALWAYS ONE MORE IDIOT.

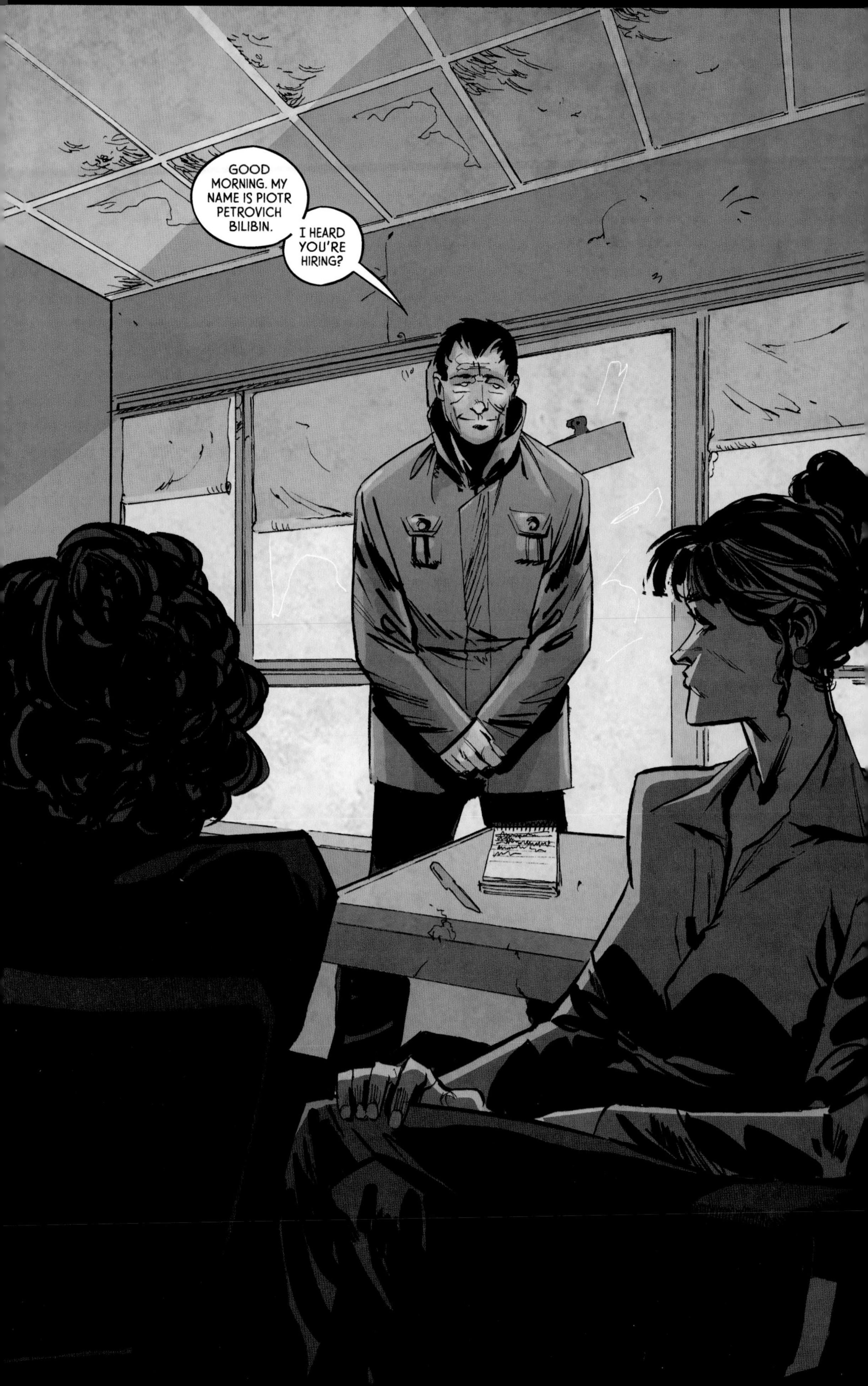
GOOD MORNING. MY NAME IS PIOTR PETROVICH BILIBIN.
I HEARD YOU'RE HIRING?

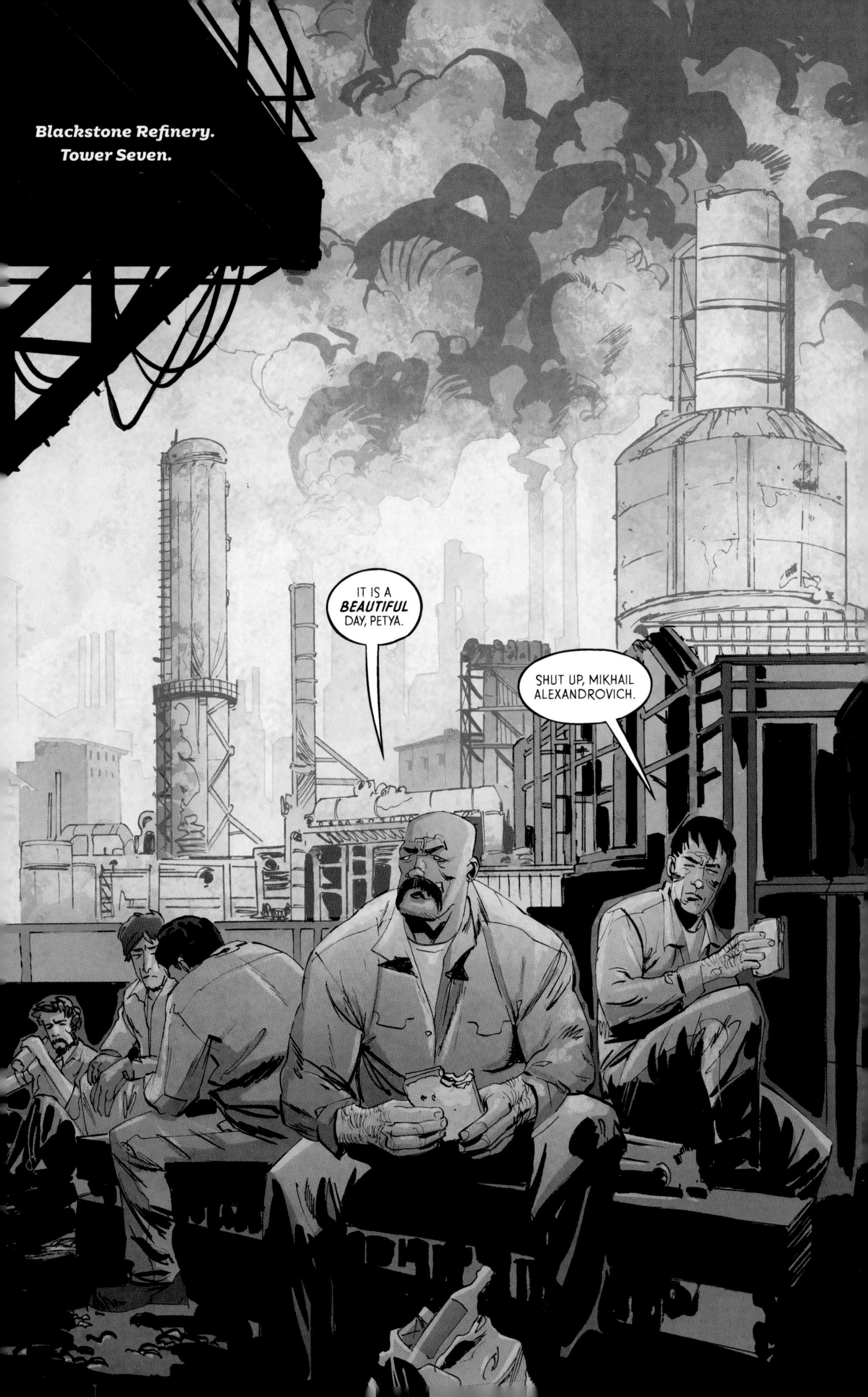
Blackstone Refinery.
Tower Seven.
IT IS A BEAUTIFUL DAY, PETYA.
SHUT UP, MIKHAIL ALEXANDROVICH.

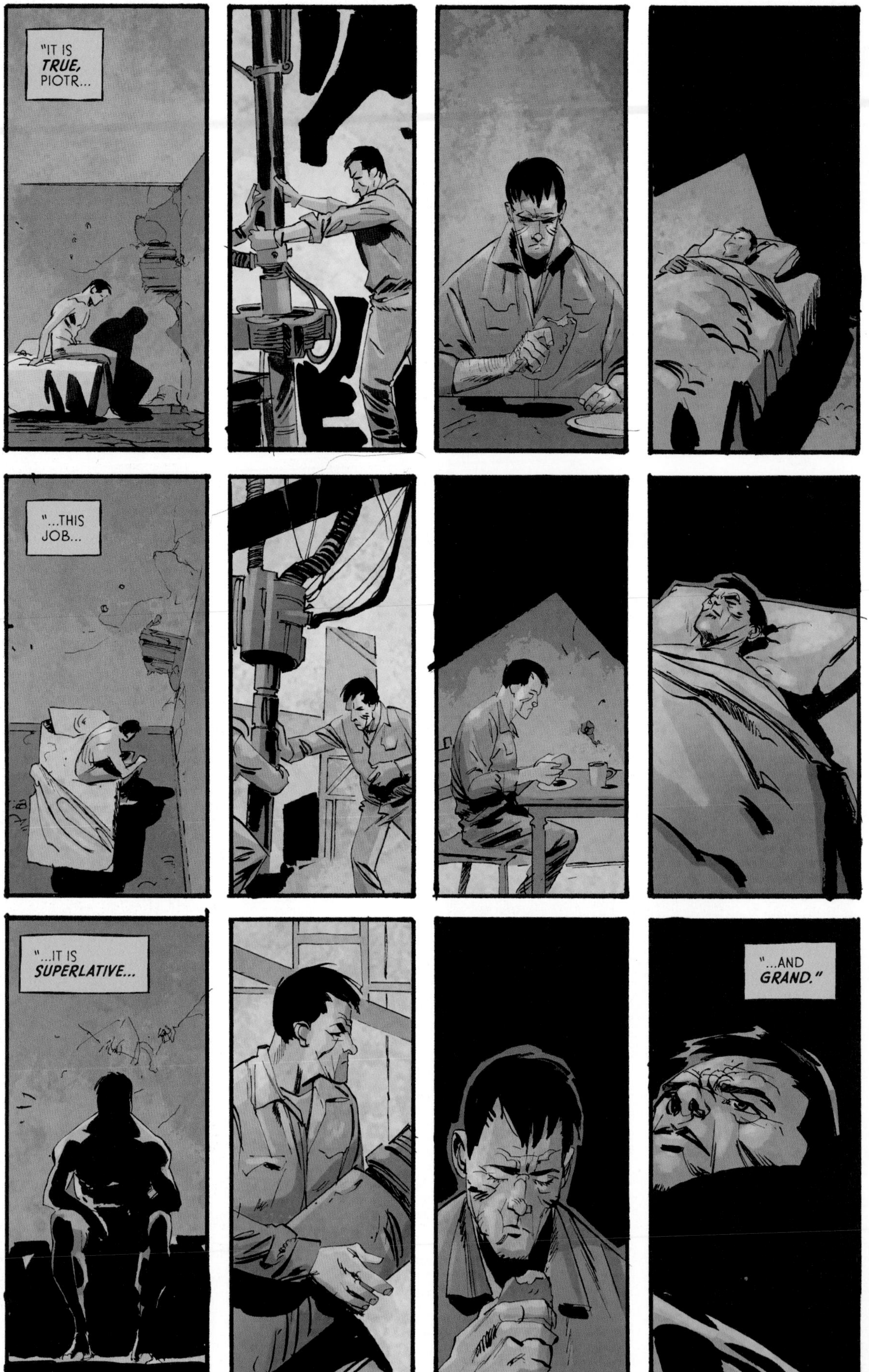
"IT IS TRUE, PIOTR...
"...THIS JOB...
"...IT IS SUPERLATIVE...
"...AND GRAND."

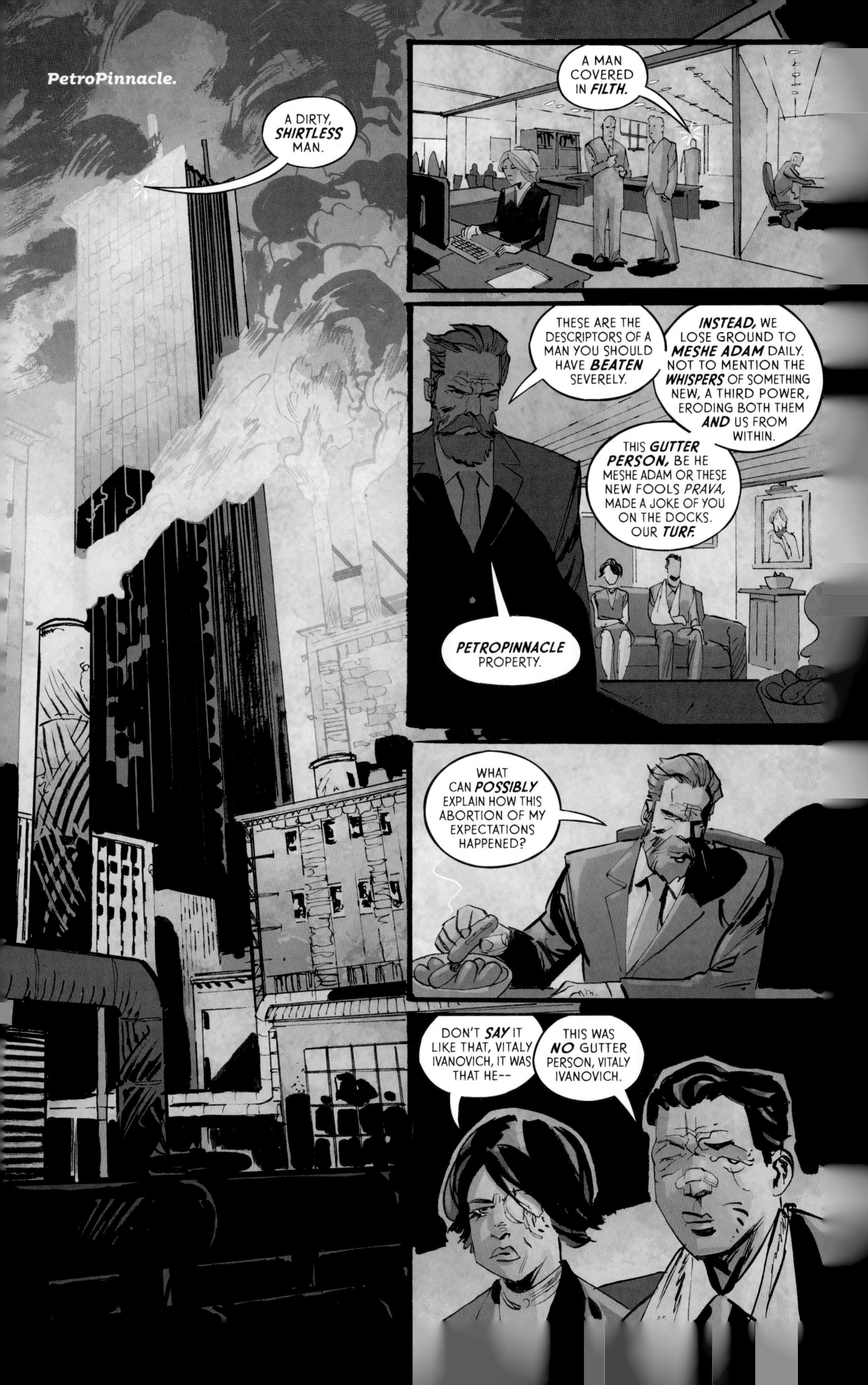
PetroPinnacle.
A DIRTY, SHIRTLESS MAN.
A MAN COVERED IN FILTH.
THESE ARE THE DESCRIPTORS OF A MAN YOU SHOULD HAVE BEATEN SEVERELY.
INSTEAD, WE LOSE GROUND TO MESHE ADAM DAILY. NOT TO MENTION THE WHISPERS OF SOMETHING NEW, A THIRD POWER, ERODING BOTH THEM AND US FROM WITHIN.
THIS GUTTER PERSON, BE HE MESHE ADAM OR THESE NEW FOOLS PRAVA, MADE A JOKE OF YOU ON THE DOCKS. OUR TURF.
PETROPINNACLE PROPERTY.
WHAT CAN POSSIBLY EXPLAIN HOW THIS ABORTION OF MY EXPECTATIONS HAPPENED?
DON'T SAY IT LIKE THAT, VITALY IVANOVICH, IT WAS THAT HE--
THIS WAS NO GUTTER PERSON, VITALY IVANOVICH.

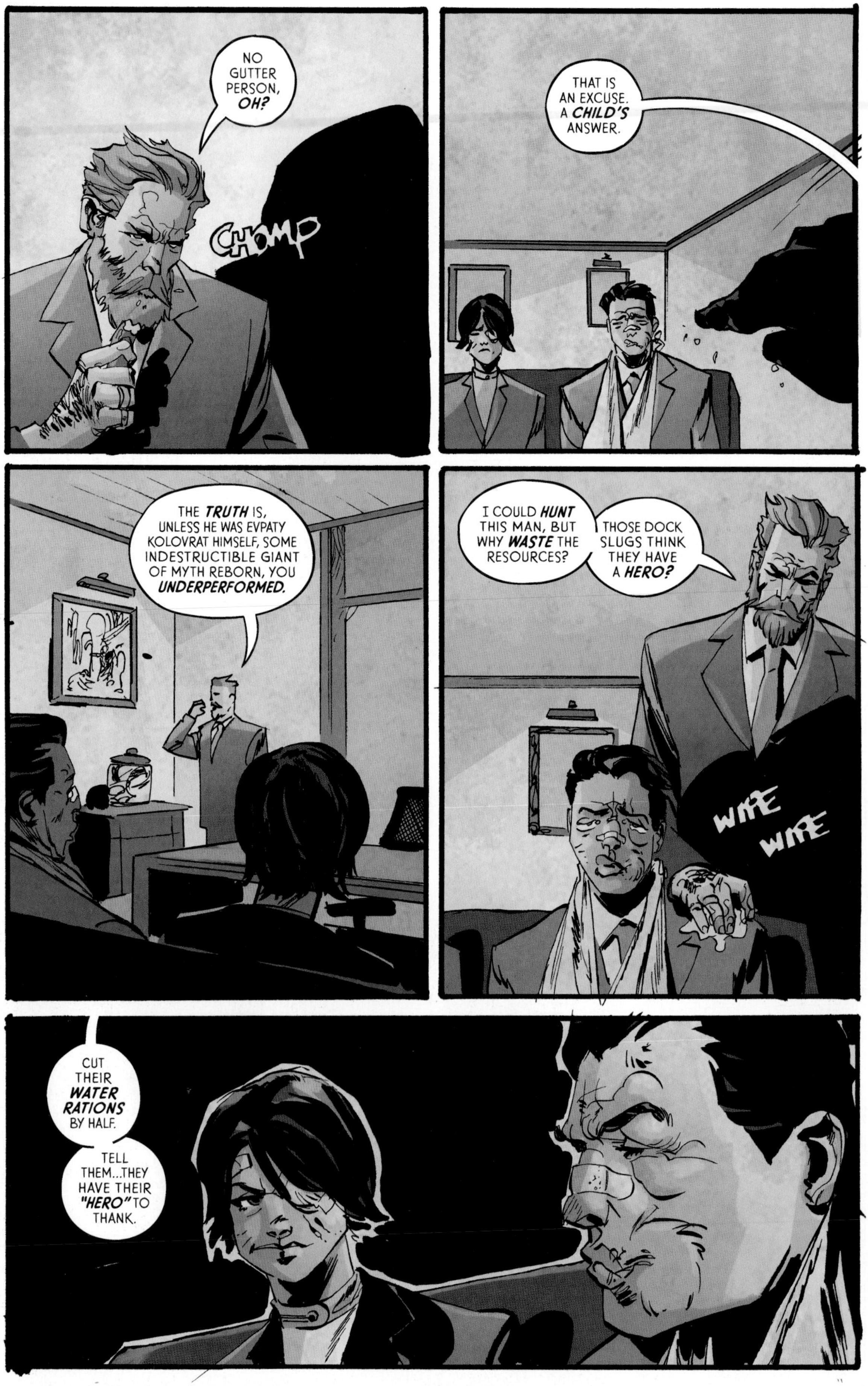
NO GUTTER PERSON, OH?
CHOMP
THAT IS AN EXCUSE. A CHILD'S ANSWER.
THE TRUTH IS, UNLESS HE WAS EVPATY KOLOVRAT HIMSELF, SOME INDESTRUCTIBLE GIANT OF MYTH REBORN, YOU UNDERPERFORMED.
I COULD HUNT THIS MAN, BUT WHY WASTE THE RESOURCES?
THOSE DOCK SLUGS THINK THEY HAVE A HERO?
WIPE
WIPE
CUT THEIR WATER RATIONS BY HALF.
TELL THEM...THEY HAVE THEIR "HERO" TO THANK.

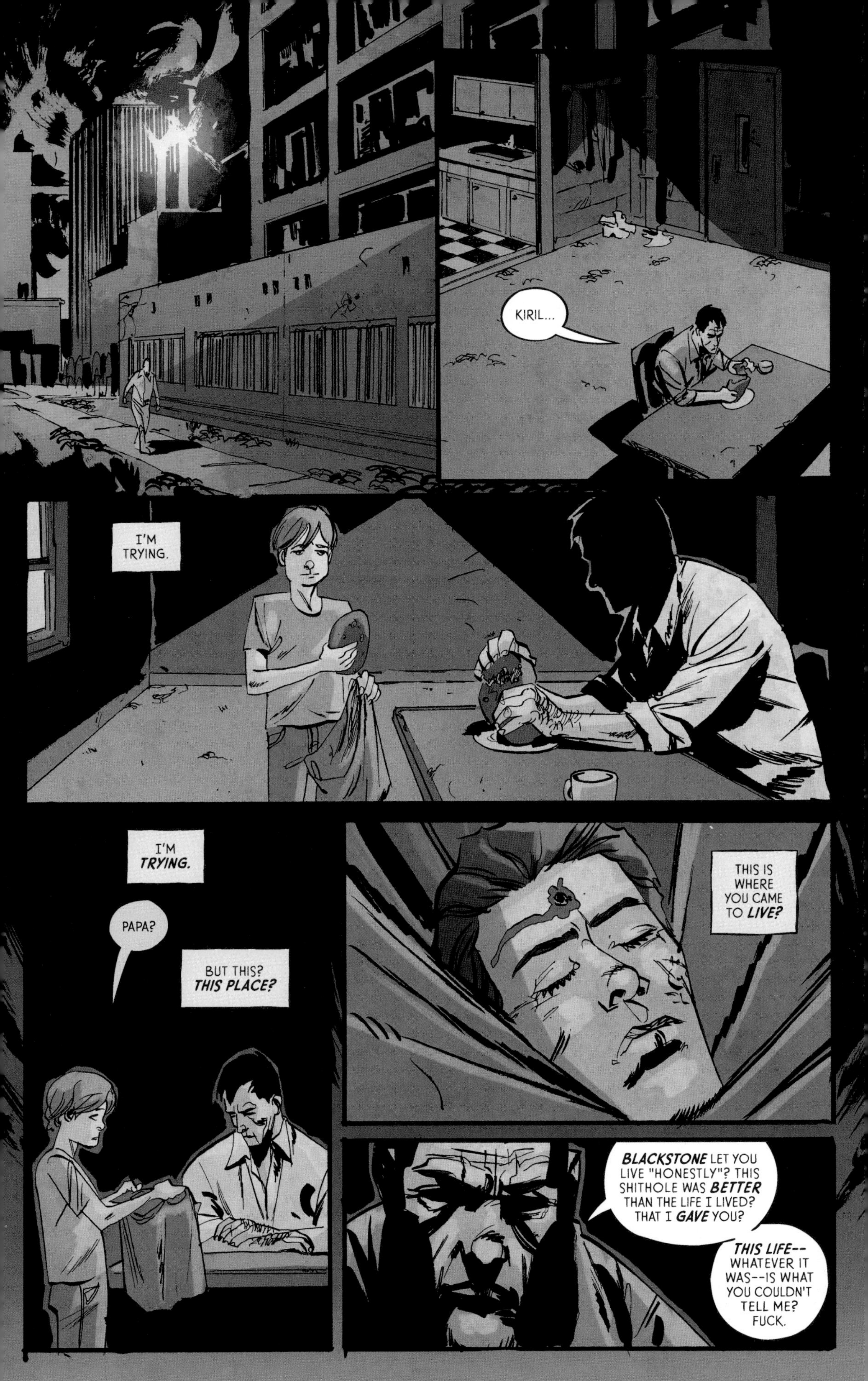
KIRIL...
I'M TRYING.
I'M *TRYING.*
PAPA?
BUT THIS? *THIS PLACE?*
THIS IS WHERE YOU CAME TO *LIVE?*
BLACKSTONE LET YOU LIVE "HONESTLY"? THIS SHITHOLE WAS *BETTER* THAN THE LIFE I LIVED? THAT I *GAVE* YOU?
THIS LIFE-- WHATEVER IT WAS--IS WHAT YOU COULDN'T TELL ME? FUCK.

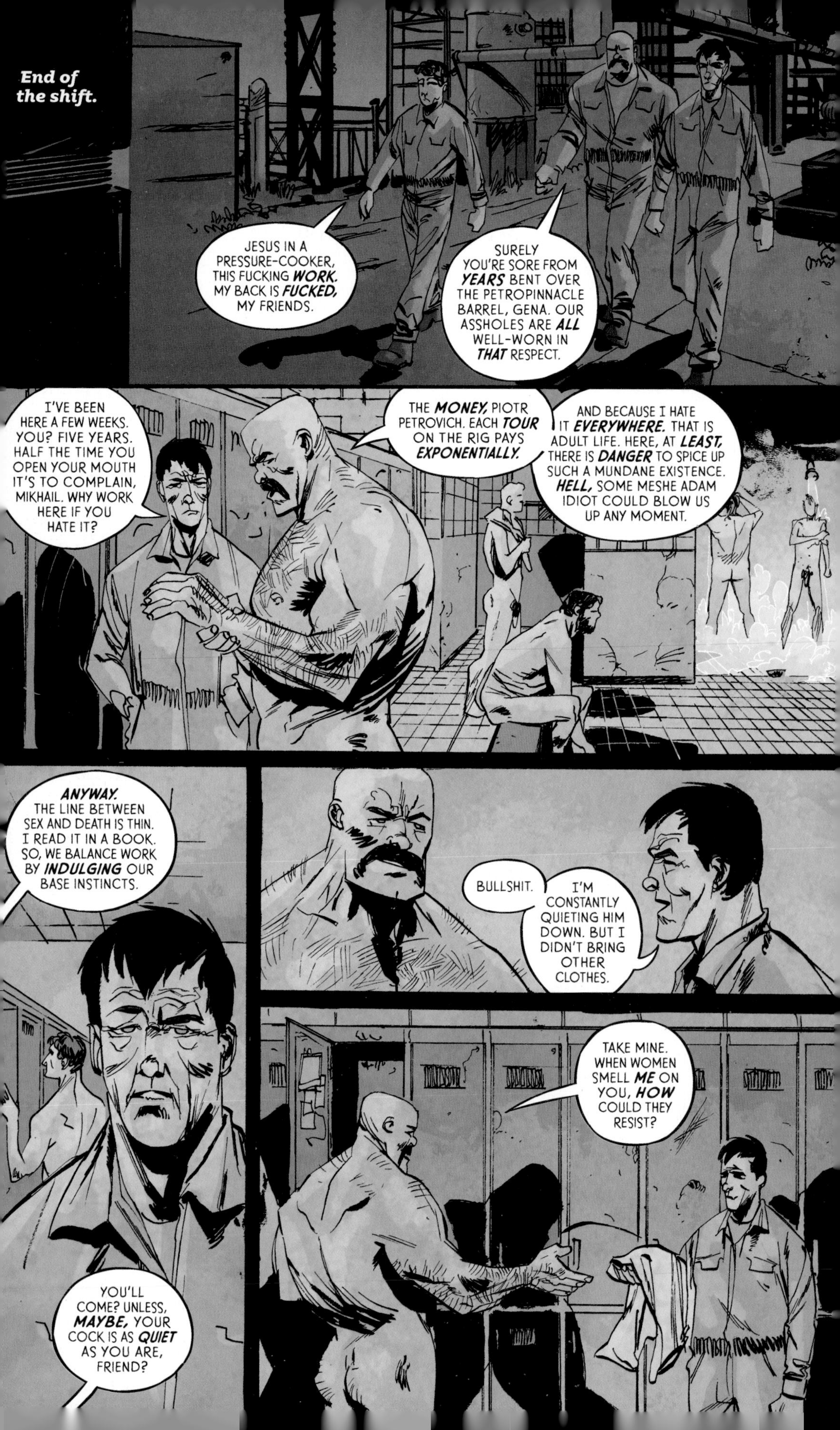

End of the shift.
JESUS IN A PRESSURE-COOKER, THIS FUCKING WORK. MY BACK IS FUCKED, MY FRIENDS.
SURELY YOU'RE SORE FROM YEARS BENT OVER THE PETROPINNACLE BARREL, GENA. OUR ASSHOLES ARE ALL WELL-WORN IN THAT RESPECT.
I'VE BEEN HERE A FEW WEEKS. YOU? FIVE YEARS. HALF THE TIME YOU OPEN YOUR MOUTH IT'S TO COMPLAIN, MIKHAIL. WHY WORK HERE IF YOU HATE IT?
THE MONEY, PIOTR PETROVICH. EACH TOUR ON THE RIG PAYS EXPONENTIALLY.
AND BECAUSE I HATE IT EVERYWHERE. THAT IS ADULT LIFE. HERE, AT LEAST, THERE IS DANGER TO SPICE UP SUCH A MUNDANE EXISTENCE. HELL, SOME MESHE ADAM IDIOT COULD BLOW US UP ANY MOMENT.
ANYWAY. THE LINE BETWEEN SEX AND DEATH IS THIN. I READ IT IN A BOOK. SO, WE BALANCE WORK BY INDULGING OUR BASE INSTINCTS.
YOU'LL COME? UNLESS, MAYBE, YOUR COCK IS AS QUIET AS YOU ARE, FRIEND?
BULLSHIT.
I'M CONSTANTLY QUIETING HIM DOWN. BUT I DIDN'T BRING OTHER CLOTHES.
TAKE MINE. WHEN WOMEN SMELL ME ON YOU, HOW COULD THEY RESIST?

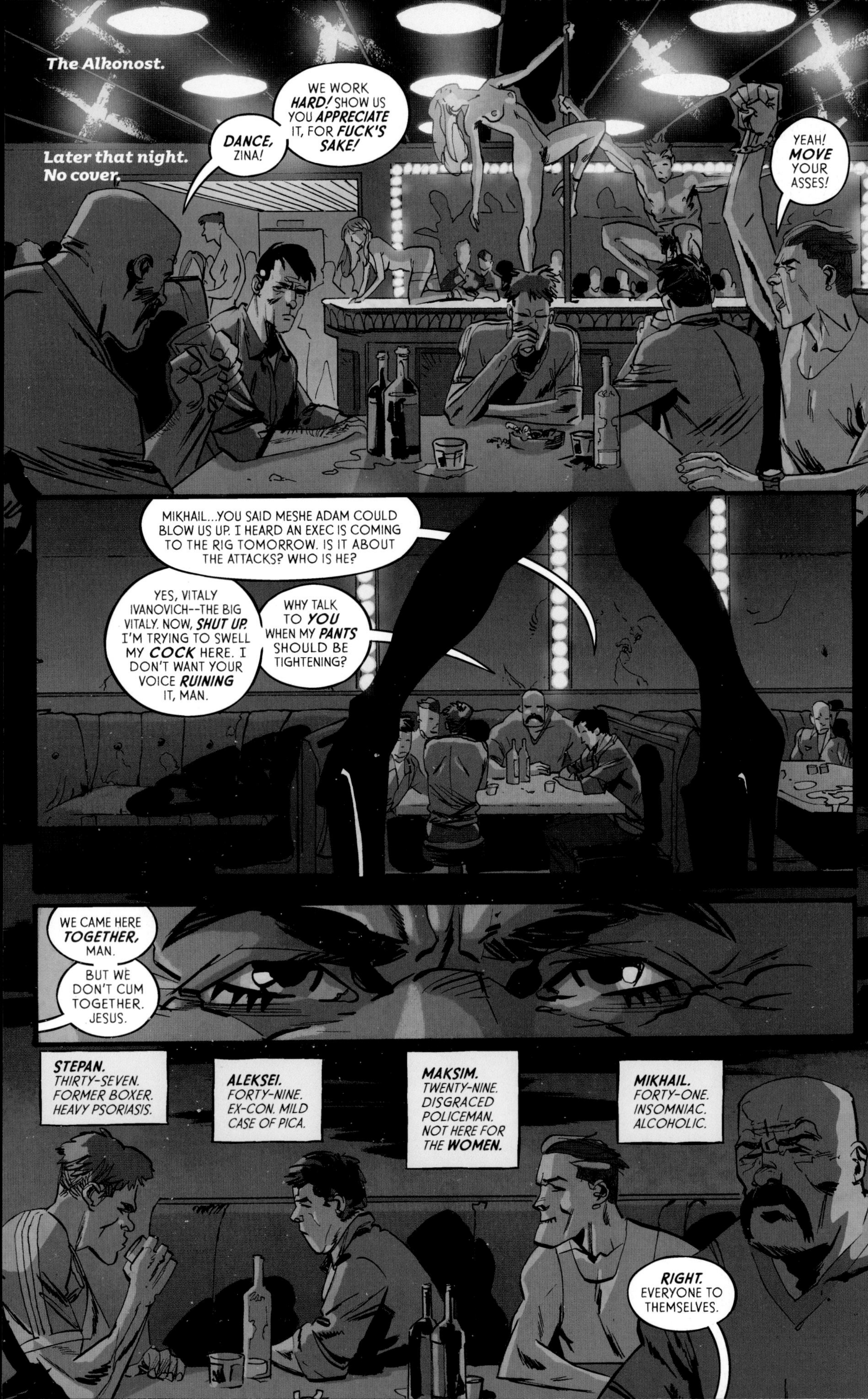
The Alkonost.
Later that night. No cover.
DANCE, ZINA!
WE WORK HARD! SHOW US YOU APPRECIATE IT, FOR FUCK'S SAKE!
YEAH! MOVE YOUR ASSES!
MIKHAIL...YOU SAID MESHE ADAM COULD BLOW US UP. I HEARD AN EXEC IS COMING TO THE RIG TOMORROW. IS IT ABOUT THE ATTACKS? WHO IS HE?
YES, VITALY IVANOVICH--THE BIG VITALY. NOW, SHUT UP. I'M TRYING TO SWELL MY COCK HERE. I DON'T WANT YOUR VOICE RUINING IT, MAN.
WHY TALK TO YOU WHEN MY PANTS SHOULD BE TIGHTENING?
WE CAME HERE TOGETHER, MAN.
BUT WE DON'T CUM TOGETHER. JESUS.
STEPAN. THIRTY-SEVEN. FORMER BOXER. HEAVY PSORIASIS.
ALEKSEI. FORTY-NINE. EX-CON. MILD CASE OF PICA.
MAKSIM. TWENTY-NINE. DISGRACED POLICEMAN. NOT HERE FOR THE WOMEN.
MIKHAIL. FORTY-ONE. INSOMNIAC. ALCOHOLIC.
RIGHT. EVERYONE TO THEMSELVES.

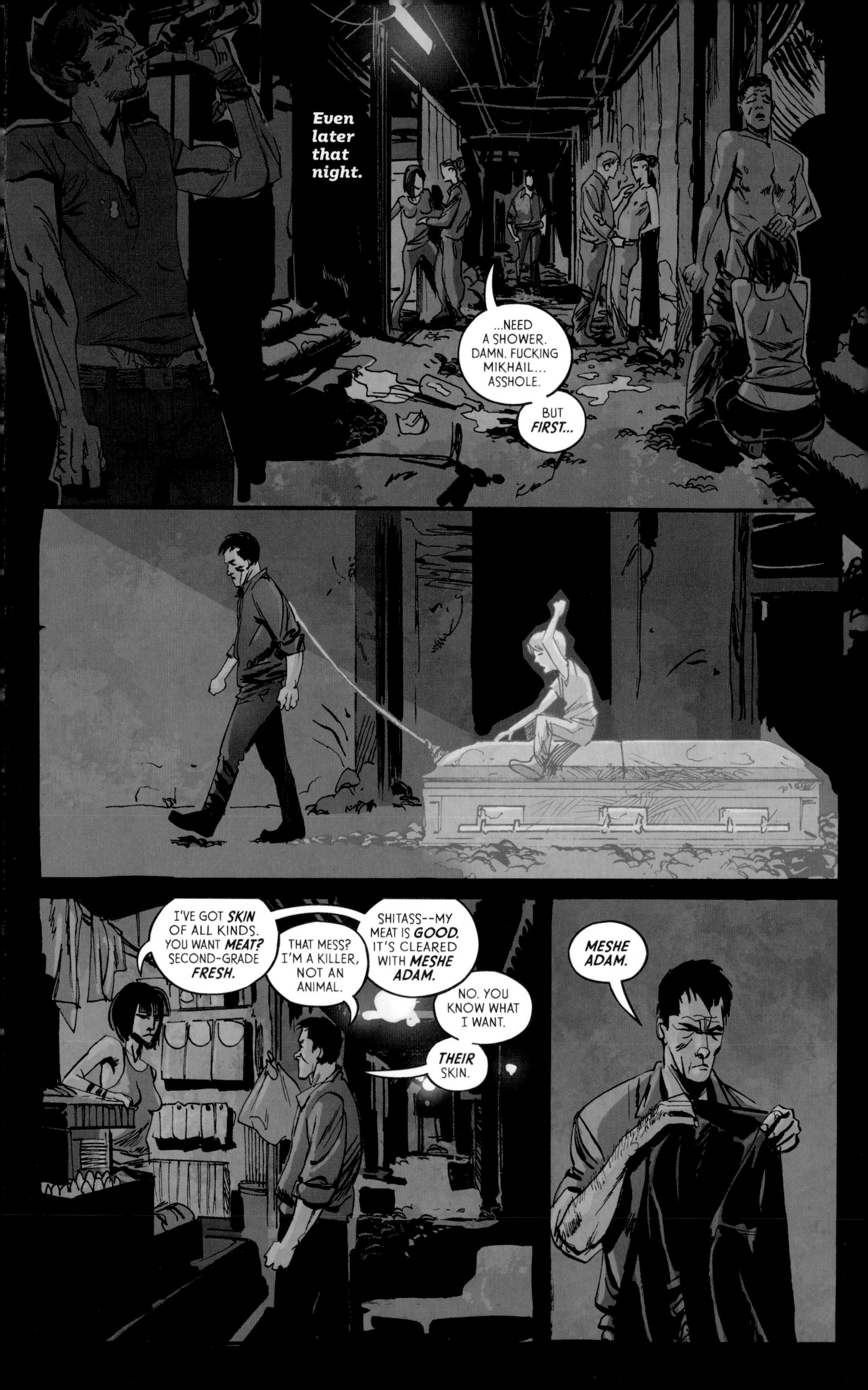
Even later that night.
...NEED A SHOWER. DAMN. FUCKING MIKHAIL... ASSHOLE.
BUT FIRST...
I'VE GOT SKIN OF ALL KINDS. YOU WANT MEAT? SECOND-GRADE FRESH.
THAT MESS? I'M A KILLER, NOT AN ANIMAL.
SHITASS--MY MEAT IS GOOD. IT'S CLEARED WITH MESHE ADAM.
NO. YOU KNOW WHAT I WANT.
THEIR SKIN.
MESHE ADAM.

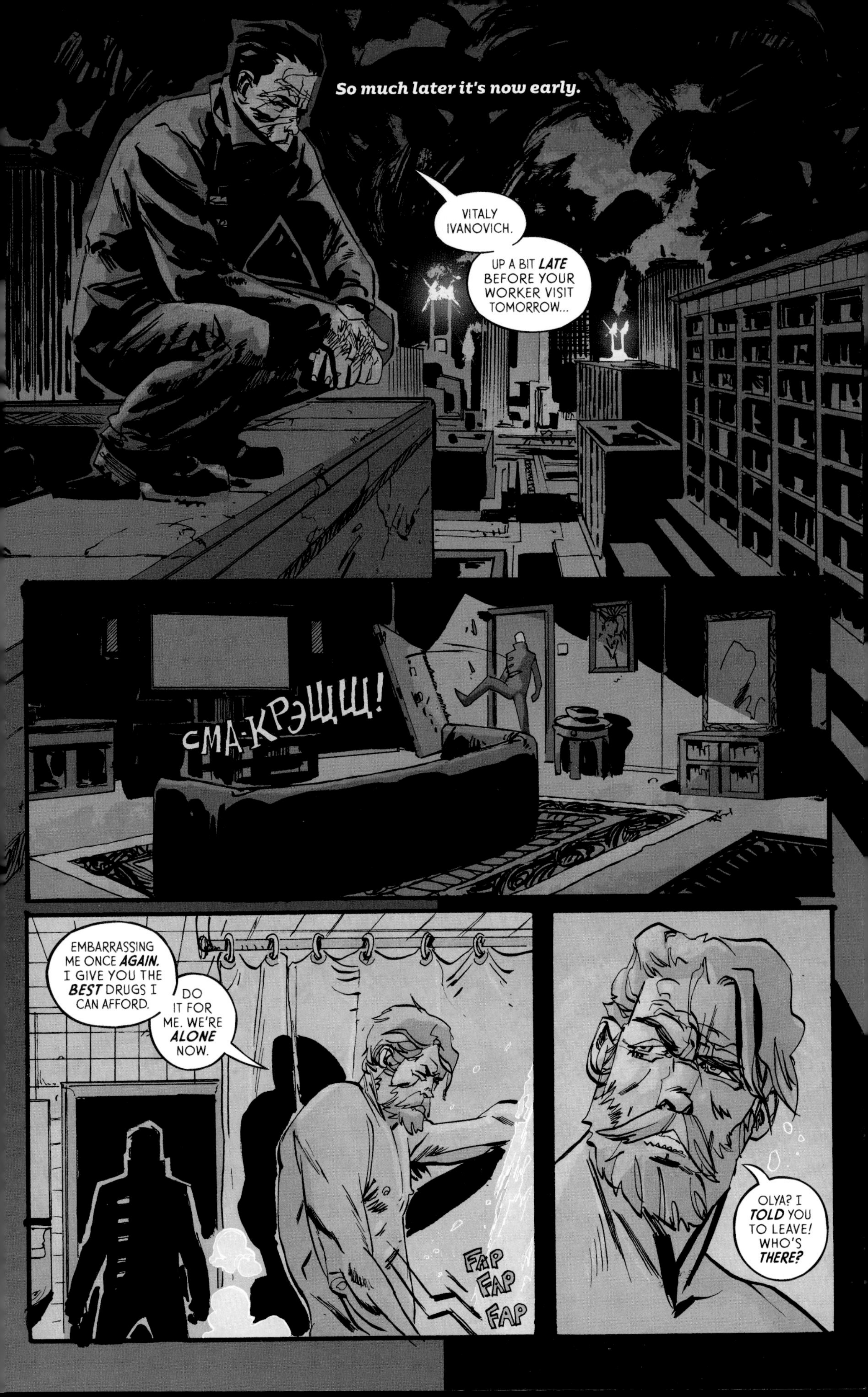
So much later it's now early.
VITALY IVANOVICH.
UP A BIT LATE BEFORE YOUR WORKER VISIT TOMORROW...
СМА-КРЭЩЩ!
EMBARRASSING ME ONCE AGAIN. I GIVE YOU THE BEST DRUGS I CAN AFFORD.
DO IT FOR ME. WE'RE ALONE NOW.
FAP FAP FAP
OLYA? I TOLD YOU TO LEAVE! WHO'S THERE?

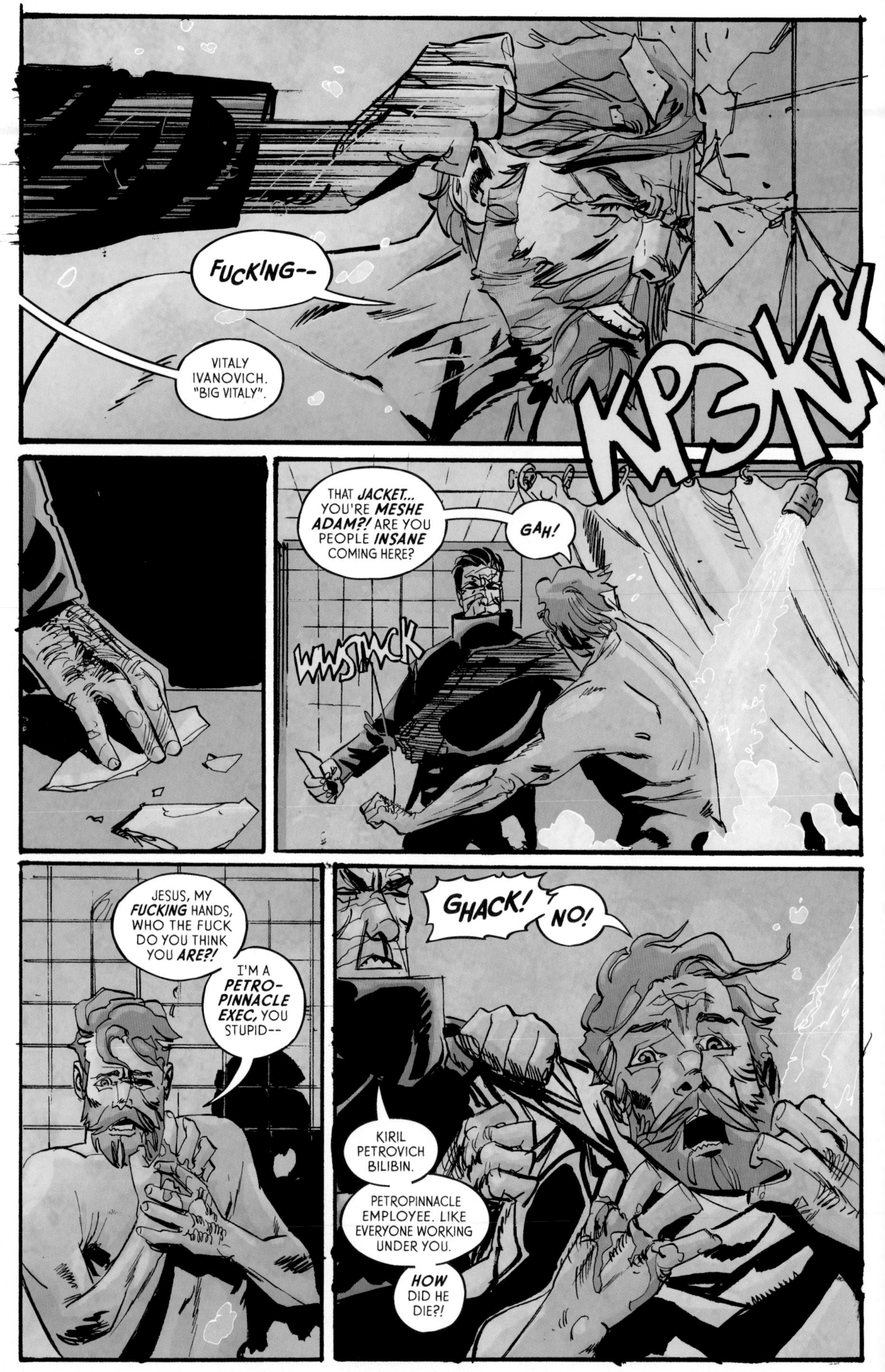
FUCKING--
VITALY IVANOVICH. "BIG VITALY".
KP3KK
THAT JACKET... YOU'RE MESHE ADAM?! ARE YOU PEOPLE INSANE COMING HERE?
GAH!
WWSTWCK
JESUS, MY FUCKING HANDS, WHO THE FUCK DO YOU THINK YOU ARE?!
I'M A PETRO-PINNACLE EXEC, YOU STUPID--
GHACK!
NO!
KIRIL PETROVICH BILIBIN.
PETROPINNACLE EMPLOYEE. LIKE EVERYONE WORKING UNDER YOU.
HOW DID HE DIE?!

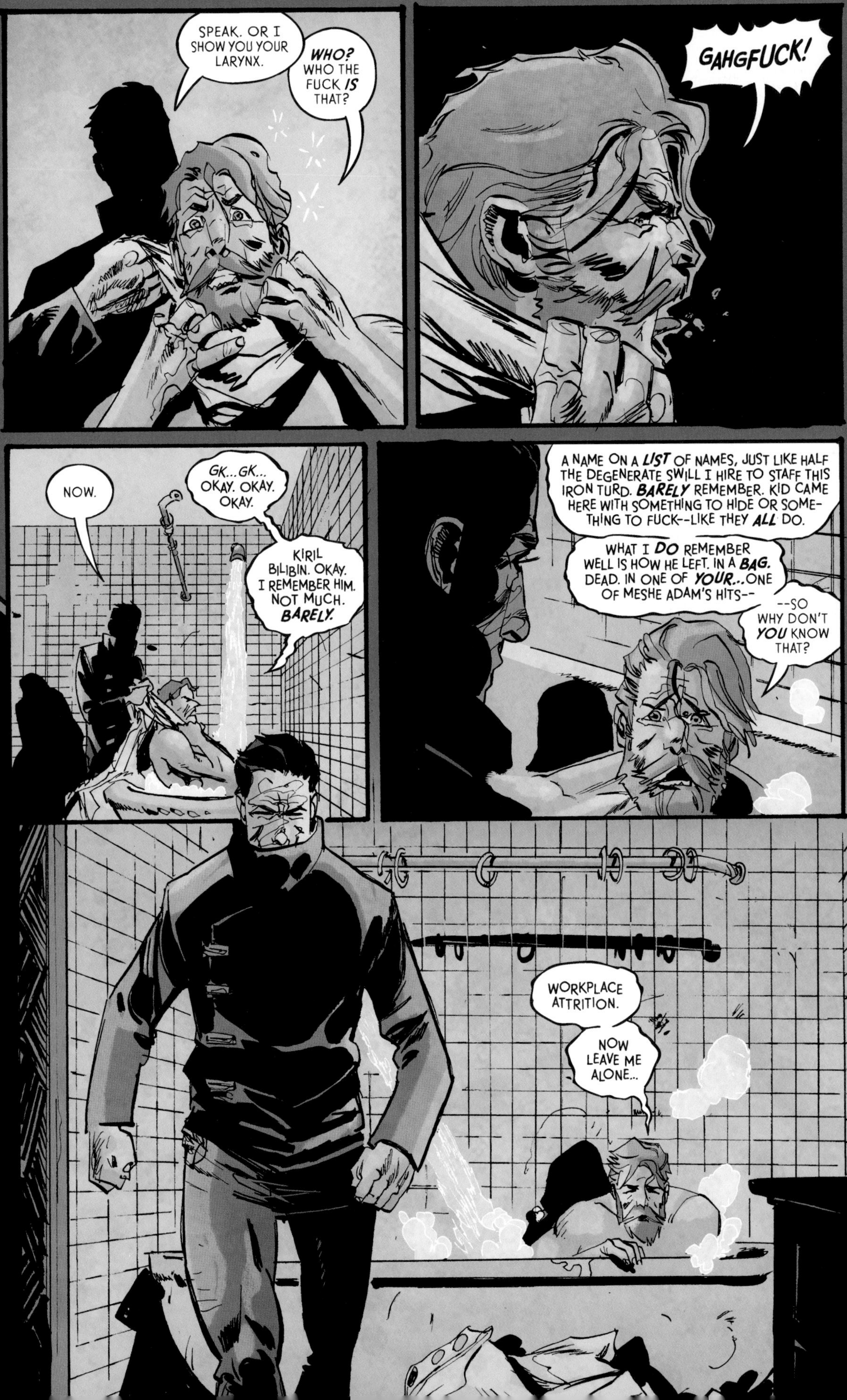
SPEAK. OR I SHOW YOU YOUR LARYNX.
WHO? WHO THE FUCK IS THAT?
GAHGFUCK!
NOW.
GK...GK... OKAY. OKAY. OKAY.
KIRIL BILIBIN. OKAY. I REMEMBER HIM. NOT MUCH. BARELY.
A NAME ON A LIST OF NAMES, JUST LIKE HALF THE DEGENERATE SWILL I HIRE TO STAFF THIS IRON TURD. BARELY REMEMBER. KID CAME HERE WITH SOMETHING TO HIDE OR SOMETHING TO FUCK--LIKE THEY ALL DO.
WHAT I DO REMEMBER WELL IS HOW HE LEFT. IN A BAG. DEAD. IN ONE OF YOUR...ONE OF MESHE ADAM'S HITS--
--SO WHY DON'T YOU KNOW THAT?
WORKPLACE ATTRITION.
NOW LEAVE ME ALONE...

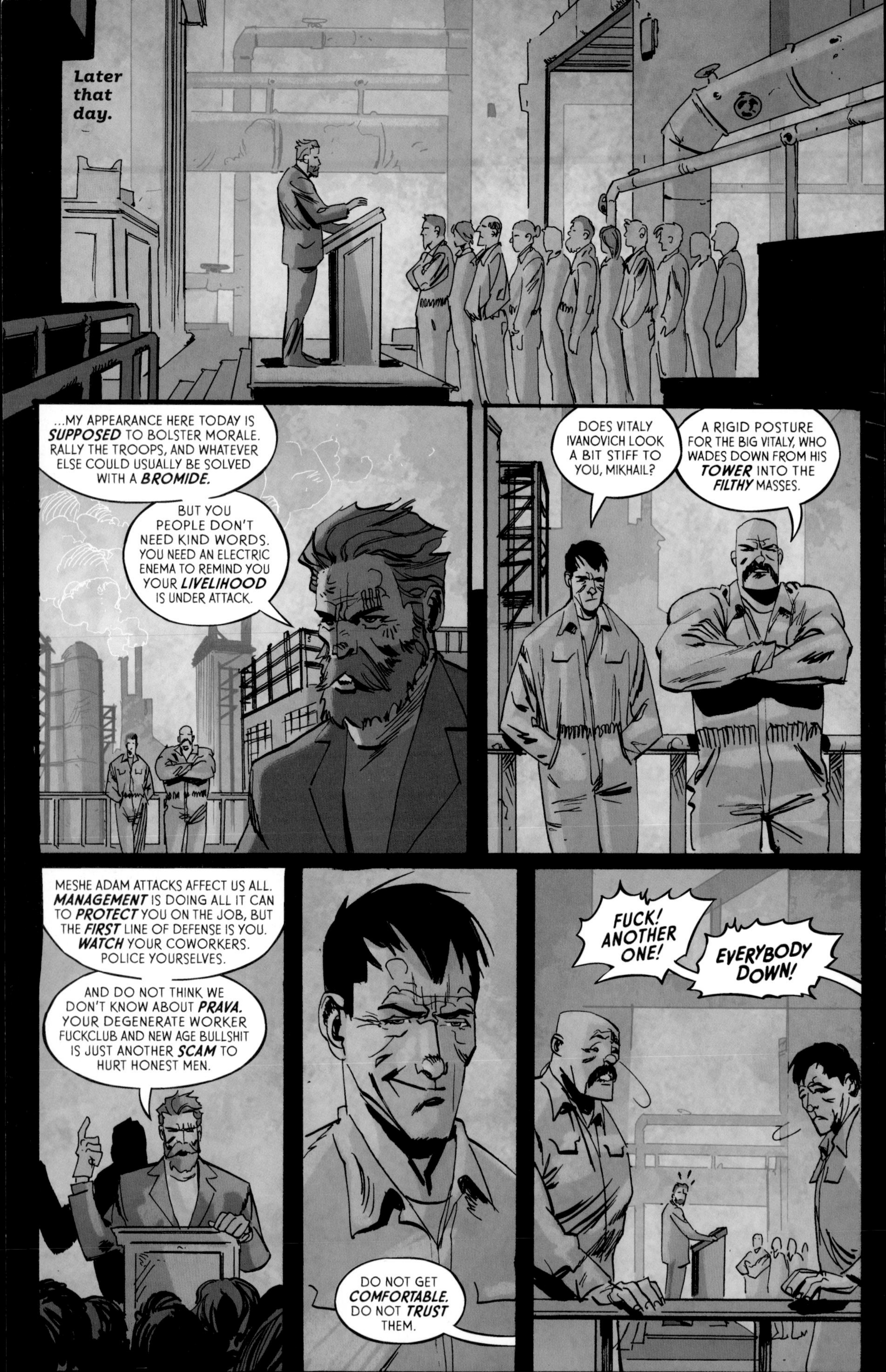
Later that day.
...MY APPEARANCE HERE TODAY IS SUPPOSED TO BOLSTER MORALE. RALLY THE TROOPS, AND WHATEVER ELSE COULD USUALLY BE SOLVED WITH A BROMIDE.
BUT YOU PEOPLE DON'T NEED KIND WORDS. YOU NEED AN ELECTRIC ENEMA TO REMIND YOU YOUR LIVELIHOOD IS UNDER ATTACK.
DOES VITALY IVANOVICH LOOK A BIT STIFF TO YOU, MIKHAIL?
A RIGID POSTURE FOR THE BIG VITALY, WHO WADES DOWN FROM HIS TOWER INTO THE FILTHY MASSES.
MESHE ADAM ATTACKS AFFECT US ALL. MANAGEMENT IS DOING ALL IT CAN TO PROTECT YOU ON THE JOB, BUT THE FIRST LINE OF DEFENSE IS YOU. WATCH YOUR COWORKERS. POLICE YOURSELVES.
AND DO NOT THINK WE DON'T KNOW ABOUT PRAVA. YOUR DEGENERATE WORKER FUCKCLUB AND NEW AGE BULLSHIT IS JUST ANOTHER SCAM TO HURT HONEST MEN.
DO NOT GET COMFORTABLE. DO NOT TRUST THEM.
FUCK! ANOTHER ONE!
EVERYBODY DOWN!

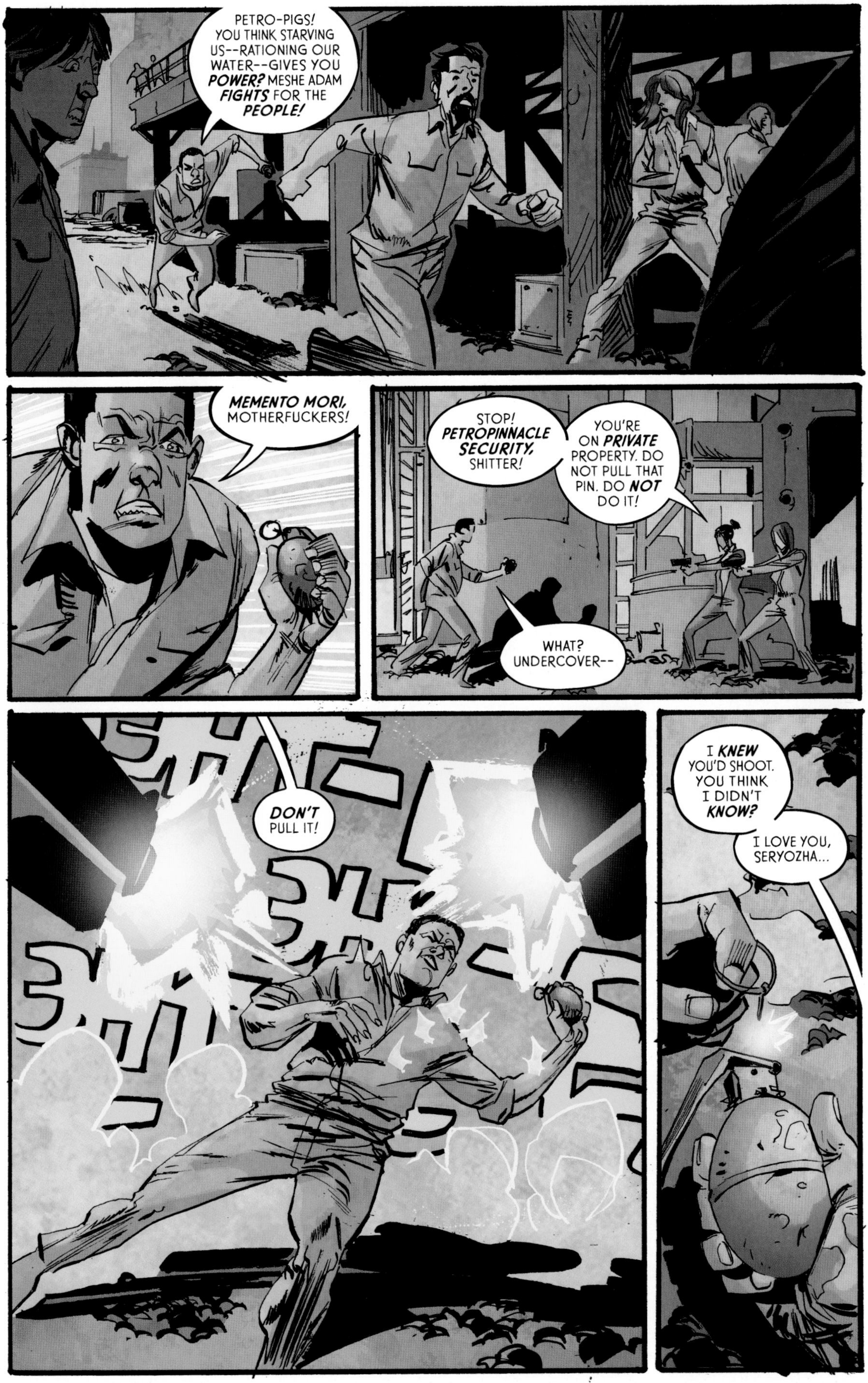
PETRO-PIGS! YOU THINK STARVING US--RATIONING OUR WATER--GIVES YOU POWER? MESHE ADAM FIGHTS FOR THE PEOPLE!
MEMENTO MORI, MOTHERFUCKERS!
STOP! PETROPINNACLE SECURITY, SHITTER!
YOU'RE ON PRIVATE PROPERTY. DO NOT PULL THAT PIN. DO NOT DO IT!
WHAT? UNDERCOVER--
DON'T PULL IT!
I KNEW YOU'D SHOOT. YOU THINK I DIDN'T KNOW?
I LOVE YOU, SERYOZHA...

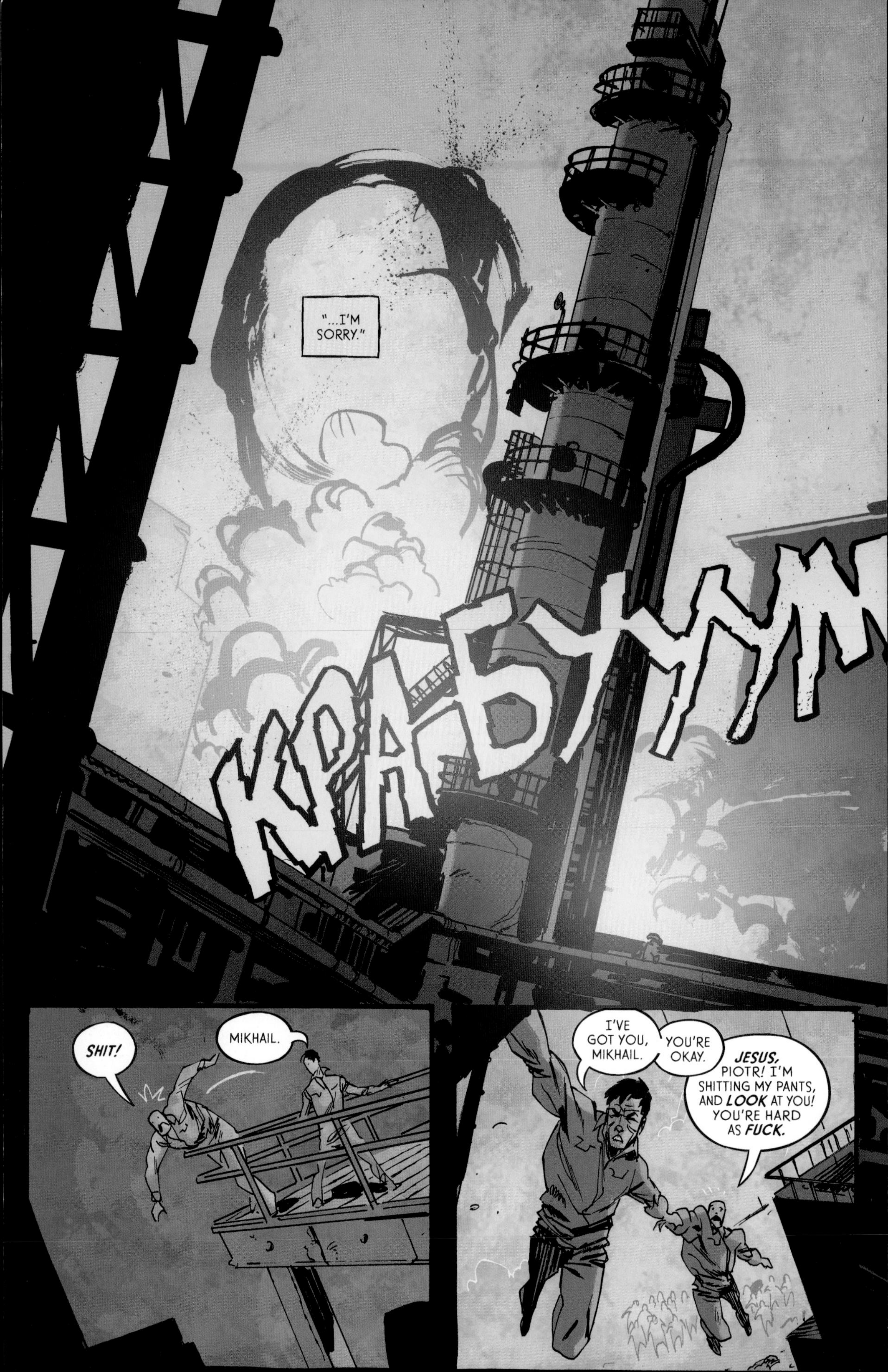
"...I'M SORRY."
SHIT!
MIKHAIL.
I'VE GOT YOU, MIKHAIL.
YOU'RE OKAY.
JESUS, PIOTR! I'M SHITTING MY PANTS, AND LOOK AT YOU! YOU'RE HARD AS FUCK.

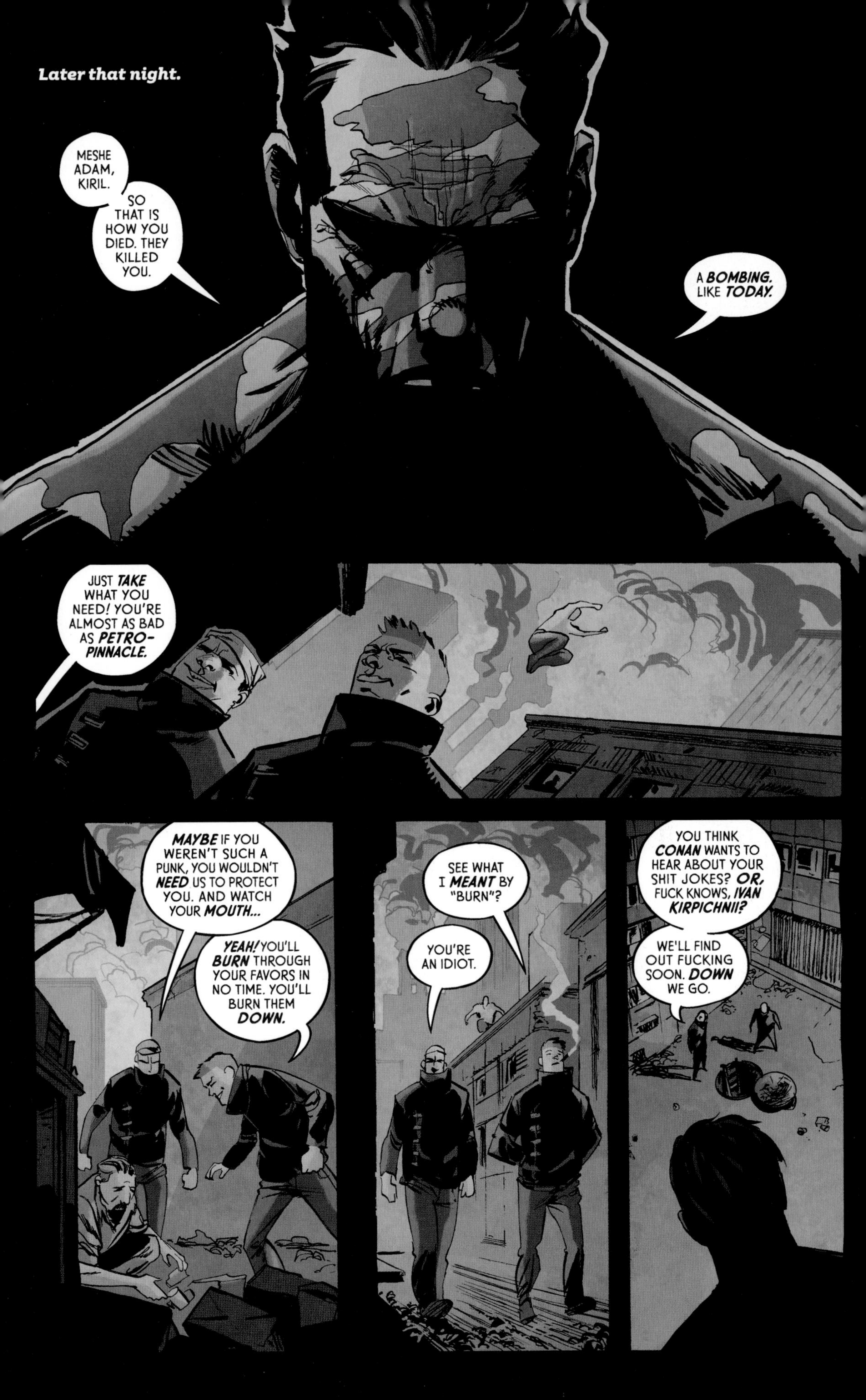
Later that night.
MESHE ADAM, KIRIL.
SO THAT IS HOW YOU DIED. THEY KILLED YOU.
A BOMBING. LIKE TODAY.
JUST TAKE WHAT YOU NEED! YOU'RE ALMOST AS BAD AS PETRO-PINNACLE.
MAYBE IF YOU WEREN'T SUCH A PUNK, YOU WOULDN'T NEED US TO PROTECT YOU. AND WATCH YOUR MOUTH...
YEAH! YOU'LL BURN THROUGH YOUR FAVORS IN NO TIME. YOU'LL BURN THEM DOWN.
SEE WHAT I MEANT BY "BURN"?
YOU'RE AN IDIOT.
YOU THINK CONAN WANTS TO HEAR ABOUT YOUR SHIT JOKES? OR, FUCK KNOWS, IVAN KIRPICHNII?
WE'LL FIND OUT FUCKING SOON. DOWN WE GO.

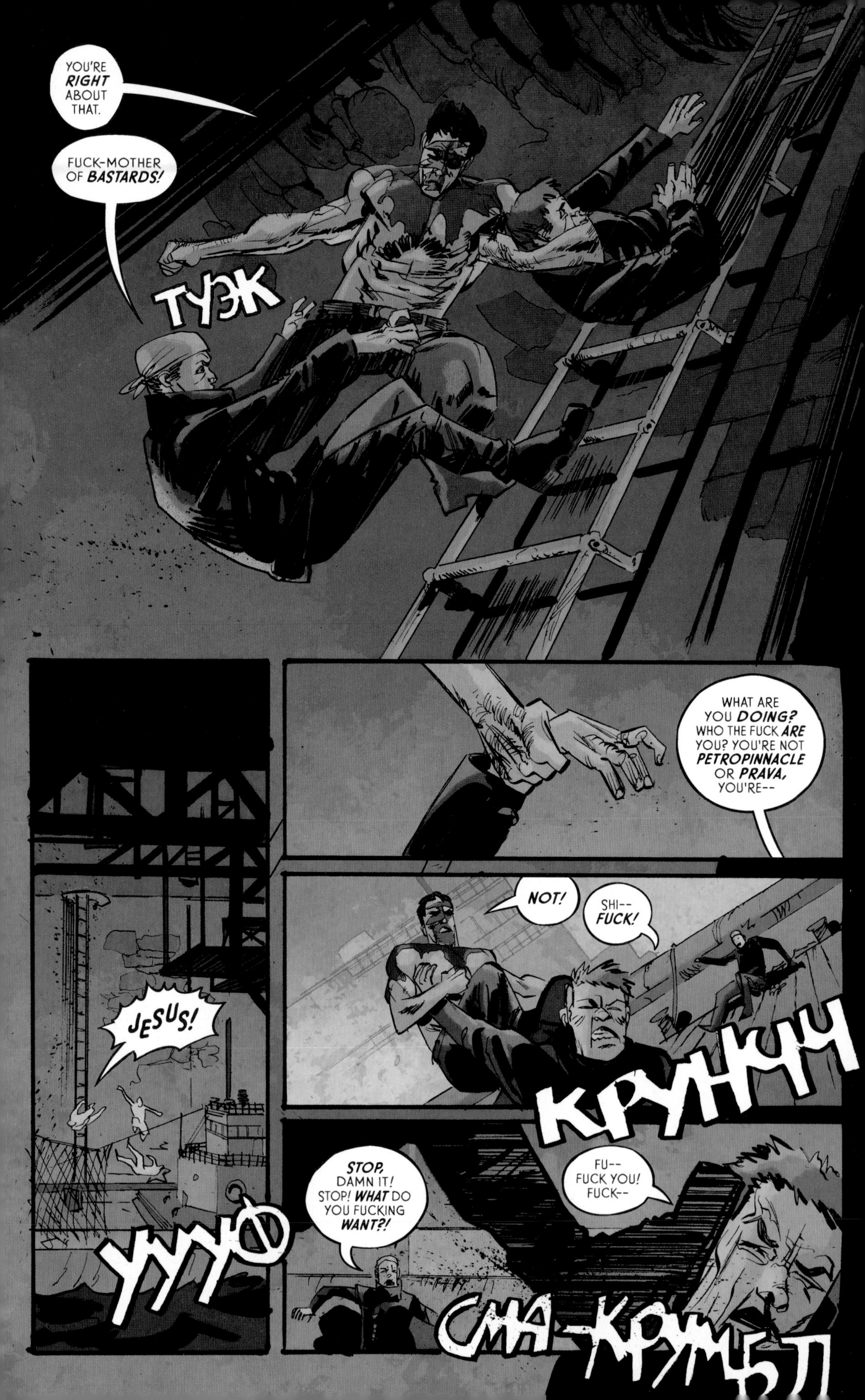
YOU'RE *RIGHT* ABOUT THAT.
FUCK-MOTHER OF *BASTARDS!*
ТУЭК
WHAT ARE YOU *DOING?* WHO THE FUCK *ARE* YOU? YOU'RE NOT *PETROPINNACLE* OR *PRAVA,* YOU'RE--
JESUS!
NOT!
SHI-- *FUCK!*
КРУНЧЧ
УУУФ
STOP, DAMN IT! STOP! *WHAT* DO YOU FUCKING *WANT?!*
FU-- FUCK YOU! FUCK--
СМА-КРУМБЛ

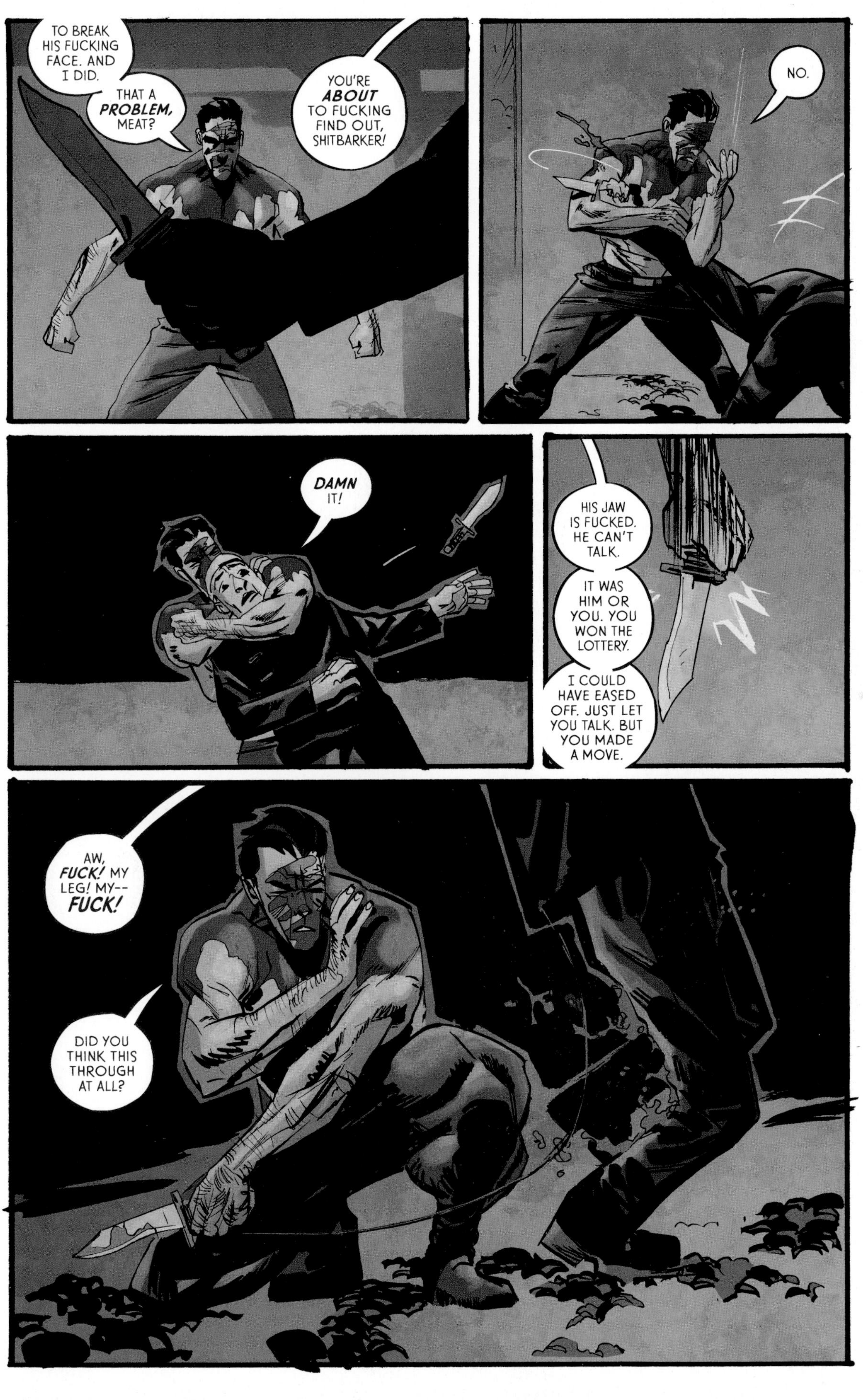
TO BREAK HIS FUCKING FACE. AND I DID.
THAT A *PROBLEM,* MEAT?
YOU'RE *ABOUT* TO FUCKING FIND OUT, SHITBARKER!
NO.
DAMN IT!
HIS JAW IS FUCKED. HE CAN'T TALK.
IT WAS HIM OR YOU. YOU WON THE LOTTERY.
I COULD HAVE EASED OFF. JUST LET YOU TALK. BUT YOU MADE A MOVE.
AW, *FUCK!* MY LEG! MY-- *FUCK!*
DID YOU THINK THIS THROUGH AT ALL?

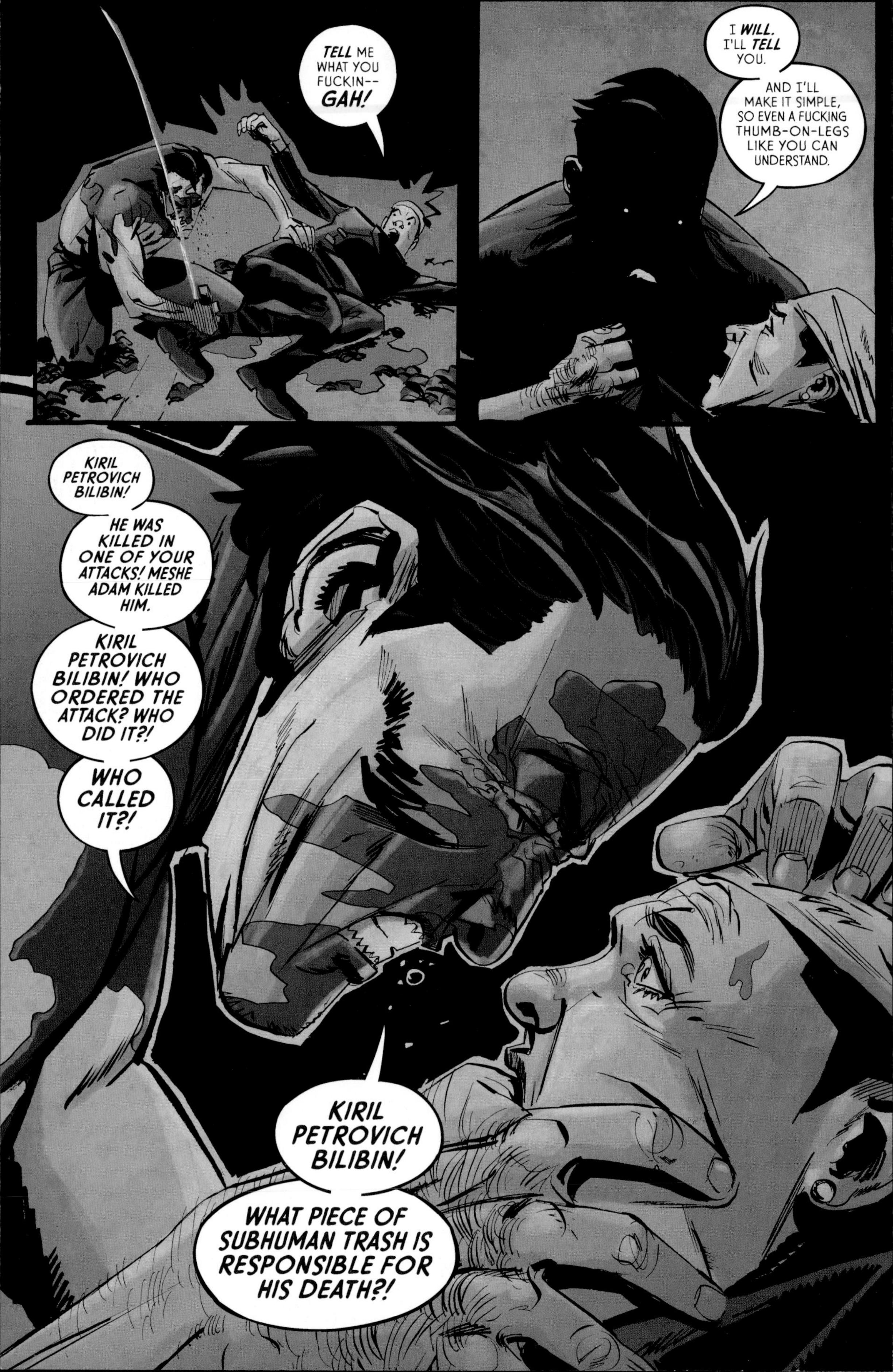
TELL ME WHAT YOU FUCKIN-- GAH!
I WILL. I'LL TELL YOU.
AND I'LL MAKE IT SIMPLE, SO EVEN A FUCKING THUMB-ON-LEGS LIKE YOU CAN UNDERSTAND.
KIRIL PETROVICH BILIBIN!
HE WAS KILLED IN ONE OF YOUR ATTACKS! MESHE ADAM KILLED HIM.
KIRIL PETROVICH BILIBIN! WHO ORDERED THE ATTACK? WHO DID IT?!
WHO CALLED IT?!
KIRIL PETROVICH BILIBIN!
WHAT PIECE OF SUBHUMAN TRASH IS RESPONSIBLE FOR HIS DEATH?!

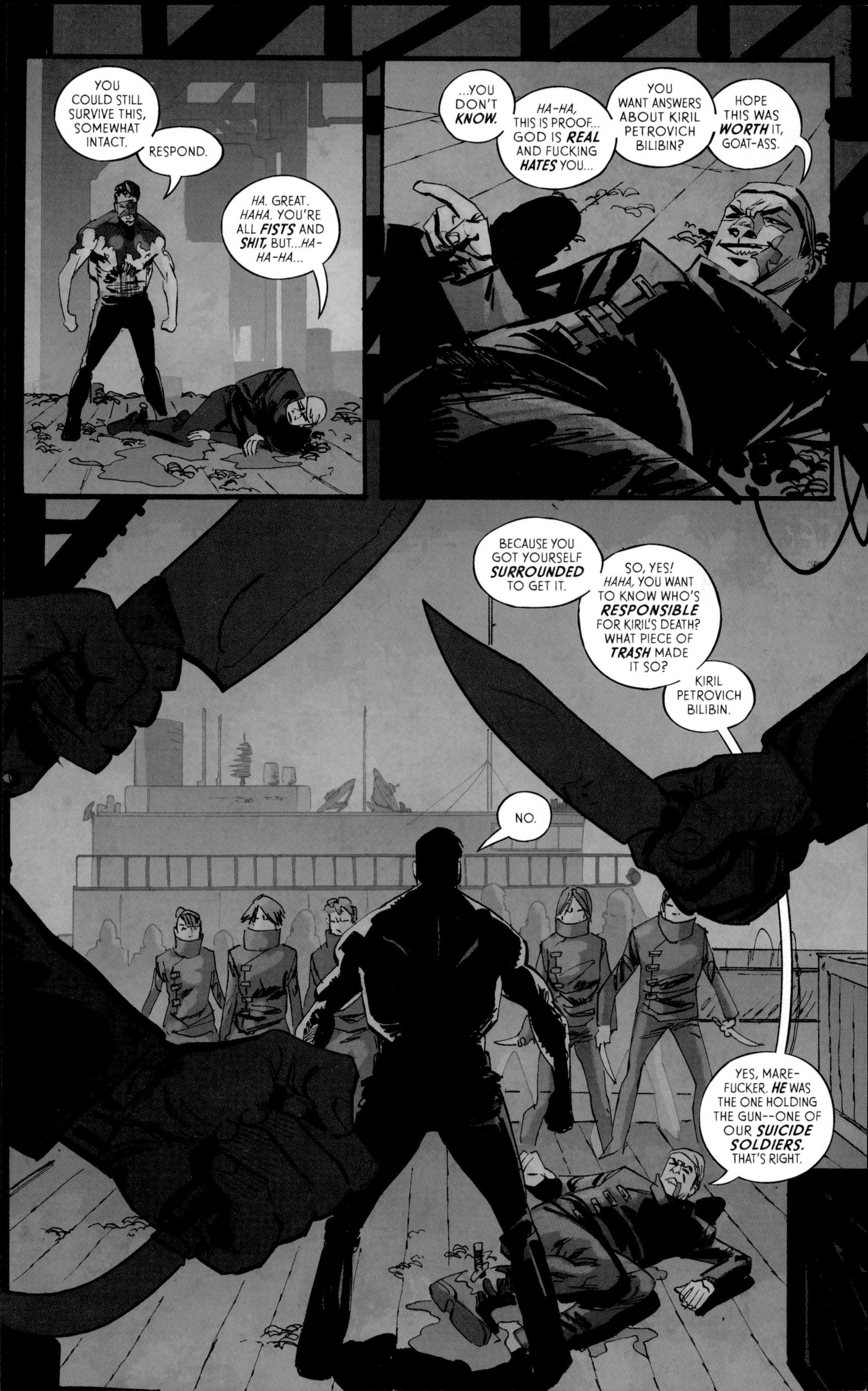
YOU COULD STILL SURVIVE THIS, SOMEWHAT INTACT.
RESPOND.
HA. GREAT. HAHA. YOU'RE ALL FISTS AND SHIT, BUT...HA-HA-HA...
...YOU DON'T KNOW.
HA-HA, THIS IS PROOF... GOD IS REAL AND FUCKING HATES YOU...
YOU WANT ANSWERS ABOUT KIRIL PETROVICH BILIBIN?
HOPE THIS WAS WORTH IT, GOAT-ASS.
BECAUSE YOU GOT YOURSELF SURROUNDED TO GET IT.
SO, YES! HAHA, YOU WANT TO KNOW WHO'S RESPONSIBLE FOR KIRIL'S DEATH? WHAT PIECE OF TRASH MADE IT SO?
KIRIL PETROVICH BILIBIN.
NO.
YES, MARE-FUCKER. HE WAS THE ONE HOLDING THE GUN--ONE OF OUR SUICIDE SOLDIERS. THAT'S RIGHT.

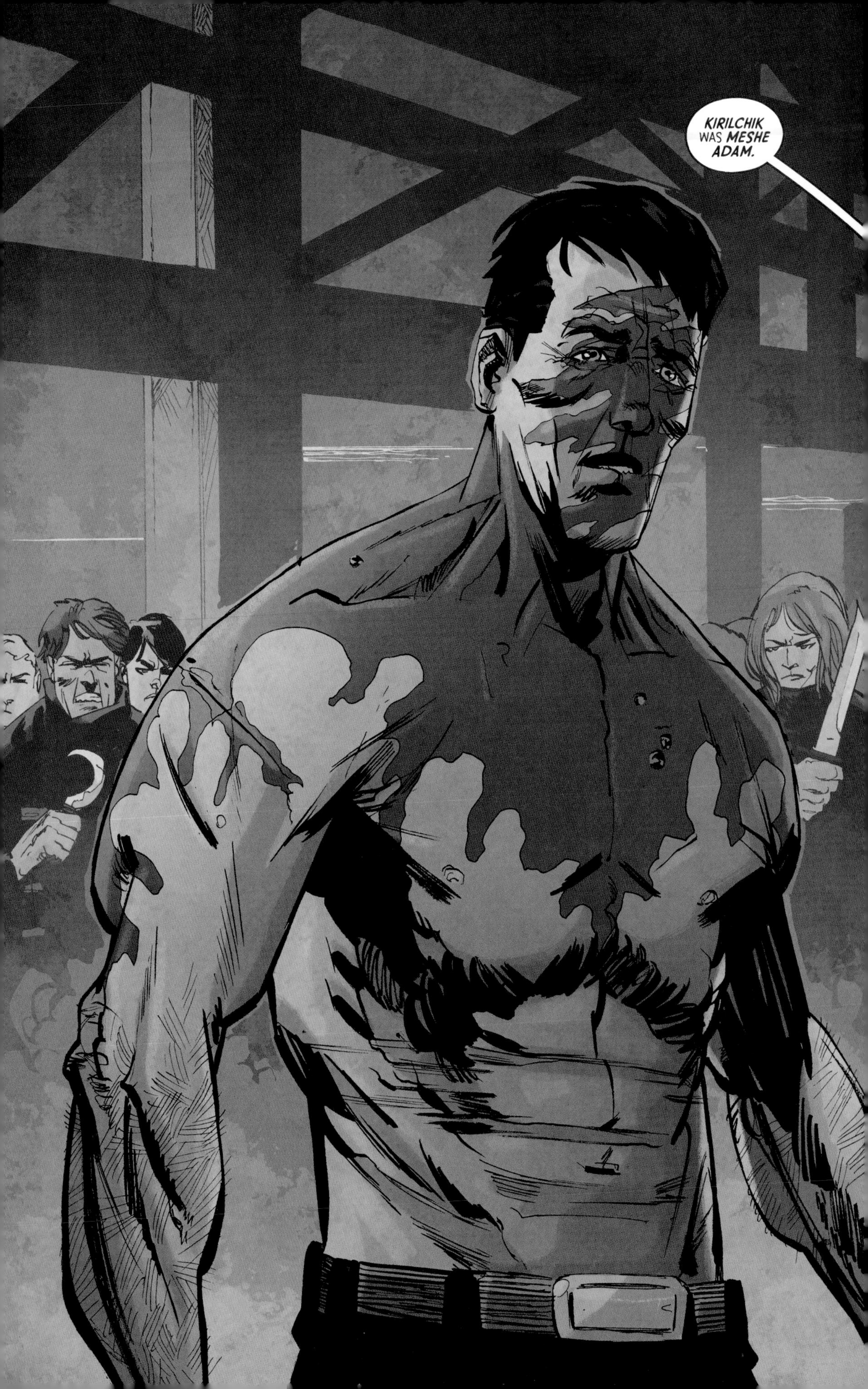
KIRILCHIK WAS MESHE ADAM.

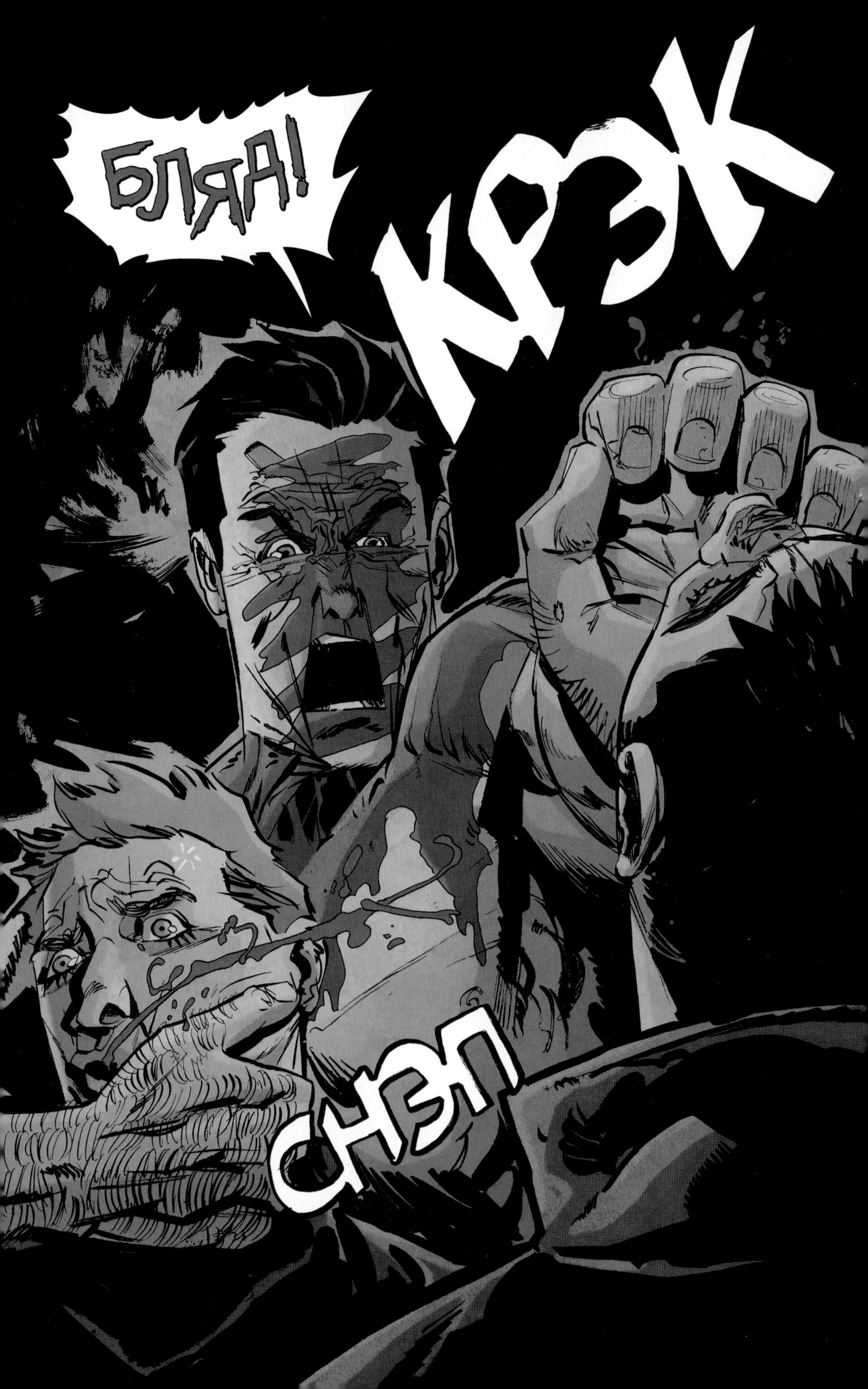
БЛЯДЬ!
КРЭК
СНЭП

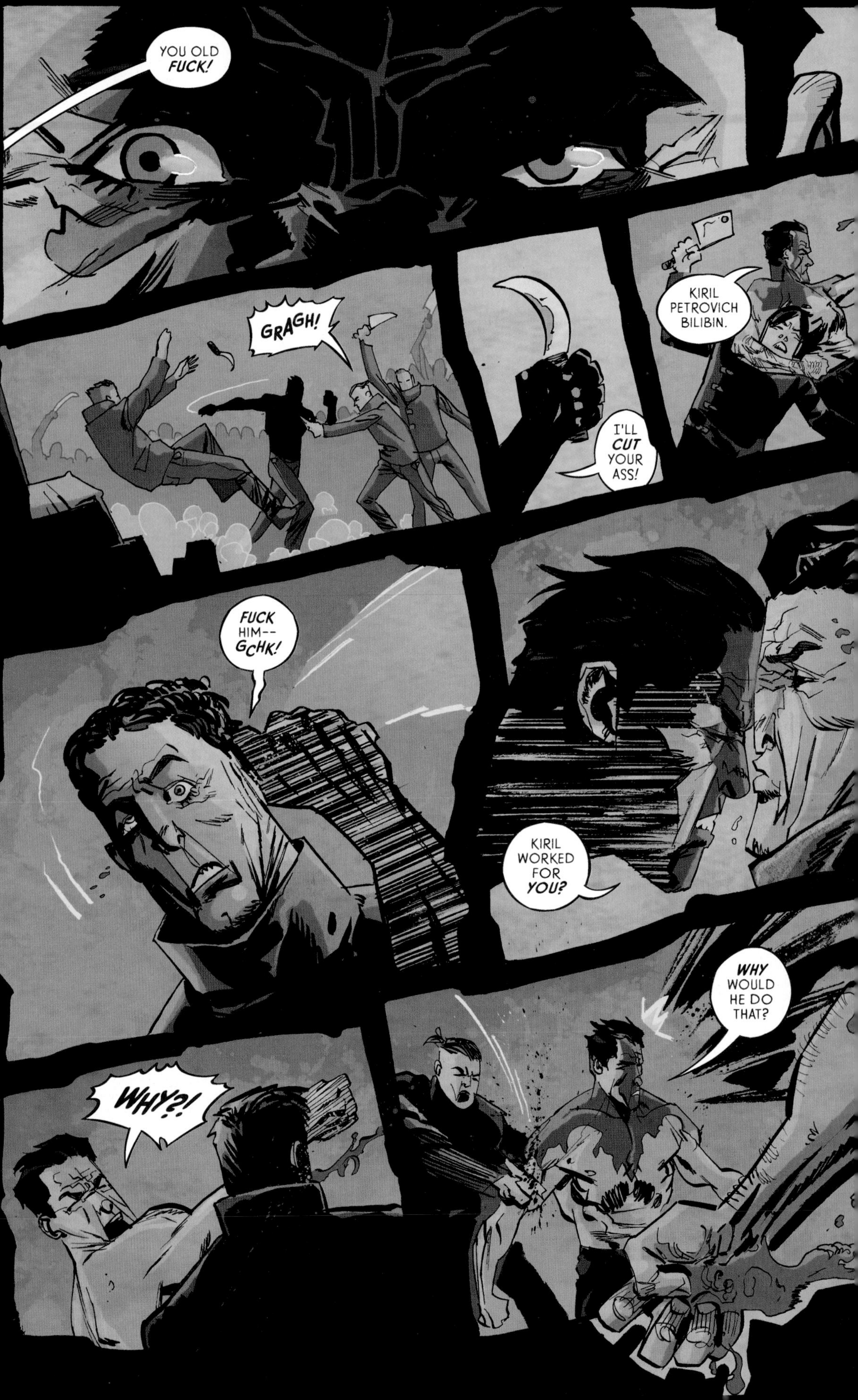
YOU OLD FUCK!
GRAGH!
I'LL CUT YOUR ASS!
KIRIL PETROVICH BILIBIN.
FUCK HIM-- GCHK!
KIRIL WORKED FOR YOU?
WHY WOULD HE DO THAT?
WHY?!

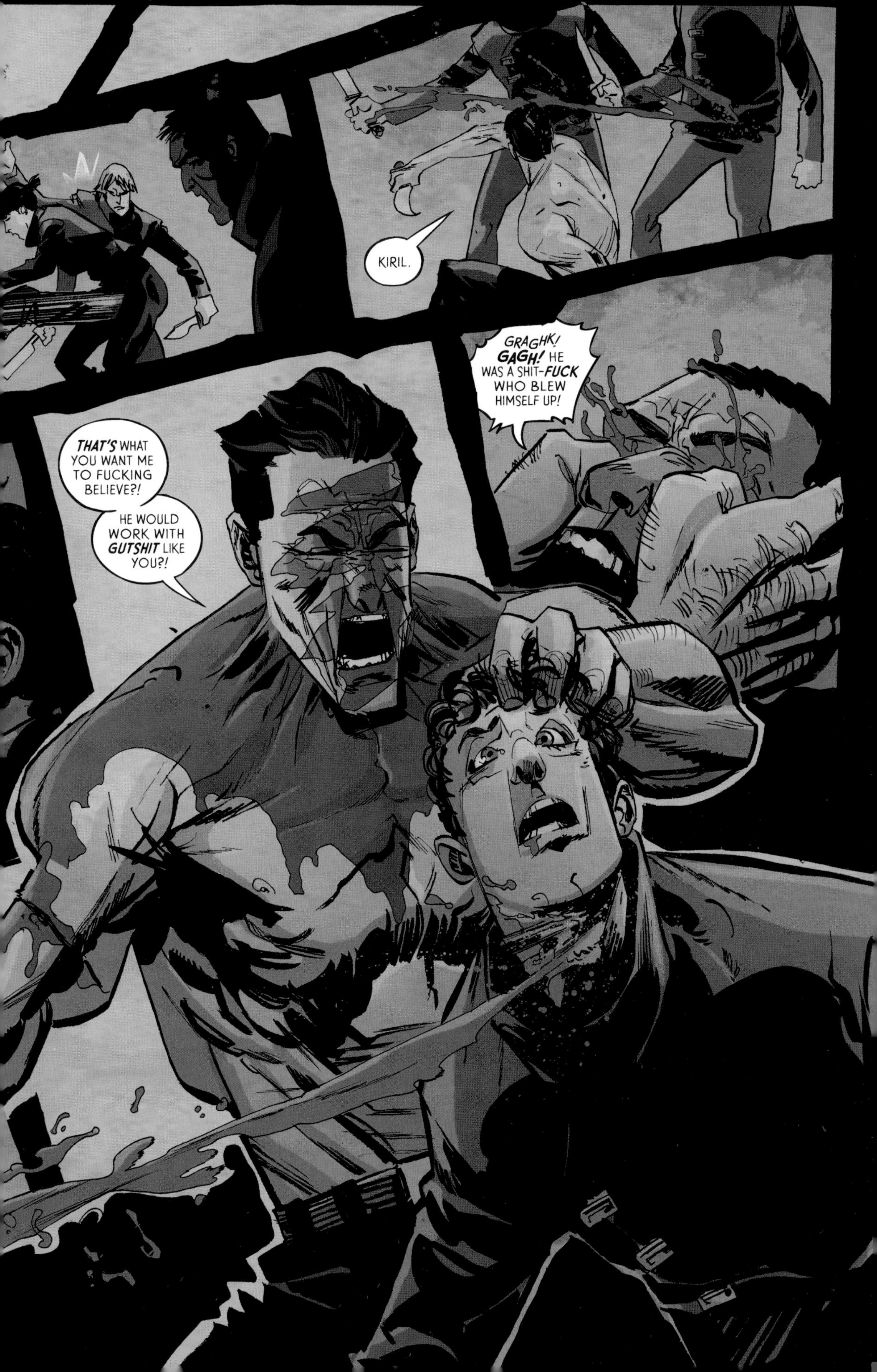
KIRIL.
GRAGHK! GAGH! HE WAS A SHIT-FUCK WHO BLEW HIMSELF UP!
THAT'S WHAT YOU WANT ME TO FUCKING BELIEVE?!
HE WOULD WORK WITH GUTSHIT LIKE YOU?!

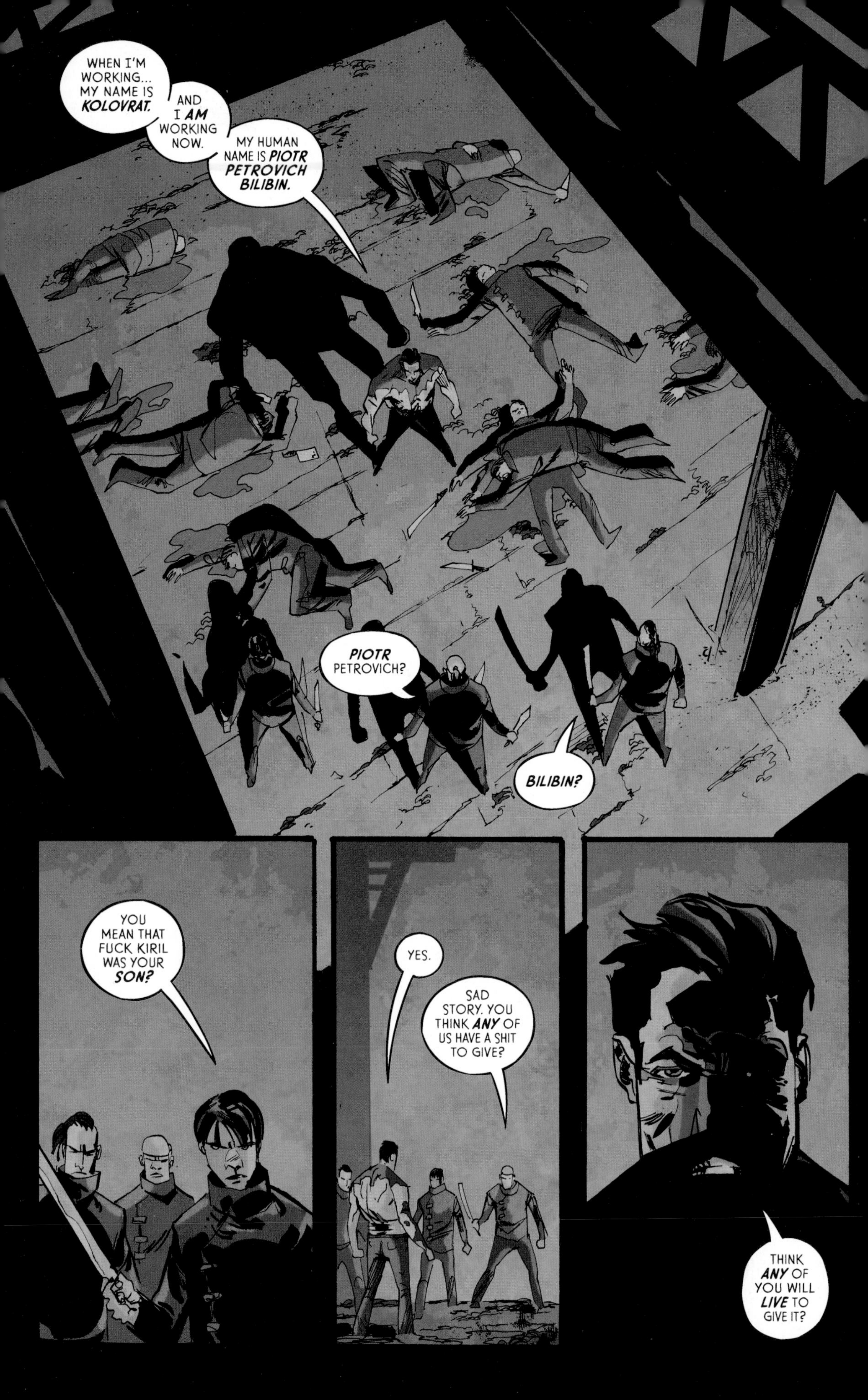
WHEN I'M WORKING... MY NAME IS KOLOVRAT.
AND I AM WORKING NOW.
MY HUMAN NAME IS PIOTR PETROVICH BILIBIN.
PIOTR PETROVICH?
BILIBIN?
YOU MEAN THAT FUCK KIRIL WAS YOUR SON?
YES.
SAD STORY. YOU THINK ANY OF US HAVE A SHIT TO GIVE?
THINK ANY OF YOU WILL LIVE TO GIVE IT?

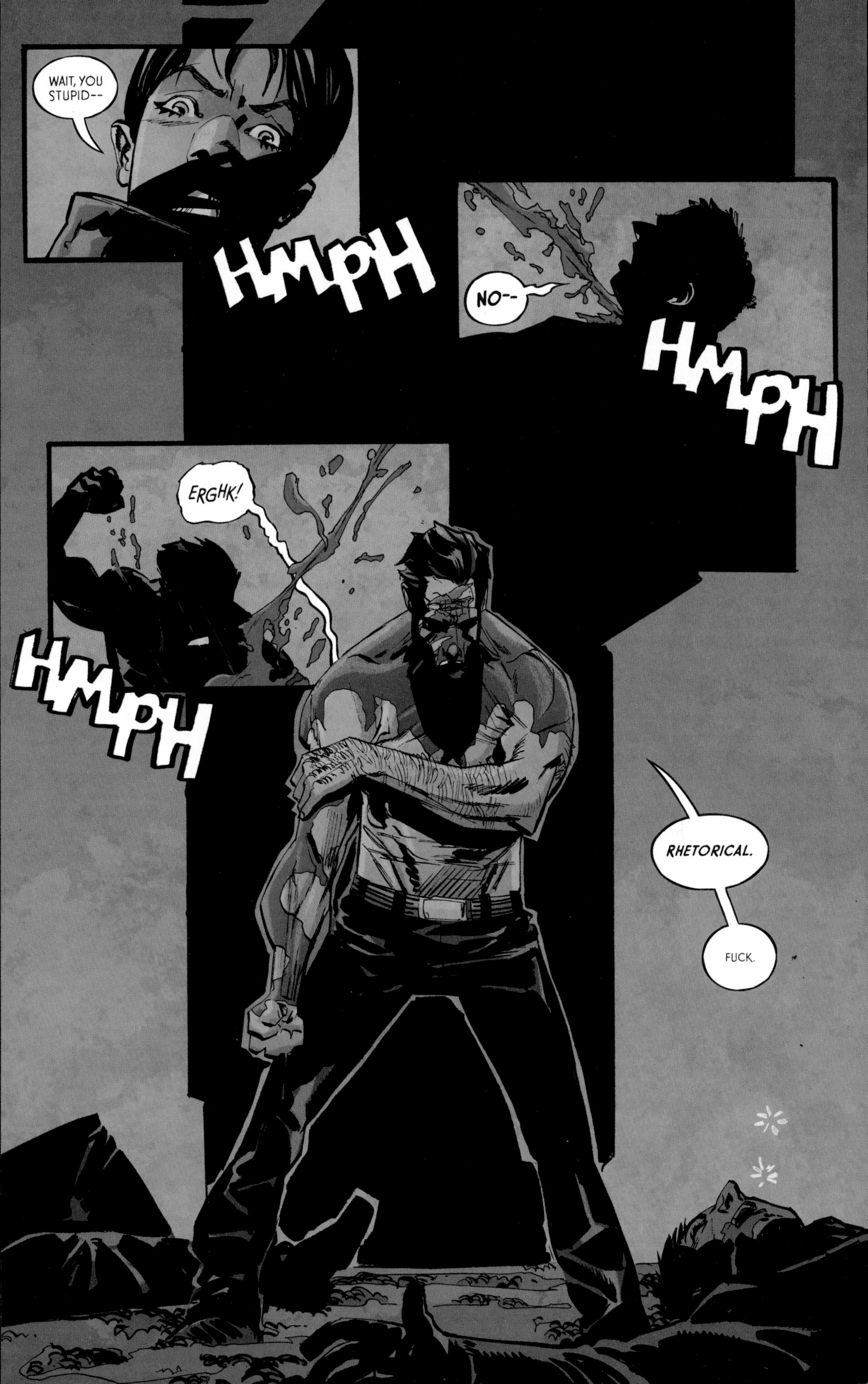
WAIT, YOU STUPID--
HMPH
NO--
HMPH
ERGHK!
HMPH
RHETORICAL.
FUCK.

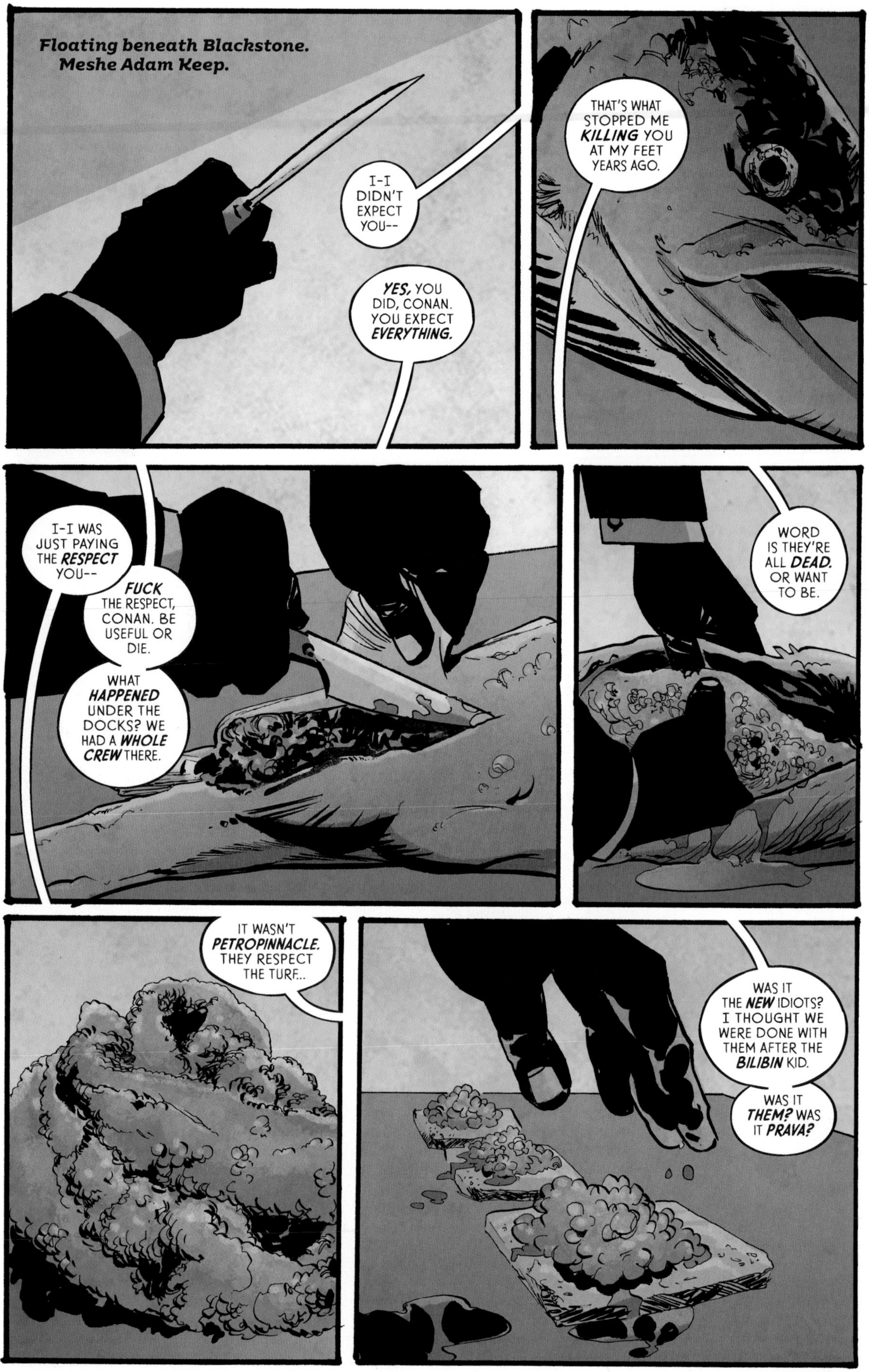
Floating beneath Blackstone.
Meshe Adam Keep.
I-I DIDN'T EXPECT YOU--
YES, YOU DID, CONAN. YOU EXPECT EVERYTHING.
THAT'S WHAT STOPPED ME KILLING YOU AT MY FEET YEARS AGO.
I-I WAS JUST PAYING THE RESPECT YOU--
FUCK THE RESPECT, CONAN. BE USEFUL OR DIE.
WHAT HAPPENED UNDER THE DOCKS? WE HAD A WHOLE CREW THERE.
WORD IS THEY'RE ALL DEAD. OR WANT TO BE.
IT WASN'T PETROPINNACLE. THEY RESPECT THE TURF...
WAS IT THE NEW IDIOTS? I THOUGHT WE WERE DONE WITH THEM AFTER THE BILIBIN KID.
WAS IT THEM? WAS IT PRAVA?

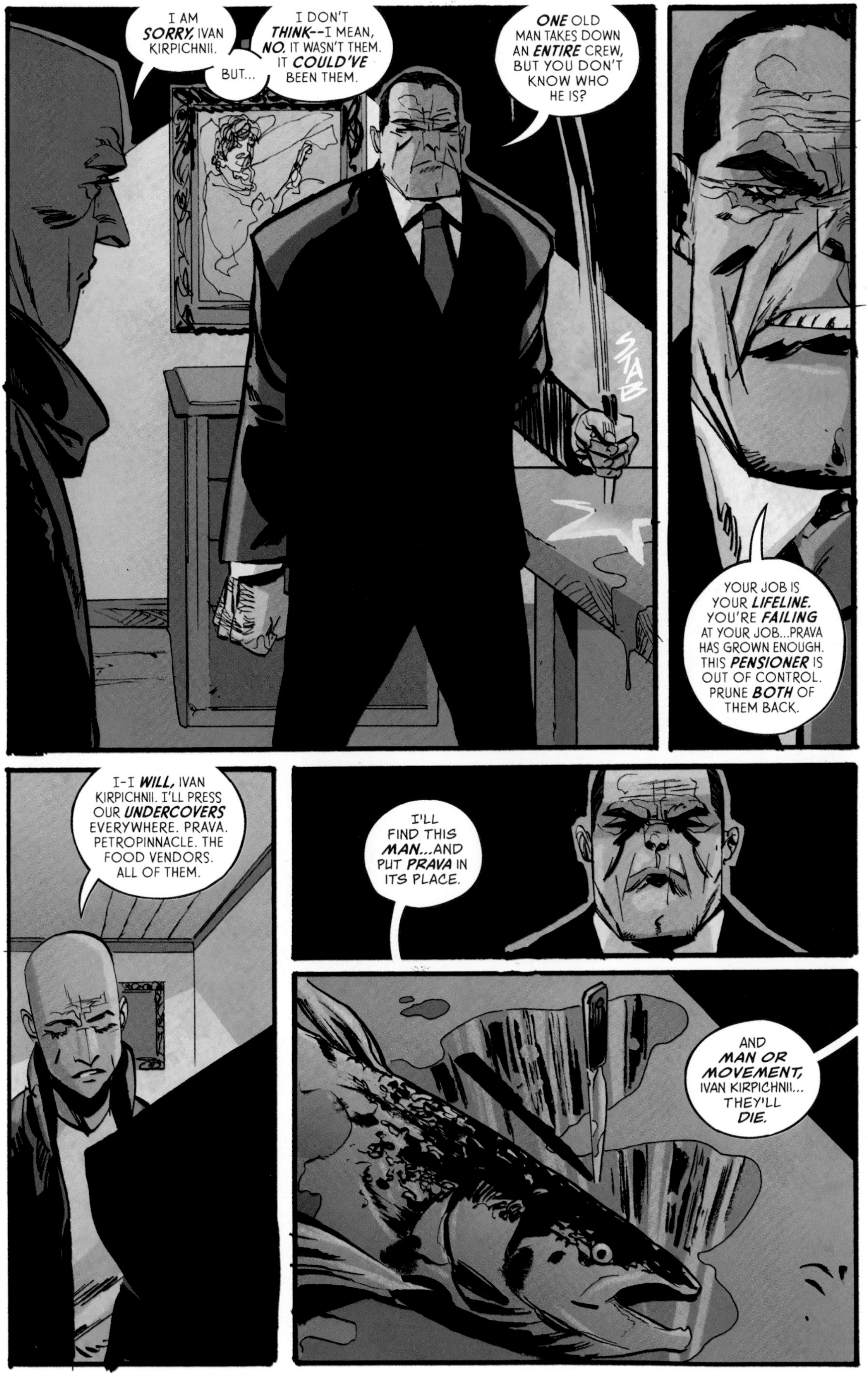
I AM SORRY, IVAN KIRPICHNII.
BUT...
I DON'T THINK--I MEAN, NO. IT WASN'T THEM. IT COULD'VE BEEN THEM.
ONE OLD MAN TAKES DOWN AN ENTIRE CREW, BUT YOU DON'T KNOW WHO HE IS?
STAB
YOUR JOB IS YOUR LIFELINE. YOU'RE FAILING AT YOUR JOB...PRAVA HAS GROWN ENOUGH. THIS PENSIONER IS OUT OF CONTROL. PRUNE BOTH OF THEM BACK.
I-I WILL, IVAN KIRPICHNII. I'LL PRESS OUR UNDERCOVERS EVERYWHERE. PRAVA. PETROPINNACLE. THE FOOD VENDORS. ALL OF THEM.
I'LL FIND THIS MAN...AND PUT PRAVA IN ITS PLACE.
AND MAN OR MOVEMENT, IVAN KIRPICHNII... THEY'LL DIE.

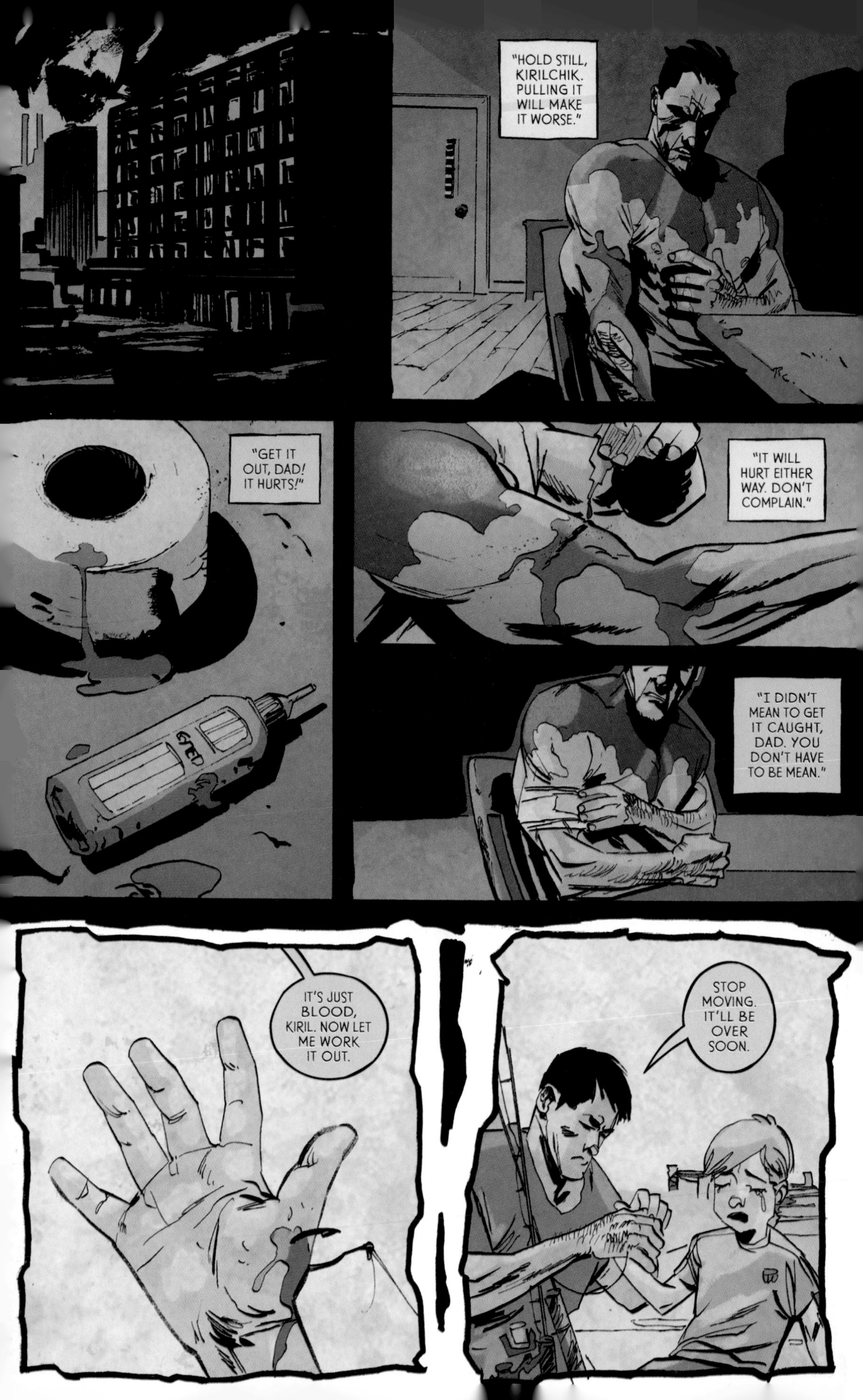
"HOLD STILL, KIRILCHIK. PULLING IT WILL MAKE IT WORSE."
"GET IT OUT, DAD! IT HURTS!"
"IT WILL HURT EITHER WAY. DON'T COMPLAIN."
"I DIDN'T MEAN TO GET IT CAUGHT, DAD. YOU DON'T HAVE TO BE MEAN."
IT'S JUST BLOOD, KIRIL. NOW LET ME WORK IT OUT.
STOP MOVING. IT'LL BE OVER SOON.

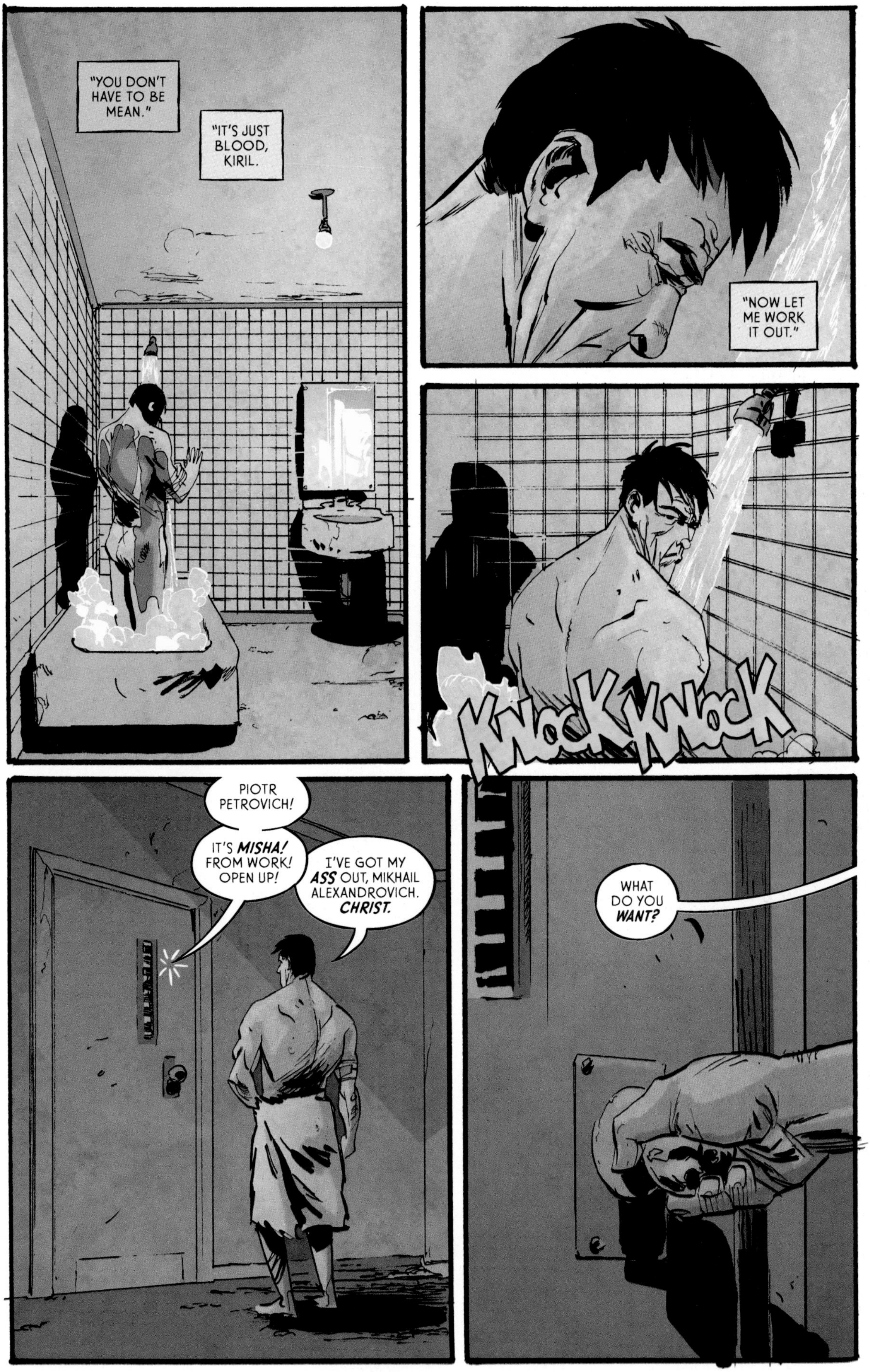
"YOU DON'T HAVE TO BE MEAN."
"IT'S JUST BLOOD, KIRIL.
"NOW LET ME WORK IT OUT."
KNOCK KNOCK
PIOTR PETROVICH!
IT'S **MISHA!** FROM WORK! OPEN UP!
I'VE GOT MY **ASS** OUT, MIKHAIL ALEXANDROVICH. **CHRIST.**
WHAT DO YOU **WANT?**

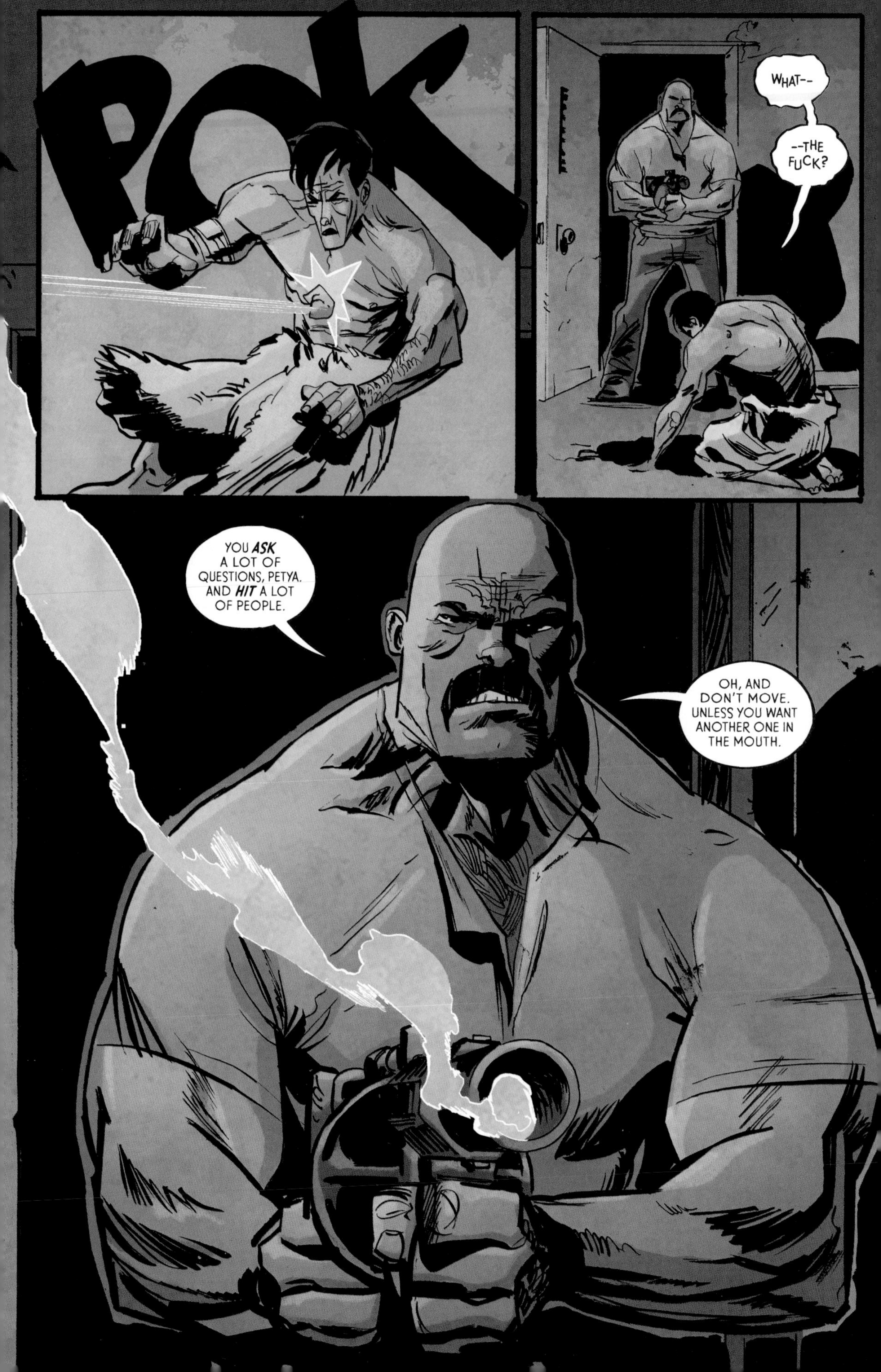
POK
WHAT--
--THE FUCK?
YOU ASK A LOT OF QUESTIONS, PETYA. AND HIT A LOT OF PEOPLE.
OH, AND DON'T MOVE. UNLESS YOU WANT ANOTHER ONE IN THE MOUTH.

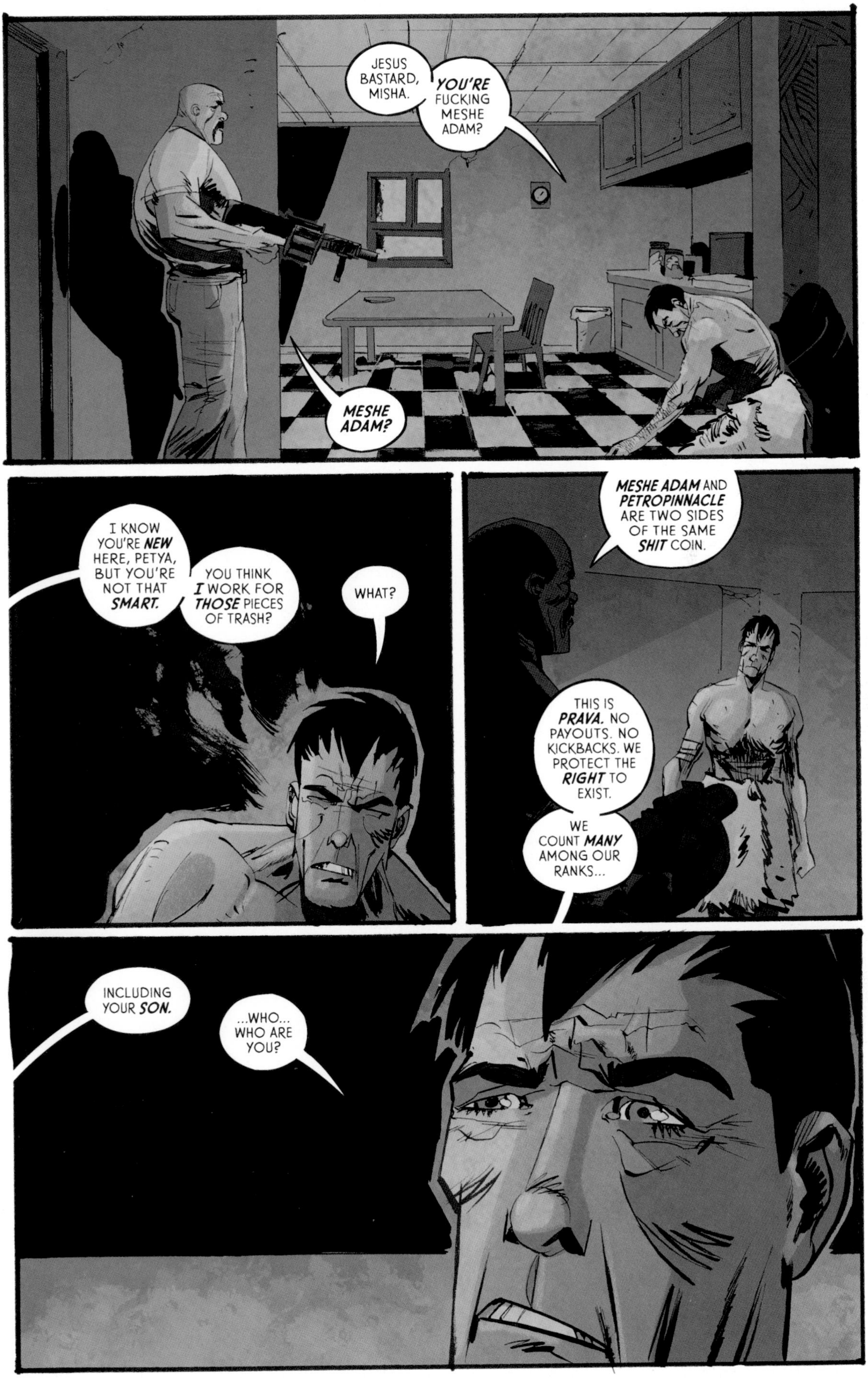
JESUS BASTARD, MISHA.
YOU'RE FUCKING MESHE ADAM?
MESHE ADAM?
I KNOW YOU'RE NEW HERE, PETYA, BUT YOU'RE NOT THAT SMART.
YOU THINK I WORK FOR THOSE PIECES OF TRASH?
WHAT?
MESHE ADAM AND PETROPINNACLE ARE TWO SIDES OF THE SAME SHIT COIN.
THIS IS PRAVA. NO PAYOUTS. NO KICKBACKS. WE PROTECT THE RIGHT TO EXIST.
WE COUNT MANY AMONG OUR RANKS...
INCLUDING YOUR SON.
...WHO... WHO ARE YOU?

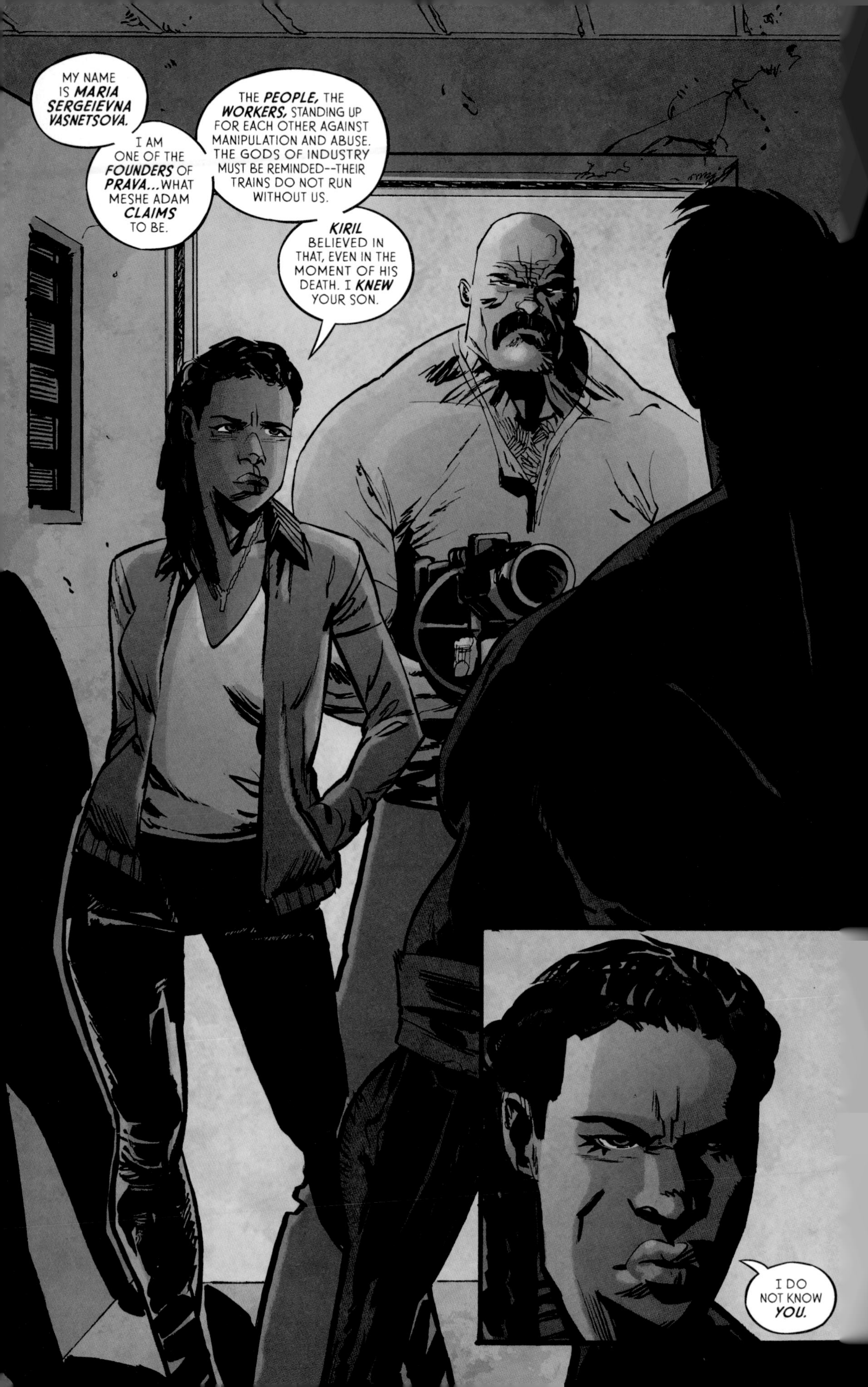
MY NAME IS MARIA SERGEIEVNA VASNETSOVA.
I AM ONE OF THE FOUNDERS OF PRAVA...WHAT MESHE ADAM CLAIMS TO BE.
THE PEOPLE, THE WORKERS, STANDING UP FOR EACH OTHER AGAINST MANIPULATION AND ABUSE. THE GODS OF INDUSTRY MUST BE REMINDED--THEIR TRAINS DO NOT RUN WITHOUT US.
KIRIL BELIEVED IN THAT, EVEN IN THE MOMENT OF HIS DEATH. I KNEW YOUR SON.
I DO NOT KNOW YOU.

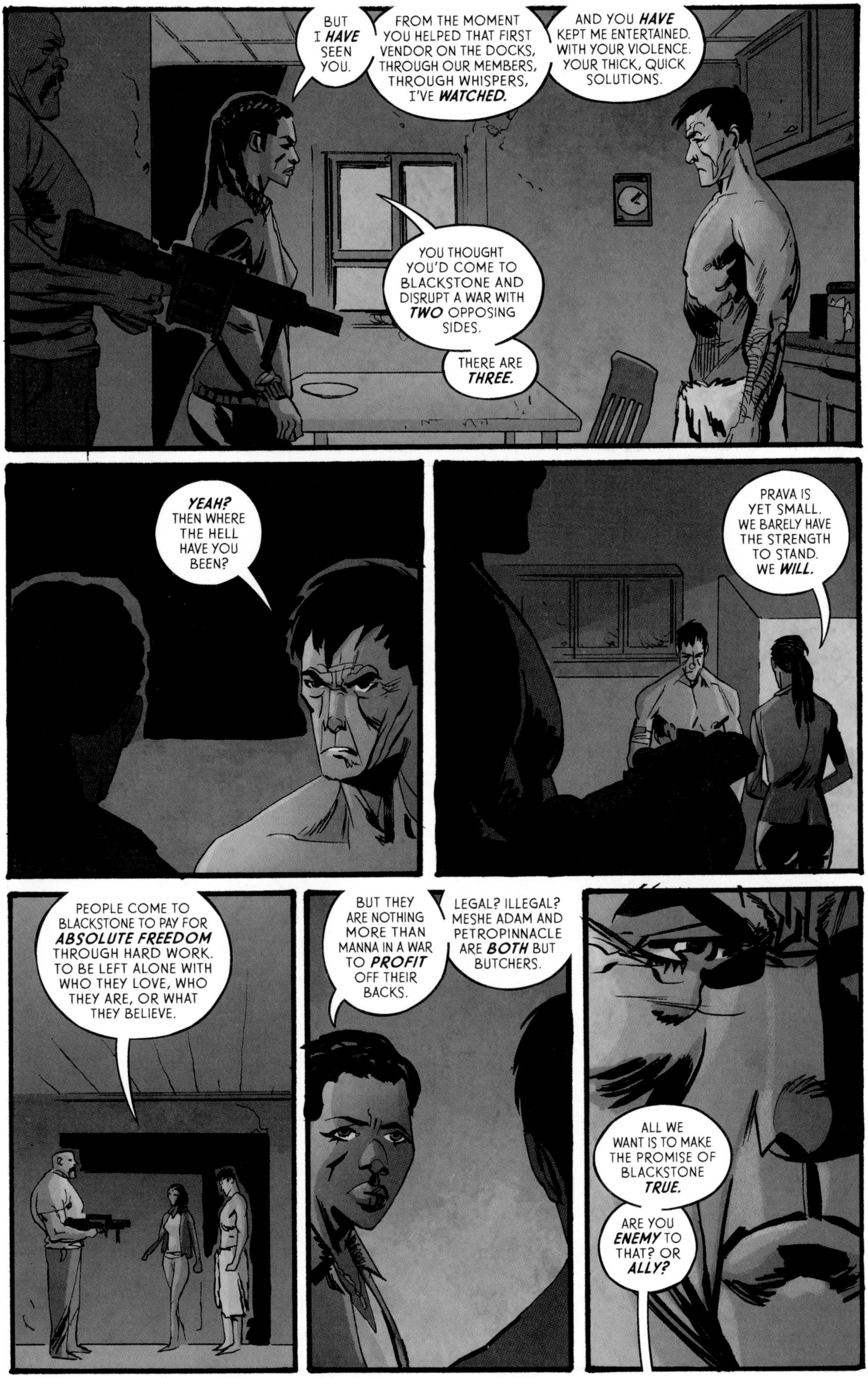
BUT I HAVE SEEN YOU.
FROM THE MOMENT YOU HELPED THAT FIRST VENDOR ON THE DOCKS, THROUGH OUR MEMBERS, THROUGH WHISPERS, I'VE WATCHED.
AND YOU HAVE KEPT ME ENTERTAINED. WITH YOUR VIOLENCE. YOUR THICK, QUICK SOLUTIONS.
YOU THOUGHT YOU'D COME TO BLACKSTONE AND DISRUPT A WAR WITH TWO OPPOSING SIDES.
THERE ARE THREE.
YEAH? THEN WHERE THE HELL HAVE YOU BEEN?
PRAVA IS YET SMALL. WE BARELY HAVE THE STRENGTH TO STAND. WE WILL.
PEOPLE COME TO BLACKSTONE TO PAY FOR ABSOLUTE FREEDOM THROUGH HARD WORK. TO BE LEFT ALONE WITH WHO THEY LOVE, WHO THEY ARE, OR WHAT THEY BELIEVE.
BUT THEY ARE NOTHING MORE THAN MANNA IN A WAR TO PROFIT OFF THEIR BACKS.
LEGAL? ILLEGAL? MESHE ADAM AND PETROPINNACLE ARE BOTH BUT BUTCHERS.
ALL WE WANT IS TO MAKE THE PROMISE OF BLACKSTONE TRUE.
ARE YOU ENEMY TO THAT? OR ALLY?

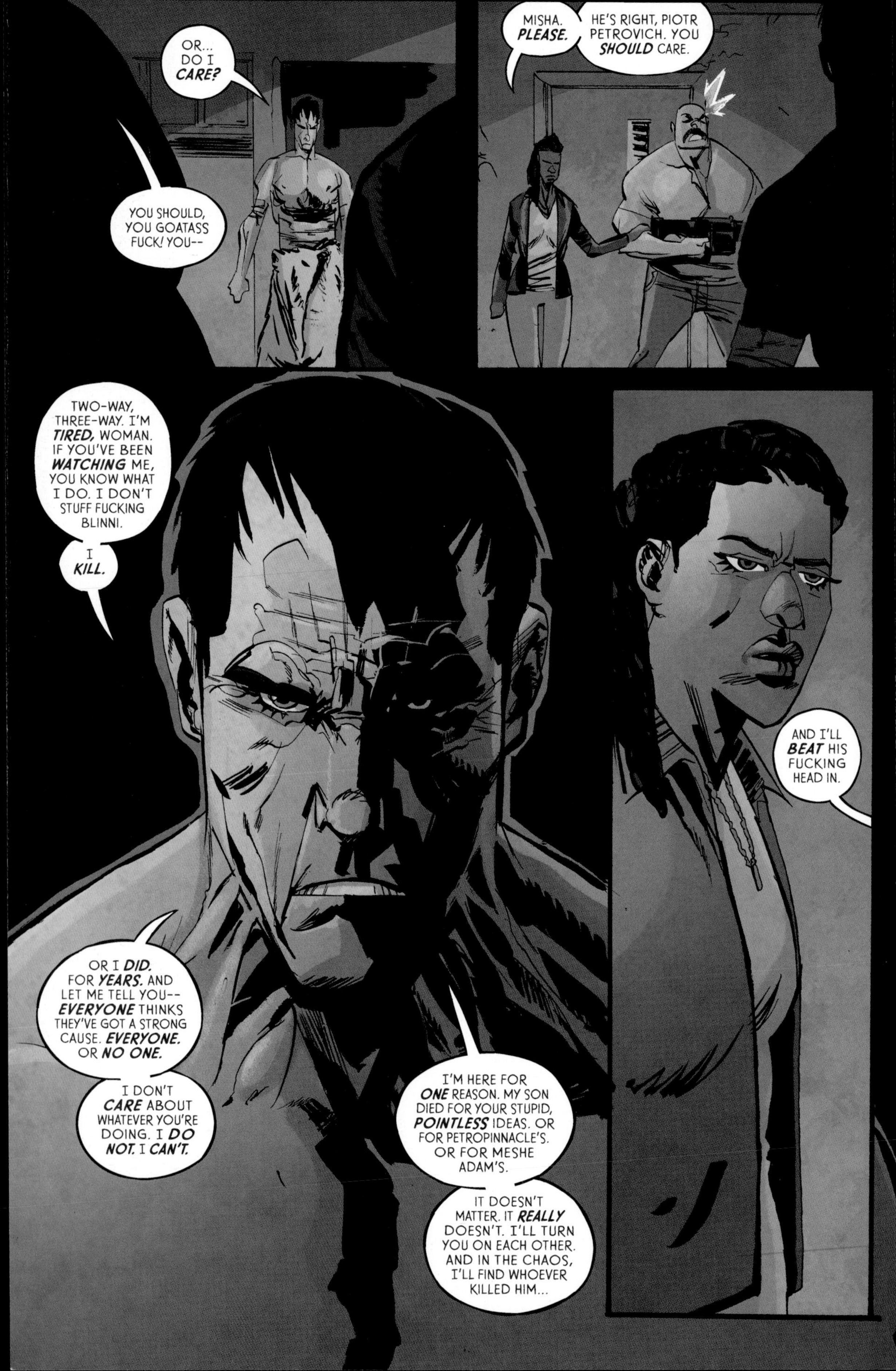
OR... DO I CARE?
YOU SHOULD, YOU GOATASS FUCK! YOU--
MISHA. PLEASE.
HE'S RIGHT, PIOTR PETROVICH. YOU SHOULD CARE.
TWO-WAY, THREE-WAY. I'M TIRED, WOMAN. IF YOU'VE BEEN WATCHING ME, YOU KNOW WHAT I DO. I DON'T STUFF FUCKING BLINNI.
I KILL.
AND I'LL BEAT HIS FUCKING HEAD IN.
OR I DID. FOR YEARS. AND LET ME TELL YOU-- EVERYONE THINKS THEY'VE GOT A STRONG CAUSE. EVERYONE. OR NO ONE.
I DON'T CARE ABOUT WHATEVER YOU'RE DOING. I DO NOT. I CAN'T.
I'M HERE FOR ONE REASON. MY SON DIED FOR YOUR STUPID, POINTLESS IDEAS. OR FOR PETROPINNACLE'S. OR FOR MESHE ADAM'S.
IT DOESN'T MATTER. IT REALLY DOESN'T. I'LL TURN YOU ON EACH OTHER. AND IN THE CHAOS, I'LL FIND WHOEVER KILLED HIM...

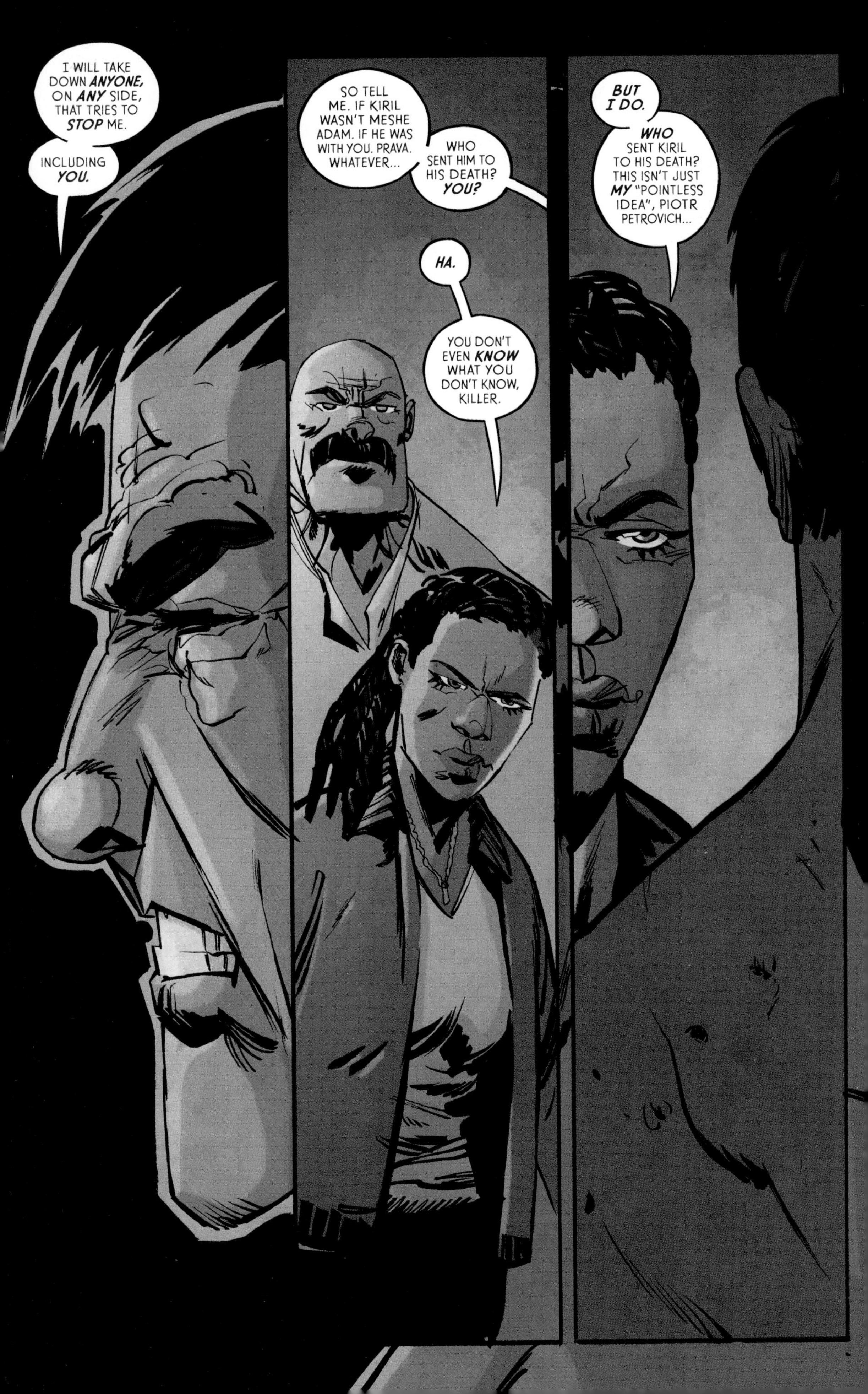
I WILL TAKE DOWN ANYONE, ON ANY SIDE, THAT TRIES TO STOP ME.
INCLUDING YOU.
SO TELL ME. IF KIRIL WASN'T MESHE ADAM. IF HE WAS WITH YOU. PRAVA. WHATEVER...
WHO SENT HIM TO HIS DEATH? YOU?
HA.
YOU DON'T EVEN KNOW WHAT YOU DON'T KNOW, KILLER.
BUT I DO.
WHO SENT KIRIL TO HIS DEATH? THIS ISN'T JUST MY "POINTLESS IDEA", PIOTR PETROVICH...

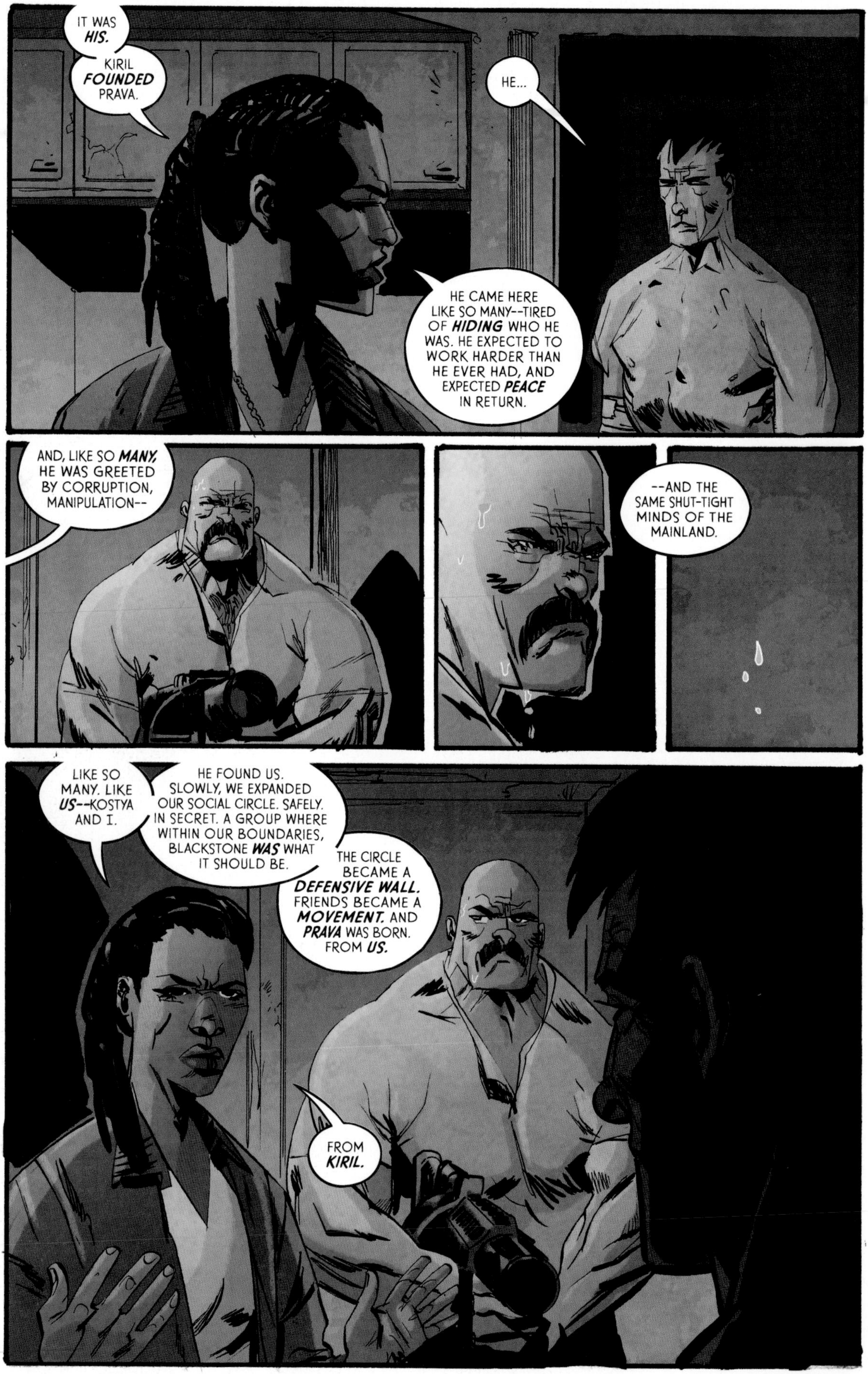
IT WAS *HIS.*
KIRIL *FOUNDED* PRAVA.
HE...
HE CAME HERE LIKE SO MANY--TIRED OF *HIDING* WHO HE WAS. HE EXPECTED TO WORK HARDER THAN HE EVER HAD, AND EXPECTED *PEACE* IN RETURN.
AND, LIKE SO *MANY,* HE WAS GREETED BY CORRUPTION, MANIPULATION--
--AND THE SAME SHUT-TIGHT MINDS OF THE MAINLAND.
LIKE SO MANY. LIKE *US*--KOSTYA AND I.
HE FOUND US. SLOWLY, WE EXPANDED OUR SOCIAL CIRCLE. SAFELY. IN SECRET. A GROUP WHERE WITHIN OUR BOUNDARIES, BLACKSTONE *WAS* WHAT IT SHOULD BE.
THE CIRCLE BECAME A *DEFENSIVE WALL.* FRIENDS BECAME A *MOVEMENT.* AND *PRAVA* WAS BORN. FROM *US.*
FROM *KIRIL.*

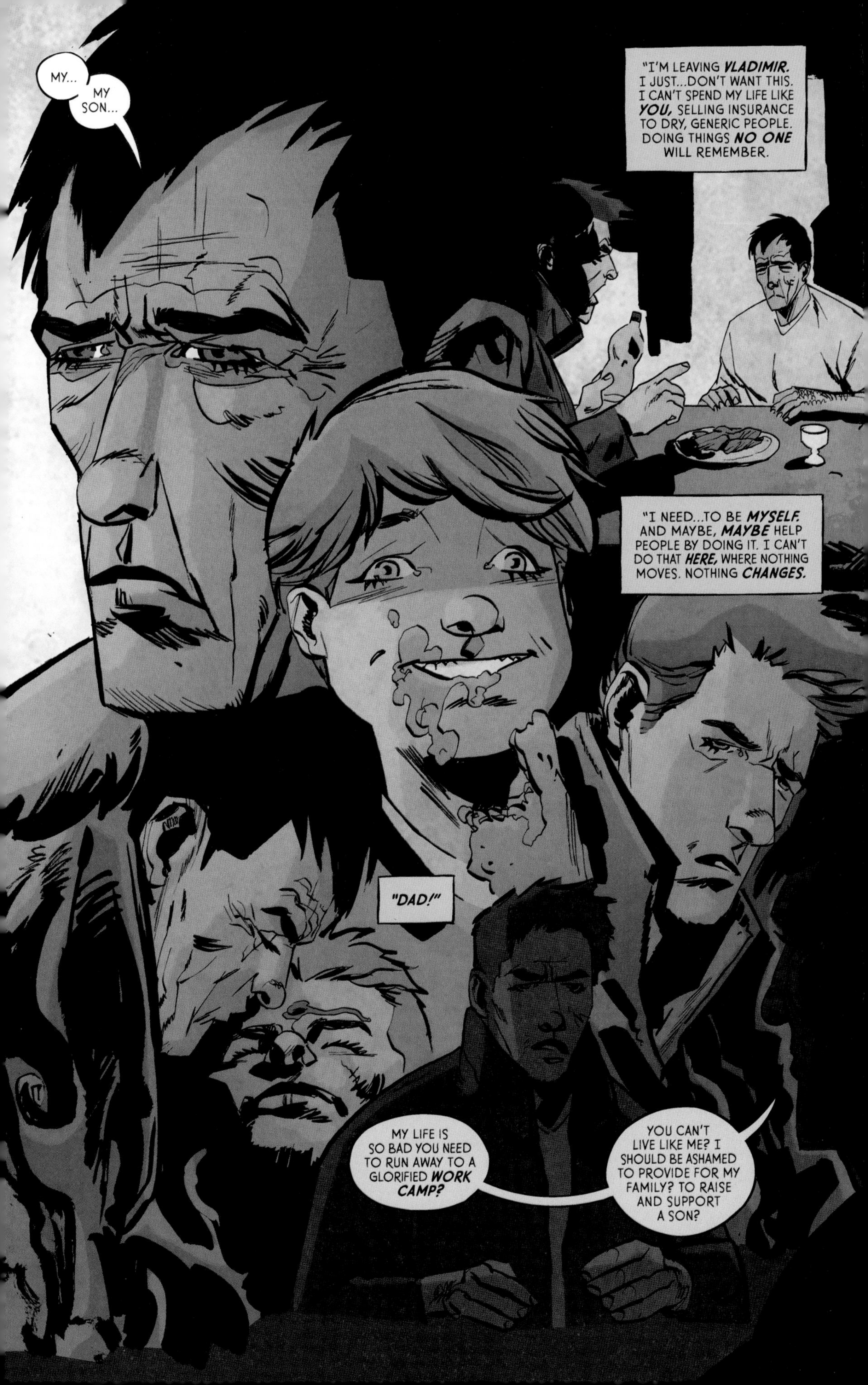
MY... MY SON...
"I'M LEAVING VLADIMIR. I JUST...DON'T WANT THIS. I CAN'T SPEND MY LIFE LIKE YOU, SELLING INSURANCE TO DRY, GENERIC PEOPLE. DOING THINGS NO ONE WILL REMEMBER.
"I NEED...TO BE MYSELF. AND MAYBE, MAYBE HELP PEOPLE BY DOING IT. I CAN'T DO THAT HERE, WHERE NOTHING MOVES. NOTHING CHANGES.
"DAD!"
MY LIFE IS SO BAD YOU NEED TO RUN AWAY TO A GLORIFIED WORK CAMP?
YOU CAN'T LIVE LIKE ME? I SHOULD BE ASHAMED TO PROVIDE FOR MY FAMILY? TO RAISE AND SUPPORT A SON?

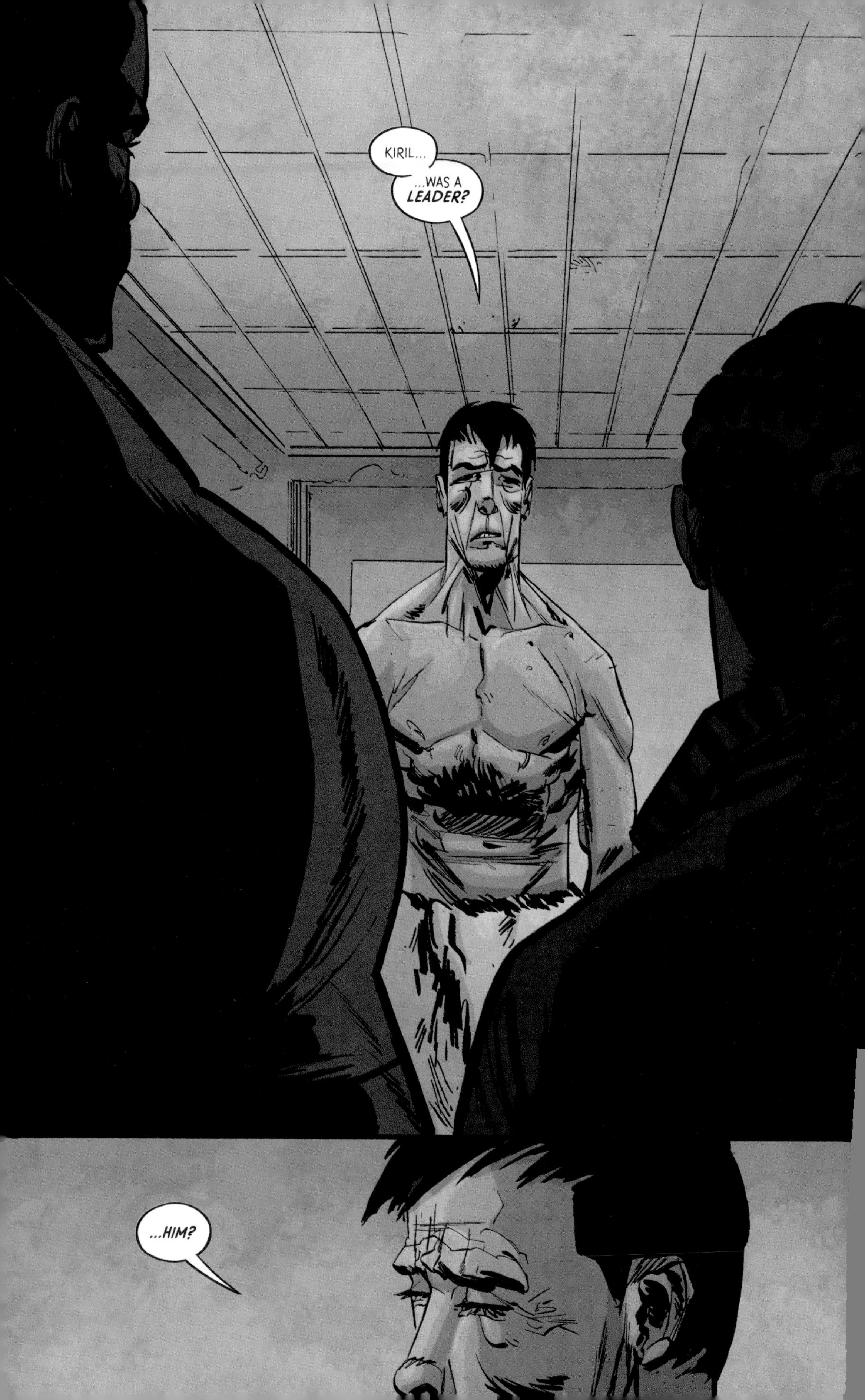
KIRIL...
...WAS A LEADER?
...HIM?

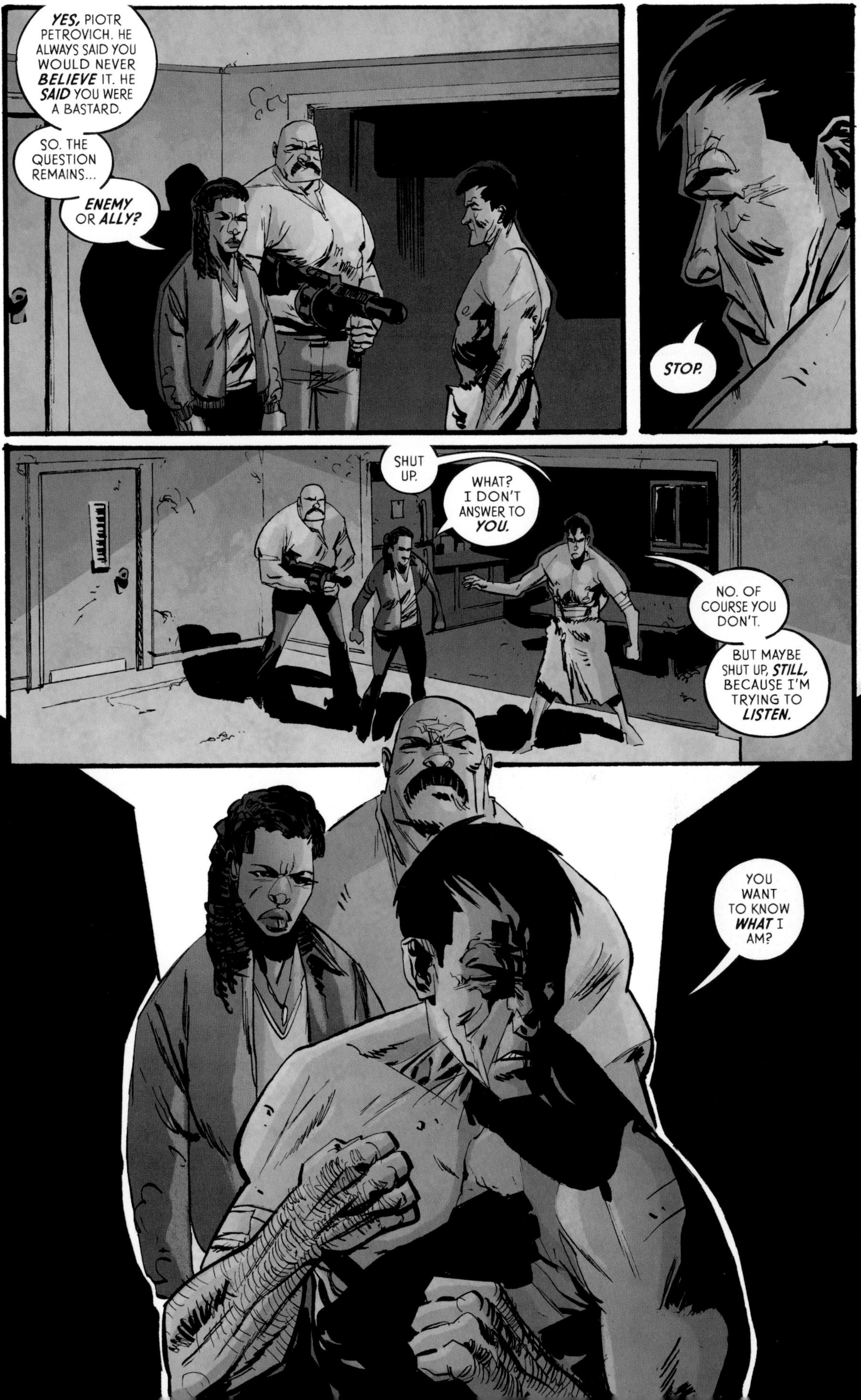

YES, PIOTR PETROVICH. HE ALWAYS SAID YOU WOULD NEVER **BELIEVE** IT. HE **SAID** YOU WERE A BASTARD.
SO. THE QUESTION REMAINS...
ENEMY OR **ALLY?**
STOP.
SHUT UP.
WHAT? I DON'T ANSWER TO **YOU.**
NO. OF COURSE YOU DON'T.
BUT MAYBE SHUT UP, **STILL,** BECAUSE I'M TRYING TO **LISTEN.**
YOU WANT TO KNOW **WHAT** I AM?

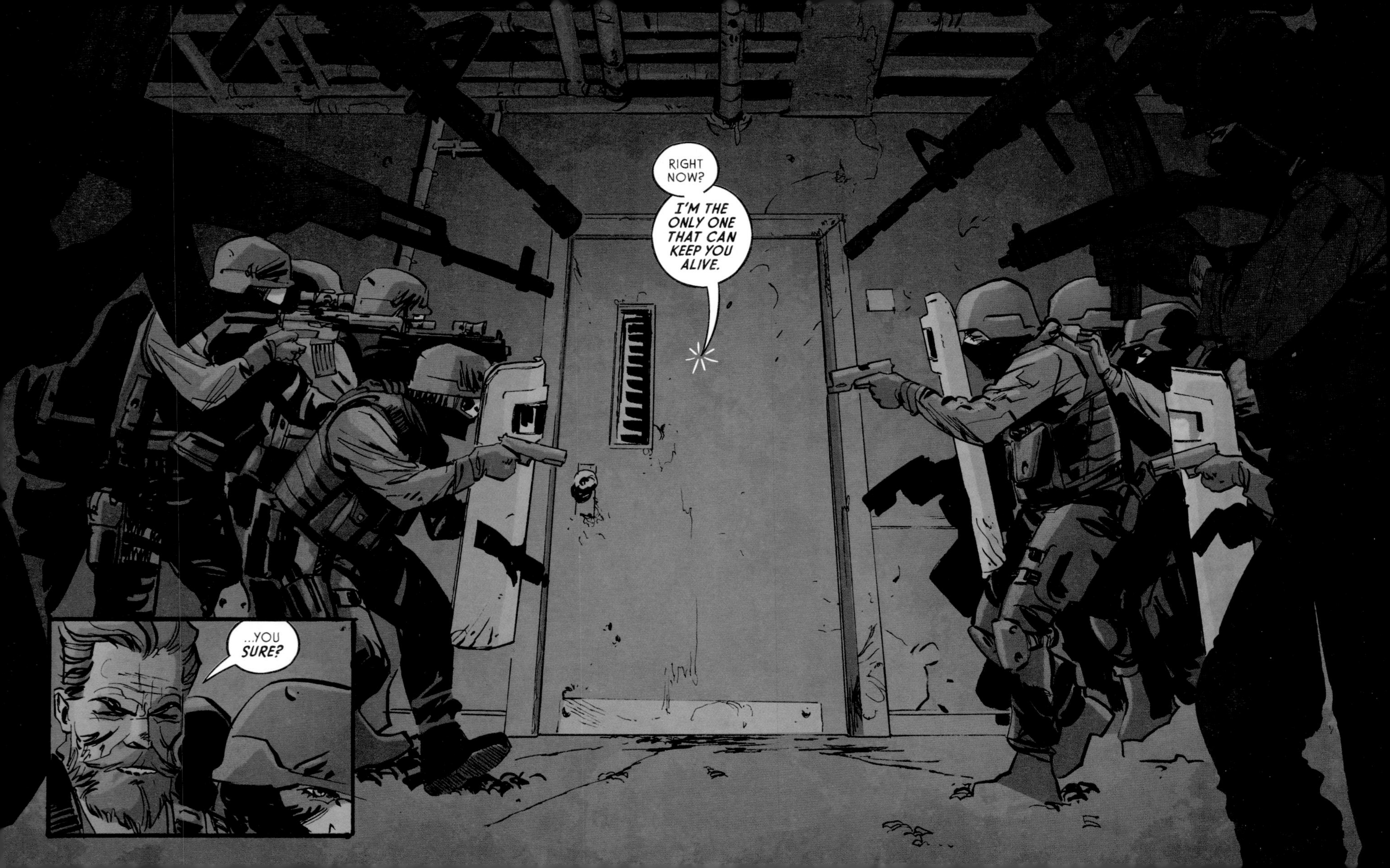
RIGHT NOW?
I'M THE ONLY ONE THAT CAN KEEP YOU ALIVE.
...YOU SURE?

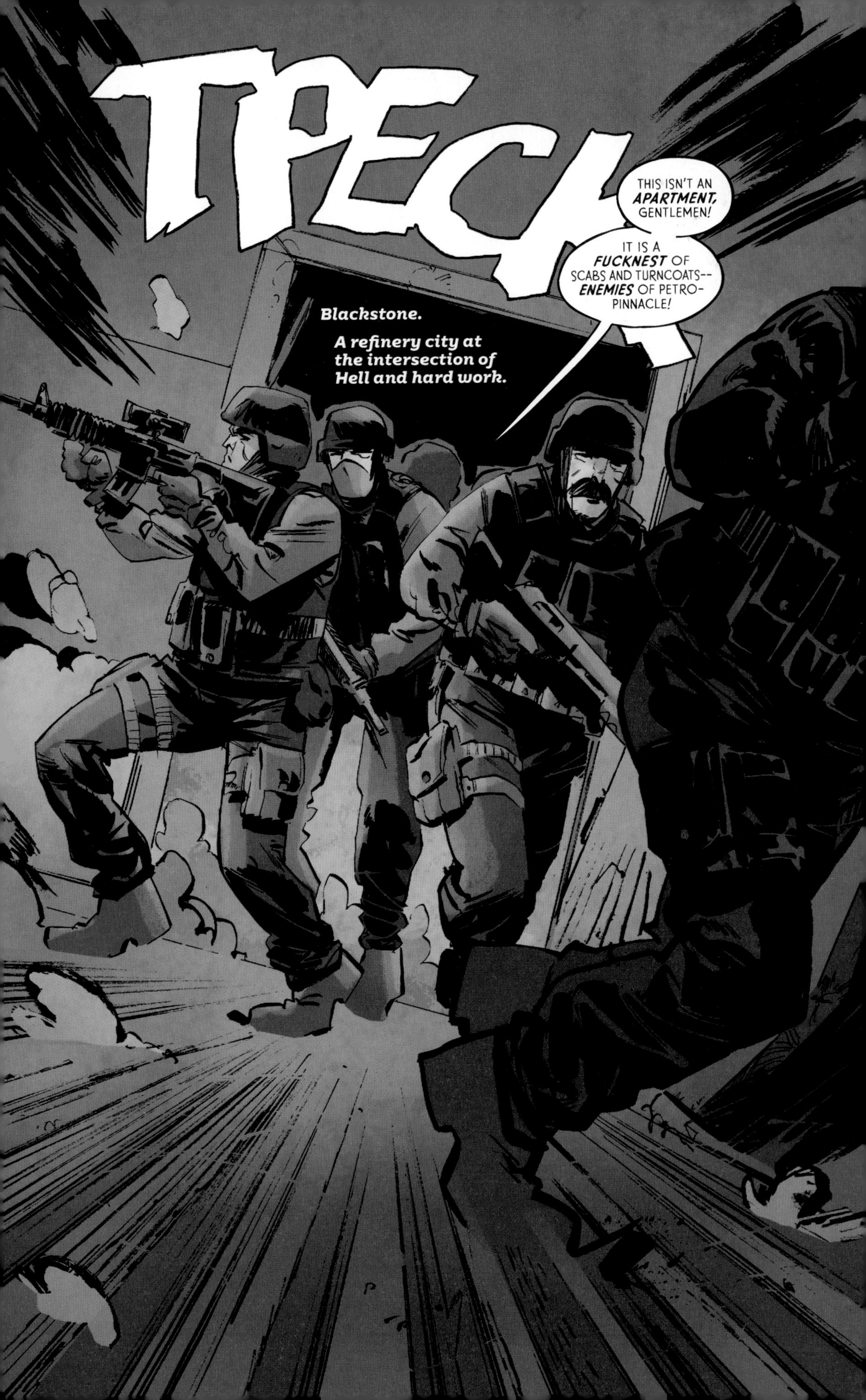
TPECH
Blackstone.
A refinery city at the intersection of Hell and hard work.
THIS ISN'T AN APARTMENT, GENTLEMEN!
IT IS A FUCKNEST OF SCABS AND TURNCOATS-- ENEMIES OF PETRO-PINNACLE!

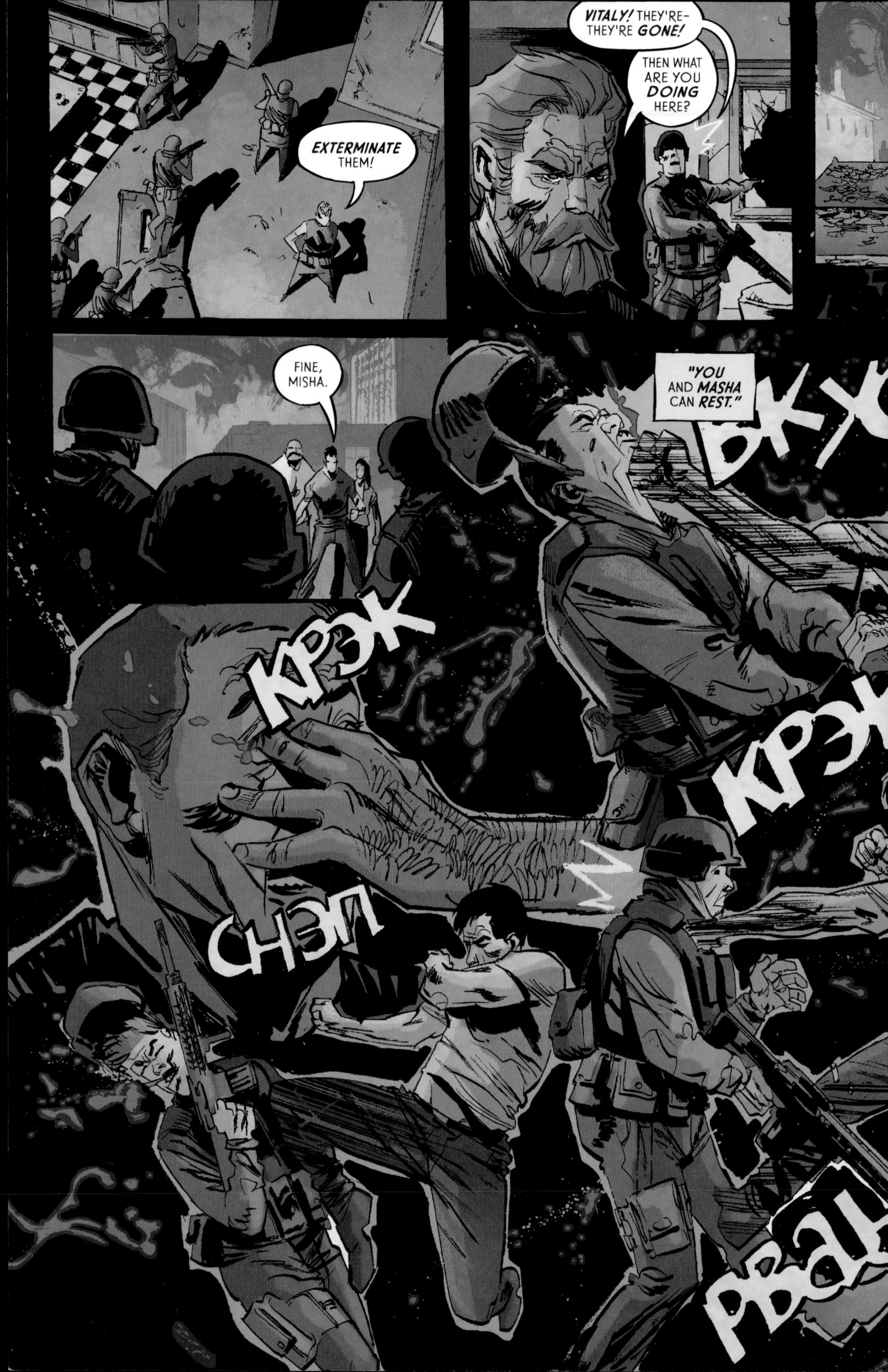

EXTERMINATE THEM!
VITALY! THEY'RE- THEY'RE GONE!
THEN WHAT ARE YOU DOING HERE?
FINE, MISHA.
"YOU AND MASHA CAN REST."
KPЭK
CHЭП

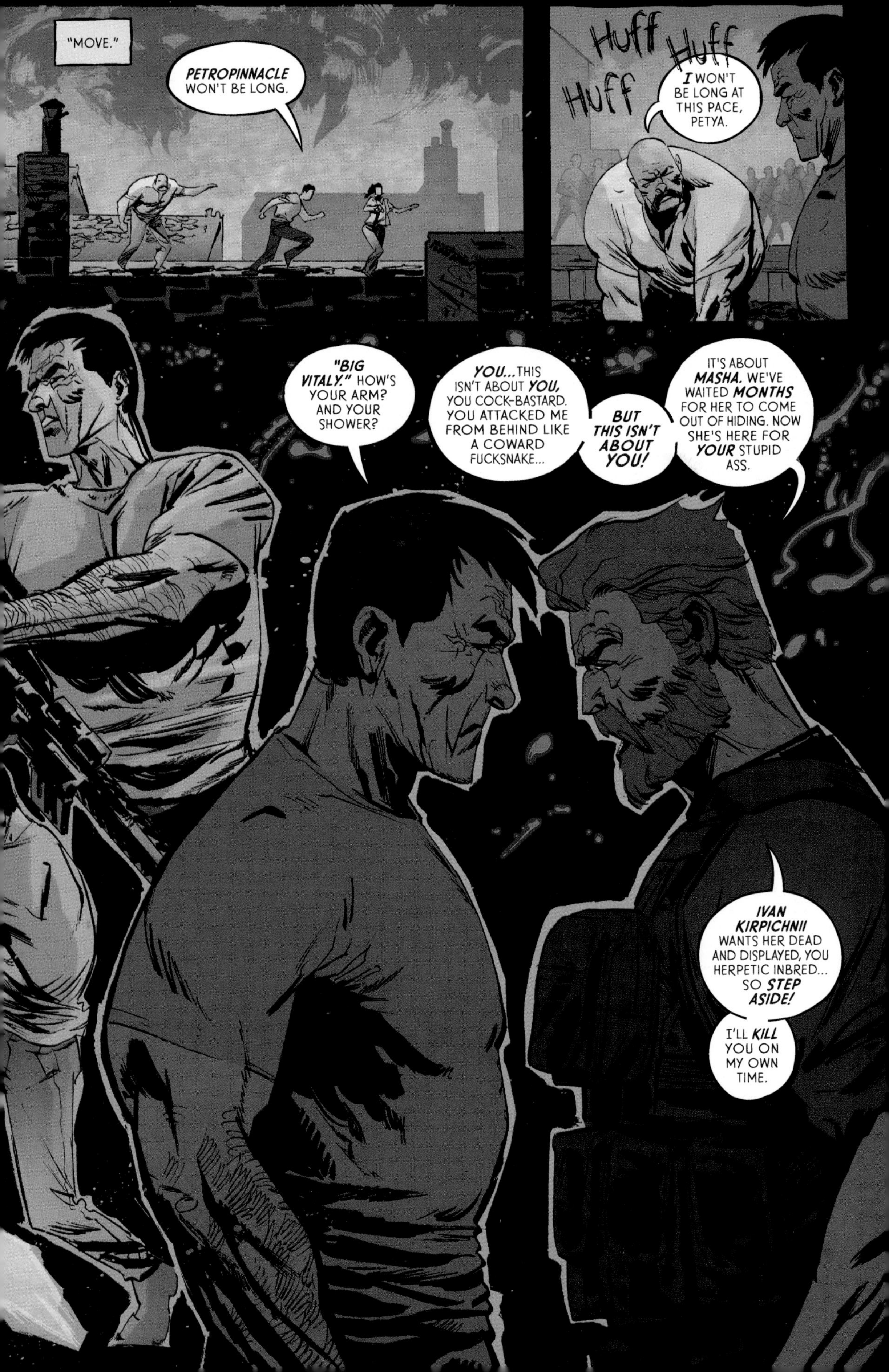
"MOVE."
PETROPINNACLE WON'T BE LONG.
HUFF HUFF HUFF
I WON'T BE LONG AT THIS PACE, PETYA.
"BIG VITALY." HOW'S YOUR ARM? AND YOUR SHOWER?
YOU...THIS ISN'T ABOUT YOU, YOU COCK-BASTARD. YOU ATTACKED ME FROM BEHIND LIKE A COWARD FUCKSNAKE...
BUT THIS ISN'T ABOUT YOU!
IT'S ABOUT MASHA. WE'VE WAITED MONTHS FOR HER TO COME OUT OF HIDING. NOW SHE'S HERE FOR YOUR STUPID ASS.
IVAN KIRPICHNII WANTS HER DEAD AND DISPLAYED, YOU HERPETIC INBRED... SO STEP ASIDE!
I'LL KILL YOU ON MY OWN TIME.

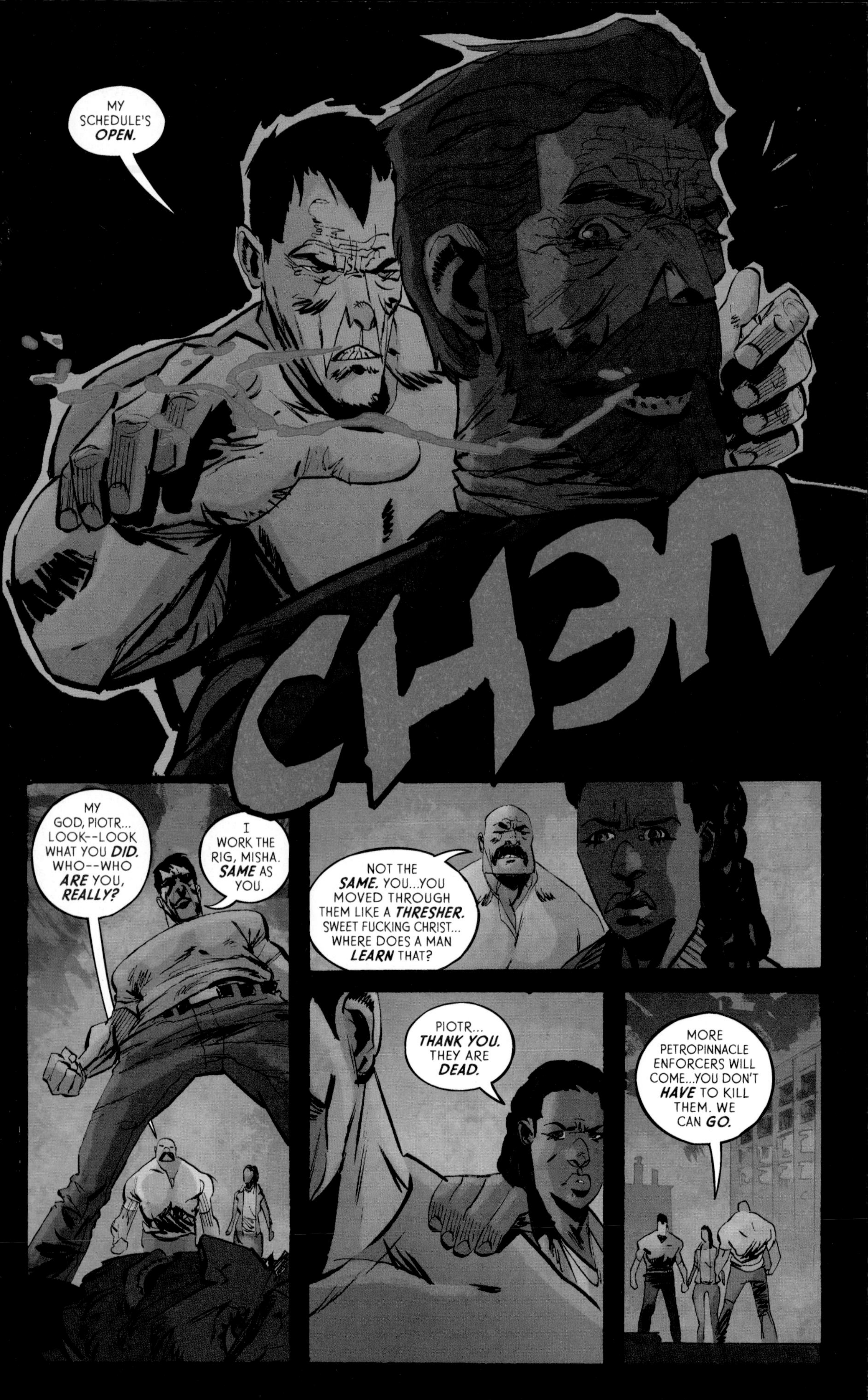
MY SCHEDULE'S ***OPEN.***
MY GOD, PIOTR... LOOK--LOOK WHAT YOU ***DID.*** WHO--WHO ***ARE*** YOU, ***REALLY?***
I WORK THE RIG, MISHA. ***SAME*** AS YOU.
NOT THE ***SAME.*** YOU...YOU MOVED THROUGH THEM LIKE A ***THRESHER.*** SWEET FUCKING CHRIST... WHERE DOES A MAN ***LEARN*** THAT?
PIOTR... ***THANK YOU.*** THEY ARE ***DEAD.***
MORE PETROPINNACLE ENFORCERS WILL COME...YOU DON'T ***HAVE*** TO KILL THEM. WE CAN ***GO.***

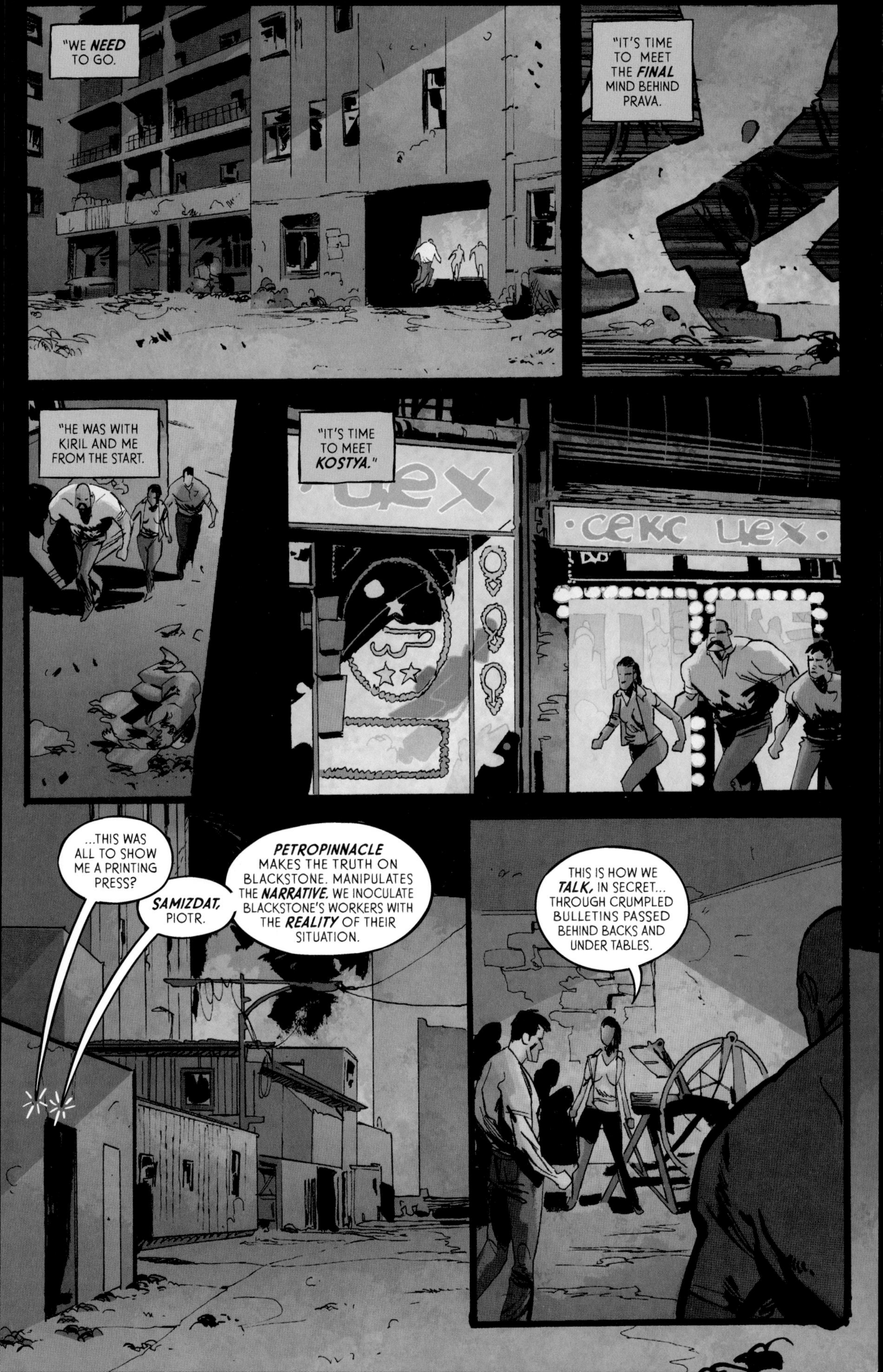
"WE NEED TO GO.
"IT'S TIME TO MEET THE FINAL MIND BEHIND PRAVA.
"HE WAS WITH KIRIL AND ME FROM THE START.
"IT'S TIME TO MEET KOSTYA."
СЕКС ЦЕХ
...THIS WAS ALL TO SHOW ME A PRINTING PRESS?
SAMIZDAT, PIOTR.
PETROPINNACLE MAKES THE TRUTH ON BLACKSTONE. MANIPULATES THE NARRATIVE. WE INOCULATE BLACKSTONE'S WORKERS WITH THE REALITY OF THEIR SITUATION.
THIS IS HOW WE TALK, IN SECRET... THROUGH CRUMPLED BULLETINS PASSED BEHIND BACKS AND UNDER TABLES.

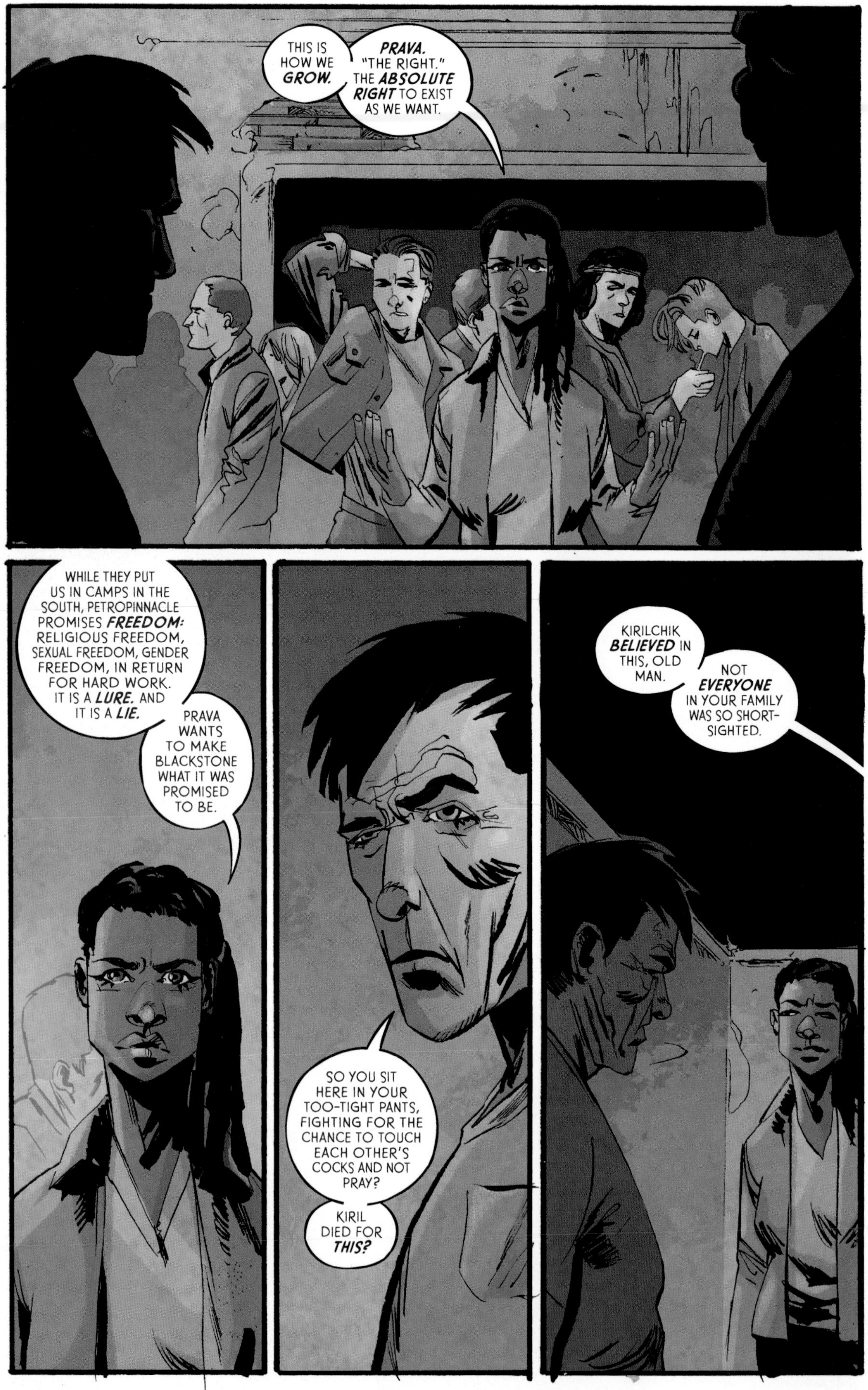
THIS IS HOW WE GROW.
PRAVA. "THE RIGHT." THE ABSOLUTE RIGHT TO EXIST AS WE WANT.
WHILE THEY PUT US IN CAMPS IN THE SOUTH, PETROPINNACLE PROMISES FREEDOM: RELIGIOUS FREEDOM, SEXUAL FREEDOM, GENDER FREEDOM, IN RETURN FOR HARD WORK. IT IS A LURE. AND IT IS A LIE.
PRAVA WANTS TO MAKE BLACKSTONE WHAT IT WAS PROMISED TO BE.
SO YOU SIT HERE IN YOUR TOO-TIGHT PANTS, FIGHTING FOR THE CHANCE TO TOUCH EACH OTHER'S COCKS AND NOT PRAY?
KIRIL DIED FOR THIS?
KIRILCHIK BELIEVED IN THIS, OLD MAN.
NOT EVERYONE IN YOUR FAMILY WAS SO SHORT-SIGHTED.

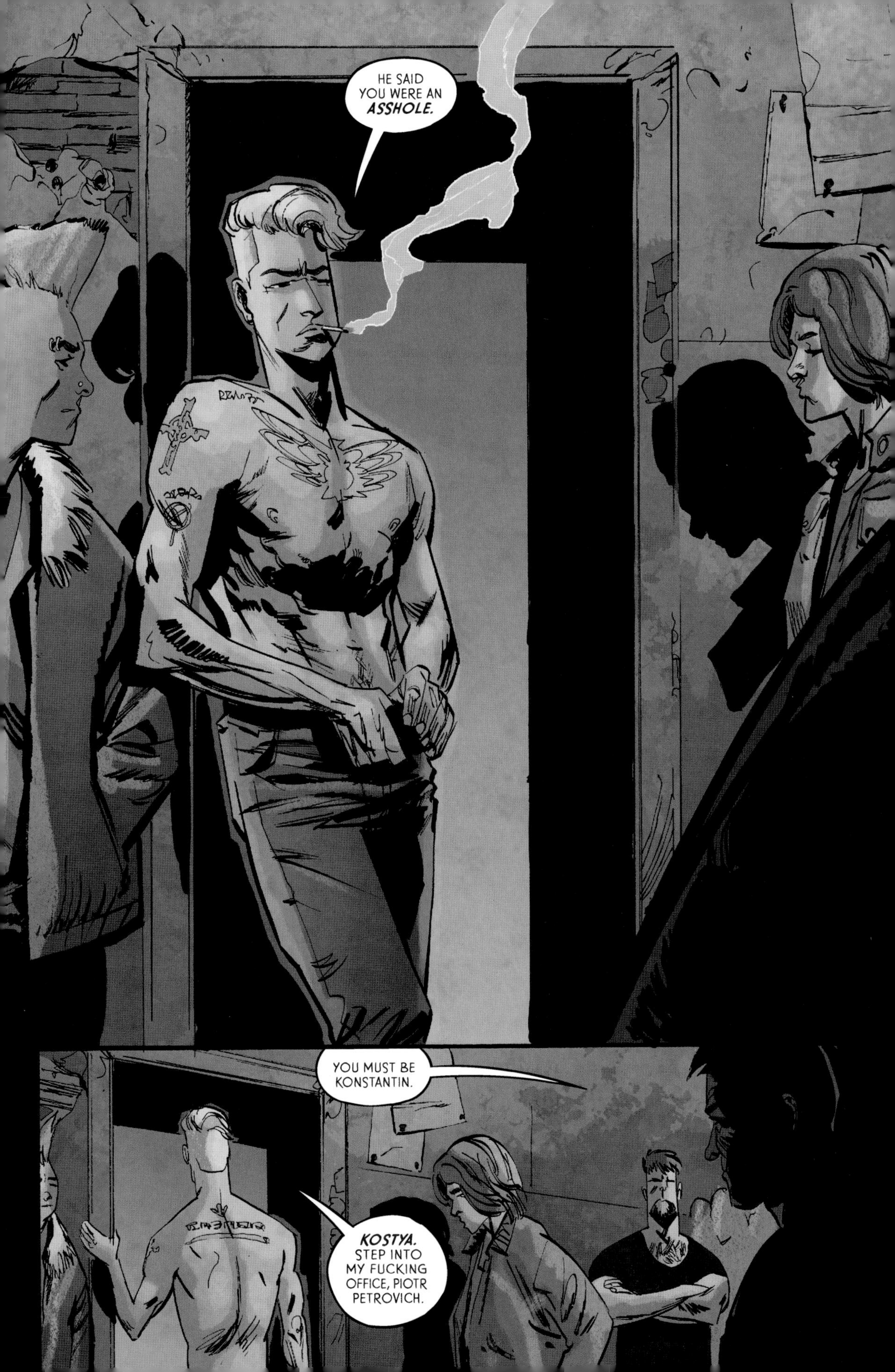
HE SAID YOU WERE AN ***ASSHOLE.***
YOU MUST BE KONSTANTIN.
KOSTYA. STEP INTO MY FUCKING OFFICE, PIOTR PETROVICH.

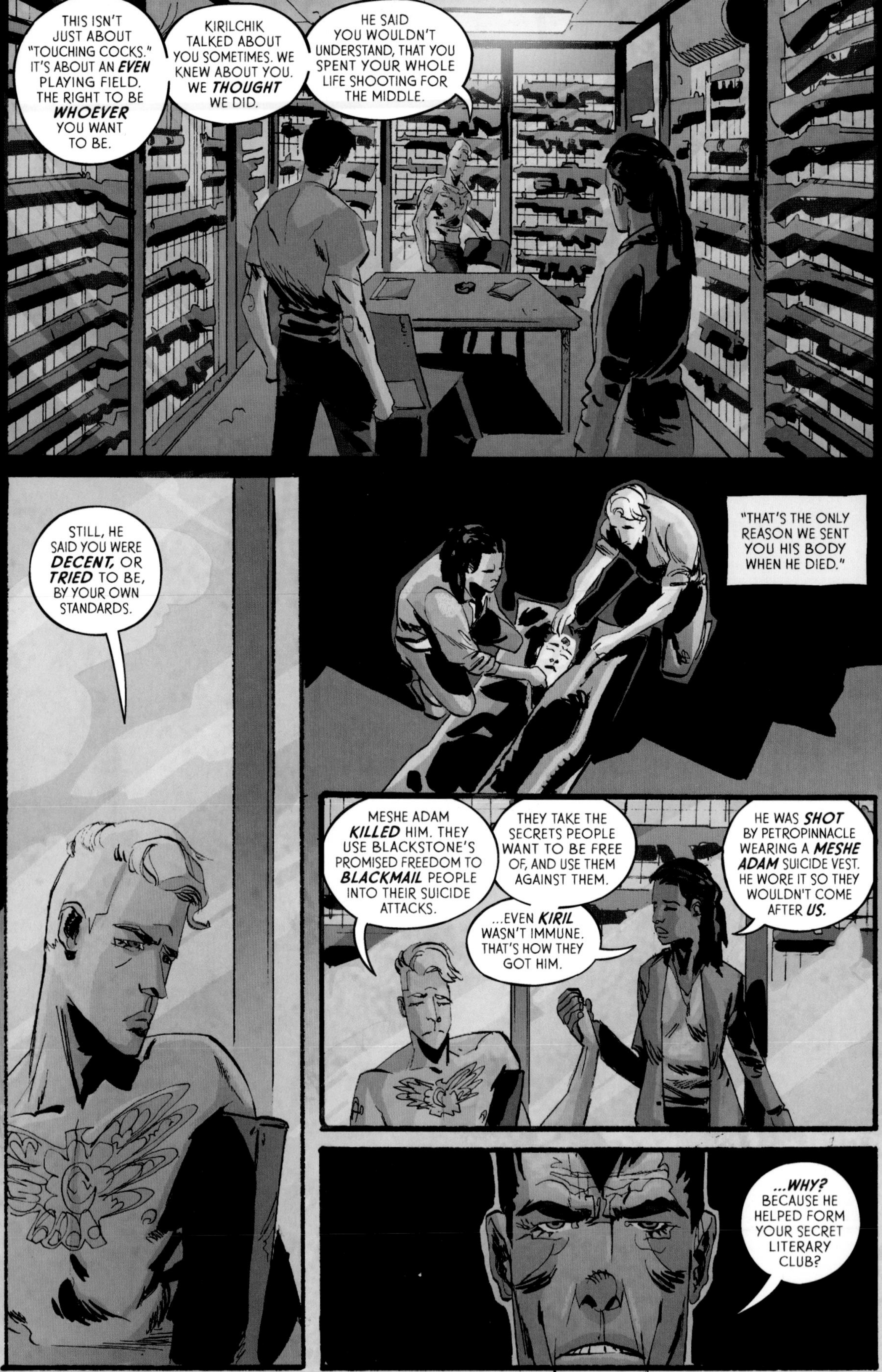
THIS ISN'T JUST ABOUT "TOUCHING COCKS." IT'S ABOUT AN *EVEN* PLAYING FIELD. THE RIGHT TO BE *WHOEVER* YOU WANT TO BE.
KIRILCHIK TALKED ABOUT YOU SOMETIMES. WE KNEW ABOUT YOU. WE *THOUGHT* WE DID.
HE SAID YOU WOULDN'T UNDERSTAND, THAT YOU SPENT YOUR WHOLE LIFE SHOOTING FOR THE MIDDLE.
STILL, HE SAID YOU WERE *DECENT,* OR *TRIED* TO BE, BY YOUR OWN STANDARDS.
"THAT'S THE ONLY REASON WE SENT YOU HIS BODY WHEN HE DIED."
MESHE ADAM *KILLED* HIM. THEY USE BLACKSTONE'S PROMISED FREEDOM TO *BLACKMAIL* PEOPLE INTO THEIR SUICIDE ATTACKS.
THEY TAKE THE SECRETS PEOPLE WANT TO BE FREE OF, AND USE THEM AGAINST THEM.
...EVEN *KIRIL* WASN'T IMMUNE. THAT'S HOW THEY GOT HIM.
HE WAS *SHOT* BY PETROPINNACLE WEARING A *MESHE ADAM* SUICIDE VEST. HE WORE IT SO THEY WOULDN'T COME AFTER *US.*
...WHY? BECAUSE HE HELPED FORM YOUR SECRET LITERARY CLUB?

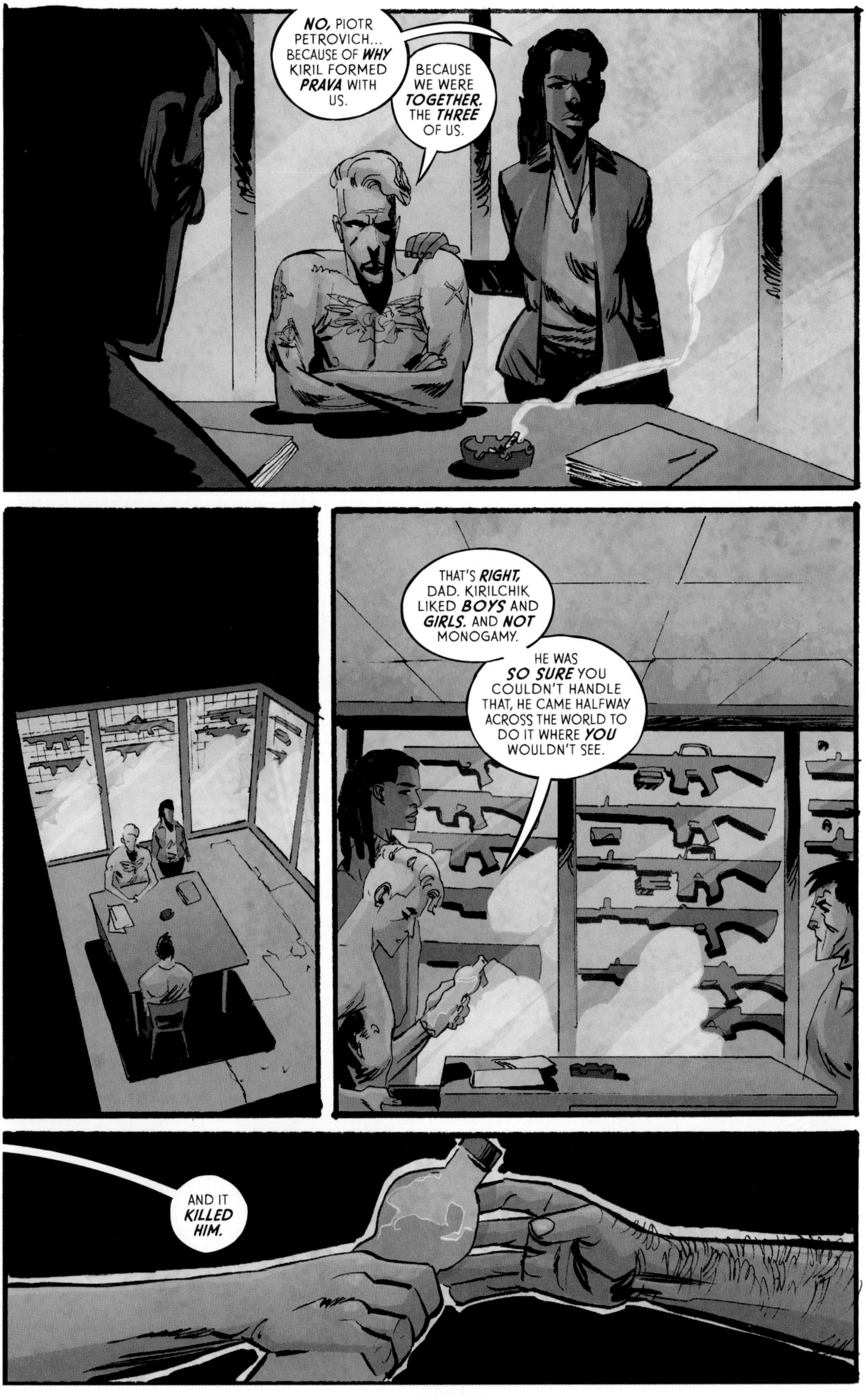
NO, PIOTR PETROVICH... BECAUSE OF WHY KIRIL FORMED PRAVA WITH US.
BECAUSE WE WERE TOGETHER. THE THREE OF US.
THAT'S RIGHT, DAD. KIRILCHIK LIKED BOYS AND GIRLS. AND NOT MONOGAMY.
HE WAS SO SURE YOU COULDN'T HANDLE THAT, HE CAME HALFWAY ACROSS THE WORLD TO DO IT WHERE YOU WOULDN'T SEE.
AND IT KILLED HIM.

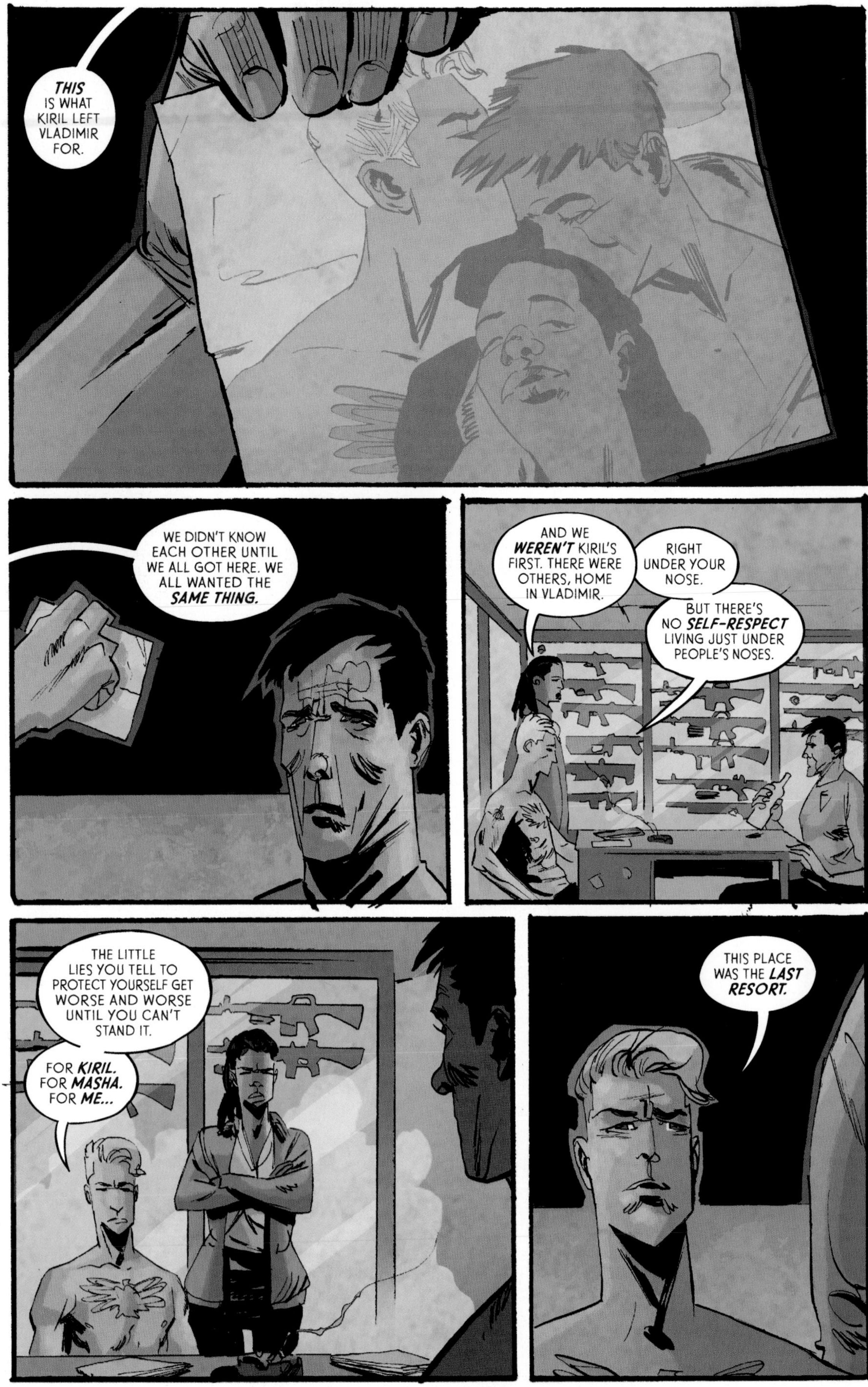
THIS IS WHAT KIRIL LEFT VLADIMIR FOR.
WE DIDN'T KNOW EACH OTHER UNTIL WE ALL GOT HERE. WE ALL WANTED THE SAME THING.
AND WE WEREN'T KIRIL'S FIRST. THERE WERE OTHERS, HOME IN VLADIMIR.
RIGHT UNDER YOUR NOSE.
BUT THERE'S NO SELF-RESPECT LIVING JUST UNDER PEOPLE'S NOSES.
THE LITTLE LIES YOU TELL TO PROTECT YOURSELF GET WORSE AND WORSE UNTIL YOU CAN'T STAND IT.
FOR KIRIL. FOR MASHA. FOR ME...
THIS PLACE WAS THE LAST RESORT.

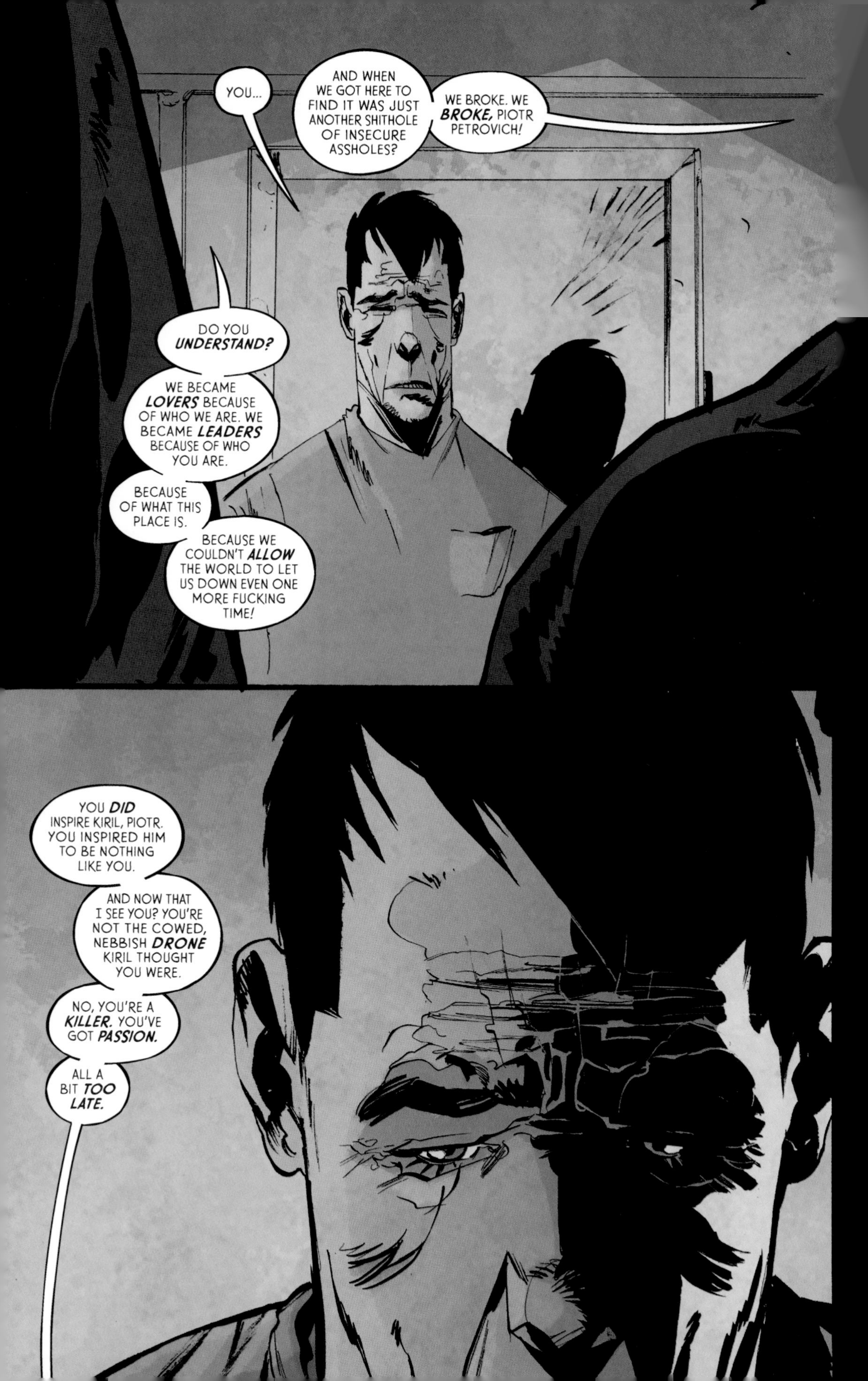
YOU...
AND WHEN WE GOT HERE TO FIND IT WAS JUST ANOTHER SHITHOLE OF INSECURE ASSHOLES?
WE BROKE. WE BROKE, PIOTR PETROVICH!
DO YOU UNDERSTAND?
WE BECAME LOVERS BECAUSE OF WHO WE ARE. WE BECAME LEADERS BECAUSE OF WHO YOU ARE.
BECAUSE OF WHAT THIS PLACE IS.
BECAUSE WE COULDN'T ALLOW THE WORLD TO LET US DOWN EVEN ONE MORE FUCKING TIME!
YOU DID INSPIRE KIRIL, PIOTR. YOU INSPIRED HIM TO BE NOTHING LIKE YOU.
AND NOW THAT I SEE YOU? YOU'RE NOT THE COWED, NEBBISH DRONE KIRIL THOUGHT YOU WERE.
NO, YOU'RE A KILLER. YOU'VE GOT PASSION.
ALL A BIT TOO LATE.

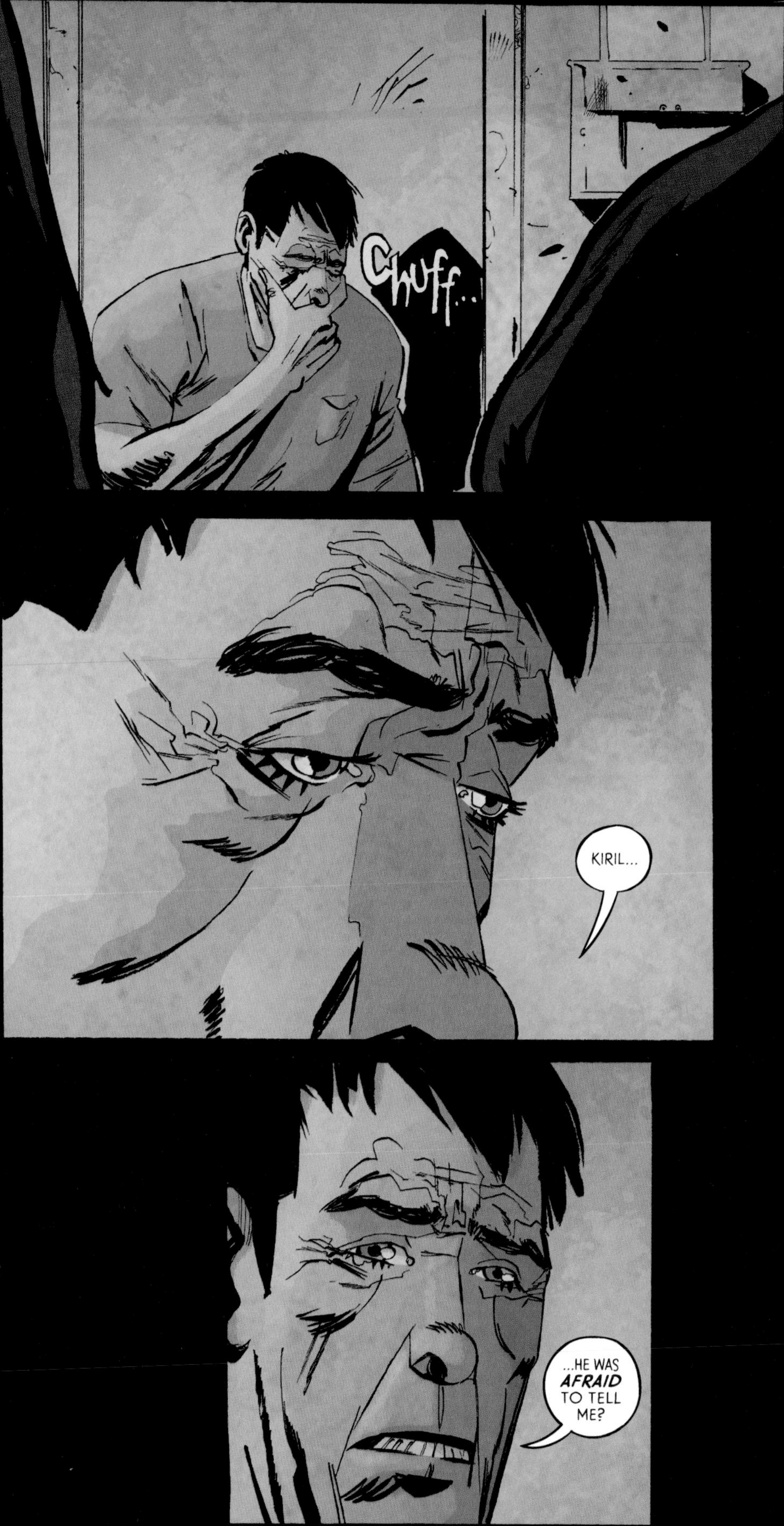
CHUFF...
KIRIL...
...HE WAS **AFRAID** TO TELL ME?

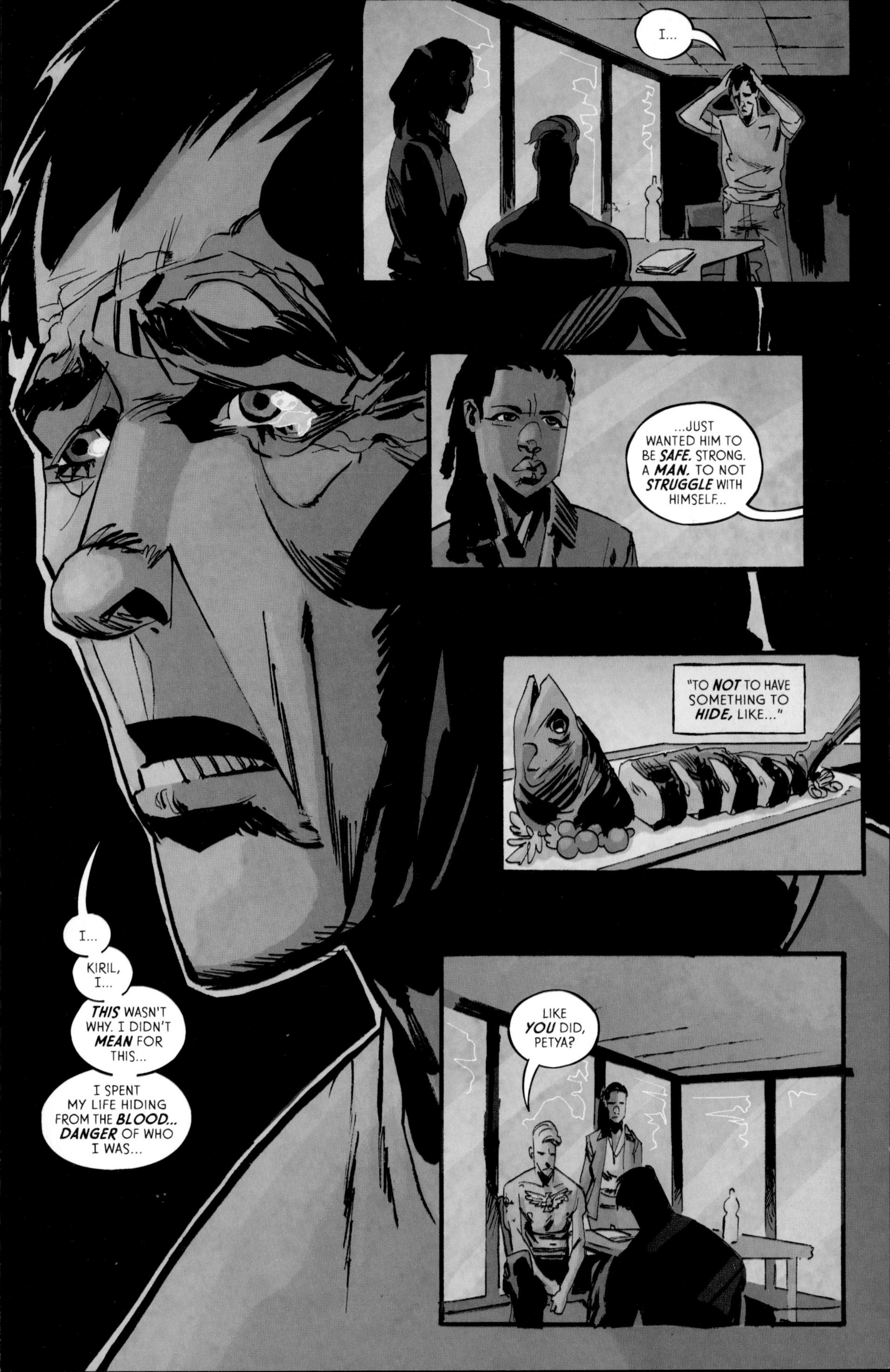

I...
...JUST WANTED HIM TO BE SAFE. STRONG. A MAN. TO NOT STRUGGLE WITH HIMSELF...
"TO NOT TO HAVE SOMETHING TO HIDE, LIKE..."
LIKE YOU DID, PETYA?
I...
KIRIL, I...
THIS WASN'T WHY. I DIDN'T MEAN FOR THIS...
I SPENT MY LIFE HIDING FROM THE BLOOD... DANGER OF WHO I WAS...

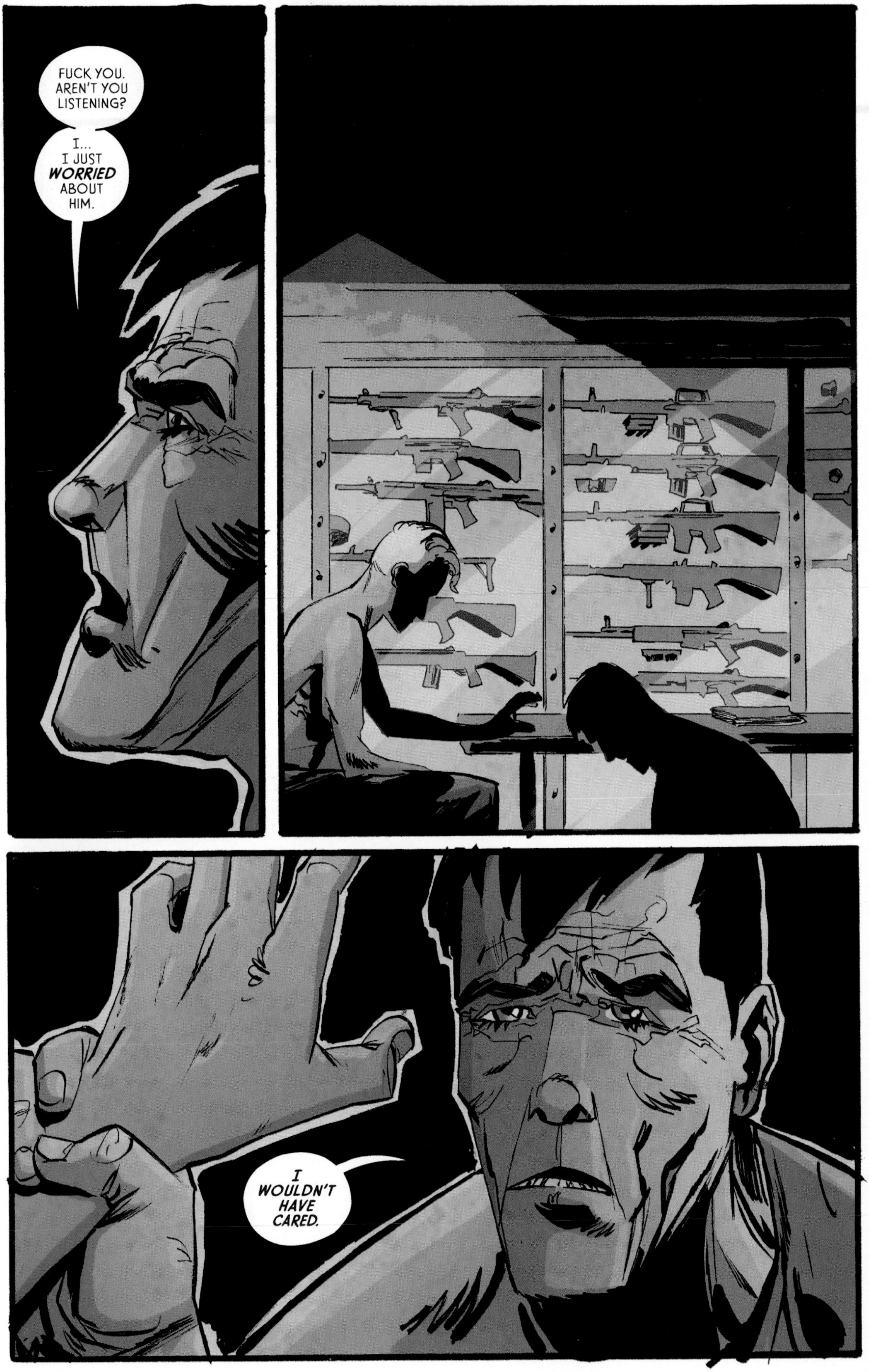
FUCK YOU. AREN'T YOU LISTENING?
I... I JUST *WORRIED* ABOUT HIM.
I WOULDN'T HAVE CARED.

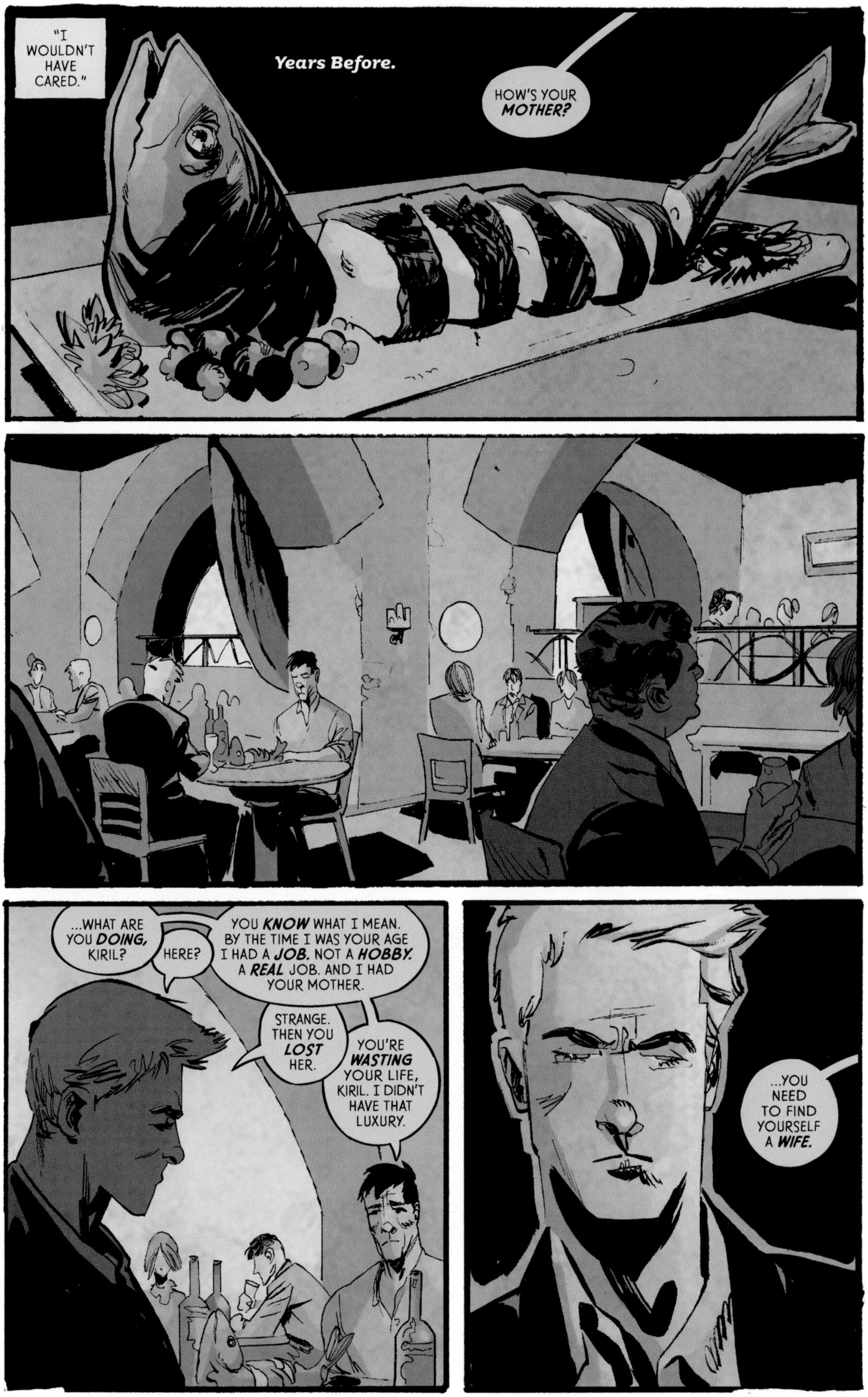
"I WOULDN'T HAVE CARED."
Years Before.
HOW'S YOUR MOTHER?
...WHAT ARE YOU DOING, KIRIL?
HERE?
YOU KNOW WHAT I MEAN. BY THE TIME I WAS YOUR AGE I HAD A JOB. NOT A HOBBY. A REAL JOB. AND I HAD YOUR MOTHER.
STRANGE. THEN YOU LOST HER.
YOU'RE WASTING YOUR LIFE, KIRIL. I DIDN'T HAVE THAT LUXURY.
...YOU NEED TO FIND YOURSELF A WIFE.

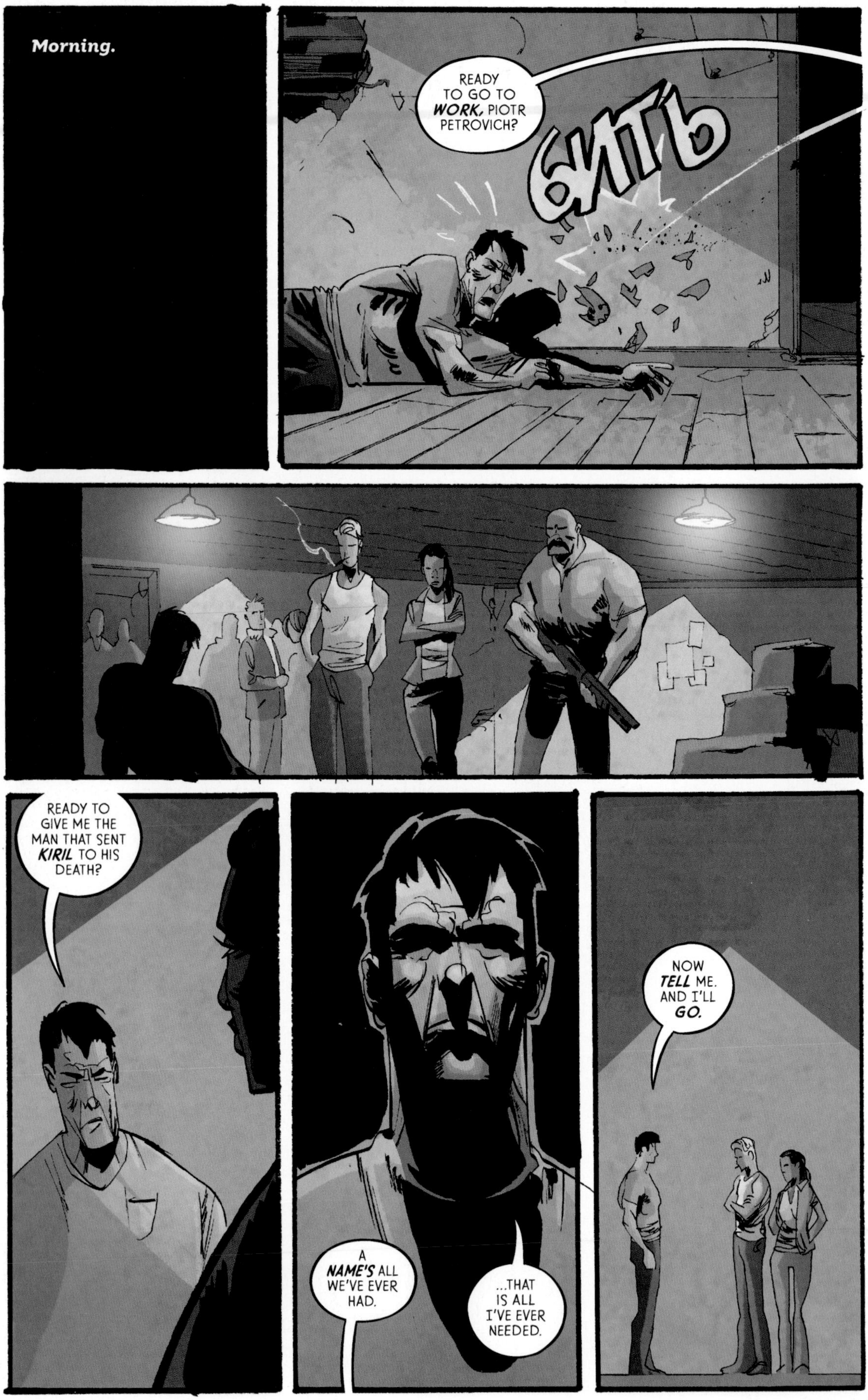
Morning.
READY TO GO TO WORK, PIOTR PETROVICH?
ЫТЬ
READY TO GIVE ME THE MAN THAT SENT KIRIL TO HIS DEATH?
A NAME'S ALL WE'VE EVER HAD.
...THAT IS ALL I'VE EVER NEEDED.
NOW TELL ME. AND I'LL GO.

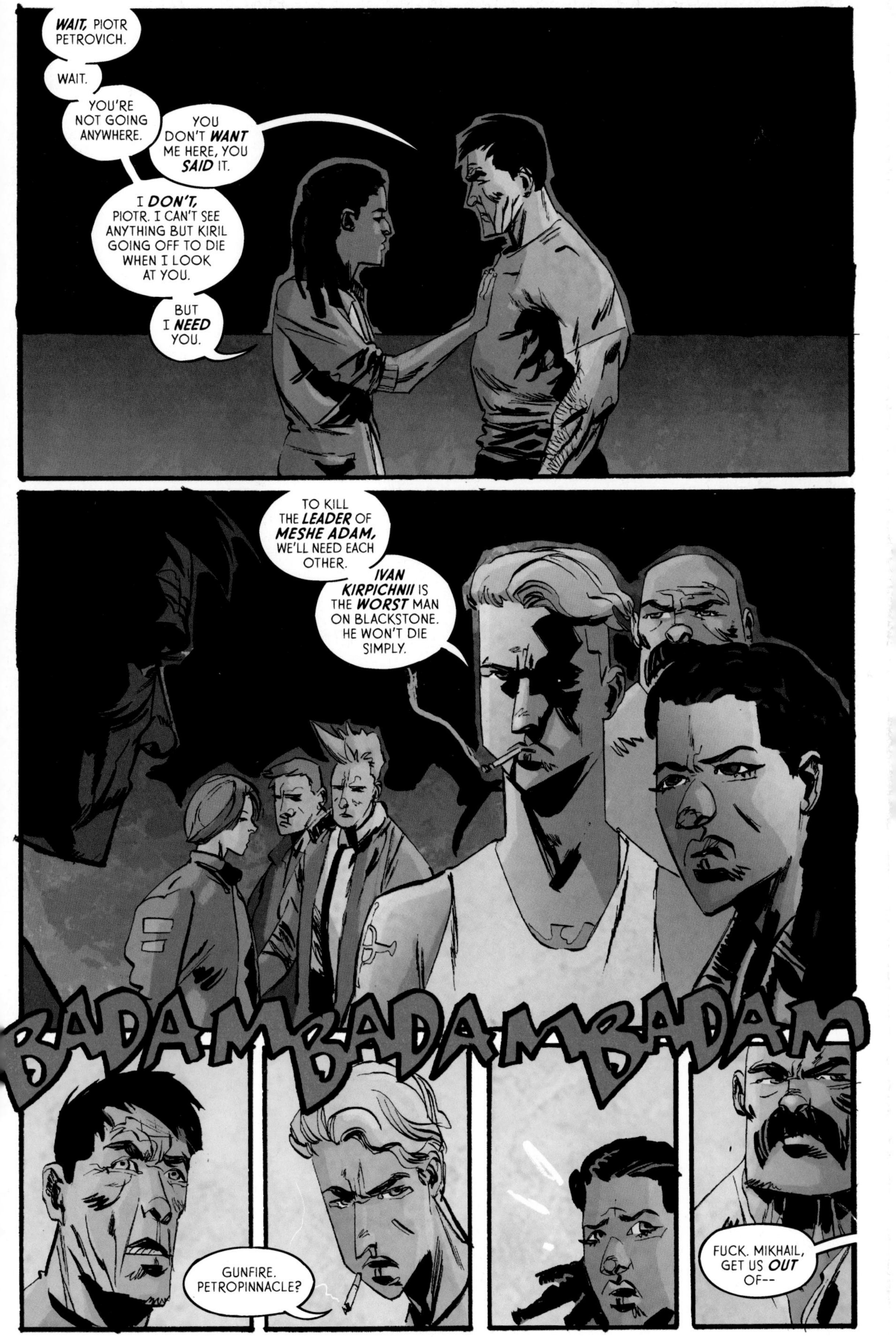
WAIT, PIOTR PETROVICH.
WAIT.
YOU'RE NOT GOING ANYWHERE.
YOU DON'T WANT ME HERE, YOU SAID IT.
I DON'T, PIOTR. I CAN'T SEE ANYTHING BUT KIRIL GOING OFF TO DIE WHEN I LOOK AT YOU.
BUT I NEED YOU.
TO KILL THE LEADER OF MESHE ADAM, WE'LL NEED EACH OTHER.
IVAN KIRPICHNII IS THE WORST MAN ON BLACKSTONE. HE WON'T DIE SIMPLY.
BADAMBADAMBADAM
GUNFIRE. PETROPINNACLE?
FUCK. MIKHAIL, GET US OUT OF--

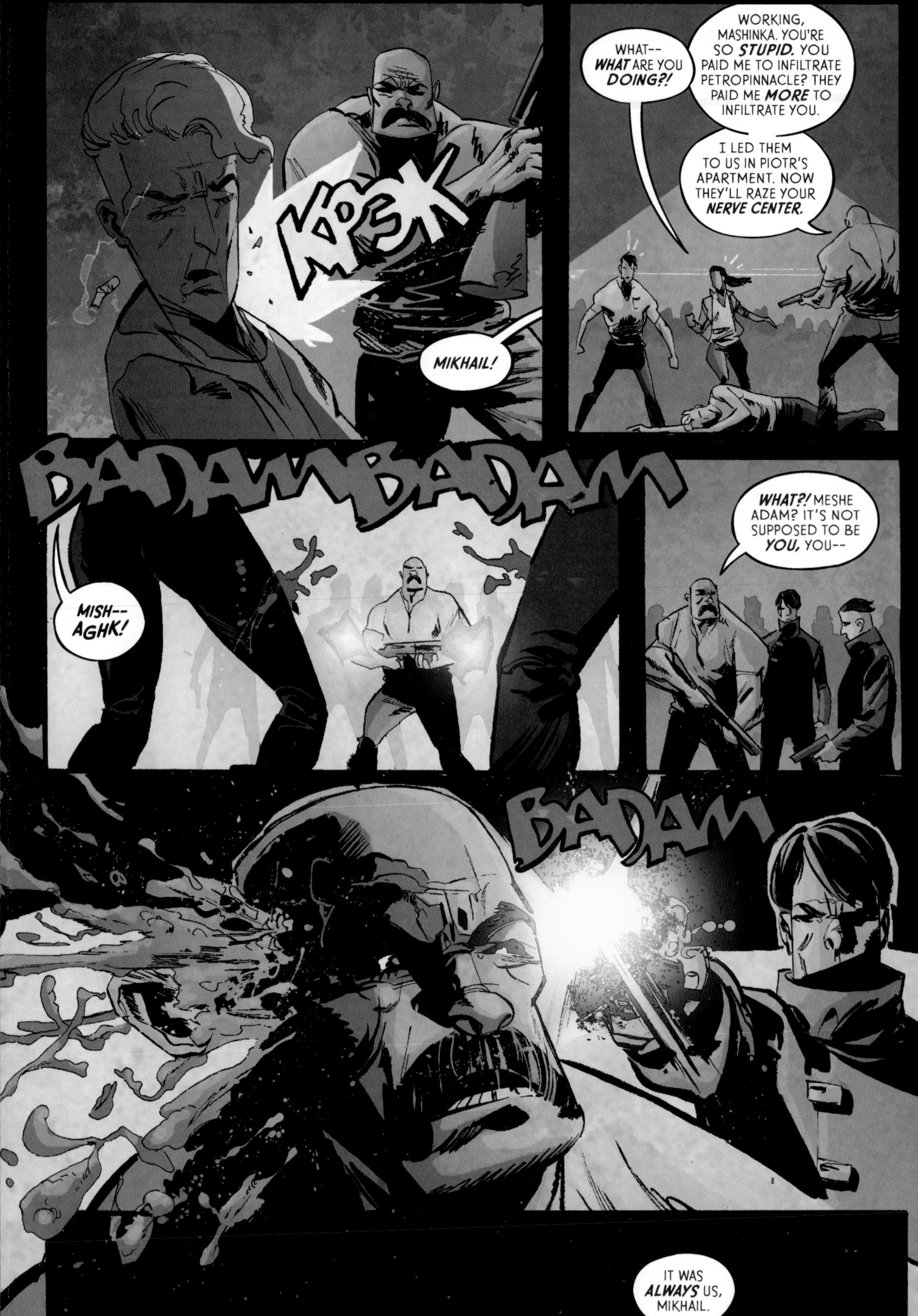
MIKHAIL!
WHAT-- WHAT ARE YOU DOING?!
WORKING, MASHINKA. YOU'RE SO STUPID. YOU PAID ME TO INFILTRATE PETROPINNACLE? THEY PAID ME MORE TO INFILTRATE YOU.
I LED THEM TO US IN PIOTR'S APARTMENT. NOW THEY'LL RAZE YOUR NERVE CENTER.
BADAMBADAM
MISH-- AGHK!
WHAT?! MESHE ADAM? IT'S NOT SUPPOSED TO BE YOU, YOU--
BADAM
IT WAS ALWAYS US, MIKHAIL.

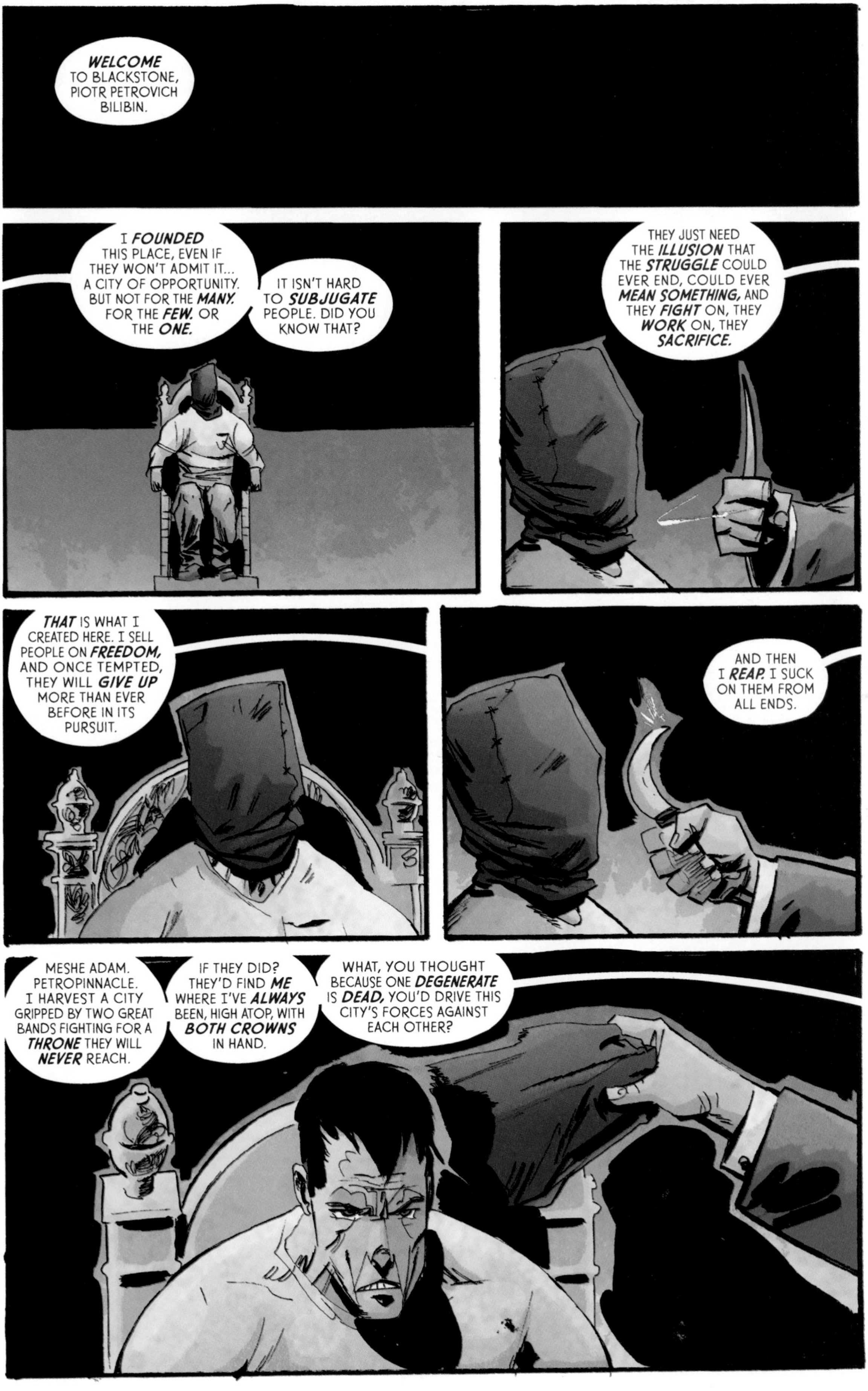
WELCOME TO BLACKSTONE, PIOTR PETROVICH BILIBIN.
I FOUNDED THIS PLACE, EVEN IF THEY WON'T ADMIT IT... A CITY OF OPPORTUNITY. BUT NOT FOR THE MANY. FOR THE FEW. OR THE ONE.
IT ISN'T HARD TO SUBJUGATE PEOPLE. DID YOU KNOW THAT?
THEY JUST NEED THE ILLUSION THAT THE STRUGGLE COULD EVER END, COULD EVER MEAN SOMETHING, AND THEY FIGHT ON, THEY WORK ON, THEY SACRIFICE.
THAT IS WHAT I CREATED HERE. I SELL PEOPLE ON FREEDOM, AND ONCE TEMPTED, THEY WILL GIVE UP MORE THAN EVER BEFORE IN ITS PURSUIT.
AND THEN I REAP. I SUCK ON THEM FROM ALL ENDS.
MESHE ADAM. PETROPINNACLE. I HARVEST A CITY GRIPPED BY TWO GREAT BANDS FIGHTING FOR A THRONE THEY WILL NEVER REACH.
IF THEY DID? THEY'D FIND ME WHERE I'VE ALWAYS BEEN, HIGH ATOP, WITH BOTH CROWNS IN HAND.
WHAT, YOU THOUGHT BECAUSE ONE DEGENERATE IS DEAD, YOU'D DRIVE THIS CITY'S FORCES AGAINST EACH OTHER?

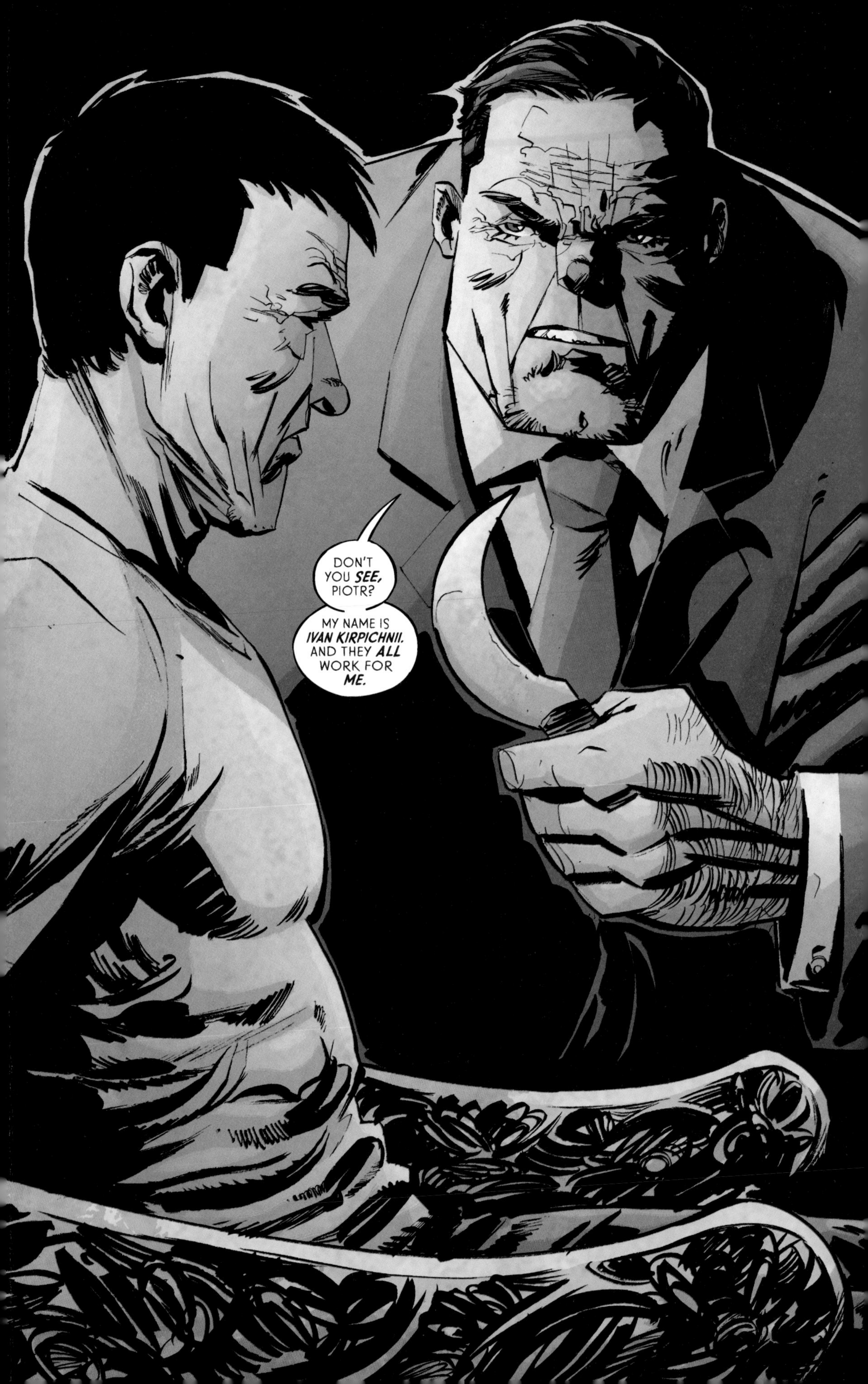
DON'T YOU **SEE,** PIOTR?
MY NAME IS ***IVAN KIRPICHNII.*** AND THEY ***ALL*** WORK FOR ***ME.***

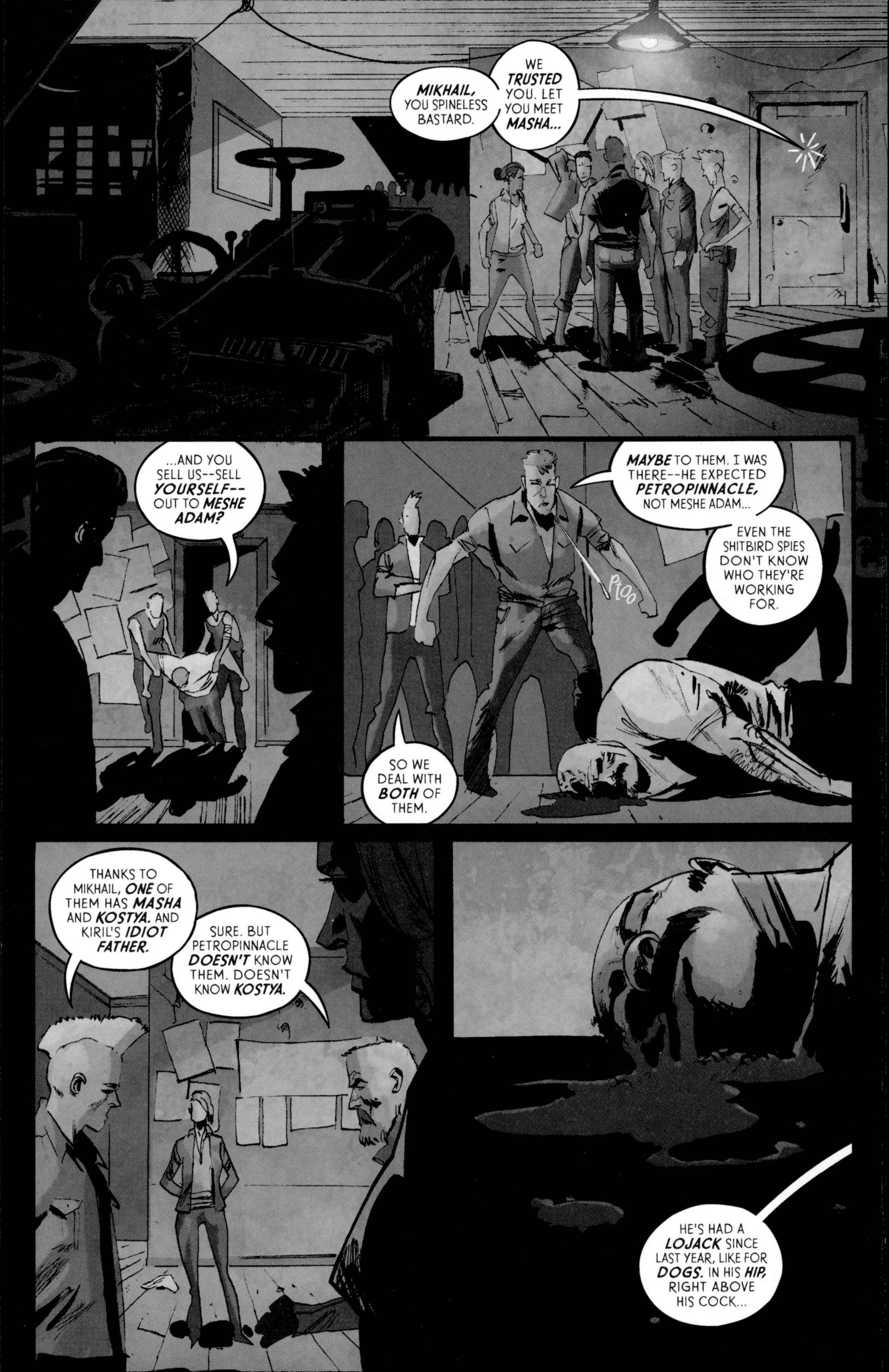
MIKHAIL, YOU SPINELESS BASTARD.
WE TRUSTED YOU. LET YOU MEET MASHA...
...AND YOU SELL US--SELL YOURSELF-- OUT TO MESHE ADAM?
MAYBE TO THEM. I WAS THERE--HE EXPECTED PETROPINNACLE, NOT MESHE ADAM...
EVEN THE SHITBIRD SPIES DON'T KNOW WHO THEY'RE WORKING FOR.
PTOO
SO WE DEAL WITH BOTH OF THEM.
THANKS TO MIKHAIL, ONE OF THEM HAS MASHA AND KOSTYA. AND KIRIL'S IDIOT FATHER.
SURE. BUT PETROPINNACLE DOESN'T KNOW THEM. DOESN'T KNOW KOSTYA.
HE'S HAD A LOJACK SINCE LAST YEAR, LIKE FOR DOGS. IN HIS HIP, RIGHT ABOVE HIS COCK...

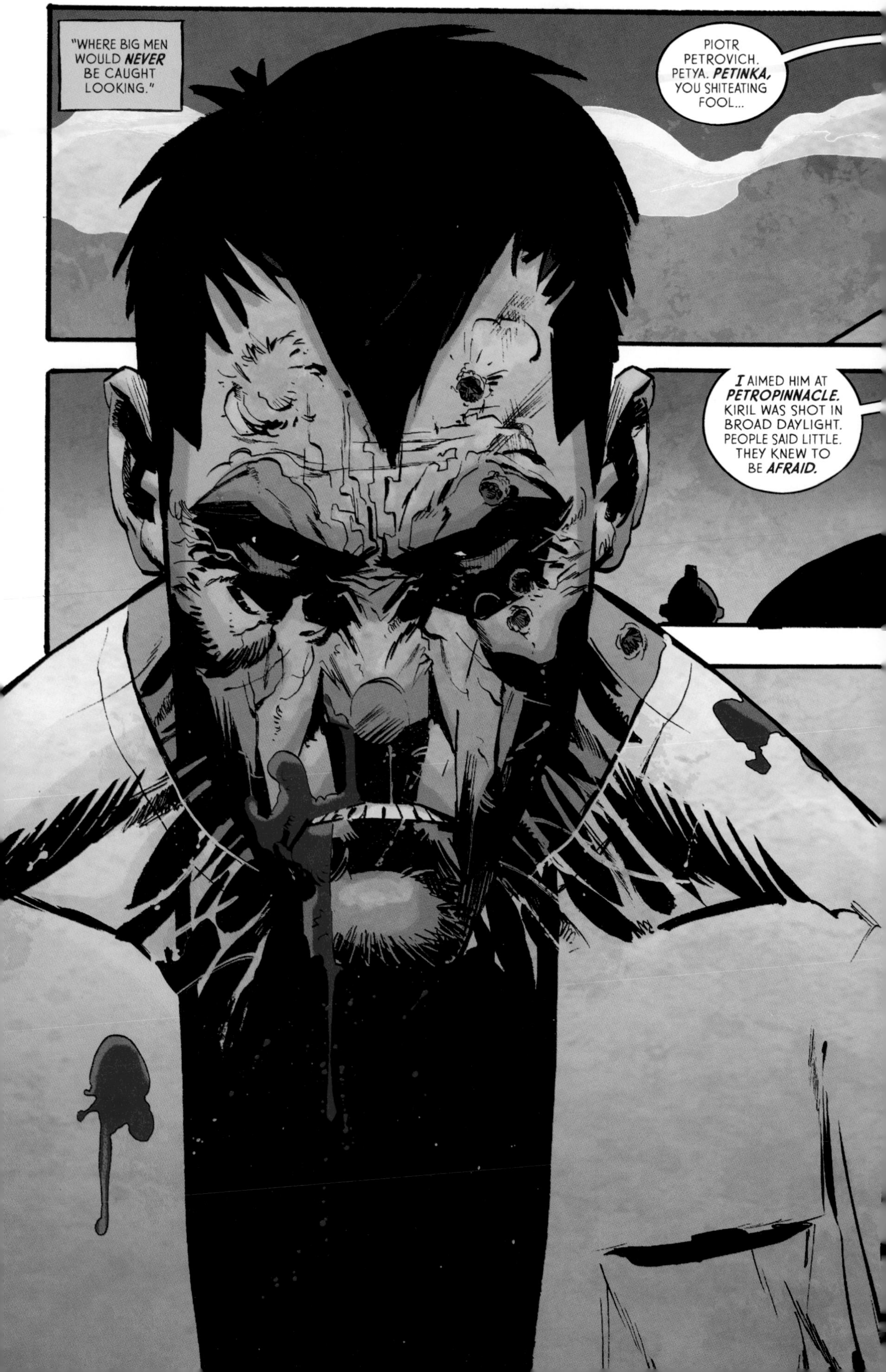
"WHERE BIG MEN WOULD NEVER BE CAUGHT LOOKING."
PIOTR PETROVICH. PETYA. PETINKA, YOU SHITEATING FOOL...
I AIMED HIM AT PETROPINNACLE. KIRIL WAS SHOT IN BROAD DAYLIGHT. PEOPLE SAID LITTLE. THEY KNEW TO BE AFRAID.

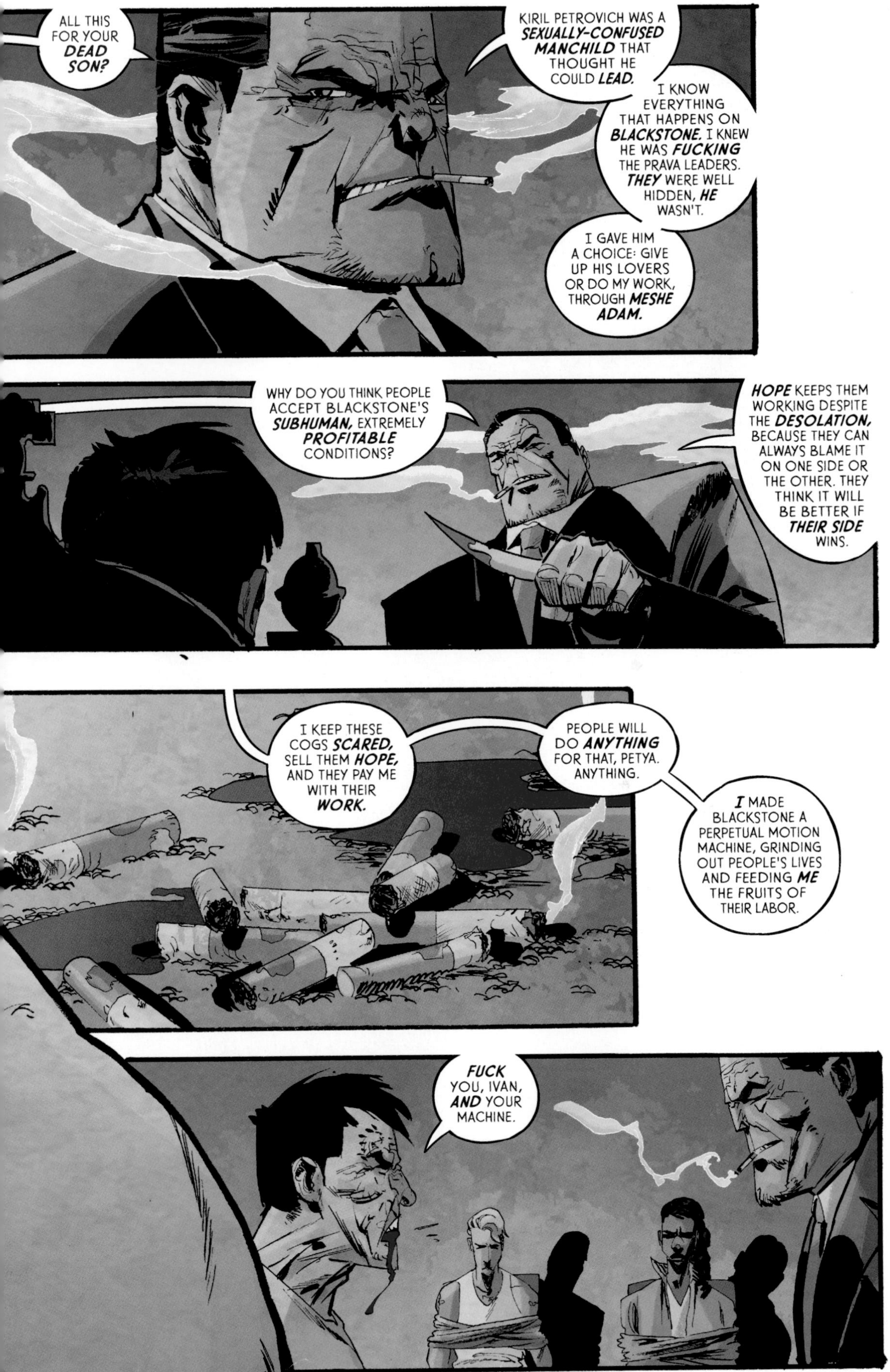
ALL THIS FOR YOUR DEAD SON?
KIRIL PETROVICH WAS A SEXUALLY-CONFUSED MANCHILD THAT THOUGHT HE COULD LEAD.
I KNOW EVERYTHING THAT HAPPENS ON BLACKSTONE. I KNEW HE WAS FUCKING THE PRAVA LEADERS. THEY WERE WELL HIDDEN, HE WASN'T.
I GAVE HIM A CHOICE: GIVE UP HIS LOVERS OR DO MY WORK, THROUGH MESHE ADAM.
WHY DO YOU THINK PEOPLE ACCEPT BLACKSTONE'S SUBHUMAN, EXTREMELY PROFITABLE CONDITIONS?
HOPE KEEPS THEM WORKING DESPITE THE DESOLATION, BECAUSE THEY CAN ALWAYS BLAME IT ON ONE SIDE OR THE OTHER. THEY THINK IT WILL BE BETTER IF THEIR SIDE WINS.
I KEEP THESE COGS SCARED, SELL THEM HOPE, AND THEY PAY ME WITH THEIR WORK.
PEOPLE WILL DO ANYTHING FOR THAT, PETYA. ANYTHING.
I MADE BLACKSTONE A PERPETUAL MOTION MACHINE, GRINDING OUT PEOPLE'S LIVES AND FEEDING ME THE FRUITS OF THEIR LABOR.
FUCK YOU, IVAN, AND YOUR MACHINE.

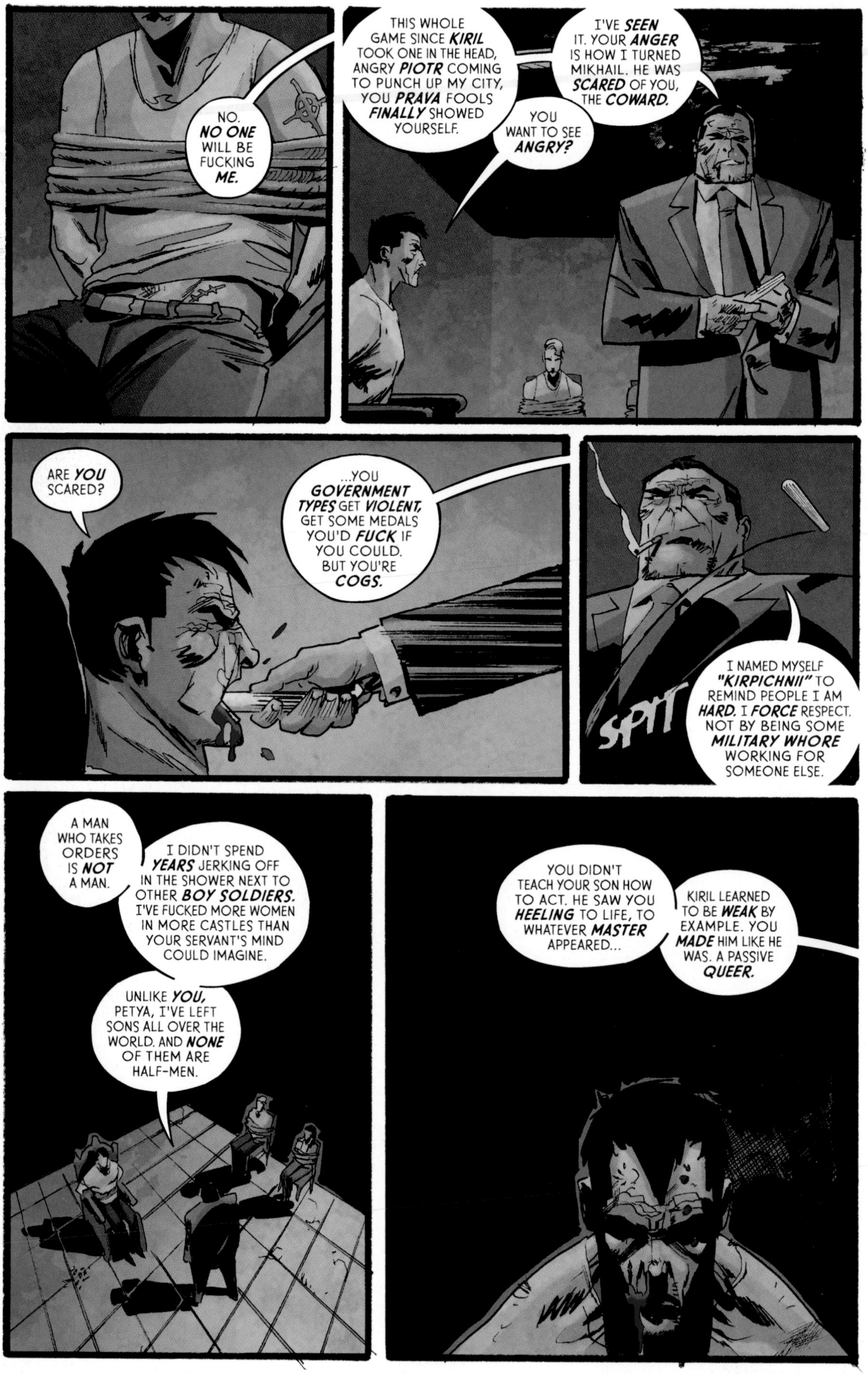

NO. NO ONE WILL BE FUCKING ME.
THIS WHOLE GAME SINCE KIRIL TOOK ONE IN THE HEAD, ANGRY PIOTR COMING TO PUNCH UP MY CITY, YOU PRAVA FOOLS FINALLY SHOWED YOURSELF.
I'VE SEEN IT. YOUR ANGER IS HOW I TURNED MIKHAIL. HE WAS SCARED OF YOU, THE COWARD.
YOU WANT TO SEE ANGRY?
ARE YOU SCARED?
...YOU GOVERNMENT TYPES GET VIOLENT, GET SOME MEDALS YOU'D FUCK IF YOU COULD. BUT YOU'RE COGS.
SPIT
I NAMED MYSELF "KIRPICHNII" TO REMIND PEOPLE I AM HARD. I FORCE RESPECT. NOT BY BEING SOME MILITARY WHORE WORKING FOR SOMEONE ELSE.
A MAN WHO TAKES ORDERS IS NOT A MAN.
I DIDN'T SPEND YEARS JERKING OFF IN THE SHOWER NEXT TO OTHER BOY SOLDIERS. I'VE FUCKED MORE WOMEN IN MORE CASTLES THAN YOUR SERVANT'S MIND COULD IMAGINE.
UNLIKE YOU, PETYA, I'VE LEFT SONS ALL OVER THE WORLD. AND NONE OF THEM ARE HALF-MEN.
YOU DIDN'T TEACH YOUR SON HOW TO ACT. HE SAW YOU HEELING TO LIFE, TO WHATEVER MASTER APPEARED...
KIRIL LEARNED TO BE WEAK BY EXAMPLE. YOU MADE HIM LIKE HE WAS. A PASSIVE QUEER.

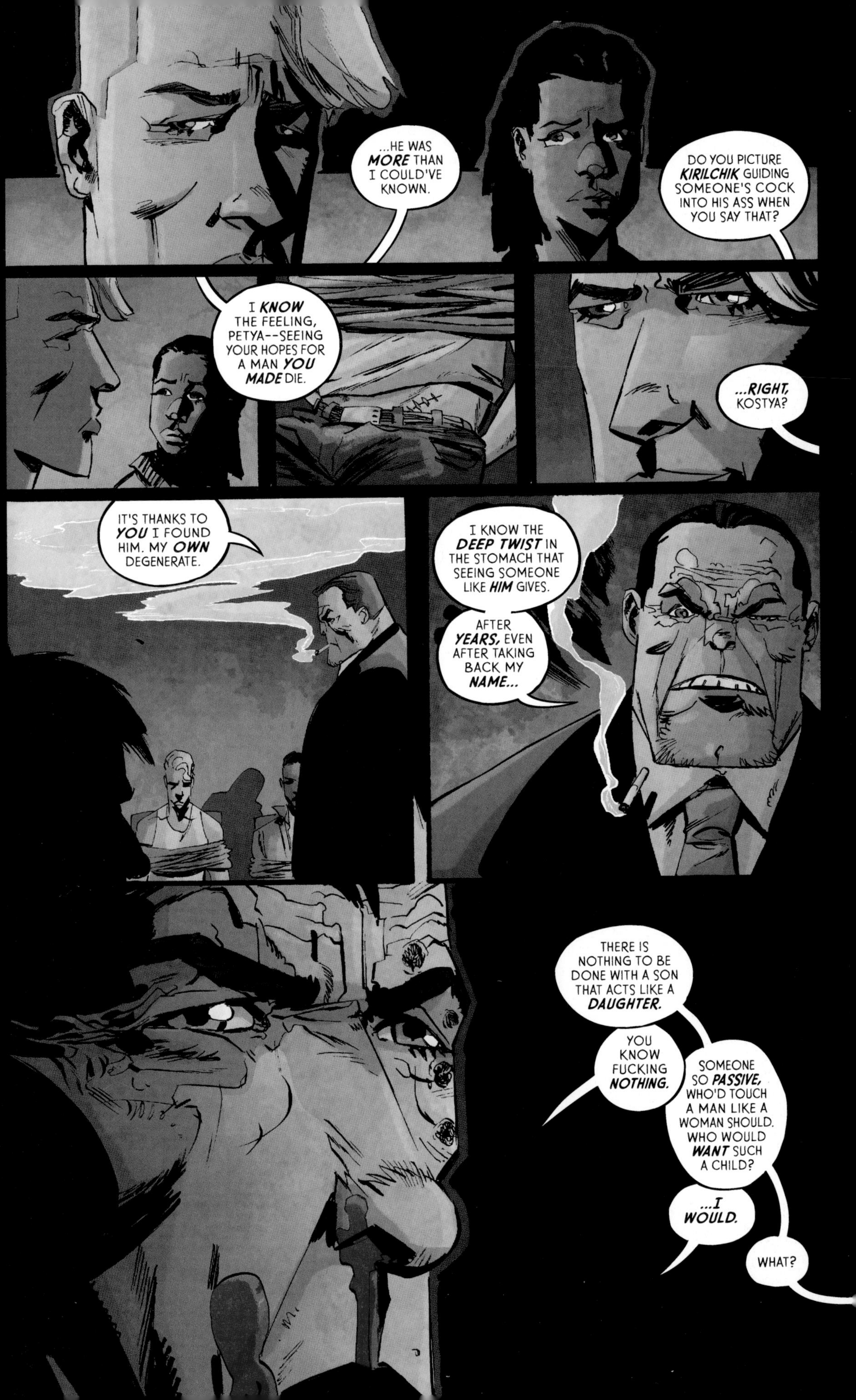
...HE WAS MORE THAN I COULD'VE KNOWN.
DO YOU PICTURE KIRILCHIK GUIDING SOMEONE'S COCK INTO HIS ASS WHEN YOU SAY THAT?
I KNOW THE FEELING, PETYA--SEEING YOUR HOPES FOR A MAN YOU MADE DIE.
...RIGHT, KOSTYA?
IT'S THANKS TO YOU I FOUND HIM. MY OWN DEGENERATE.
I KNOW THE DEEP TWIST IN THE STOMACH THAT SEEING SOMEONE LIKE HIM GIVES.
AFTER YEARS, EVEN AFTER TAKING BACK MY NAME...
THERE IS NOTHING TO BE DONE WITH A SON THAT ACTS LIKE A DAUGHTER.
YOU KNOW FUCKING NOTHING.
SOMEONE SO PASSIVE, WHO'D TOUCH A MAN LIKE A WOMAN SHOULD. WHO WOULD WANT SUCH A CHILD?
...I WOULD.
WHAT?

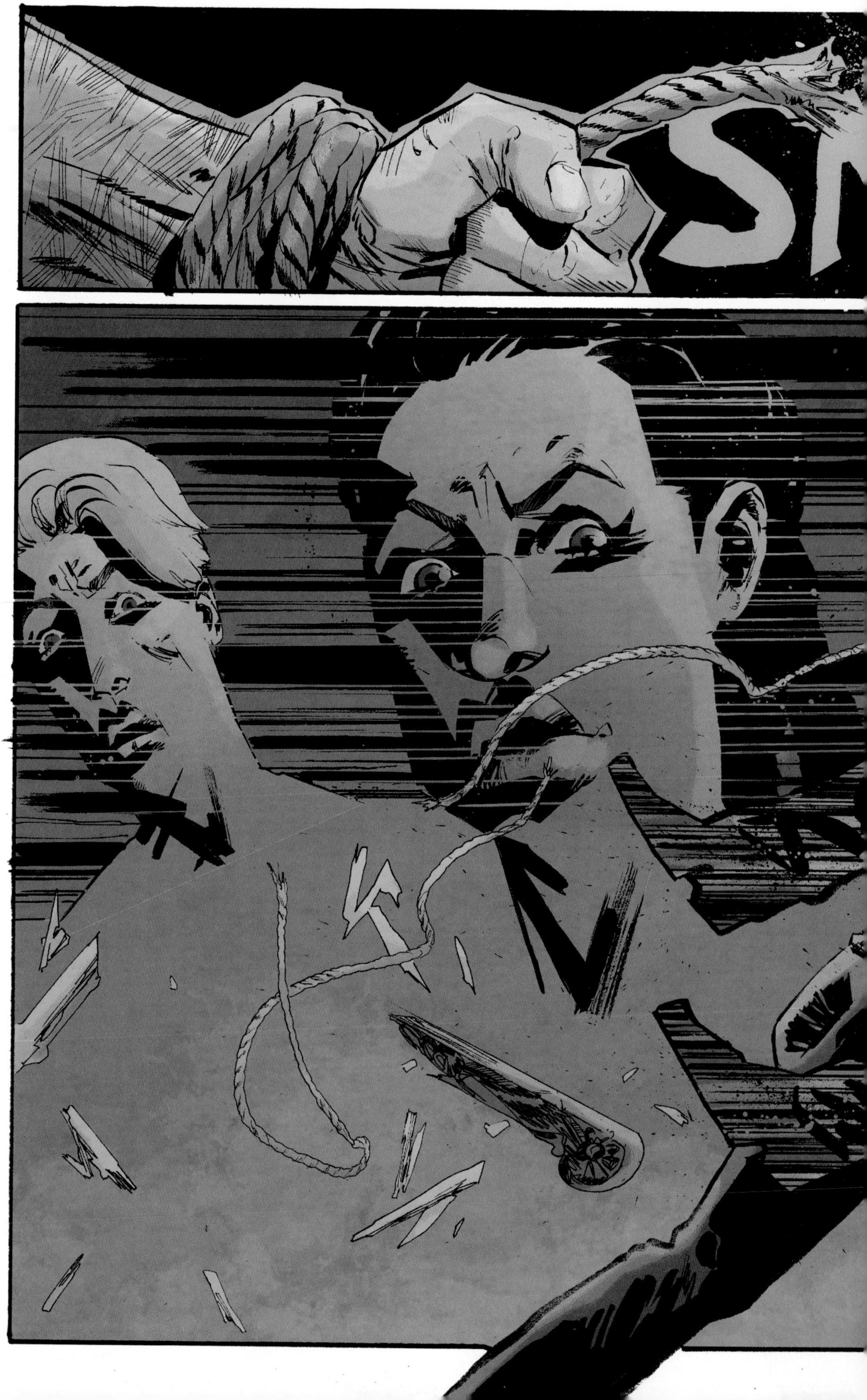
SN

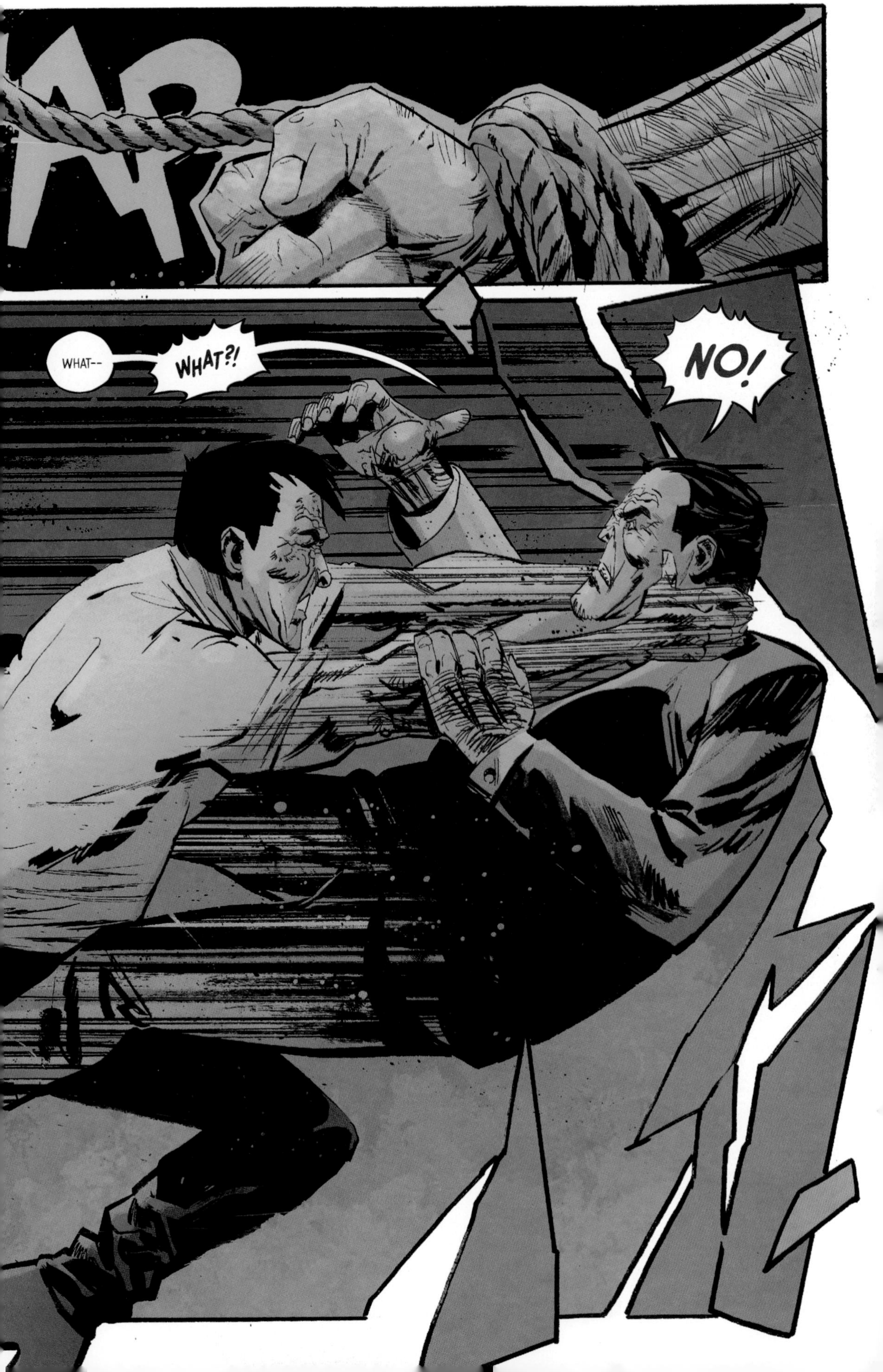
WHAT--
WHAT?!
NO!

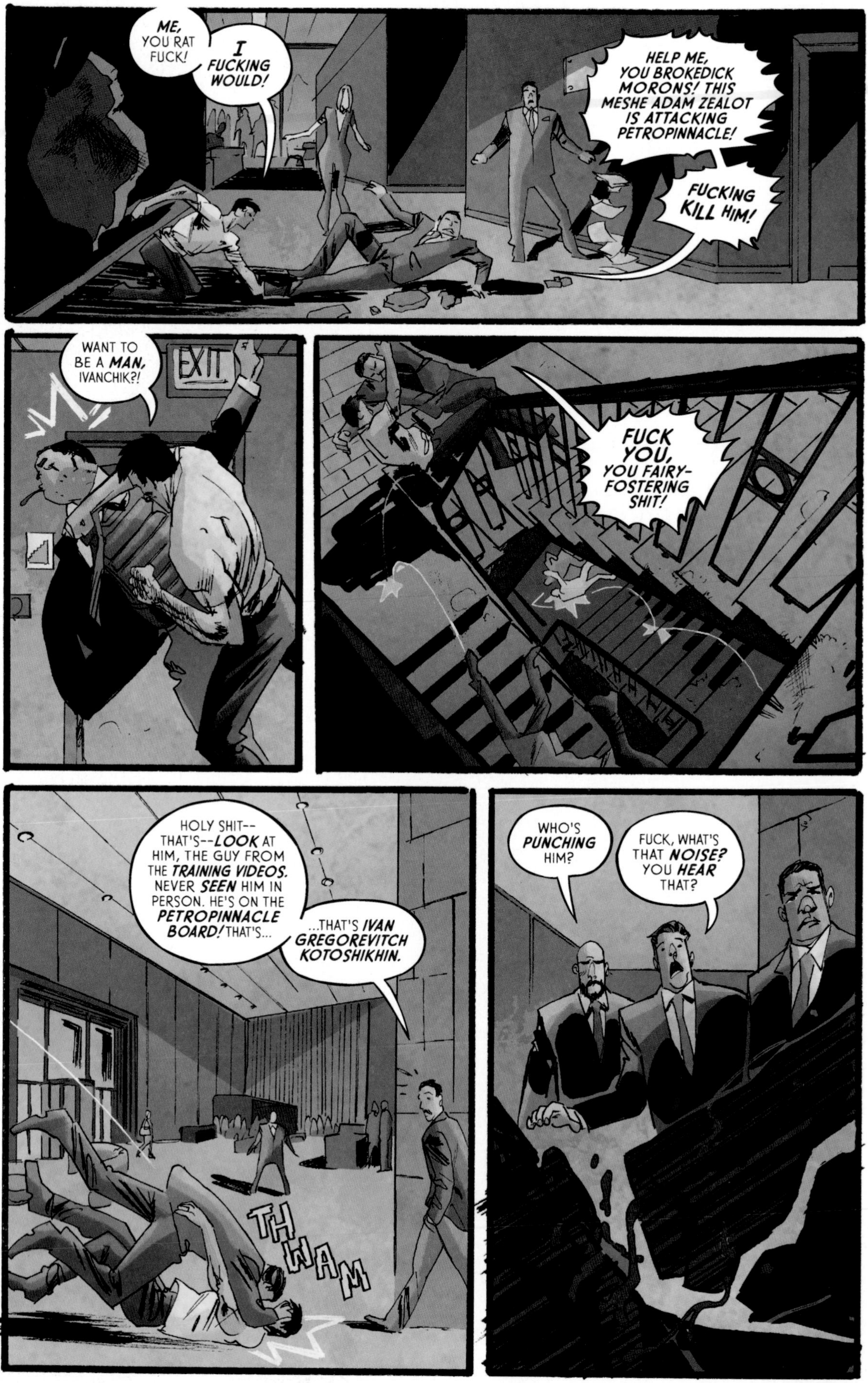
ME, YOU RAT FUCK!
I FUCKING WOULD!
HELP ME, YOU BROKEDICK MORONS! THIS MESHE ADAM ZEALOT IS ATTACKING PETROPINNACLE!
FUCKING KILL HIM!
WANT TO BE A MAN, IVANCHIK?!
EXIT
FUCK YOU, YOU FAIRY-FOSTERING SHIT!
HOLY SHIT--THAT'S--LOOK AT HIM, THE GUY FROM THE TRAINING VIDEOS. NEVER SEEN HIM IN PERSON. HE'S ON THE PETROPINNACLE BOARD! THAT'S...
...THAT'S IVAN GREGOREVITCH KOTOSHIKHIN.
THWAM
WHO'S PUNCHING HIM?
FUCK, WHAT'S THAT NOISE? YOU HEAR THAT?

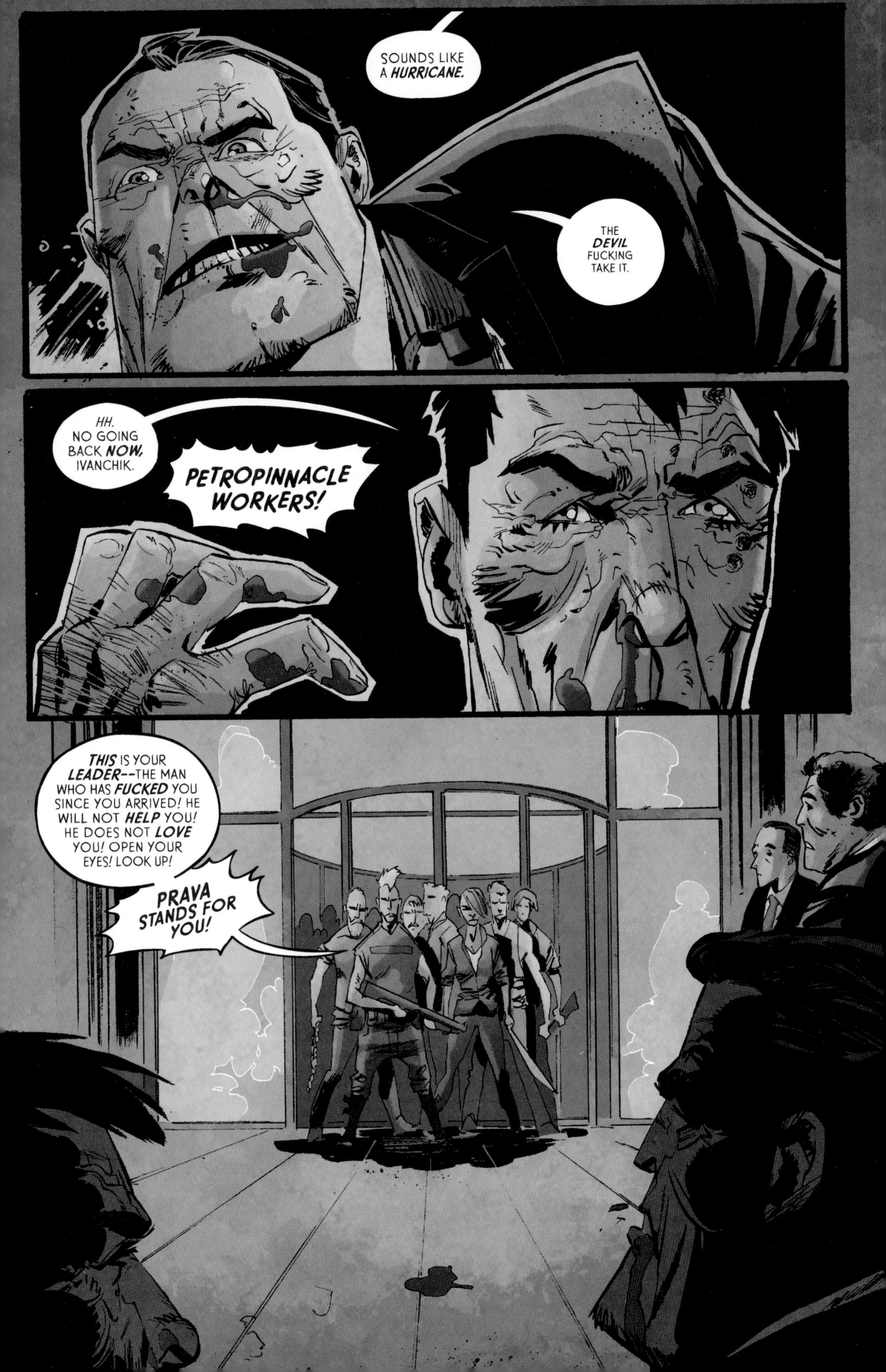
SOUNDS LIKE A *HURRICANE.*
THE *DEVIL* FUCKING TAKE IT.
HH. NO GOING BACK *NOW,* IVANCHIK.
PETROPINNACLE WORKERS!
THIS IS YOUR *LEADER*--THE MAN WHO HAS *FUCKED* YOU SINCE YOU ARRIVED! HE WILL NOT *HELP* YOU! HE DOES NOT *LOVE* YOU! OPEN YOUR EYES! LOOK UP!
PRAVA STANDS FOR YOU!

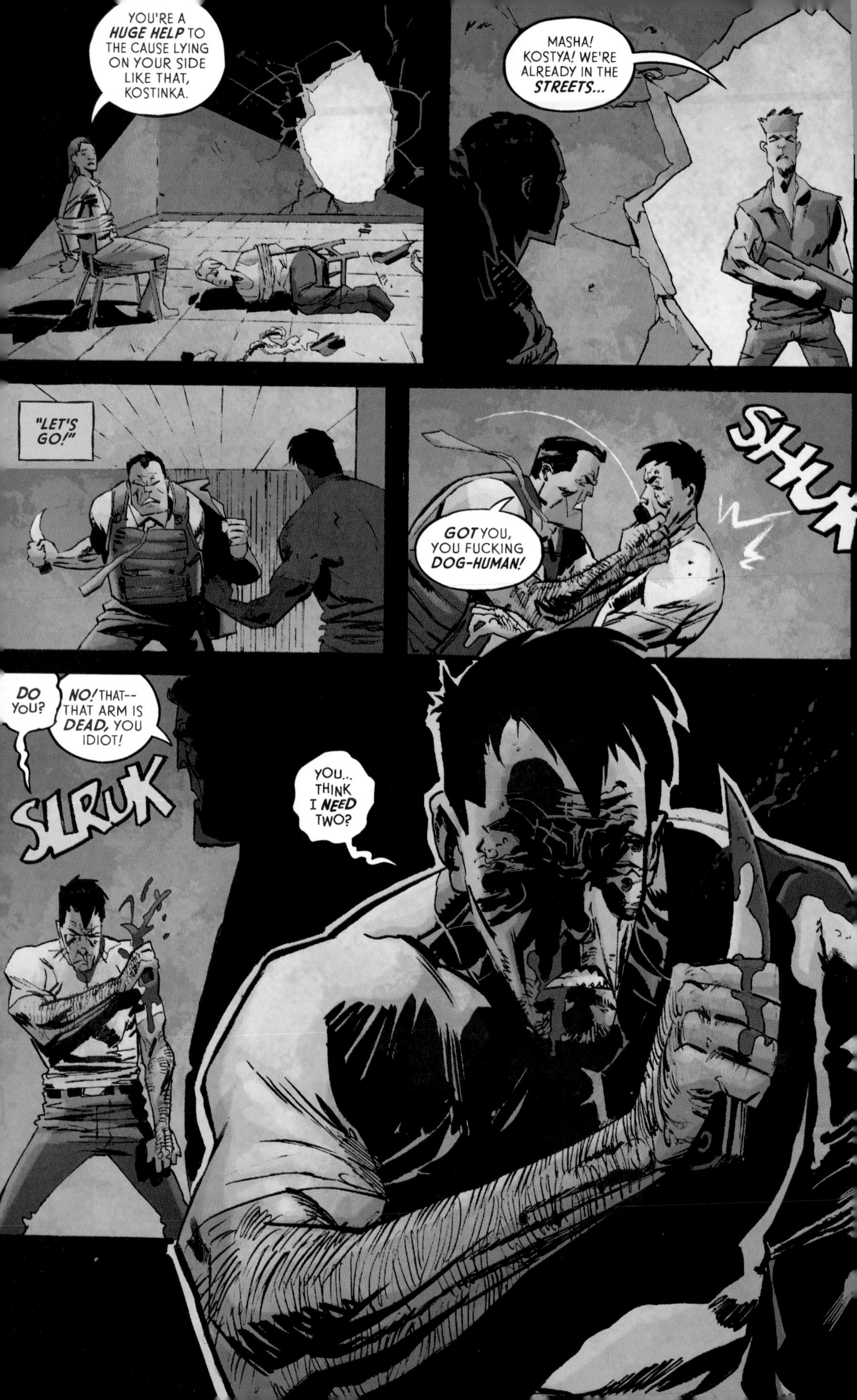
YOU'RE A **HUGE HELP** TO THE CAUSE LYING ON YOUR SIDE LIKE THAT, KOSTINKA.
MASHA! KOSTYA! WE'RE ALREADY IN THE **STREETS...**
"LET'S GO!"
GOT YOU, YOU FUCKING **DOG-HUMAN!**
SHUK
DO YOU?
NO! THAT-- THAT ARM IS **DEAD,** YOU IDIOT!
SLRUK
YOU... THINK I **NEED** TWO?

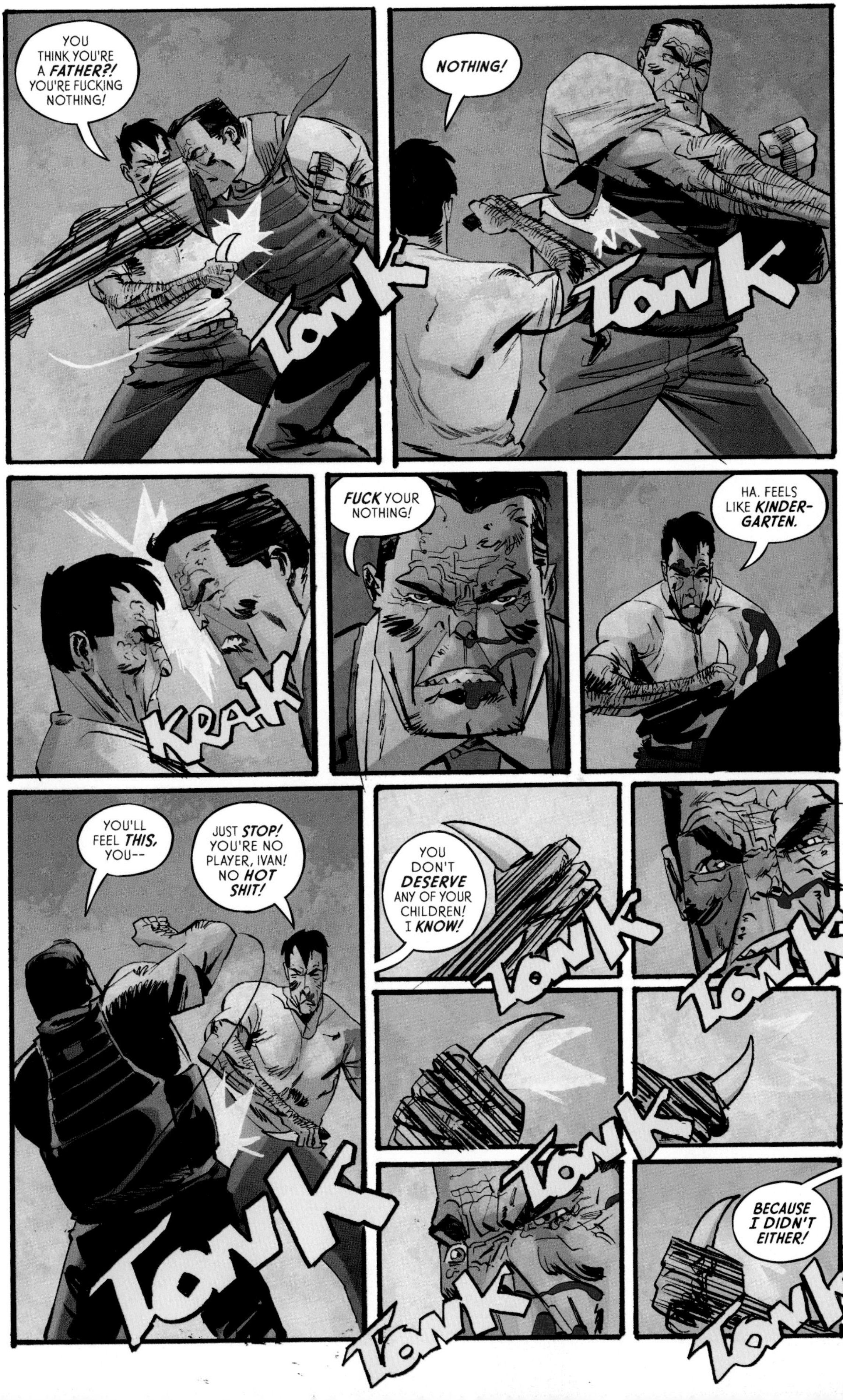

YOU THINK YOU'RE A FATHER?! YOU'RE FUCKING NOTHING!
TONK
NOTHING!
TONK
KRAK
FUCK YOUR NOTHING!
HA. FEELS LIKE KINDER-GARTEN.
YOU'LL FEEL THIS, YOU--
JUST STOP! YOU'RE NO PLAYER, IVAN! NO HOT SHIT!
TONK
YOU DON'T DESERVE ANY OF YOUR CHILDREN! I KNOW!
TONK
TONK
TONK
TONK
TONK
BECAUSE I DIDN'T EITHER!
TONK

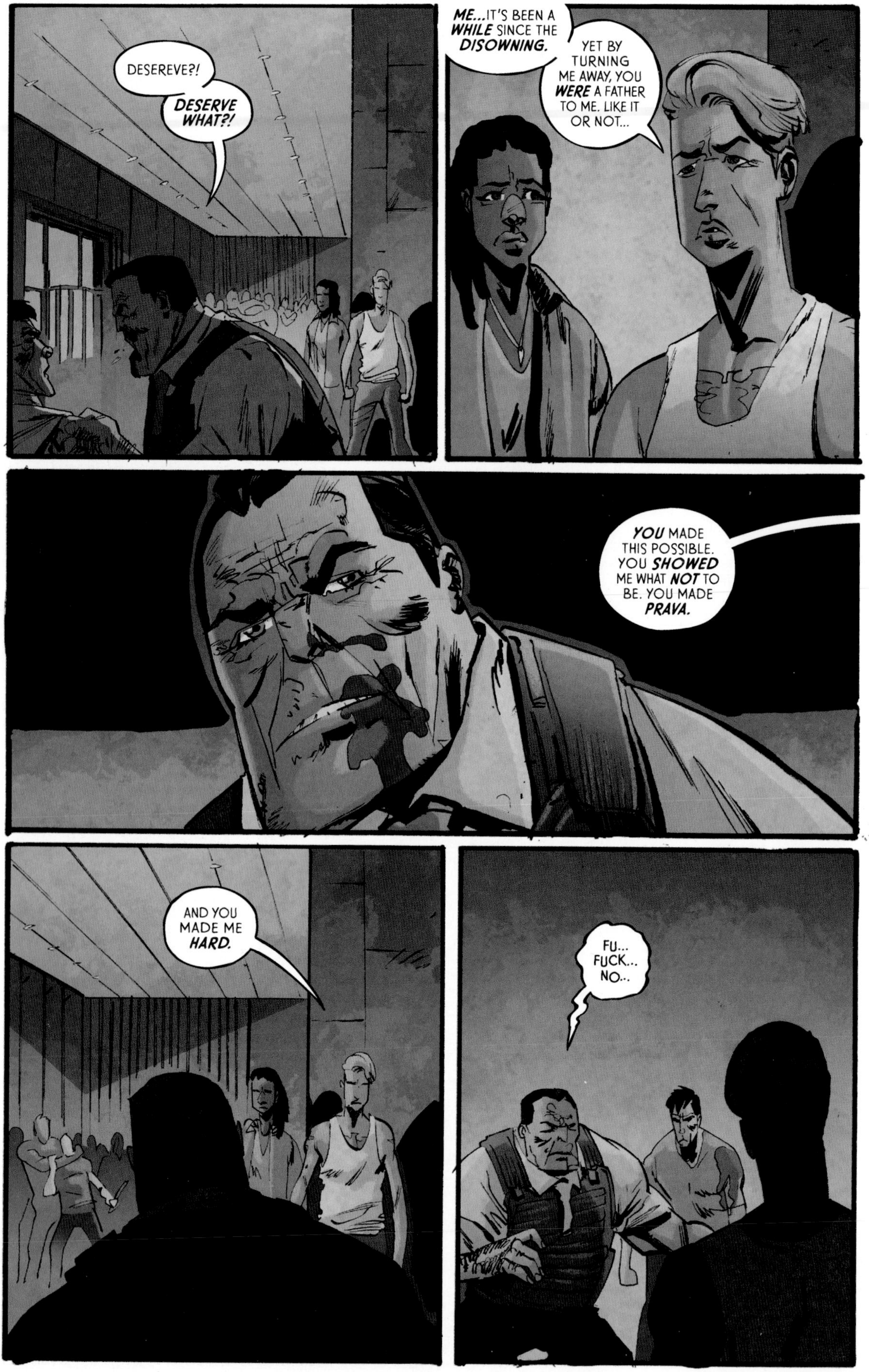
DESEREVE?!
DESERVE WHAT?!
ME...IT'S BEEN A WHILE SINCE THE DISOWNING.
YET BY TURNING ME AWAY, YOU WERE A FATHER TO ME. LIKE IT OR NOT...
YOU MADE THIS POSSIBLE. YOU SHOWED ME WHAT NOT TO BE. YOU MADE PRAVA.
AND YOU MADE ME HARD.
FU... FUCK... NO...

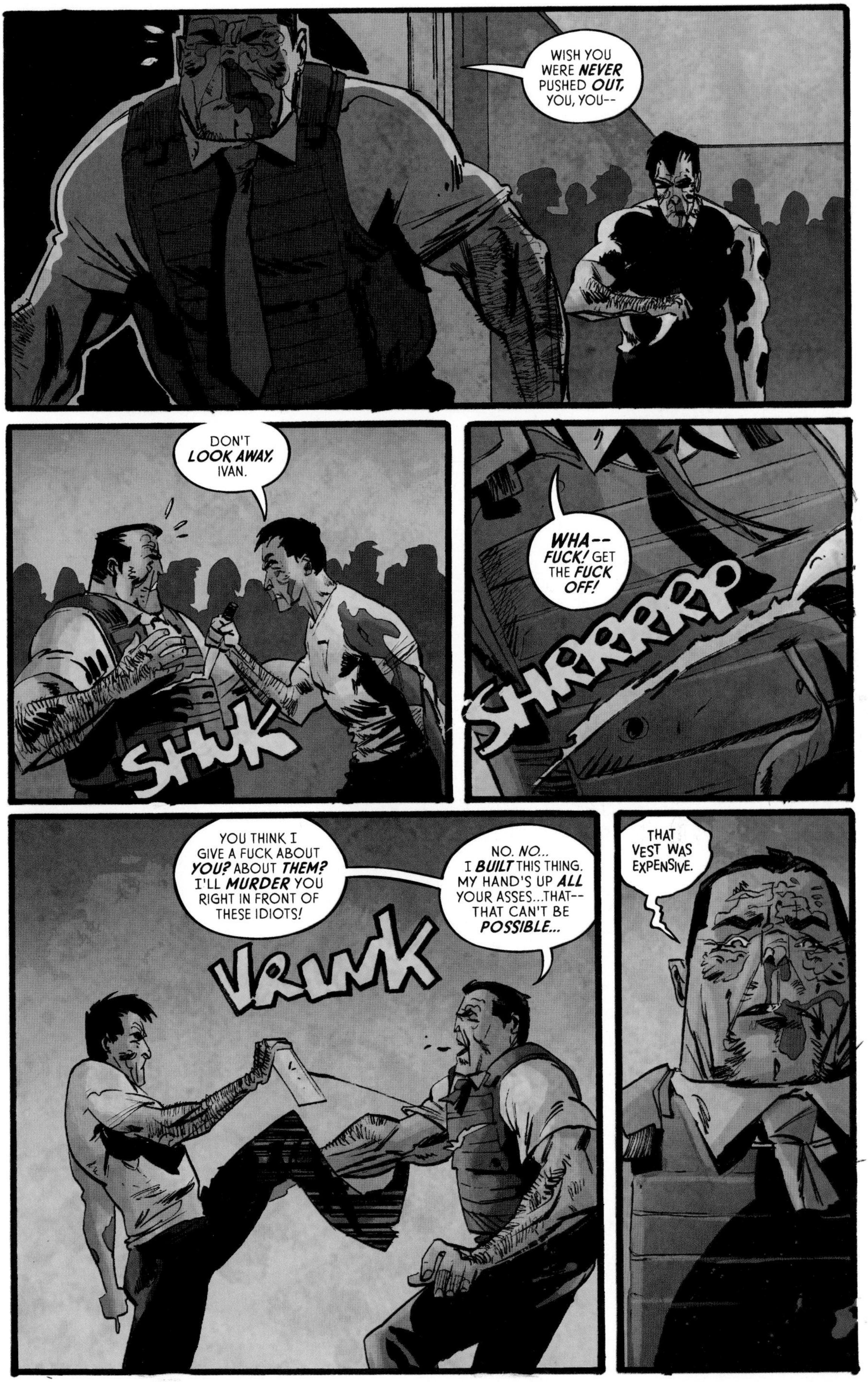
WISH YOU WERE NEVER PUSHED OUT, YOU, YOU--
DON'T LOOK AWAY, IVAN.
SHUK
WHA-- FUCK! GET THE FUCK OFF!
SHRRRRRP
YOU THINK I GIVE A FUCK ABOUT YOU? ABOUT THEM? I'LL MURDER YOU RIGHT IN FRONT OF THESE IDIOTS!
NO. NO... I BUILT THIS THING. MY HAND'S UP ALL YOUR ASSES...THAT--THAT CAN'T BE POSSIBLE...
VRUNK
THAT VEST WAS EXPENSIVE.

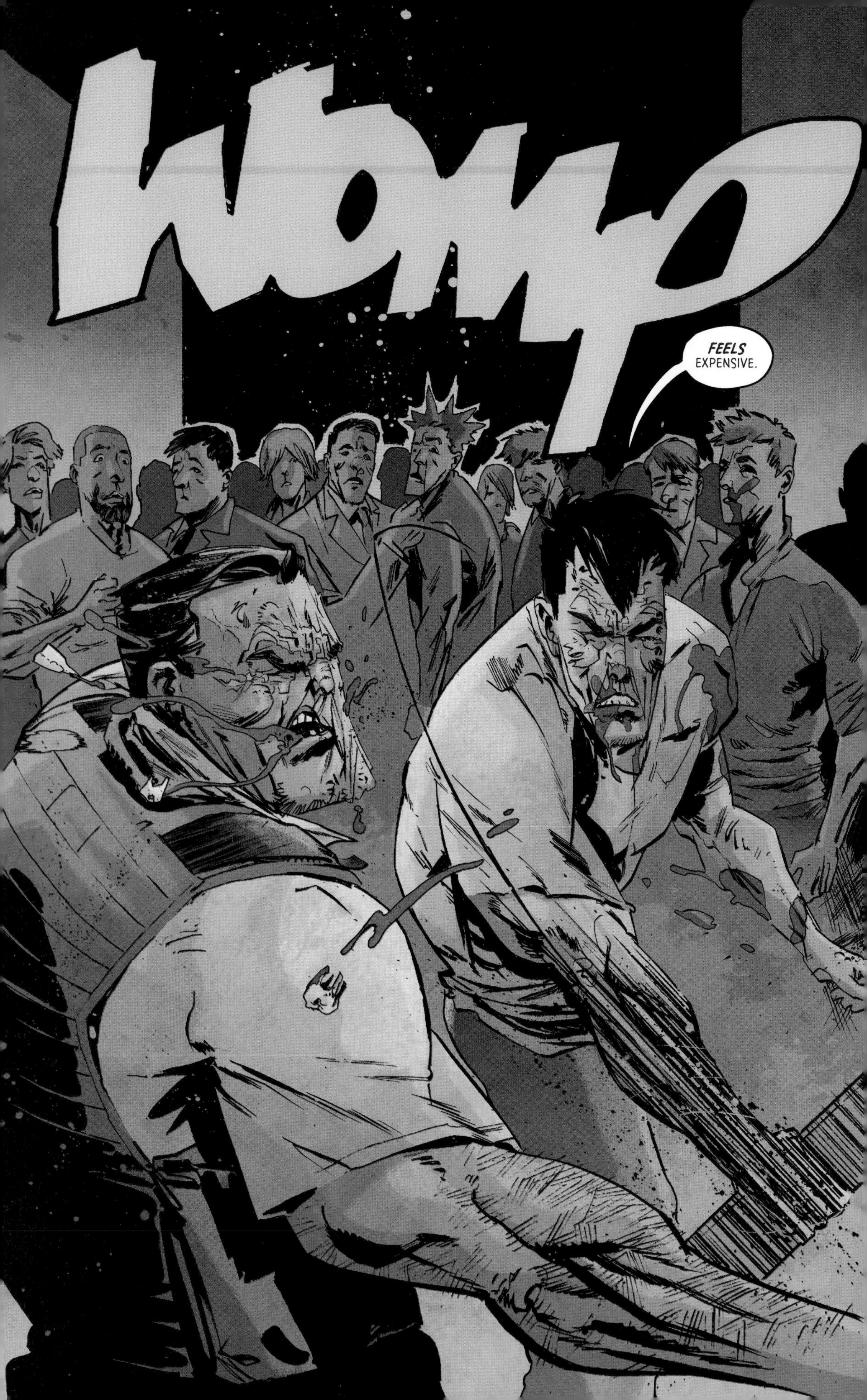
FEELS EXPENSIVE.

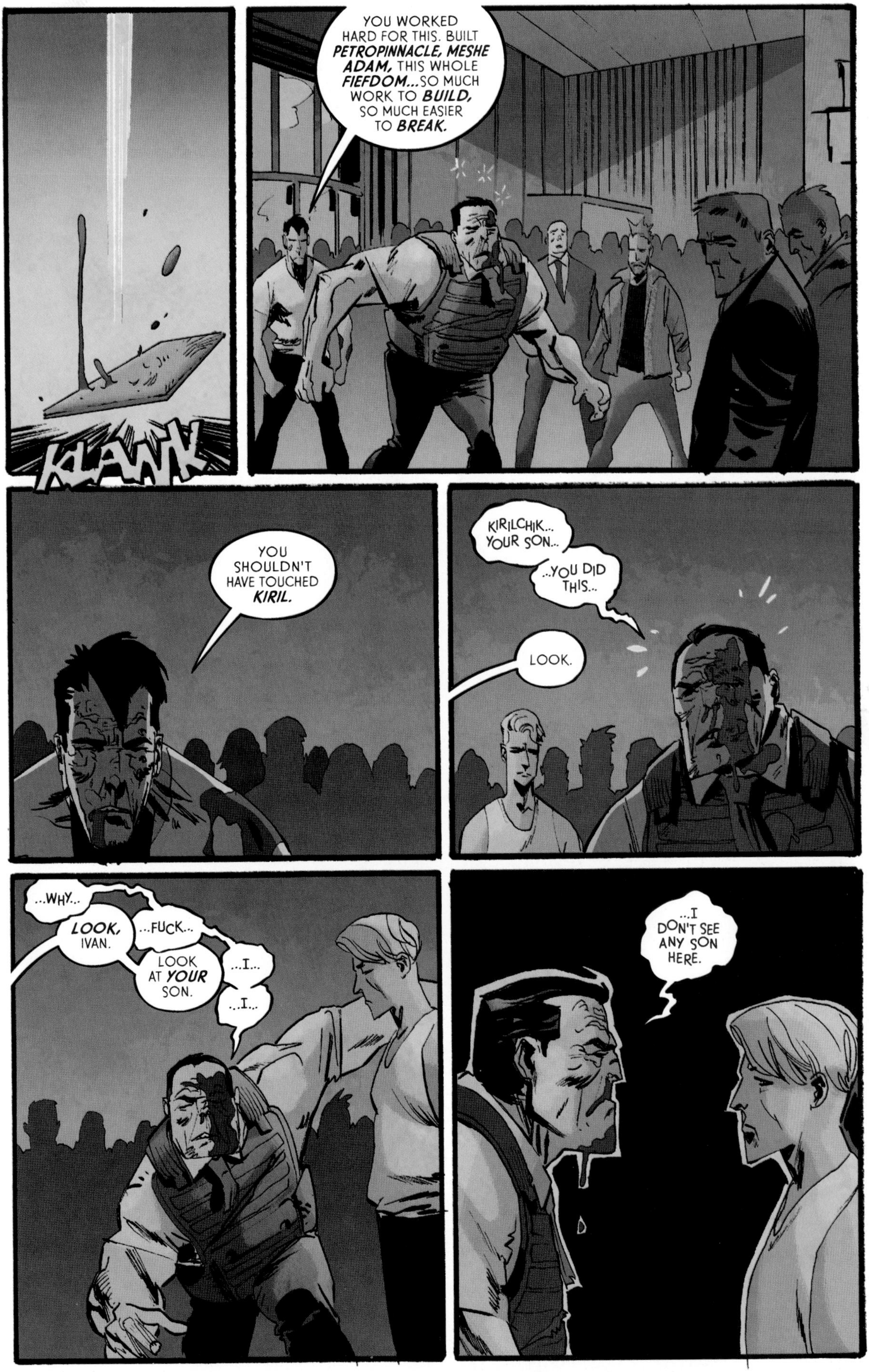
KLANK
YOU WORKED HARD FOR THIS. BUILT PETROPINNACLE, MESHE ADAM, THIS WHOLE FIEFDOM...SO MUCH WORK TO BUILD, SO MUCH EASIER TO BREAK.
YOU SHOULDN'T HAVE TOUCHED KIRIL.
KIRILCHIK... YOUR SON...
...YOU DID THIS...
LOOK.
...WHY...
LOOK, IVAN.
...FUCK...
LOOK AT YOUR SON.
...I...
...I...
...I DON'T SEE ANY SON HERE.

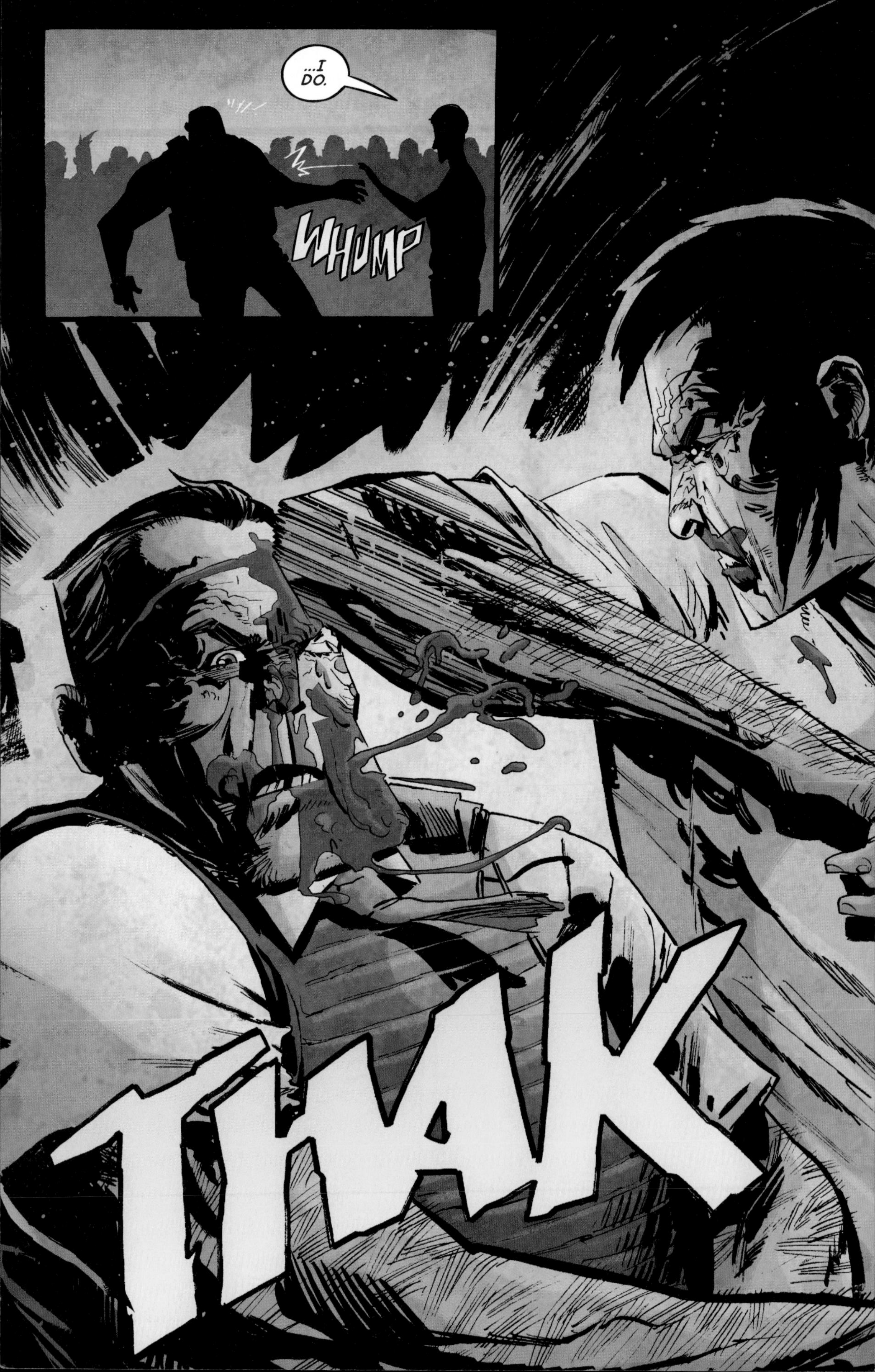
...I DO.
WHUMP
THAK

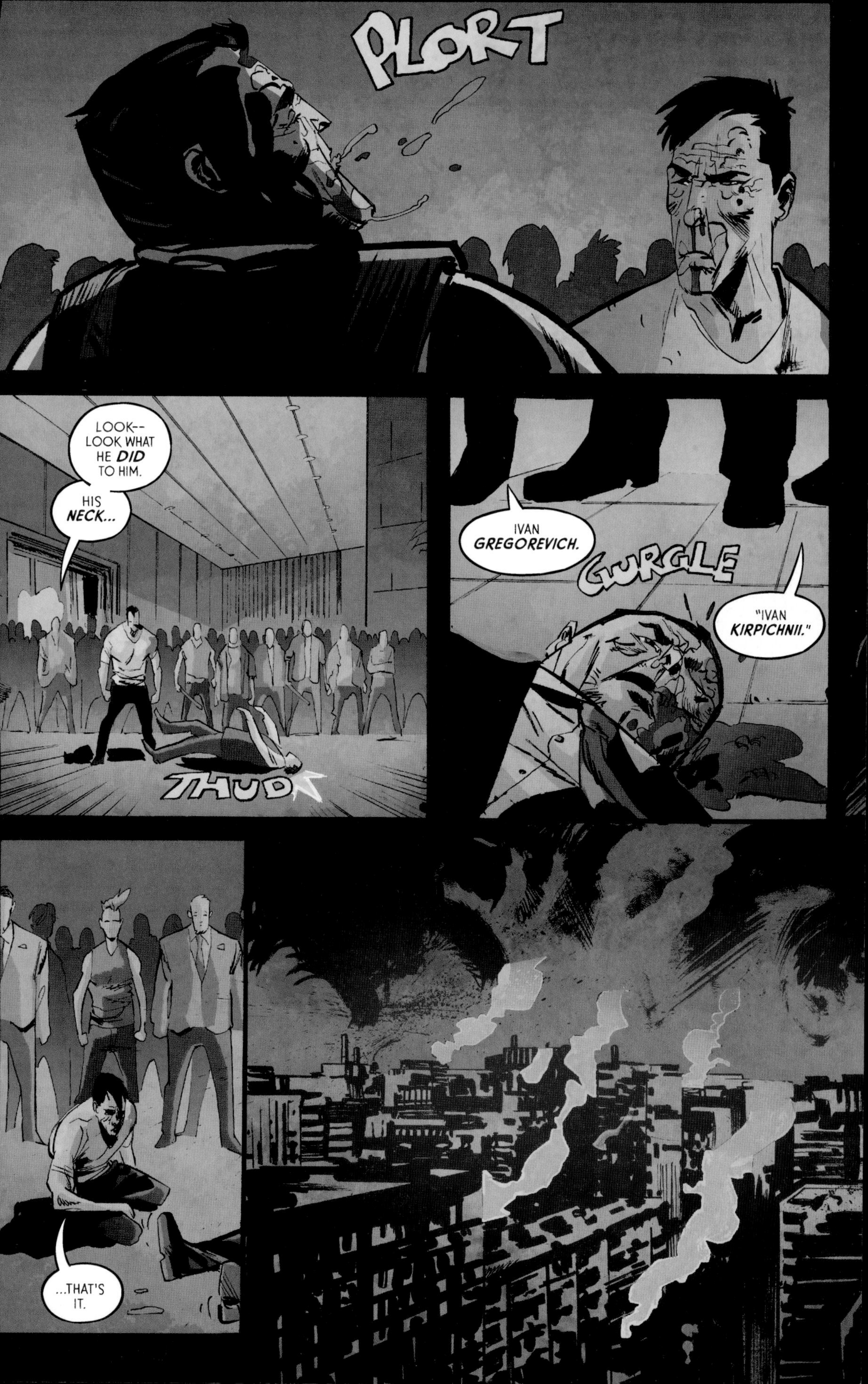
PLORT
LOOK-- LOOK WHAT HE *DID* TO HIM.
HIS *NECK...*
THUD
IVAN *GREGOREVICH.*
GURGLE
"IVAN *KIRPICHNII."*
...THAT'S IT.

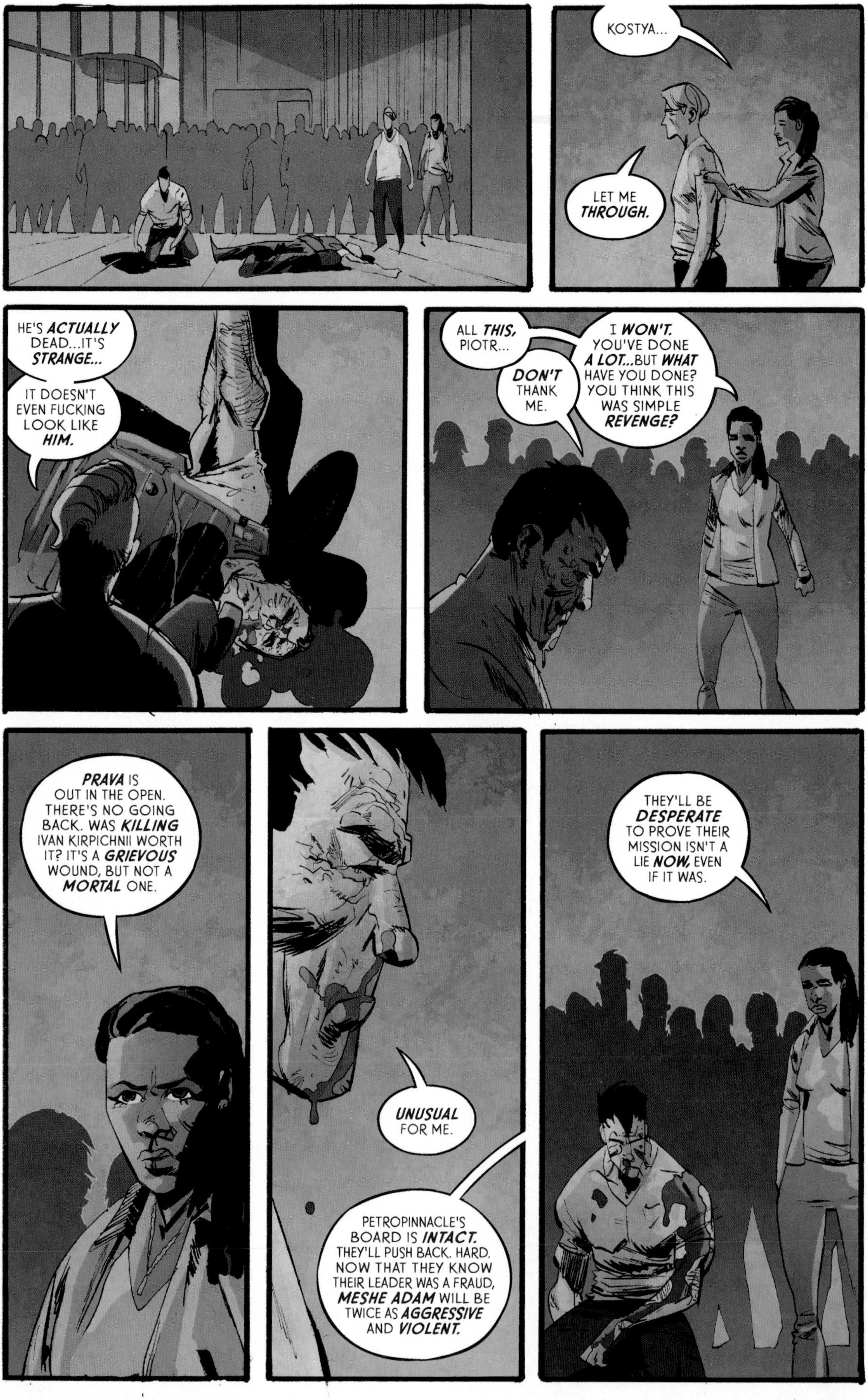
KOSTYA...
LET ME THROUGH.
HE'S ACTUALLY DEAD...IT'S STRANGE...
IT DOESN'T EVEN FUCKING LOOK LIKE HIM.
ALL THIS, PIOTR...
DON'T THANK ME.
I WON'T. YOU'VE DONE A LOT...BUT WHAT HAVE YOU DONE? YOU THINK THIS WAS SIMPLE REVENGE?
PRAVA IS OUT IN THE OPEN. THERE'S NO GOING BACK. WAS KILLING IVAN KIRPICHNII WORTH IT? IT'S A GRIEVOUS WOUND, BUT NOT A MORTAL ONE.
UNUSUAL FOR ME.
PETROPINNACLE'S BOARD IS INTACT. THEY'LL PUSH BACK. HARD. NOW THAT THEY KNOW THEIR LEADER WAS A FRAUD, MESHE ADAM WILL BE TWICE AS AGGRESSIVE AND VIOLENT.
THEY'LL BE DESPERATE TO PROVE THEIR MISSION ISN'T A LIE NOW, EVEN IF IT WAS.

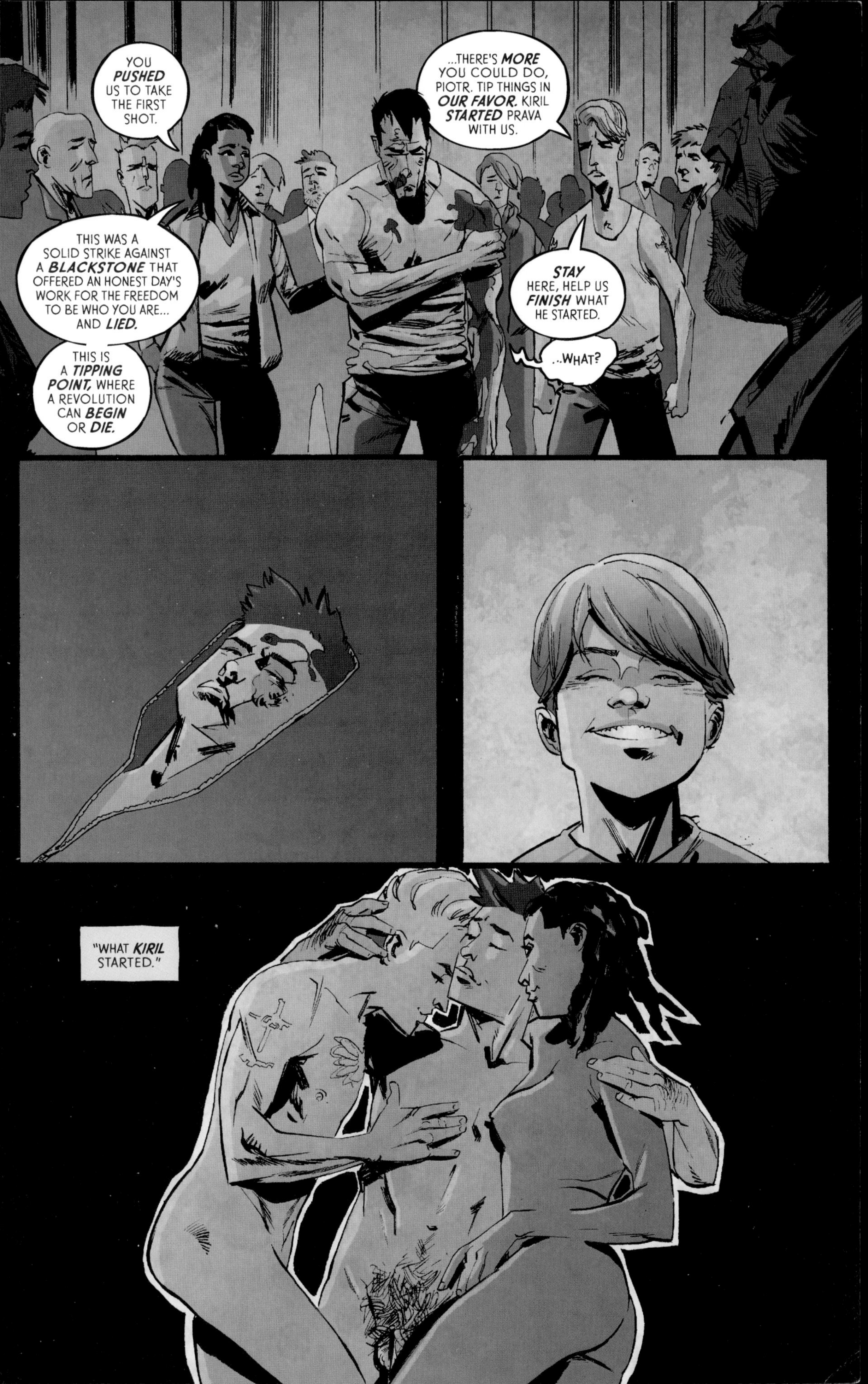

YOU PUSHED US TO TAKE THE FIRST SHOT.
THIS WAS A SOLID STRIKE AGAINST A BLACKSTONE THAT OFFERED AN HONEST DAY'S WORK FOR THE FREEDOM TO BE WHO YOU ARE... AND LIED.
THIS IS A TIPPING POINT, WHERE A REVOLUTION CAN BEGIN OR DIE.
...THERE'S MORE YOU COULD DO, PIOTR. TIP THINGS IN OUR FAVOR. KIRIL STARTED PRAVA WITH US.
STAY HERE, HELP US FINISH WHAT HE STARTED.
...WHAT?
"WHAT KIRIL STARTED."

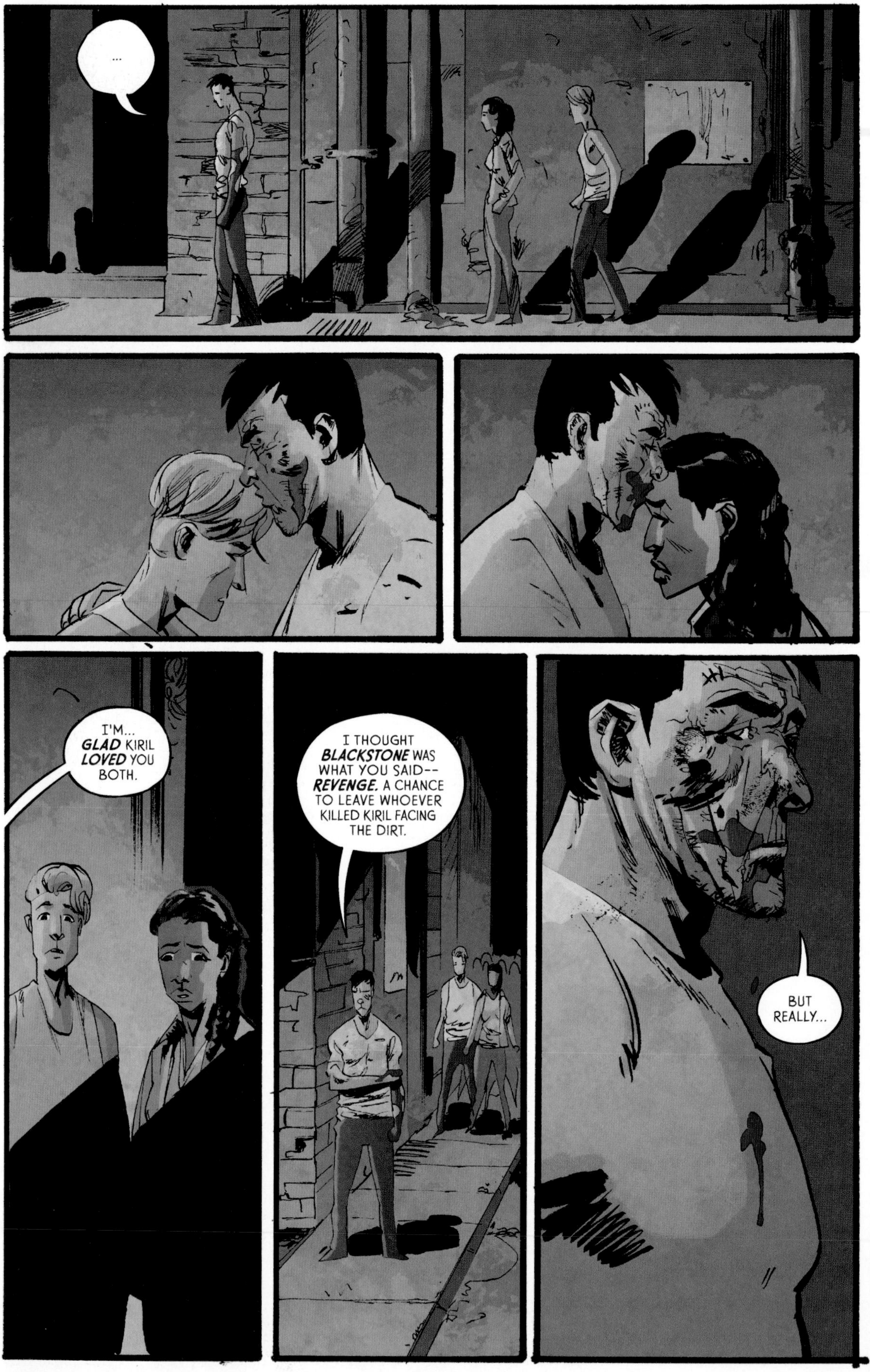
...
I'M... GLAD KIRIL LOVED YOU BOTH.
I THOUGHT BLACKSTONE WAS WHAT YOU SAID-- REVENGE. A CHANCE TO LEAVE WHOEVER KILLED KIRIL FACING THE DIRT.
BUT REALLY...

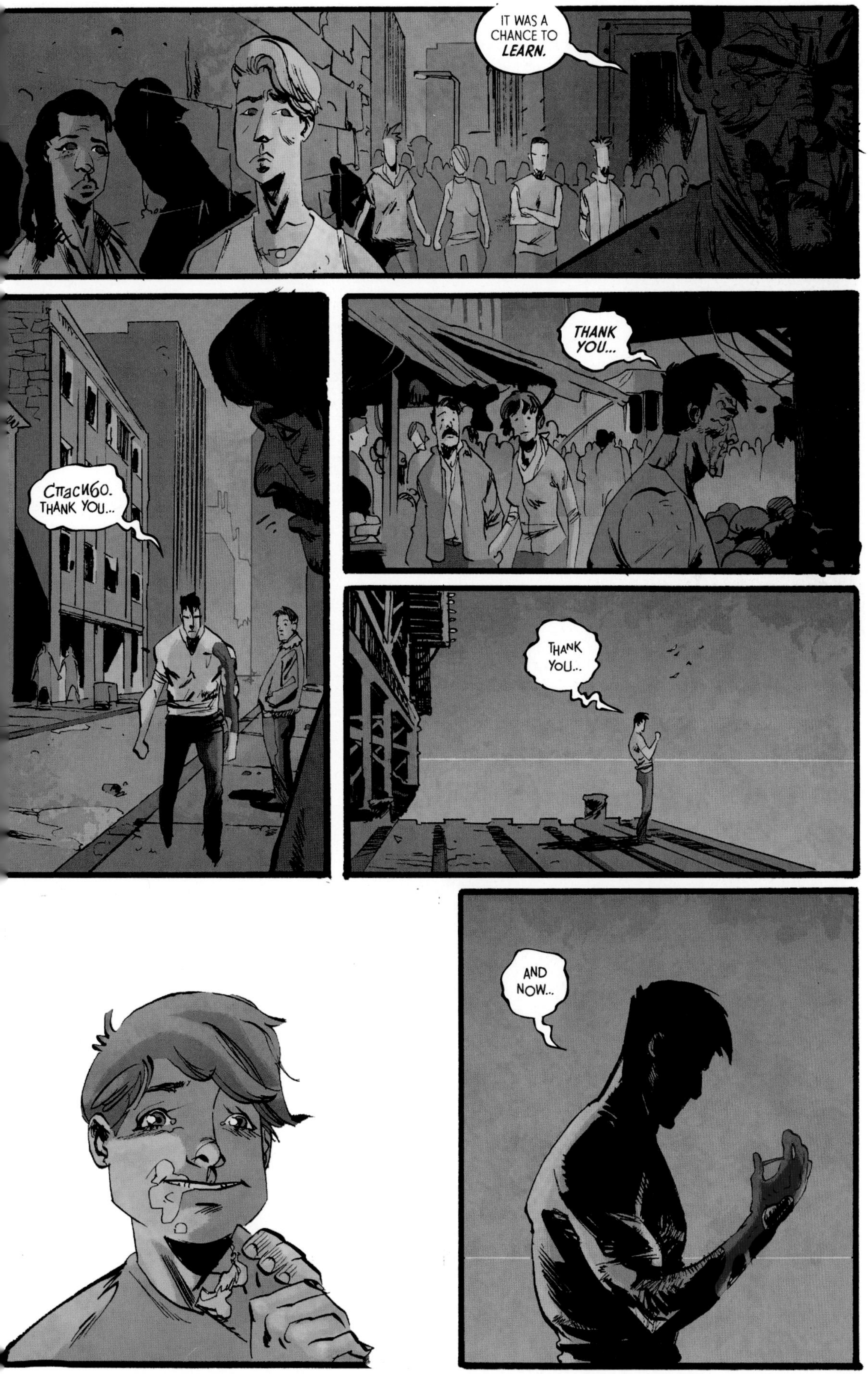
IT WAS A CHANCE TO LEARN.
Спасибо. THANK YOU...
THANK YOU...
THANK YOU...
AND NOW...

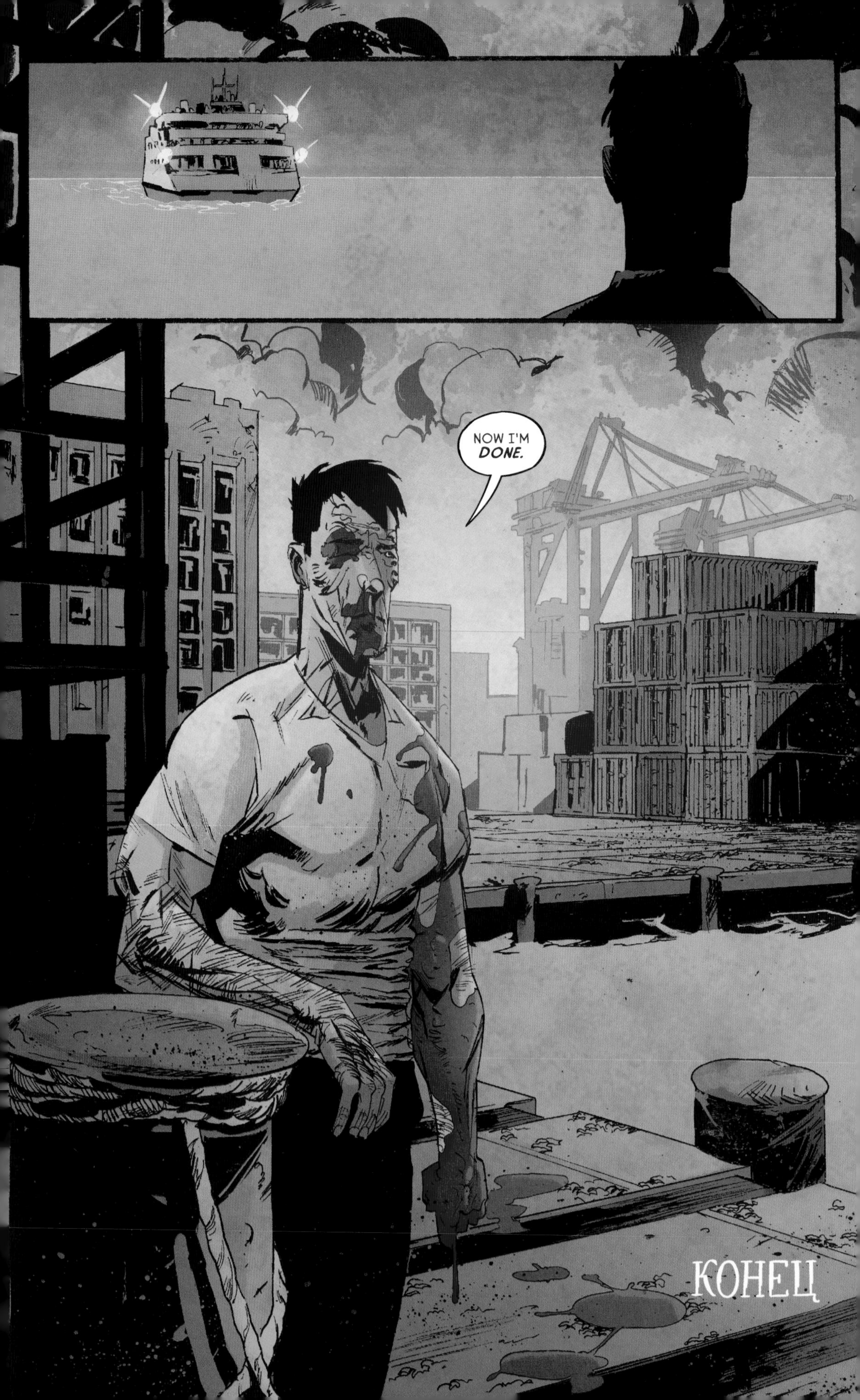
NOW I'M DONE.
КОНЕЦ

THE END

CRUDE – BLINI RECIPE

(THIS ARTICLE ORIGINALLY APPEARED IN THE APRIL 2018 ISSUE OF IMAGE+)
ESSAY: VERNON MILES   CHEFS: STEVE ORLANDO AND GARRY BROWN

Piotr and his son Kiril both live in Russia, but in two very different worlds. For Piotr, Russia is the relic of an era defined by strict etiquette in cohabitation with brutal violence. For Kiril, Russia is a nation of moral grays. Piotr worked for years as a hitman, a life he kept hidden from Kiril. The secrets that define Piotr's life are abhorred in his son's world, but when Kiril's life comes crashing down, Piotr must leave the Russia he's familiar with and venture into his son's emergent version.

Throughout the book, Piotr and Kiril's love and divisions are expressed through their shared meals.

CRUDE opens with a rare breakfast between the two characters where, even at a young age, the disparity between father and son becomes evident. "The entire thesis of the book is stated in that opener, as Piotr sees Kiril with the jam on his mouth and is triggered into a memory where, for him, the jam was blood," Orlando says. "That's the generational conflict–brutality (in blood) to innocence (in jam). Similarly, caviar with blini is quite traditional, as are any number of other savory pairings. But caviar is ubiquitous. Yet, for American readers who largely think of pancakes (which blini essentially are–crepes) as vessels for sweet, leisurely foods, it's also a moment of stark contrast. We're in somewhere new. And Kiril, young, uninterested in his father's traditions, immediately and still-innocently rejects it as gross. This whole discussion, this breakfast, the food choices made and the words said, is a microcosm of the book's entire conflict."

Fittingly, nearly half of the first issue takes place inside Piotr's kitchen. "The kitchen is the heart of the home, and in CRUDE, it's a broken heart," Orlando says. "This goes back in Slavic culture to the fact that many homes in early times would have a massive stone oven, (Russkaya Pech), which the entire home was built around. It was used for heating, cooking, often even for sleeping on top of to keep warm. So the kitchen, this area, has always been the gathering place. It's where the family finds its core."

INGREDIENTS

2/3 CUP ALL-PURPOSE FLOUR
½ CUP BUCKWHEAT FLOUR
½ TABLESPOON SALT
1 CUP MILK (WARM)
2 TABLESPOONS BUTTER (MELTED)
1 LARGE EGG (COMBINED/WHISKED)
½ TEASPOON BAKING SODA
½ TEASPOON WHITE VINEGAR
½ TEASPOON VEGETABLE OIL

DIRECTIONS

1. In a medium pot, warm milk and butter without bringing to a boil, until butter is integrated.

2. Once milk/butter mixture is warm, maintain lowest heat setting.

3. With a whisk, slowly add first egg, then salt, all-purpose flour, and buckwheat flour. Add slowly, allowing to integrate and form a batter.

4. Once a batter is formed, whisk in vegetable oil.

5. Combine baking soda and white vinegar and whisk into batter. Alternatively, pour vinegar over baking soda in a spoon, directly over batter, and stir in.

6. Heat a medium-sized (6-inch) nonstick skillet over medium heat. Lightly oil or butter skillet.

7. Fill skillet with enough batter to thinly coat the flat bottom of the skillet.

8. Cook for about 1 minute or until bubbles form and break. Turn and cook for about 30 seconds more.

9. Cover blini and keep warm. Repeat with remaining batter.

10. Serve with toppings of choice: caviar, smoked fish, chopped hard-boiled eggs, minced onion, sour cream, chopped dill, lemon, jam, or meat filling.

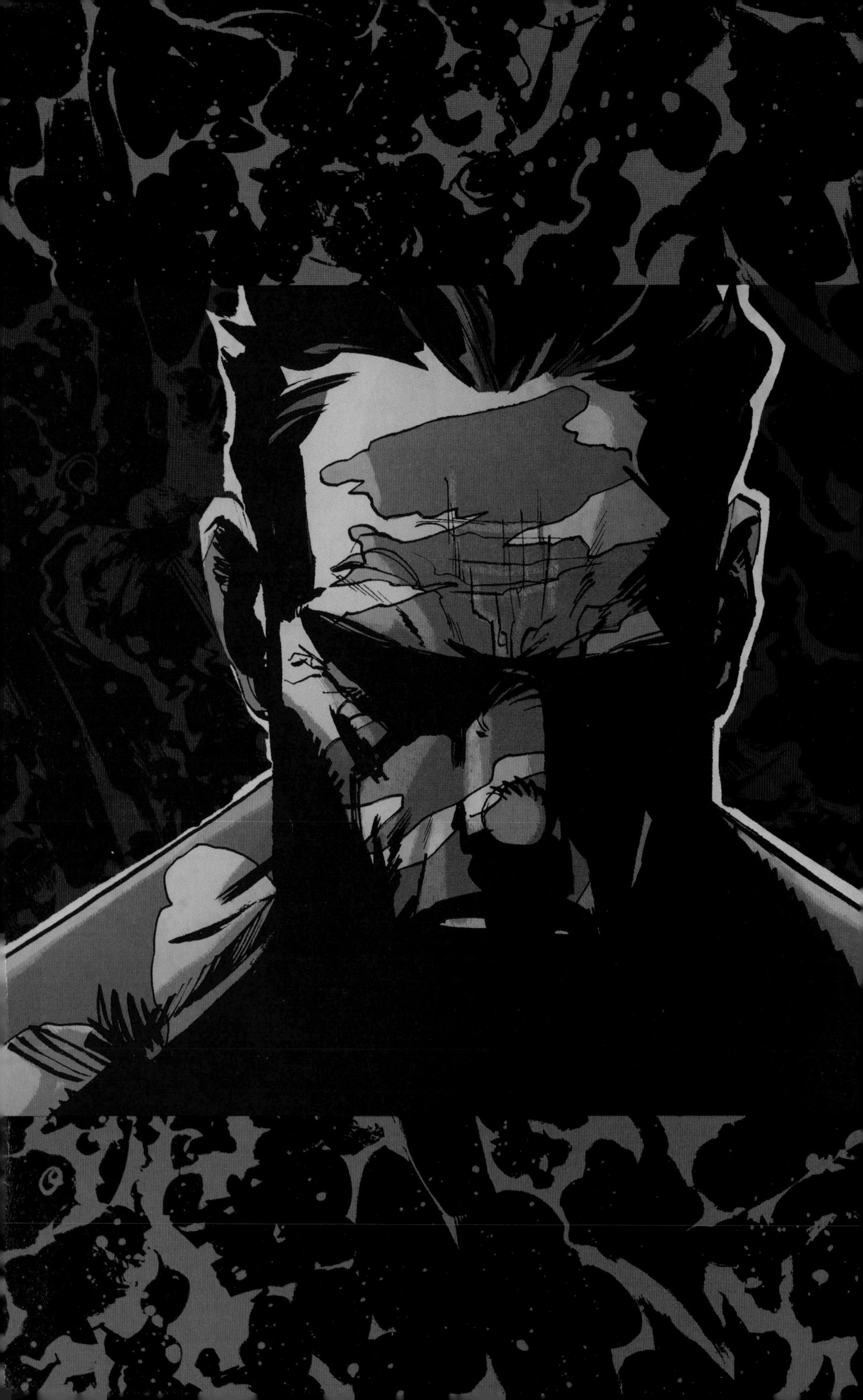

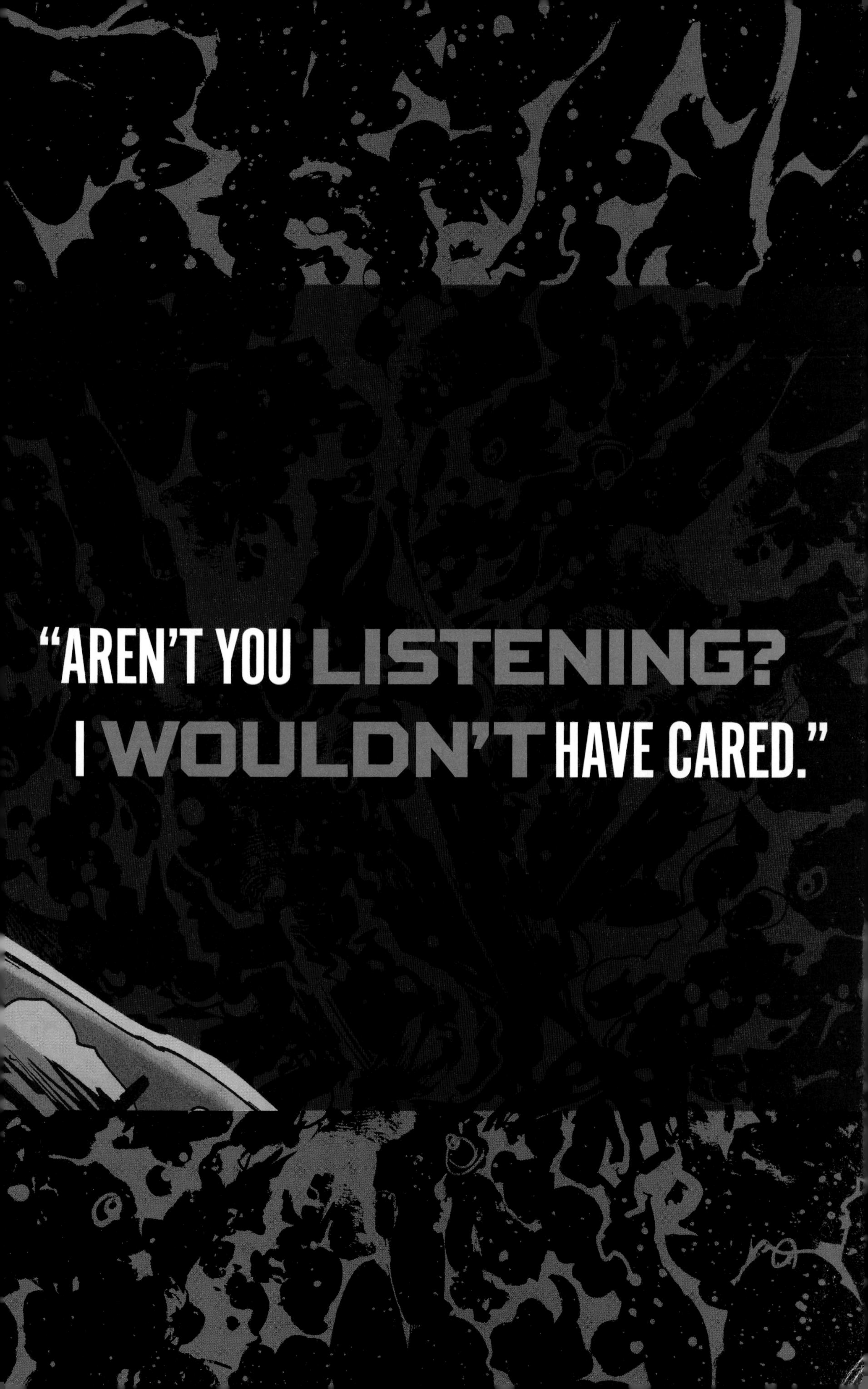
"AREN'T YOU LISTENING?
I WOULDN'T HAVE CARED."

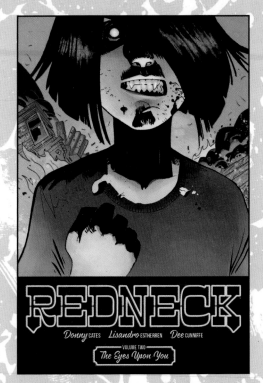

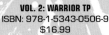

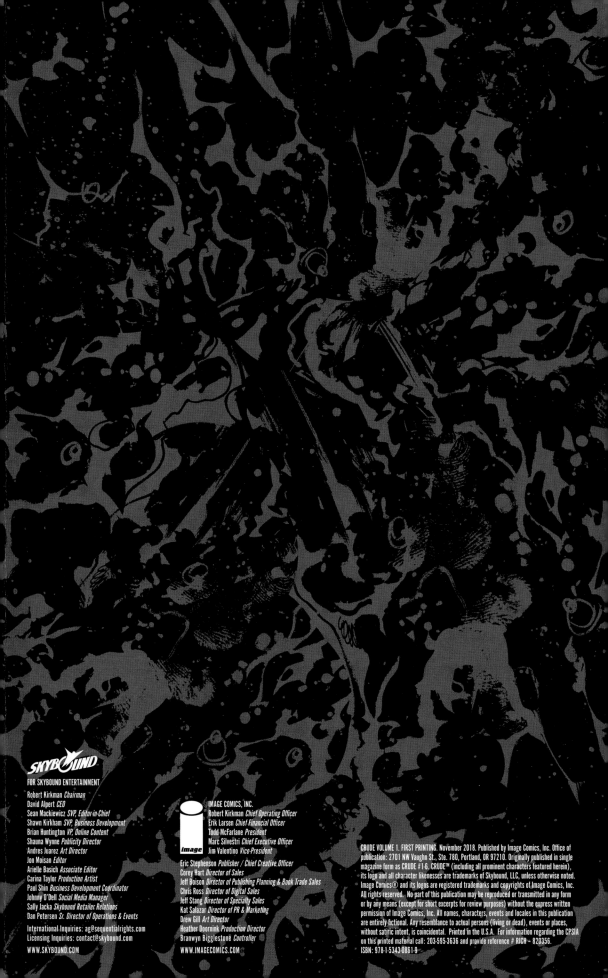

IMAGE COMICS, INC.
Robert Kirkman *Chief Operating Officer*
Erik Larsen *Chief Financial Officer*
Todd McFarlane *President*
Marc Silvestri *Chief Executive Officer*
Jim Valentino *Vice-President*

Eric Stephenson *Publisher / Chief Creative Officer*
Corey Hart *Director of Sales*
Jeff Boison *Director of Publishing Planning & Book Trade Sales*
Chris Ross *Director of Digital Sales*
Jeff Stang *Director of Specialty Sales*
Kat Salazar *Director of PR & Marketing*
Drew Gill *Art Director*
Heather Doornink *Production Director*
Branwyn Bigglestone *Controller*

WWW.IMAGECOMICS.COM

CRUDE VOLUME 1. FIRST PRINTING. November 2018. Published by Image Comics, Inc. Office of publication: 2701 NW Vaughn St., Ste. 780, Portland, OR 97210. Originally published in single magazine form as CRUDE #1-6. CRUDE™ (including all prominent characters featured herein), its logo and all character likenesses are trademarks of Skybound, LLC, unless otherwise noted. Image Comics® and its logos are registered trademarks and copyrights of Image Comics, Inc. All rights reserved. No part of this publication may be reproduced or transmitted in any form or by any means (except for short excerpts for review purposes) without the express written permission of Image Comics, Inc. All names, characters, events and locales in this publication are entirely fictional. Any resemblance to actual persons (living or dead), events or places, without satiric intent, is coincidental. Printed in the U.S.A. For information regarding the CPSIA on this printed material call: 203-595-3636 and provide reference # RICH – 820356.
ISBN: 978-1-5343-0861-9

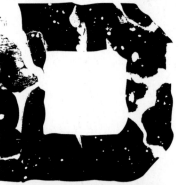

CREATED BY
**STEVE ORLANDO
& GARRY BROWN**